Elvi Rhodes was born and educated in Yorkshire, and now lives in Sussex. Her best-selling novels include: *Opal*, *Doctor Rose*, *Ruth Appleby*, *The Golden Girls*, *Madeleine*, *The House of Bonneau*, *Cara's Land*, *The Rainbow Through the Rain*, *The Bright One*, *The Mountain*, *Portrait of Chloe*, *Spring Music* and *Midsummer Meeting*. A collection of stories, *Summer Promise and Other Stories*, is also published by Corgi Books.

Also by Elvi Rhodes

DOCTOR ROSE
THE GOLDEN GIRLS
THE HOUSE OF BONNEAU
MADELEINE
OPAL
RUTH APPLEBY
CARA'S LAND
SUMMER PROMISE AND OTHER STORIES
THE RAINBOW THROUGH THE RAIN
THE BRIGHT ONE
THE MOUNTAIN
PORTRAIT OF CHLOE
SPRING MUSIC
MIDSUMMER MEETING

and published by Corgi Books

THE BIRTHDAY PARTY

Elvi Rhodes

THE BIRTHDAY PARTY
A CORGI BOOK : 0 552 14792 3

Originally published in Great Britain by Bantam Press,
a division of Transworld Publishers

PRINTING HISTORY
Bantam Press edition published 2000
Corgi edition published 2001

1 3 5 7 9 10 8 6 4 2

Set in 11/13pt New Baskerville by
Kestrel Data, Exeter, Devon.

Corgi Books are published by Transworld Publishers,
61–63 Uxbridge Road, London W5 5SA,
a division of The Random House Group Ltd,
in Australia by Random House Australia (Pty) Ltd,
20 Alfred Street, Milsons Point, Sydney, NSW 2061, Australia,
in New Zealand by Random House New Zealand Ltd,
18 Poland Road, Glenfield, Auckland 10, New Zealand
and in South Africa by Random House (Pty) Ltd,
Endulini, 5a Jubilee Road, Parktown 2193, South Africa.

Printed and bound in Great Britain by
Mackays of Chatham PLC, Chatham, Kent.

Acknowledgements

I thank my son Stephen and his wife Christine in whose home part of this book was written, and who have, through their hospitality over the years, instilled in me a love of New York and New Yorkers. I thank Stephen, yet again, for translating my English English into New York speak.

I also thank Liz Morgan who, in spite of being at school and studying for her GCSE exams, did many hours of valuable research for this book – all done with intelligence and thoroughness, and often taking it beyond the questions I had thought to ask.

I thank, too, Shirley Hall, friend and secretary, for her skill and unending patience.

This book is for the Morgan family, Martin, Sylvia, Ann, John and Liz, with much love.

1

Poppy awakened reluctantly as the daylight, penetrating the too-thin curtains, hit her eyes. She turned her head towards the clock: 4.15 a.m. But then, she remembered, it was mid June; there was nothing one could do about dawn breaking at this uncivilized hour except buy thicker curtains. The trouble was, she knew from experience that she would be unable to fall asleep again, though she longed to do so with every bone and muscle in her body. She had had exactly four and a quarter hours sleep, and it was not enough with which to face the day.

When she had last looked at her radio clock it had shown eleven fifty. The clock had been a present from her ever-considerate daughter Beryl, and as far as Poppy was concerned it was a magic clock. It soothed her to sleep at night with the gentle music from Classic FM, then somehow, when it knew she was asleep, it switched itself off. She had never been awake to find out just when this happened. It was much the same thing as when she had sung lullabies to her babies, only ceasing to sing when she could see they were fast asleep. The clock had large illuminated figures which were intrusively bright in the darkness, but at least she didn't have to fumble among the litter on her bedside table looking for her glasses whenever she wanted to know the time.

She always wanted to know the time, as though she had to account for it, or be somewhere at a given hour, which was simply not true. She was free, should she so wish, to stay in bed every day until noon, though if she decided to do so even once, Edith Prince, who arrived promptly at eight thirty three mornings a week to do the housework, would assume she was ill and would phone the doctor. I am not really free, Poppy thought. Most of all, she was not free from habit – a lifetime's habit of getting up at seven every morning.

She debated now, since she was awake, whether she would go along to the bathroom for a pee. But no, she decided; she would hang on. There was no point in starting another habit that would get her out of bed every morning, possibly for the rest of her life, at this unearthly hour.

She turned over, away from the light. It was not easy to turn because she was encumbered by a small pillow which her surgeon, Mr Barton-Foster, after her hip replacement a year ago, had told her she must place between her knees when she went to bed to prevent her crossing her legs, which was bad. She had not realized that she was an inveterate leg-crosser, and probably always had been, but Mr B.F., as he was affectionately known, had sussed it out in no time in the ten days she had spent in a rather posh hospital, courtesy of her good medical insurance.

On the whole, she thought as she heaved herself over while still trying to retain the pillow between her knees, and failing to do so, it was a good thing she slept alone: none of her husbands would have put up with a pillow between the knees. On the whole, it had not been a bad ten days, or at least not after the first two or three, when male nurses had given her bedpans, though they did it with complete detachment, chatting all the while. Wonderful food, a wide view of the Sussex Downs and the sea from her bed, a G and T before supper, lots of visitors bringing goodies – flowers, glossy magazines, toiletries and Belgian chocolates which, thankfully, a hip operation did not prevent her eating to her heart's content.

She pummelled her pillows into submission, pulled up the sheet around her shoulders, closed her eyes and determinedly invited sleep. It didn't come, of course. Sleep is capricious. There she was, warm and reasonably comfortable, except for a few familiar aches here and there, everything conducive to sleep, yet it eluded her. If it had been the middle of the day, especially if she had been in boring company, she would have been clenching her jaws in an effort not to yawn her head off.

'This will *not* do,' she said after twenty futile minutes. 'I am clearly not going to fall asleep, therefore I will concentrate on something else.'

She said the words out loud, as she often did, if only to assure herself that her voice was still there and had not faded away from lack of use. People living alone who were fortunate enough to have dogs or cats could use them as sounding boards, with at least the hope of a degree of response. Since Fred, her Yorkshire terrier, had gone to doggy heaven, she had not allowed herself to have another animal because, as she was old, it might outlive her and be as bereft as she had been after Fred's death. So she talked to herself; sometimes she even answered herself.

There was no doubt in her mind as to what she would concentrate on. The day after tomorrow would be her eightieth birthday, for which Beryl – who else? – had arranged a family party to be held here. Everyone, it seemed, had accepted, except possibly Joe, who would come if he could. The possibility of Joe's absence was a disappointment to Poppy, since her American grandson was the person she would most like to see. Still, it couldn't be helped. He hadn't said a definite no, and she would live in hope.

All three of her children would be there with their spouses – or, in Richard's case, his partner. She was not sure Graham could be described as a spouse, though the two of them had lived together for some time, as happily as any married couple – her grandchildren, with or without their lovers, and even one great-grandchild, Daisy, who was four months old.

She looked forward to seeing Daisy. She hadn't seen her since her baptism, when she had been tiny, somewhat wrinkled and red with furious anger at what was going on. In retaliation for having water poured over her head she had been sick over the vicar's rather nice vestments.

Beryl and Rodney would be the advance party, arriving today from Bath in their caravan, which Beryl had pointed out would be useful because, as well as carrying some of the baked meats they were bringing with them, it would also sleep four.

I am not, at this moment, Poppy decided, burying her head further into the pillow as if to drive out the thought, going to try to work out where everyone will sleep. She had driven herself mad about that in the last week. I shall leave it to Beryl. In any case, they were mostly Beryl's brood, or their appendages, since Mervyn, Maria and Georgia were to stay at the Splendide. My daughter did well for herself, marrying Mervyn Leverson, Poppy thought.

It had all been quite swift. Maria had saved up enough money to pay her fare to New York, where she would stay for a month with a well-heeled American girlfriend she had met at university. There, within the first week, she had sat next to Mervyn at a dinner party. From that moment, according to what the friend let slip at a later date, she had pursued, captivated and snared Mervyn within the month, with only a day or two to spare before returning to England wearing a splendid engagement ring of sapphires and diamonds. She had stayed in England just long enough to shop for a wedding dress and pack her bags before flying back to New York.

Yes, her elder daughter had done well for herself – at least materially. Certainly better in that way than her sister, who had trained as a nurse, then married a teacher and was still nursing part time to make ends meet. Possibly, though, Beryl was the happier of the two. It was not easy to tell with Maria; she had a harder shell.

I do not want this celebration, Poppy thought suddenly. She was not one for birthdays, never had been, and what was so special about one's eightieth, except, perhaps, the fact that one had survived long enough to reach it? But Beryl had been the driving force in organizing it – and 'driving' was the right word, since she had succeeded in getting Maria and her family to come to England, and it was a long time since they had done so.

Possibly, Poppy thought, they had accepted because they had felt a degree of guilt. They needn't have done. Mervyn was a fashionable, clever dentist with a busy practice and Maria had thriving beauty salons. It was not easy for either of them to take time off, and even less for it to coincide with a particular date. It was more convenient for her to visit New York which, truth to tell, she preferred to do.

All the same, this party was apparently what her family wanted. She had not always done what her family wanted, perhaps she hadn't even always done what was best for them, so on her eightieth birthday she would. She would be compliant, co-operative and very, very good.

Somehow, after that firm resolve, she must have fallen asleep, because when she next looked at the clock it was seven thirty and the sun was streaming into the room. She sat up at once, flung off the duvet and swung herself round onto the edge of the bed in the manner of those who have gone through the hip business. Legs held straight and together, cutting an elegant arc through the air. These days she could get into the front seat of a car as elegantly as the Queen.

She was good at getting up; one minute fast asleep, the next open-eyed and conscious, ready to go. She was always curious about what the day might bring, and was usually resolved to spend it well and do at least several of the things that were crying out to be done. Letters to write, purchases to be made, clothes to take to the dry-cleaners, weeds to be eradicated. The fact that she seldom achieved even half this programme didn't deter her from making a fresh one each morning.

It hadn't been like that when she was a girl.

Her mother had almost had to drag her out of bed, and that pattern had followed with her own children, especially when they were teenagers. Richard had been the worst. He would have stayed in bed until teatime if she'd let him, and at weekends he'd grumbled when she wouldn't allow it.

She wriggled her feet into her slippers, not easily because her feet were always swollen first thing in the morning, and put on her summer dressing gown. She had dressing gowns for every season of the year because people gave them to her. Perhaps they thought them a suitable present for a lady getting on in years. 'Robes' Maria called them, which had a touch of splendour to it. This was a silky, floral affair with large, tawny chrysanthemums on a black background. She hoped she wouldn't be given any more on this birthday.

She toddled along to the bathroom, though not yet for her shower. That she would take when she'd had a cup of English Breakfast tea, a slice of wholemeal toast spread with Fortnum & Mason apricot preserve, and done *The Times* Two crossword. The fact that there was a great deal to do this morning was no reason to miss out on the crossword. At one time she had done the real *Times* crossword, not the easier one hidden away at the back with the sports news. She could no longer do that; perhaps it was a sign that she was getting old. Of course she never admitted to not doing it. 'Oh, yes,' she would say, 'I finish *The*

Times crossword every day.' It was not entirely a lie, except to herself.

Minutes later she was seated at the kitchen table, toast in one hand, pen in the other, tea cooling in its mug while she attacked the crossword. 'Shine wetly', seven letters. That was easy. 'Talent; bent for', eight letters. Aptitude, of course. Talent seemed easy these days, she thought. Anyone could do anything, and not just one thing, either. You could be a concert pianist and sail around the world single-handed in your spare time. You could be an Olympic athlete, and at the same time a well-known interior designer. Everyone could write books, or at least *a* book, except those who were too busy. 'I've always thought I could write a book,' they'd say, 'if only I had the time.' She had yet to hear anyone say, 'I've always thought I could be an opera singer if only I had the time.' So perhaps there were still a few things left which needed a special talent?

That was the thing about crosswords. The words set one's thoughts moving. And I will have to move more than my thoughts, she admonished herself. Edith would arrive quite soon, and later so would Beryl and Rodney, parking their caravan on the side lawn at the back.

Caravans were so middle-aged, but then, at fifty-three, so was Beryl. Though really my younger daughter has been middle-aged since she was about twelve, Poppy thought. She and

Rodney were well matched, they had each chosen well and they were – she searched for the right word – happy would do, but contented was better. Well adjusted. She could not imagine either of them abandoning themselves to the heights of delirious passion, not even in the conception of their three children. Time, place, date of birth – which would include prospective weather at the season of the year – and financial obligations would all have been sensibly discussed. Beryl was nothing if not sensible. But also kind, Poppy reminded herself. So very kind. Today they would leave their home in Bath at the hour they'd previously decided on, and arrive here exactly three hours later. It would all go according to plan.

How come I have such an organized daughter? Poppy asked herself.

But then Beryl, and for that matter Maria, must have taken after their father. Edward would never have made all that lovely lolly had he not known what he was doing and where he was going. Her first husband's talent, and a most useful one at that, had been for making money.

What a pity he had not lived long enough to enjoy it, Poppy thought with a swift, affectionate memory of Edward. And how terribly unfortunate that his death had been so undignified, since he was easily the most dignified of her husbands. He had been sitting on the lavatory in his own house when a stray bomb jettisoned from a returning plane had badly damaged the house next door, and the blast had affected part of Edward's house. He had been hit by a small but lethal piece of flying debris. Caught with his pants down.

Poppy was out of the bathroom, drying her hair in the bedroom, when she heard Edith's arrival. She switched off the hairdryer and called out.

'I'll be down shortly, Edith.'

'Right ho, Mrs Marsh,' Edith shouted back.

Edith Prince had been coming to her for almost ten years. She had been recently widowed at the time and had, and still did, let it be known that, but for her husband's demise, there was no way she would be doing some other woman's housework.

'Henry would never have let me,' she said. 'He cherished me. A prince by name and a prince by nature, my Henry was.'

Poppy had quickly learned to let Edith believe she was doing her a favour by coming, and that her employer, in spite of paying quite good wages plus several small perks, was the recipient. Poppy didn't mind. It worked well, and anyway, what would she have done without Edith? She hated housework. Fortunately, through three marriages she had never had to do much.

Poppy herself had been widowed for the third time well before Edith came to work for her, and Edith mourned and sometimes shed a few tears for both of them. Poppy never liked to confess that, in her case, it was superfluous. Gregory

Marsh had walked out two years before news had reached her of his death in an accident. Or rather, he had taken a plane, and the local barmaid, and fled to Australia, taking his wife's pearls and a pair of diamond earrings with him. Poppy had been especially sorry about the pearls; they had been rather fine ones, given to her by Edward. The earrings she had bought herself and seldom wore. She should have sold them, or given them to one of her daughters, so in a way it served her right.

No, she had not minded the jewellery, or even Gregory, as such. She had been bored with him for quite some time before he flew away, and the idea of divorce had been flitting through her mind. It was the fact that *he* had left *her* which rankled. She was not used to things happening that way round.

She dressed now in a pair of well-cut black trousers and a long-sleeved T-shirt, combed through her hair, applied lipstick, a spot of eye shadow and the mascara without which she would not dream of facing the day. As she went down the stairs a shower of envelopes shot through the letterbox. She gathered them up and joined Edith in the kitchen.

'You get a lot of post,' Edith remarked, 'though it's nothing to what you'll get on the day.'

Poppy cleared a space on the kitchen table and started to open the post. Even though none of it looked important, she would have preferred to do it on her own, but she always spent a little time with Edith immediately after her arrival and it would look unfriendly not to do so. Added to which, Edith took a keen interest in who the post was from, no matter that she might not know the senders.

'I've put the coffee on,' Edith said. 'It's a bit early, but I thought you might be ready for it.'

There was nothing of interest in the post. One or two bills, the usual catalogues and charity appeals, and the once-a-fortnight envelope that told her, even before she opened it, that she was in line to win a quarter of a million pounds. Now *that* would be a nice birthday present! There was an early birthday card from Maisie Carstairs. Every year they sent each other birthday and Christmas cards, though it was years since they had met in the flesh. Only once, in fact, since that ill-fated Mediterranean cruise Poppy had taken on a sudden whim. Ill-fated because it was there she had met Gregory Marsh, and under indigo-blue, starry skies, with the moonlight on the water and three powerful cocktails inside her, he had wooed and won her.

It had been Poppy's first and last cruise; she didn't take to the life, and though it was by no means Gregory's first, it was also his last, since he had found what he was looking for, the prize for which he had invested his meagre means: a well-to-do widow of fifty-one. She was his senior by quite a few years, but one couldn't have everything, and she was well-preserved, generous and amusing.

Yes, Poppy thought, reading Maisie's card, I have not seen her since she attended my wedding at Akersfield Registry Office. And would that she had never met her at all, for Maisie's vicarious interest in the love affair had done a great deal to drive it forward.

She tossed Maisie's card aside. It was the last she would hear from her until Christmas.

'So who's coming today?' Edith asked.

'Only Beryl and Rodney today,' Poppy said. 'Maria and her husband are flying into Heathrow tomorrow. I'm not sure what time they'll be here. Georgia will be with them, but even his own mother isn't sure about Joe. Joe is a law unto himself.'

'They are at that age,' Edith said indulgently.

She speaks as though he's a wayward sixteen-year-old, Poppy thought, even though he is twenty-four. But I will be disappointed if he doesn't come. She knew it was wrong, but among her children and grandchildren Joe was her favourite. Always had been. He was the only one who seemed to have anything of her in him. Not so much physically, though he had her dark eyes and fair complexion, but because there was something of her temperament there. That might or might not be a good thing, of course.

'I thought you might be nipping off to the hairdresser's this morning,' Edith said.

'Tomorrow,' Poppy told her. 'I had lowlights and a cut ten days ago, so it's not too bad. I sometimes wonder what colour my hair really is! I haven't seen the original for years.'

'Those beigy streaks suit you,' Edith said, 'and I like it short, the way you have it now.' She would say nothing about the red stripes intermingled with the rest. They were not quite the thing for a woman of Mrs Marsh's age. Her Henry would not have approved if she'd had her hair tinted. In fact, it had only just started to go grey when he'd died, though now it was as white as the driven snow, and she kept it that way for his sake.

'Short is a lot less trouble,' Poppy said.

'Will Mervyn and Maria get the train from Heathrow?' Edith asked. She was interested in the minutiae of other people's lives.

'I wouldn't think so. Too complicated. No, they'll get a car.'

'That'll cost a packet,' Edith said.

'Mervyn can afford it,' Poppy replied. 'Being a dentist in New York puts him high in the money.' And ensured, of course, that he and his family saved a fortune on their near-perfect teeth. She must visit New York again before too long and get hers attended to. Mervyn was quite generous that way. He would not do it for free – that would be against his principles – but he would give her a hefty discount. And with his skill and up-to-the-minute knowledge he would preserve her ageing teeth a little longer. The day she had to part with her teeth she would possibly depart from life.

'Where everyone's going to sleep, I can't imagine!' Edith said.

'I'm not sure, either,' Poppy admitted.

What actually exercised her mind was whether or not she would give up her bedroom to Fiona and David. Presumably they would bring the baby in a carrycot? It would mean relinquishing her wondrously comfortable large bed with its Swedish mattress which had cost a small fortune, and sleeping on a narrow, rocklike put-you-up in a tiny bedroom. Was this the kind of thing one should be doing aged eighty. She would like to think her family would not allow this sacrifice, but she was by no means sure.

'In fact,' she said, 'Maria and her husband have booked in at the Splendide – and Georgia, too, of course.'

'Very posh,' Edith said, 'though I like somewhere more homely myself. There are some quite nice bed-and-breakfast places.'

Can I see my elder daughter in a B & B, Poppy asked herself? No, I cannot! But how about if I were to move into such a place for the next four nights? I could leave them all to it and sleep comfortably in peace. Reluctantly, she relinquished the idea. No way could she walk out on them and, by the same token, no way could she *not* give up her bed to Fiona and David.

'I'll sleep in the little room,' she informed Edith. 'Will you make up the bed for me and see that I have a lamp?' No way, either, would she not have a bedside lamp. Given the state of the mattress in that room, she would probably lie awake reading deep into the night.

'That doesn't seem right to me,' Edith said. 'If you'll allow me to say so, Mrs Marsh, you're no spring chicken. We need our sleep when we get older.'

Poppy sighed.

'I know. But I can't expect Fiona and David to sleep anywhere other than in my room. There's the baby to think of, you see.'

'Well, yes,' Edith admitted, 'there is that. Babies need their sleep, too, bless 'em!'

But everyone sees to it that babies get their sleep. They are bathed, dressed, fed, tucked up warm and dry in a pram, perhaps, and pushed around the park. Totally without responsibility. What utter bliss. What a pity one couldn't remember being a baby oneself. The older she became, the further back she could recall things, but never quite that far. What, in fact, *was* her earliest memory?

2

I was sitting on top of a stone wall. Not sitting on my own, I was too small for that, but my mother had lifted me up and was holding me there, her arms around me while I leaned back against her shoulder, quite safe. I knew she wouldn't let me go. The surface of the wall was rough and the stone prodded into my legs through my cotton dress, but I didn't mind. Seated as I was, with my head close to my mother's, I saw the same view as she did. That was a nice change from mainly seeing people's legs.

From the wall where I was sitting a steep, grassy hill ran down to a narrow valley at the bottom, and then climbed up again, just as steeply, on the other opposite side.

'Please! I want to go down the hill,' I begged.

'You can't do that, Poppy love,' my mother said. 'It's far too steep for a little girl of two.'

'I would hold your hand,' I promised.

'In any case,' she said, 'it's not allowed. Even I am not allowed. No-one is. There's a notice there.' She pointed it out to me. 'You can't read it yet but it says, "Trespassers Will be Prosecuted".'

I laughed at that.

'What's funny?' my mother asked.

'What you said: funny words.' I loved the sound of words, even when I had no idea what they meant.

'I suppose they are,' she agreed. 'What they mean is that if we go down this hill someone might come along and be very cross with us, and that's because, as you very well know, the trains run down at the bottom. It wouldn't be safe.'

'I want to see the train,' I said.

'I know you do, Poppy,' she always spoke to me patiently, 'and so do I. That's why we've come here, isn't it?'

'Where *is* the train?' I was by no means patient.

'If you watch over there' – she let go of me for a second with one arm to point out the way – 'quite soon you'll see the signal, and then the train will come.'

My mother was always right. In any case, I knew what would happen because this wasn't the first time we'd come to watch for the train; we did it quite often, and always in the afternoon. Sure enough, not many minutes later there was the click of the signal and then, in the distance, what I had been waiting for.

'Smoke!' I cried. 'Smoke!'

'Steam, not smoke,' my mother corrected me. 'And now here comes the train.'

First there was the big engine with the chimney on top with white steam pouring from it, filling the sky, and then the long carriages. The engine was the same colour as the grassy hill, only darker, and the front of it was black. The carriages were yellow. I knew all my colours by now, and a few letters. 'She's a bright child,' people used to say. There were three large letters on the engine, written in gold and shining brightly in the afternoon sun.

'G – N – R,' my mother said. 'Great Northern Railway.'

We always counted the carriages. One, two, three, sometimes as many as six. They had windows all along the sides, and there were men who all looked alike crowded around the windows.

'Wave to the soldiers,' my mother instructed.

I waved my hand and she fluttered a white handkerchief.

'See,' she cried. 'They're waving back to us!'

Very soon the train passed out of sight, disappearing into a hole in the hillside, leaving only a cloud of steam curling around the entrance to show that it had been there.

'All the trains live in the hole,' I said, 'and all the soldiers live in the hole.'

My mother laughed.

'No, Poppy darling, the train comes out on the other side of the hole, which is called a tunnel. The men are going home from the war in France. It's quite disgraceful. All these months after the war ended and there are thousands not yet back in England. There was nearly a mutiny about it in the army.' She sounded very angry.

'Mutiny?' I asked. I had no idea what she was talking about, but I liked the sound of that word, too. Trespassers, prosecuted, mutiny.

'Mutiny,' I repeated. 'What's mutiny?'

'It's what you do when I tell you to pick up your toys and you won't.'

'Naughty,' I said.

'But sometimes necessary. Except for little girls,' she added. 'Come along then. Time to go home for tea.' She held me firmly by the waist and lifted me through the air in a wide arc from the top of the wall to the ground so that I could pretend I was flying like a bird.

It was a long walk home and the sun was hot. Our house was at the top of a hill, the very last house before the road ended at the farm. When I was a small girl I thought every road, every street was a hill, I suppose because many of them were and my legs were short. As I grew older the roads didn't seem hills at all. On this particular afternoon I was hot and weary so, deciding I would go no further, I let go of my mother's hand and sat down on the pavement.

'Poppy, what are you doing?' my mother said. 'Stand up at once. You'll get your dress all dirty.'

'No,' I said. 'Poppy is tired.'

'Mother is tired, too. Come along. Get up and take my hand. It's not far now.'

I shook my head.

'Carry me,' I demanded.

'Oh no, Poppy, you're much too heavy.' She didn't sound cross, she just sounded sad. 'And on top of everything else.'

'Now this *is* mutiny,' she said. Nevertheless, she stooped down, lifted me up and carried me the rest of the way home. She walked quite slowly, and when we reached the top of the hill the lady next door was just leaving her house.

'Why, Harriet,' she said – Harriet was what other people called my mother. 'You look quite worn out. You shouldn't be carrying Poppy; she's big enough to walk.'

'I know, Mrs Harris,' my mother said, 'but you try telling her that.' Her voice sounded funny.

'Why, I do believe you're crying,' Mrs Harris said. 'That's not like you. Now I'll come in the house with you, I'll put the kettle on and make you a nice cup of tea. As for you, Poppy, you can get down this minute and walk up the path on your own two feet.'

I did as I was told. In the house, Mrs Harris set the kettle to boil on the fire and my mother sat down at the table and burst into tears.

'There, look what you've done,' Mrs Harris said in a stern voice. 'You've made your mother cry. What a naughty girl you are.'

My mother raised her head and wiped her eyes with the handkerchief with which she had waved to the soldiers. 'It's not Poppy,' she said. 'It's just everything. I get so tired of waiting, and he never comes. Nearly three years since he had his last leave, and the war's well over. I sometimes wonder whether he'll ever come home.'

'Of course he will, love. Don't you fret. One of these days, very soon, you'll look out of the window and see him walking up that path,' Mrs Harris reassured her. 'And you be a good girl and do as you're told,' she said to me. 'You've got to look after your mother until your Daddy comes home.'

I didn't like Mrs Harris and I was quite sure she didn't like me. Even when you're small you can tell who likes you and who doesn't.

I knew who Daddy was. He was the man in the photograph on the sideboard. He wore a jacket with lots of buttons and a funny cap on his head. Mother said it was his uniform and that he was a soldier fighting for his king and country. 'And for you and me,' she added.

Of course, I don't remember every single thing that happened that day, or exactly what everyone said, but I *do* remember sitting on the wall, watching the train, and the soldiers waving. When I told my mother about it she filled in the rest, about being carried up the hill and Mrs Harris and so on.

'Mrs Harris was quite a kind lady, actually,' she said. 'It was just that she didn't know how to talk to children because she'd never had any. She wasn't prepared for a little mutineer like you.'

'I just longed for your dad,' she told me. 'All the time. Of course, you'd never seen him, and what you don't know you don't miss.'

For that matter, she said, she hadn't seen much of him herself. She had met him at a party in October 1916. The world was full of parties of a sort: young men leaving and having a last fling before they went back to the war; younger men, recently called up, making the most of what was left to them before they were sent overseas. Hugh was eighteen and handsome in his immaculate new uniform. My mother was the same age. They married in no time at all, and three months later he was in France, helping to fill the vast black hole left by hundreds of thousands of men who had been killed on the Somme that summer.

My father did come back not many weeks after that afternoon when I saw my mother cry for him. I expect she had a telegram and I expect she told me, but I don't remember any of that. All I do recall is that one day there was a knock on the door, my mother ran to open it and there was this tall man standing there. My mother shrieked, ran into his arms and then burst into tears, and he put his arms around her. It seemed quite a long time before either of them noticed me, and it was my mother who did.

'This is your daughter, Poppy,' she said proudly. 'Poppy, this is your daddy. Are you going to give him a big kiss?'

He picked me up and lifted me quite high – he was very strong – and started to kiss me. I didn't like it at all; his face was all prickly. I wriggled away from him and put my arms out to my mother to lift me down, which she did.

'Poppy isn't used to men,' she said.

'I'm pleased to hear that,' my father replied.

I didn't really need my father and I couldn't see why my mother did, either. We had each other. We had our outings to the park, to the shops and to the railway embankment. She bathed me, cooked me nice dinners and baked little cakes for my tea. She helped me draw pictures, read stories to me and taught me letters and numbers, and she continued to do that after my father's return.

'She's too young for all that,' he objected.

It was one of the few things on which my mother contradicted him.

'No, she's not,' she said. 'No-one is ever too young to learn. And she's a clever little girl; she needs to use her mind.'

My father didn't think little girls had minds, except to be awkward, which my mother afterwards told me I was.

'You weren't very nice to him,' she said. 'You turned away when he came near you and yelled if he tried to pick you up. It was no homecoming for a man who'd been in the trenches.'

The worst thing for me was that he slept in my mother's bed, which had always been *our* bed, mine and hers. Of course, I had my cot, but whatever time of the night or early morning I awoke and crept into her bed, I was sure of a welcome. Sometimes, if I wasn't well, I would sleep in the big bed from the beginning and we'd spend the whole night together.

All that changed from the very first night my father returned. He made it quite plain that he didn't want me in the bedroom, let alone in the bed, and he made my mother move my cot into the spare room. If I turned up at the side of the bed during the night he would send me back to my room, no matter what my mother said. Only very occasionally, when he was ready to get up anyway, would he give in to my mother's plea and let me in. But it wasn't the same. For a start it had a funny smell.

The worst time of all was that terrible morning when I left my cot and walked into the big bedroom to find my father lying on top of my mother and bouncing on her. He was a big man and I could hardly see my mother underneath him. She was giving little cries and I thought he was killing her. I screamed and screamed.

I can't remember what happened next. I know he went out and stayed out all day, which pleased me. It didn't please my mother, but she wouldn't talk to me about it, either then or later.

I don't remember the next few months very clearly. It was Christmas, and then it was very cold and I got chilblains – or perhaps that was another time. I got chilblains every year in the winter.

'Don't sit so near the fire,' my mother would say. 'It makes them worse.'

It was June and it was my third birthday;

we had jelly and custard for tea, and my mother baked a cake in the shape of a flower. I was given a box of wax crayons and a colouring book.

The months went by, and all the time I knew my father didn't like me. I could never please him. He didn't even like my name.

'What sort of a name is Poppy?' he grumbled. 'It's a stupid name.'

'I think it's a nice name,' my mother said.

'I think it's the best name in the whole world,' I added. We were both being quite courageous because it was not a good idea to defy my father.

'Your father gets cross because he can't find work,' my mother explained to me later when we were alone together. 'He wants to earn money to look after you and me. We thought when the war was over it would be easier for everyone, but that's not true.'

A little while later my mother announced that she was to go out to work doing housework five mornings a week for a lady who was well-off. The lady had agreed that I could go with my mother because I wasn't old enough to go to school.

'You will have to behave well,' my mother warned me. 'She is a very particular lady. But you can take your colouring book with you.'

I went with her every morning, but unfortunately it didn't last because in the second week I knocked over a vase of flowers, broke the vase and spilled the water all over the floor.

'I'm sorry,' the lady told my mother, 'I'm

afraid you'll have to come on your own from now on.'

This meant that I had to stay with my father, which he didn't like – he said I got on his nerves – and nor did I.

One day he said, 'I'm going out. Your mother will be back in less than an hour. There's a note for her on the table.' He had put the note in an envelope and stuck the flap down.

I was quite happy on my own. I could read now – my mother had taught me – and I had a book called *Little Frolics* which was all about a family of children who had lovely times, going on picnics, roundabouts and to the fair.

Eventually my mother came home, took off her coat and said, 'Where's Daddy?'

'Out,' I said. 'There's a note.'

I never saw my father again, and I learned later that neither did my mother. I didn't mind; in fact, I was pleased. It was much better with just my mother and me and, with the self-centredness of an only child, I thought it would be better for her, too.

But all this was more than seventy years ago. I don't know how I remember it, but I do.

3

On the dot of eleven, passing through the hall to go upstairs, Poppy looked out of the window and saw the caravan, with Beryl driving, turn into the drive. Beryl, small of stature so that she was almost hidden behind the wheel, made the awkward turn into the drive with great skill and confidence and almost no decrease of speed. Poppy watched with admiration. She herself was a dashing but erratic driver and not good at parking. Her daughter was one of those women who, had she been in the army during war, would be driving a tank through the desert or an ambulance under fire across the battlefield. And she would have got there on time.

But were Beryl's skills a mite heavy for a nurse? Perhaps not. It had been her own experience, when in hospital, that those nurses who were the size of midgets, or vertically challenged as she must now remember to say, were the ones who could fling you around as if you were a bag of feathers.

She went out to greet them and Beryl wound down the window.

'Hi, Mummy,' she said in a cheerful voice. 'Are you all right? I'll just drive down to the side garden and park out of sight.'

'I'm fine, darling. I'll follow you.'

Rodney, seated beside his wife, gave Poppy a smile and a wave. He never had much to say, probably because he didn't often get the chance. As a school teacher, Poppy thought, he must wield authority in other parts of his life. But Beryl was not a small child.

Poppy followed the caravan round to the back of the house where Beryl, with a few deft movements, parked it exactly where she wanted it, on the gravelled area of the side garden, then jumped down with ease. Rodney followed at a more leisurely pace.

'Is Jeremy not with you?' Poppy asked. 'I thought he would be. The vacation has started, hasn't it?'

'Oh, yes,' Beryl replied. 'He'll be here tomorrow. And I'm afraid he's bringing a friend. I hope you don't mind. I told him he should ring up first and ask you.'

'That's perfectly all right,' Poppy said. 'He'll be very welcome.'

'A "she", not a "he",' Beryl said.

'His new girlfriend,' Rodney volunteered.

'Oh. I didn't know he had a new girlfriend. What happened to Carol?'

'Who knows?' Rodney said. 'But Megan is nice.

She's also at LSE in the same year. She's reading Politics and Russian.'

'Good heavens!' Poppy said. 'She must be awfully clever.' She had never thought of Jeremy choosing a brainbox. His girlfriends, even from his school days, had, without exception, been pretty and on the dumb side.

'She is clever,' Beryl said. She sounded less than enthusiastic. Perhaps this one was serious, and Beryl was a mother hen who liked to keep her chicks under her wing.

'They're at a conference in Swindon today,' Rodney explained. 'Something to do with the Labour Party.'

So that was it! A clever girl who was also, presumably, a member of the Labour Party, or why would she be attending a conference? That would certainly be too much for Beryl. Beryl was a true-blue, dyed-in-the-wool Tory; a prop and stay of her local party, and in her time a stalwart of the Young Conservatives. Poppy gave her daughter an enquiring look.

'Oh, I know what you're thinking, Mummy,' Beryl said. 'And you're right. I never wanted Jeremy to go to the London School of Economics. It's a hotbed of socialism. Why couldn't he have tried for Oxford or Cambridge? He would have met a much better type of person there.'

'Oh, come on love,' Rodney said soothingly. 'I'm sure it's not all that bad. I daresay there are quite a few members of the Conservative Party at the LSE.'

As well as socialists at Oxbridge, Poppy reckoned.

'They might be when they start. Who knows how they'll come out in the end?' Beryl said.

Poor Beryl, Poppy thought. She was such a nice person at heart, and a good mother, but she did rather like everyone, especially her family and close friends, to conform to her way of thinking; as if, were they to stray, she might lose them altogether.

'Let me take some of those things,' Poppy offered. 'And we'll have some coffee. I expect you'd both like a cup.'

She bent down to pick up a large tin box, but Beryl put out a hand and prevented her.

'Not that one, Mummy, it's far too heavy for you. Actually, it's your birthday cake. Anyway, I don't want you to see it before the day.'

'How kind of you to bother,' Poppy said. 'I'll take this, then.' She picked up a plastic bag and led the way into the house, followed by Beryl and Rodney. Edith was at the sink, washing dishes.

'Good morning, Mrs Dean. Mr Dean,' she said.

'I think we could do with some coffee, Edith,' Poppy said. 'If you have time.'

Beryl gave her mother a look. But what my daughter doesn't understand, Poppy thought, is that with the Ediths of this world one doesn't order, one requests. Politely. Not that one had the slightest intention of making the coffee oneself; that was understood by both parties.

Beryl, of course, had never had an Edith. She eschewed domestic help, going through her house like a whirlwind in her off-duty hours from the hospital. Vacuum, dust, polish, pull the furniture out to clean behind it, pummel the cushions, empty the bins, wash the kitchen floor. Crash! Bang! Wallop! Poppy had seen her at it. It was quite exhausting for the onlooker, though Beryl came out of it apparently unscathed.

'Instant will be fine,' Beryl instructed Edith. 'So much quicker.'

Edith ignored her, measuring the coffee into the cafetière.

It was amazing how Beryl always managed to say the wrong thing, though without the slightest malice, within five minutes of arriving anywhere. But if she thought she could boss Edith around she was mistaken. Edith would now make a point of taking orders only from her employer.

'I'm sure we have time to sit down with a coffee,' Poppy said smoothly. 'It will refresh you after your journey.'

'The journey was a doddle,' Beryl replied. 'As smooth as silk.'

'Good!' Poppy said.

It would be, wouldn't it? When had Beryl ever had a flat tyre? When had she had to sacrifice her tights as a substitute for a broken fan belt, or when had her exhaust fallen off? How often had she run out of petrol three miles from the nearest garage? The answers were never, never, never and never. And why am I being so mean so early in the day, and with a daughter I love, who is here to help me?

Edith put the coffee on the table. Poppy and Rodney sat down, and Beryl hovered.

'Mummy,' she asked, 'have you sorted out where we're all sleeping?'

'Not yet,' Poppy said. 'I thought I'd consult you. You're good at these things. But we won't have to worry about Maria and Mervyn, or Georgia. They're staying at the Splendide.'

Beryl gave a sniff that might have been disapproval or the beginning of a head cold.

'And I've definitely decided that Fiona and David, and little Daisy, are to have my room.'

Beryl's face lit up in a smile. How different she looked when she smiled. The two vertical lines disappeared from her brow, her mouth turned up at the corners, becoming generous rather than simply large, and her eyes softened to a warm grey. It was her new grandmotherly look. 'How kind of you. You're going to see quite a difference in Daisy, Mummy. She changes almost every day now, bless her.' There was a short silence, then Beryl put down her coffee cup, the moment of grandmotherly tenderness having passed. 'We'd better make a start, hadn't we? We should bring in the food from the caravan. It can get quite hot in there.'

'We shall have to find room for it in the study,' Poppy said. 'The fridge is fairly full. But since it faces north, the study is quite cool . . .'

She was about to add how she envied Maria,

who had one of those American fridges the size of a double wardrobe, plus a freezer equally spacious, but she clamped her jaw and held it back.

'Right,' Beryl said. 'Rodney, you and I will bring in the rest of the stuff. No need for you, Mummy.' She looked at Edith, who quickly turned away.

Poppy watched them as they traipsed to and fro between the caravan and the house, bearing dishes, bowls and boxes, presumably full of food. What could it all be, she asked herself? Do we need it? 'It's very good of you to do all this,' she said. 'You must let me make a contribution.'

'Certainly not, Mummy,' Beryl replied. 'It's your birthday. But don't worry, I'm sure Maria will contribute. She's quite generous when she remembers.' It was just that Maria didn't always stop to think about the difference in their positions, moneywise. As for Richard, their little half-brother – though no longer little since he was forty-nine and now that he had given up squash and all those other energetic pastimes he was rapidly putting on weight – he certainly couldn't be relied upon to contribute of his own free will. Not because he wouldn't think about it, but because he was downright mean. But not to worry, she would ask him outright.

'Well,' Edith said presently, 'it's time I wasn't here.' She took off her apron, folded it carefully and replaced it in the shopping bag which always hung behind the kitchen door when she was in residence.

'I don't think there's anything else,' she said. She had washed up the coffee cups, and that was that, as far as she was concerned. Let Bossy Beryl deal with the rest. 'I'll see you in the morning, Mrs Marsh. Don't work too hard.'

It doesn't look as though I'm going to have to work at all, Poppy thought as she saw Edith off. Beryl and Rodney had taken over, even to the extent that Beryl had brought a quiche and salad for lunch, and something in a large plastic box labelled, 'Supper, Thursday'.

'It's a lasagne,' Beryl said. 'All I have to do is heat it up.'

'Oh, Beryl, you've thought of everything,' Poppy said. 'It's so kind of you.'

'I just don't want you tiring yourself out before your birthday arrives,' Beryl told her. 'You can take it easy for the rest of today, and hopefully for a little while tomorrow before they start arriving. And you should try to get an early night.'

Which is precisely what I am doing, Poppy thought nine hours later, sitting up in bed, reading a new novel. She couldn't remember when she'd last been in bed as early as half-past nine. It was rather pleasant. All afternoon and evening Beryl had acted like a strict but loving nanny, though she had stopped short of giving Poppy a nice warm bath and hearing her say her prayers.

It was lovely in the short term, say for twenty-four hours, but longer than that and it would drive her mad. Having retired early, would she sleep through the night? But if she didn't she would at least be lying awake in her own blissfully comfortable bed. How long before she would sleep in it again?

It had not been made clear how long Fiona would be staying. Mervyn, she knew, could not stay long. He had appointments in New York, and with Mervyn, work came first. It would probably be the same with Maria. They were a driven couple. But how nice if Georgia could be persuaded to stay on a bit. Beryl was taking a few days of her holiday, but Rodney had to be back in school on Monday. She was not sure how he had managed to get two days off. Oh well, it would sort itself out.

At the point when the lines of print in her book began to blur into each other, she put it down and switched off the light. Then, miracle of miracles, she slept through the night. She was woken next morning by the sunlight on the bedroom wall and Beryl entering, bearing a breakfast tray.

'I can't believe it,' Poppy said, sitting up, wide awake. 'I don't know when I've slept so well. Are you sure you didn't drug my Ovaltine?'

'I did not,' Beryl assured her. 'I expect you needed the sleep. There's no need for you to get up just yet; I purposely brought your breakfast early to stop you doing so. So stay a bit; there's nothing in particular for you to do.'

But there is, Poppy thought when Beryl had left the room. I have to sort out the clean linen so that Edith can change this bed. I must move my belongings into the little room: make-up, hairbrush, sleeping pills, nightdress, clean clothes and all the rest. It was a pity she couldn't take the television. She had an appointment with the hairdresser at nine o'clock, but she had time to eat her breakfast at leisure. It looked tempting: cornflakes, a small jug of milk, toast, marmalade, a pot of tea and even three tiny purple violas in a minute vase.

The hairdo went well. She viewed herself in the mirror with some satisfaction. Fran, the stylist, was also pleased. 'Eighty tomorrow, Mrs Marsh, and you don't look a day over seventy,' she said.

'Thank you,' Poppy said, but she was piqued. She had not thought she looked anywhere near seventy. She lifted her chin high, sucked in her cheeks, opened her eyes wide and looked defiantly in the mirror.

She was back at home before eleven o'clock and now the three of them were taking a breather in the sitting room, or at least Poppy and Rodney were. Beryl was on her feet, anxious to get going again. 'We still have things to do,' she reminded Rodney.

Poppy, gazing out of the window for no reason at all, saw a smart limousine draw to a smooth halt at the entrance to the drive. Clearly, the driver wasn't going to attempt to manoeuvre his shiny black vehicle between those gateposts.

She sprang to her feet.

'Good heavens! It's Maria.'

Rodney rushed to the window, followed by Beryl, then the two of them immediately made for the door, with Poppy close behind. Maria, Mervyn and Georgia stepped out of the car, and the driver opened the boot and began to extract several items of matching Louis Vuitton luggage, piling it on the pavement.

'Why didn't they go to the Splendide first and leave the luggage there?' Rodney whispered to his wife.

Beryl shrugged. 'Who knows?'

The driver stood by the luggage, waiting for the greetings to finish. They were soon over; the new arrivals were clearly not in the mood for them.

'Why didn't you go to the Splendide first, darlings?' Poppy enquired. 'It would have been easier, wouldn't it? Not that I'm not thrilled to see you all.'

But there was something wrong. They looked, all three of them . . . furious was the word. Had they had a terrible quarrel?

'Oh, we did,' Maria said grimly. 'We sure did. Would you believe they didn't have rooms for us? Said they hadn't had the reservations, or the wrong dates, or some such garbage, and they were full to the skies with a convention.'

Mervyn was red with ill-suppressed rage. 'I shall sue them,' he stormed. 'Believe me, they'll hear from my lawyer.'

'Oh dear,' Poppy said. 'How very unfortunate.' It was also unfortunate that, at that moment, she saw a dog, taking a walk along the road, lift his leg against one of their elegant suitcases. Luckily it seemed that only she and the driver had observed this. They gave each other a look and said nothing.

'Shall we go in?' Rodney suggested.

Before another dog comes along, Poppy thought. In her experience dogs always peed where another dog had peed before them.

Rodney picked up three pieces of luggage, the driver three, Beryl and Maria two each and Poppy one. Mervyn was empty-handed and Georgia carried a minuscule handbag. Together they walked up to the house.

Edith, almost ready to leave, was waiting in the hall. She blanched at the sight of the cases.

'A little misunderstanding,' Poppy said. 'We'll just stack these here, wherever we can, and go into the sitting room and have a nice calming drink!'

Mervyn looked as though it would take a general anaesthetic to calm him and Maria was only a little less tense. Like a sheepdog with a recalcitrant flock, Poppy guided them until they were safely penned.

'Do sit down,' she said, but the rage was too strong in Mervyn to allow him to sit. He stood, his shortish legs astride, his back to the window, commanding the attention of the whole room.

'Now,' Poppy said, combining encouraging brightness with lots of sympathy, plus the assurance of an eighty-year-old who has seen it all before and knows how to deal with it – though she hadn't and she didn't. 'What's it to be? Gin and tonic? Martini? Whisky? Or perhaps coffee? Or orange juice?' She turned to her granddaughter who, so far, had not spoken and looked as though she was far removed from the whole scene. 'What about you, Georgia darling?'

'A diet Coke, please.'

Poppy made for the kitchen, Rodney following to lend a hand. Edith's whole face was a question mark. Poppy raised a hand.

'Not now, Edith. We have a teeny crisis on our hands. Think of drinks as first aid! Do we have diet Coke?' Personally, she could down two large G and Ts in quick succession.

'Diet Coke?'

'Not to worry,' Rodney said. 'We have some in the van. I'll get it.'

'Beryl would like coffee, and Maria Earl Grey tea, weak, with lemon. Will you see to those, Edith? Rodney and I will do the rest.'

'Right, Mrs Marsh,' Edith said, 'but what I'm wondering is, where will everyone . . . ?'

'It is what we're *all* wondering,' Poppy said. 'And until I've had a stiff drink I refuse even to contemplate it.'

She dropped ice cubes into a tumbler, added

Gordon's generously, filled it to the brim with Schweppes and drank deep.

They returned to the sitting room, Rodney with drinks for himself and Mervyn, Edith with tea and coffee and Poppy bringing up the rear with her gin in one hand and a diet Coke in the other. Edith fussed about with sugar and milk, reluctant to leave.

'Thank you, Edith,' Poppy said.

'If you want anything else . . .' Edith offered.

'Thank you, Edith. I'll let you know. But I'm sure it's time you were going.'

Everyone was positioned exactly as she had left them, like people on a stage, though it was clear that Mervyn and Maria had been having a go at each other.

She took another sip of her drink, then sat down. 'Now, dears,' she said, 'do tell me all about it. What happened?'

Mervyn and Maria spoke at the same time. 'It's unbelievable. Somebody's going to hear about this, big time!'

'The driver and the porter took all our bags into the lounge,' Maria said. 'We went to the desk to register, planning to freshen up and then come straight here. Would you believe they said they had no reservations for us—'

'They did *not* say that,' Mervyn interrupted. 'They said our reservations had been made for *next* weekend, not this.'

'I told them that was a flat lie,' Maria said. 'My secretary made the reservations directly with the hotel. One double room, one single, and a connecting lounge. A suite, in fact.'

'You should never have left it to your secretary,' Mervyn shouted. 'She shouldn't have booked direct. Why the hell didn't she go through the usual travel agency, like anyone else would? She's no good, I tell you. Get rid of her.'

'She is perfectly good,' Maria shrieked. 'Perhaps you should have made the bloody reservations yourself. We all know *you* never make a mistake.'

'*I* do *not* make reservations.'

Mervyn's voice cut through the air like a dagger. For a man who was short, plump, crumpled from travelling and now a purplish-red in the face, Poppy thought, he suddenly showed a surprising hauteur. Of course he was a man who wouldn't make his own reservations, or carry his own suitcase.

'If I did,' he continued, 'I would make sure I got the goddam date right.'

'We only have the hotel's word that *they're* right,' Maria said. 'I'd back Claudette any day. And if you think they are in the right, how come you're threatening to sue them?'

Mervyn looked at her in astonishment. 'Someone has to be sued,' he said. He had been denied shelter, more or less thrown out, his word doubted, made to lose face in front of several people, and in a foreign country. And not a word about compensation. Of course he would sue.

'We should have stayed in London,' he said.

'Had a car bring us to the party. This would never have happened if we'd stayed at the Dorchester!'

'Didn't you get confirmation? I mean written confirmation?' Beryl interrupted.

'No,' Maria said. 'We booked late because, as you know, my husband wasn't quite sure whether he could make it.'

'I knew it would come down to me,' Mervyn said bitterly.

'Couldn't the hotel offer you anything else?' Poppy queried. 'Perhaps not a suite, but a couple of rooms?'

'Mummy, I already told you,' Maria said impatiently, 'the place was full. This convention, conference, whatever. Catering equipment suppliers, if you please. The whole town's full of them; no rooms anywhere.'

A glimmer of hope came to Poppy.

'Well,' she said brightly, 'I'm sure all isn't lost! We'll try Eastbourne. It's not as close as Brighton, but it's not too bad.'

'No go,' Mervyn barked. 'They tried Eastbourne. Another conference. International morticians, would you believe. I guess we must hope no-one worldwide is inconsiderate enough to die.'

'I daresay it's the off-season for them,' Poppy said reasonably. 'I suppose not as many people die in June.'

'While we're at it,' Mervyn said, 'the same thing applies all along your south coast. Conventions, conferences, carnivals, car rallies – whatever the hell *they* are – you name it.'

'Concerts, cat shows,' Beryl offered.

'And then,' Mervyn said, 'we had to watch – and so did everyone else; it was a free show – while the bellhop took everything back to our car. And having tipped him to bring them in, I had to tip him to take them out again!'

'Oh dear,' Poppy said. 'It's quite clear my birthday's in the wrong week.'

'No-one's blaming you,' Mervyn said gruffly. 'It's that goddam secretary.'

'It is *not*,' Maria reiterated, her voice rising skyward.

'*Please*,' Poppy begged. 'Can we move on? What we have to sort out is,' she took a deep breath, then willed herself to say it, '*where are we all going to sleep?*'

'Mervyn and Maria,' Beryl said sweetly, 'are most welcome to share the caravan with Rodney and myself!'

She was rewarded with a look of horror from her sister and brother-in-law.

Poppy cast around for something less controversial.

'Aside from all that, darlings, did you have a good flight?'

She had said the wrong thing again. Mervyn's face darkened further and Maria let out a long, long sigh. Georgia, though, gave no sign of having heard. She was turning the pages of a magazine.

'We did not,' Mervyn said.

'What went wrong?' Poppy asked. Did she want to know? But it would be impolite not to ask, and anyway, she was going to be told.

'Turbulence.'

It was amazing how much loathing could be put into one word.

'Thousands of dollars I paid for First Class seats. What use is champagne and fancy food if it's served up with turbulence?'

'It wasn't all that bad,' Maria objected. 'A few little tremors.'

Mervyn glared at her.

'When I book First Class I don't expect turbulence, and especially not in June. And if you call feeling as though the bottom of the plane's dropping out a little tremor, well, I can't agree with you.'

'Don't exaggerate, Mervyn,' Maria said wearily.

'I don't. Other passengers felt the same. Did you hear that woman call out?'

'She was hysterical.'

'What did she say?' Beryl sounded truly interested. Mervyn gave her a hostile look. This was a private argument between husband and wife.

' "Lord Jesus save us" if you must know, and if I were a religious guy I might have said the same.'

'You're being silly,' Maria said. 'The trouble is simple: you're afraid of flying. You are simply *afraid*.'

Mervyn's face went from dark red to ashen white. There was a deep silence while everyone waited for the explosion. Maria had gone too far. It didn't come, but Mervyn's tightly controlled words, quietly spoken and spaced out to add emphasis, were more telling than any tantrum.

'I . . . am . . . not . . . afraid . . . of . . . flying!'

Oh but you *are*. You poor man, you really are. Poppy was immediately convinced. The strength of Mervyn's denial made it all too false.

A dentist of whom so many people – if she was anything to go by – were afraid, a rich, successful man, and he was terrified of flying. What was more, he had endured it to be at her party. She wanted to put her arms around him and say, There, there, it's all right, as if he were a small boy faced with a nasty nightmare. She was also very annoyed with her daughter. Maria had shown real cruelty.

'I'm not keen on flying myself,' Rodney said swiftly.

Dear Rodney, he could be relied upon to say something nice. My daughters have done better than they deserve, Poppy thought, even if Mervyn *is* pompous and Rodney *is* dull.

'What I think,' she said, 'is that you are tired out and suffering from jet lag, Mervyn. I expect you have been working hard and you got no sleep on the plane. You, too, Maria. And you, Georgia. You should all get some sleep before you do anything else.'

'I *never* suffer from jet lag,' Maria said.

'Then count yourself damned lucky,' Poppy said sharply.

'You could have a kip in the caravan,' Rodney offered. 'There's a double bunk made up. It's quite comfortable.'

'Thank you, Rodney. I don't need to go to bed,' Maria said.

'While I', Mervyn said, temporarily restored to a sort of distant dignity, 'would be glad to take you up on your kind offer for just a couple of hours.'

'As long as you like, old man,' Rodney said. 'I'll show you the way.'

'Georgia,' Poppy said, 'you could have a nap on what is to be my bed for the night.' Heaven knew whether it ever would be, or indeed where any of them might find a place to rest their heads, let alone a bed.

'OK,' Georgia said listlessly.

Poppy took her, plus one suitcase from the collection in the hall, upstairs and showed her the room.

'It's rather small,' she apologized, 'and not very smart. Everything for which there isn't a home gets dumped in here.'

'It doesn't matter,' Georgia said.

'Then I'll leave you to it,' Poppy said.

How disappointing, she thought as she went back downstairs. It hadn't always been like that between them. Two years ago, when she'd last visited New York, Georgia had been a lively extrovert sixteen-year-old; she'd been fun;

they'd gone shopping together – not to Bloomingdales or Macy's, but to small, trendy boutiques. Georgia knew all the way-out places. And they had taken in several movies and even been to a pop concert. In Georgia's company she'd felt almost young, whereas in the company of her daughters she always felt the age she knew herself to be.

But it was no longer so with Georgia. There was a chasm between them. Poor child; she was probably in love. Either unrequited love, of which there is no worse hell, or the reverse, and she'd been torn apart from her beloved in order to visit her grandmother thousands of miles away. She probably hates me, Poppy thought. And with good reason.

4

As far as I was concerned, life was much better after my father had left. I hardly missed him at all, and if I did it was with a sense of relief. It was probably not better for my mother, but with the selfishness of a small and only child – spoilt, I suppose, because for the first two and a half years of my life I had had my mother's whole attention – that didn't occur to me. Now her attention was all mine again.

We did everything together. Of course, we no longer went to the railway; we hadn't done that since the day my father came home.

'I used to like watching the trains,' I complained. 'It was exciting.'

'The men have all come home now,' my mother said. 'Though whether any of them are the same as they were when they went away, I doubt. It's a new world, and it's not one we expected. Anyway, you're getting too big to watch the trains. And we do other things, don't we?'

That was true. We went to the park most days, where my mother would push me on the newly erected swings. I learned afterwards that this was a real sacrifice on her part. 'I hated it,' she told me, but not until I had outgrown the craze for it. 'Just watching swings makes me dizzy in the head and sick in the stomach.'

The next great thing which beckoned me was school. Park Street Mixed Infants. I had longed to go there at least a year before I was old enough to be admitted to the nursery class, and the longing was partly due to Esmé Infield, who lived next door, on the other side to Mrs Harris. She was a year older than me and she would come home from school every day with something she had made: a lantern, a crown or a small basket with a handle – all made from paper, cut and folded and stuck together with a white paste called 'Gloy'.

At last the day came. I had badgered my mother into letting me grow my hated fringe until it was long enough to be drawn to the side and fastened with a small tortoiseshell hairslide, of which I was inordinately proud. At school, under the guidance of Miss Fawcett, our class teacher, I soon learned to make those things myself. If we did the basket well, Miss Fawcett would pop two jelly babies into it, which we could eat at playtime. I can make a paper basket to this day.

Esmé and I had something else in common, apart from Miss Fawcett. She also had no father;

he had been killed early on in the war, so she hardly remembered him. She also had neither brothers nor sisters, but for me she had the attributes of a big sister: care, kindness and a certain bossiness. She liked to put me right, and she could do this because she knew more about almost everything than I did. But I was her equal, or perhaps ahead of her, in reading because my mother had taught me that long before I went to school.

'Reading', my mother said, 'is the key to everything. If you can read, there's nothing you can't learn.'

One day, I suppose I might have been seven, I came home from Sunday school very excited. 'There's to be a day trip to Morecambe,' I said. 'We'll go on the train, and we have to take sandwiches; it'll cost two shillings and the vicar would like mothers to go as well. You will go, won't you?'

'Of course,' she agreed.

There is a photograph of me, taken by the vicar on his Box Brownie. It shows me standing with my mother at the very edge of the sea. My dress is tucked unevenly into the top of my navy-blue knickers, which are elasticated around the legs. My feet are bare, because I'm about to paddle, but my mother is dressed in her best outfit: a cream, knee-length, knife-pleated skirt, with a matching square-necked top, Magyar sleeves and a belt slung around below her waist. She is wearing a hat like an upturned plant pot, pulled well down over her ears and forehead, so that she peers out from underneath it. Actually, the jumper and skirt would get by today. Perhaps not the hat. She looks beautiful, even through today's eyes. She had a timeless beauty which only deserted her in her last illness.

I was a skinny child – long-limbed, as I still am, with arms and legs like sticks.

'Oh, Poppy, what can I do to fatten you?' my mother used to ask in despair, as if she were feeding up a turkey for the Christmas dinner.

Fattening me was not easy, partly because my body seemed resistant to it, partly because my mother, though she took what work she could get – still cleaning other people's homes – could never earn enough money to feed the two of us well.

'Thank goodness there aren't half a dozen of you,' she said once. 'Praise the Lord your father left before that, and thank goodness he didn't leave a bun in the oven.'

'Why would my father have left a bun in the oven?' I asked her. After all, he never lifted a finger in the house, let alone baked buns.

'Never you mind,' my mother said. 'It's just a figure of speech. It doesn't mean much, but perhaps it's best not to repeat it. It's not a thing little girls say.'

We started to eat better when the first of my 'uncles' appeared. Instead of an apple or half a banana doled out once or twice in the week, we actually had a bowl of fruit which stayed on the sideboard and to which you could help yourself whenever you wished. And when we had fish and chips from the fish shop, my mother and I would have a portion each instead of sharing one.

Lodgers, they were really, but 'it would be friendlier if you called them "uncle",' my mother said. 'They'd feel more welcome.'

Uncle Harry, Uncle Bob, Uncle Raymond. Not altogether, of course; just one at a time.

Apart from the abundance and greater variety of food on the table at those times, and the coppers I was given to take myself off to the matinee at the Elysian Cinema, with an orange to suck while watching Felix the Cat, or white-hatted cowboys performing incredible feats with horses and ropes – or, on the best days, being carried off in my imagination, by Rudolph Valentino or Ramon Novarro – I didn't much care for the times when we had a lodger. My mother was different then. Skittish, little-girlish, opening her beautiful dark eyes wide and pouting her lips.

In any case, I had no time for men. As I've already said I was pleased when my father left, and if my mother knew what became of him she never said. No, I had no time at all for men. All that changed later, of course. I won't say I became *exactly* like my mother – I like to think I was more discriminating – but there was more than a little of her in me.

I suppose Uncle Harry left after about

eighteen months. I know I had left the Mixed Infants and was in 'big' school at the time he departed, which he did after a noisy row, with my mother throwing a pair of boots that he had forgotten to pack after him. I was walking up the path on my way home from school when one of them flew past me, missing me by an inch.

'And don't bother to come back!' she shouted at the top of her voice, which brought out the neighbours on either side. Fair enough. Rows in our street were public property; anyone could join in.

'And that's it,' she said, glaring at them in turn. 'You might as well go in; the performance is over.'

'Poppy, go into the house at once,' she ordered me.

I was sorry about that. I would like to have stayed and heard what Mrs Infield and Mrs Harris had to say.

After that our standard of living went down with a bump. No more bowls of fruit – all through my childhood the presence or absence of a bowl of fruit was my barometer to how well-off or poor we were. There was a slump on, my mother explained, so that not as many people could now afford to have their housework done, so she spent more time at home. All the same, I agreed with the neighbours: it *was* nice to have quieter nights.

'It's no use,' my mother said after six months

or so. 'We shall have to have another lodger. I can't manage. And with Christmas coming on . . .'

'I'll do without a Christmas present,' I offered.

'What a dear little soul you are,' she said, giving me a hug.

I wasn't a dear little soul at all. It was a sacrifice I was willing to make in order to not have another Uncle Harry.

'As a matter of fact,' she added, 'I've met someone who might just fill the bill, and he's looking for a place to stay. You'll like him, Poppy.'

No I won't! I thought.

'Where did you meet him?' I asked.

'Oh . . . in the Co-op,' she said vaguely.

I didn't believe that. The Co-op was full of women with shopping baskets. In fact, I was wrong. He was the new under-manager, and he worked on the bit of the counter where they had bacon, ham, cheese, ox tongue, butter and that kind of thing.

'Provisions,' my mother said, 'which is a step up from groceries. And a regular job. The Co-op's a very safe place. You can be there for life, if you play your cards right. He could be manager, one day.'

So Uncle Bob moved in.

He wasn't too bad, really. I quite liked him, certainly at first. We also had a steady supply of bacon pieces, the ends of cheese, ham shanks that were too small to sell and offcuts of tongue, brawn and other cooked meats. Not that he stole them; he just got them very cheaply. They were the perks of his position, he explained.

I don't remember many details about the next few years, which I suppose means they were reasonably happy, or at least that they passed without incident. I remained friends with Esmé. She went to the high school, and I followed her a year later. Uncle Bob stayed on, both with us and at the Co-op.

Then, unfortunately for him, but fortunately for Uncle Bob, the manager of the Co-op died of pneumonia – 'carried off in three days,' my mother said – and Uncle Bob inherited the position. 'One man's loss is another man's gain,' she said with suitably serious satisfaction.

As I said, I didn't dislike Uncle Bob, but he liked me more than I did him. He used to bring me small presents: tablets of scented soap, chocolate bars, packets of custard creams – all Co-op brands, of course. I suppose they were manager's perks.

'Since he's been here so long,' I said one day to Esmé, 'why don't he and my mother get married? You and I could be bridesmaids.'

'So we could,' Esmé agreed. 'What should we wear?'

After endless discussion, we decided on primrose taffeta dresses with frilled hems, gold shoes, silver and gold leaves entwined in our hair and fine gold chains with crosses on as gifts from the bridegroom to the bridesmaids.

'What about bouquets?' Esmé asked.

I thought about that, then said, 'No bouquets for the bridesmaids. We'll have small muffs entirely made from primroses.'

'Will you still call him "Uncle Bob", or will you call him "Dad"?' Esmé enquired.

'I'm not sure,' I admitted. ' "Dad" would be nice.'

I was not able to put the plan to my mother that evening, as she and Uncle Bob went out dancing, but in any case, the next day Esmé shot all our plans to pieces.

'My mother says he can't marry your mother because he has a wife in Huddersfield, and she won't divorce him because she's a Catholic. She says everyone around here knows that.' I had completely forgotten that my mother was also married.

We made the best of it by deciding that whichever one of us married first, the other would be chief bridesmaid and would wear the outfit we had planned. Then I had a better brainwave: 'The bride wears much the best clothes,' I said. 'What we could do is, we could get married, have a wonderful wedding, all written about in the newspaper, then we could get divorced, then married again. Different outfits each time. If we both did it at exactly the same time we could have double weddings. How many divorces can you have?'

'I don't know,' Esmé admitted. 'But we'd have to be careful not to marry Catholics!'

A while after this I began to develop a bust,

and so did Esmé. Although she was a year older than I, she was no more developed in that department. It was a happening much looked forward to by both of us, and discussed frequently. The criterion, jointly agreed, was that until, if you shook the upper part of your body and your breasts sort of swung free, you didn't really have a bosom. The slight, then increasing, swelling one had at the beginning didn't count as a bust (the word 'breasts' was not much used in polite society; 'bosom' or 'bust' had to do).

I would frequently monitor the growth of my bosom with a tape-measure and would look in the mirror and shake myself to check for free movement. Then there was the business of hair growing in places which had hitherto been smooth and pale. It was altogether a strange time.

As for my bust, after an agonizingly slow start, and at a time when Esmé seemed set to overtake me, it suddenly went mad, developing from thirty-one to thirty-six inches in no time at all.

'Poppy', I overheard Uncle Bob saying to my mother, 'is developing into a big girl!'

The very next morning my mother said, 'That liberty bodice is doing nothing at all to flatten you. I shall have to buy you a brassiere. I'll meet you after school and we'll go to Jenkins.'

I don't think my mother liked me growing up. It spoiled her image to have a daughter whose figure threatened to become more voluptuous than her own. That didn't occur to me at the time; it was a thought that came to me later.

Not long after that Uncle Bob moved out. There was nothing dramatic about it, at least not as far as I knew. He was there one day, and the next, a Wednesday and early closing, which meant he should have been in the house when I got home from school, he simply wasn't. Nor was there any sign of his pipes, tobacco or newspaper, all of which were usually strewn around the room.

'He's left,' my mother said when I enquired.

'Why? What for?'

She shrugged and went on polishing the table.

'He wanted a change. Men do. You'll discover that. Off with the old, on with the new.'

'Has he left the Co-op?' I asked.

'Oh, no, he's the manager, isn't he? He'd not get tired of *that*!'

We ceased to shop at the Co-op. There were no more bacon ends and out went the fruit bowl.

And then we heard that Uncle Bob had left his job.

'So he did get tired of it,' I said to my mother, who was doing the ironing.

'I don't know about that,' she said. 'It seems he's had a step up. He's been made manager of a Huddersfield branch.'

'Oh, Huddersfield,' I said. 'Has he gone back to his wife, then?'

She banged the iron down so hard the table shook.

'Don't mention that woman's name in this house!' she said fiercely.

5

Downstairs, though Mervyn had disappeared in the direction of the caravan, the rest of the family were hard at it; all quite amiably, as if a truce had been declared. They crowded the kitchen and rushed in and out of the dining room, laying the table and preparing the cold lunch – under Beryl's direction, of course.

'Well dears,' Poppy said, standing in the kitchen doorway, 'what can I do to help?'

'You can go into the garden and cut some chives, Mummy,' Beryl said. 'I need them for the cream cheese. And some parsley for garnishing. Do you have parsley and chives?'

'Of course. And coriander and thyme, sage and tarragon. In fact, most herbs, except basil. I don't do too well with that outside. I think it needs more sun than we have.'

She took the scissors from their hook and went out. The herbs grew in the long border in the side garden. From the shed she fetched her kneeling contraption. It had strong metal handles by which, once on her knees, she could pull herself upright again. Alas, she could no longer do much gardening without it.

It was a wonderful June day, calm and sunny, white vapour trails from planes which passed over all too often but today flew so high as to be inaudible criss-crossed the blue sky. How peaceful it was, out here in the garden. A couple of pigeons perched side by side on the top of the caravan, cooing and dipping their heads. She had read in a magazine that a mating pair of pigeons never strayed far away from each other. How sweet. It also said that they copulated very, very often. How exhausting! However, there was nothing like that going on at the moment. Just tender murmurings.

Suddenly, the air was riven with a noise like an express train rushing through a tunnel. The pigeons cried out, rose into the air with a great flapping of wings and departed in a hurry. Poppy dropped the scissors on the ground and clutched at the handles of the kneeler, but only momentarily, because she quickly recognized the sound.

It was Mervyn, snoring. He was in full throttle, and rising to a crescendo. When the climax was reached, he gave an extra-special snort before relapsing into silence. Everything stood still. Seconds later, he started at the bottom again and gave a repeat performance. She swore she could see the caravan shake and hear the snores reverberate. After all, what was it other than a large tin box in which every sound was magnified?

He was in mid-flow again, and she knew exactly what was to come. Victor had been a world-class snorer. When he reached that unearthly silence after the climax, she used to count the seconds in which it seemed he didn't breathe at all and be relieved when the cycle started over again.

It was the second time today that Mervyn had reminded her of Victor, which was surprising because her second husband was not often in her thoughts. After all, they had been married only six years before he had died of pneumonia. Rather boring years, except for the birth of Richard, whom she had enjoyed immensely when he was a baby and as a small boy. More than she enjoyed him now that he was a man.

I have not been a good picker of husbands, she thought as she went back to cutting chives against the background of Mervyn's snores. None of them have lasted long and none of them have been the least bit exciting. Lovers are more exciting than husbands; you can never be quite sure of lovers.

On the other hand, she congratulated herself, putting the chives in the trug and moving on to the parsley, I *was* good, except in the case of Gregory, at choosing men with money. One can't have everything. If one is going to be widowed – and she had spent more time being a widow than being a wife – money is a great comfort. And never boring.

She heaved herself to her feet and pressed both hands against the small of her back to straighten herself out. Why had she not noticed Mervyn's snoring when she'd stayed in New York? Of course, theirs was a large apartment, not a tin box on wheels. Or perhaps he had only recently started the habit?

She had gathered all the parsley and chives she thought they could possibly need, but instead of taking them into the house at once she crossed the garden to the far side and sat on a seat in the sun. She was well out of view of the kitchen window, so she could not be seen to be shirking her duty. In any case, it was her birthday; she had a right to sit down for a few minutes and do nothing.

She put the trug on the bench beside her, leaned back and closed her eyes. Mervyn's snores were not so loud here, more like background music and quite relaxing really from this distance. It was quite different when one had to share a bed with a snorer. Scores of times she had elbowed Victor quite fiercely, but it had never worked for long; it had simply interrupted the rhythm for a minute or two.

She sat for a little while, fought hard against dozing off – and won – then went back into the house.

'Here you are,' she said. 'Chives and parsley. I'll just give them a rinse.'

'Lunch is almost ready,' Beryl said. 'I don't think we need to wait for Jeremy and Megan. They weren't quite certain when they'd be here. Or for Fiona. We all know how it is with babies.'

'What about Mervyn and Georgia?' Poppy asked. 'I rather think Mervyn is fast asleep. It seems a pity to disturb him.'

'I expect you mean he's snoring,' Maria said. 'He snores like a pig. And if he's woken before he's ready he can be very bad-tempered. As for Georgia, she's a law unto herself these days. Everything I say or do is wrong.'

'Is she in love?' Poppy asked.

'Of course she's in love. What girl of eighteen isn't? But I'm sure it never made me behave the way she does.'

Oh yes it did, Poppy thought. I remember it well – and long before you were eighteen. There had been the whole of one summer when Maria was . . . what? Fourteen? And she had changed her library books every single day because she was besotted by a rather spotty assistant librarian named Kevin. All that had come of it on Maria's part was a wide knowledge of romantic fiction – her chosen reading. And for Kevin, presumably nothing came of it, since at the end of the summer he had married a fellow librarian.

'So why don't we have a nice glass of sherry, and then just the four of us can have lunch together,' she suggested. 'The others can eat when they're ready. Or we could open a bottle of wine.' It would fortify them for what she feared was in store.

Throughout the lunch, which the four of them ate with good appetite while drinking freely of a rather nice South African Chardonnay, not a word was uttered about who would sleep where and how, or indeed with whom. It was as if they had taken some monastic vow of silence on the subject. Fashion; politics; the weather in New York and England; food – the high quality of what they were consuming; wine – 'So nice that we can now buy South African with a clear conscience,' were all touched on, but the words 'bed', 'bedroom' and 'sleep' were tacitly avoided.

All the same, Poppy thought as the meal drew to an end with an apple tart Beryl had brought with her, it will have to be faced. Before long everyone would have arrived and eventually night would fall, and where would they all be then? Where indeed? She took a deep breath.

'That was a delicious lunch,' she said. 'Thank you. But before we move on to anything else, we have to decide what we're going to do about the sleeping arrangements.' She held up her hands and began to count on her fingers.

'Maria, Mervyn, Georgia, Beryl, Rodney . . .'

'Rodney and I have the caravan,' Beryl interrupted. '*And* two spare single bunks.'

'I know,' Poppy said. 'Just let me finish counting, will you, dear.'

'Fiona, David, Daisy . . .'

'Daisy is just a baby,' Maria said.

'I know that, too. She'll still need a place to sleep, though. We can't put her away in a cupboard. Richard, Jeremy and Megan . . . I make that twelve. Thirteen if Joe comes. Do you think he will?' she asked Maria.

'He *wants* to,' Maria said. 'He'll make it if he possibly can.'

'Thirteen, then. We mustn't let him travel all that way with nowhere to sleep at the end of it,' Poppy said. 'Well, we have thirteen people. My room with a double bed, one bedroom with two single beds, and then there's the little room with the put-you-up. One double and two singles in the caravan. If my arithmetic's right I make that thirteen bodies for nine places. Thirteen into nine won't go.'

'There must be *somewhere* in Brighton,' Beryl said. 'Or Eastbourne. All those hotels. You know the places, Ma. Why don't you ring around and see what you can do?'

'The thing is, I *don't* know the places,' Poppy said. 'I sleep in my own home. I've never stayed in Brighton or Eastbourne, nor has anyone who's visited me. My visitors have stayed here. I've just never had thirteen at once!'

'It might be worth a try,' Rodney said.

'Then why don't *you* make a few phone calls,' Poppy suggested. 'Look in the *Yellow Pages*.'

'You could do that better than I, Maria,' Rodney said pleasantly. 'You know best what would suit the three of you.'

'Oh, so we're assuming that it's we three who won't find a bed in this house?' said Maria.

'Well, after all,' Beryl said in a pleasant voice, 'it was the three of you who didn't get in at the Splendide. As Mervyn said, if your secretary hadn't—'

'Now, dear, I don't think we need to go into that again,' Poppy said hurriedly.

'I was simply pointing out—'

'All right,' Rodney said. 'I'll do the telephoning. But who and what am I to book for?'

'Never mind the who at the moment,' Poppy said. 'Try for a minimum of two rooms, with a total of three or four beds. Use my name and address and I'll give you my credit card. Throw yourself on their mercy. When you've got the rooms we can decide who's going to occupy them.' She picked up her handbag, which was never far from her side, and handed him her credit card.

Whoever had the idea of them coming together for her birthday – and she didn't quite know who it was, but it certainly wasn't her – it had *not* been a good one.

Fifteen minutes later, while Rodney was still on the telephone, Mervyn appeared.

'Ah, there you are,' Poppy greeted him. 'Did you have a good sleep? Are you hungry?'

'Very good,' Mervyn said. 'And, yes, I am hungry. I didn't eat a thing on the plane.'

'We've lunched,' Poppy said. 'We didn't like to wake you, but yours will be on the table in five minutes. Unless you want to wait until the others are here. I mean, if you'd rather not eat on your own, though I don't quite know *when* they'll arrive.'

'In that case, I'll eat now,' Mervyn said.

Poppy turned to Maria.

'What about Georgia? Do you want to wake her? If she stays in bed much longer she'll not sleep tonight.'

'The way things are', Maria said tersely, 'she might not have the chance to sleep tonight. Let her do it while she can.'

'It's all rather difficult,' Poppy told Mervyn.

Thirteen people, she thought, and nine places – all complicated even more because some were married and some not. One hesitates these days to put two members of the same sex in a bed together, though in my day we wouldn't have thought anything of it.

'I don't think Rodney's having any luck,' Beryl said, coming back into the room. 'Oh, hello, Mervyn. Did you sleep well?'

Oddly, she found Mervyn, self-important and opinionated though he was, easier than her sister. In her view, Maria treated him badly, which was unfair, because he was the best meal ticket any woman could have, and that was precisely the reason Maria had married him. So why should she complain?

She was always more attractive than I was, Beryl thought. All that red hair – still no sign of grey – and those green eyes. She'd inherited her green eyes from their father, or so it was said. Beryl had never seen her father. He had met his death two months before she was born. Maria had been not quite a year old, so she had no memory of him, either.

Victor was the only father they had known, and they hadn't even known him for long. She had been less than two years old when her mother had married him and seven when he'd died. She had liked Victor. They – she and Maria – had called him 'Pops'. He'd been fat and cuddly, with a pink face and a big smile. She would have liked to have had him for a father for longer.

'What's Rodney doing?' Mervyn asked.

'He's phoning hotels to see if he can get rooms,' Beryl said. 'He's been at it nearly half an hour now.'

Rodney appeared.

'No luck, I'm afraid. Everywhere's full. I've also rung the tourist offices in both towns, and they tell the same story.'

'Oh dear,' Poppy said. 'We shall just have to have another think. Now let me see . . . Fiona, David and Baby Daisy will have my room—'

'Why?' Maria demanded.

'Why not?' Poppy asked. 'They have the baby. Oh! Do you mean I shouldn't give up my room? That's thoughtful of you, dear, but in the circumstances I think I should.'

'I didn't mean that.'

'Then what?'

'I am, after all, your eldest. Mervyn and I have

travelled a long way to be with you on your eightieth birthday, only to be turned away from the Splendide.'

'Through no fault of mine,' Poppy said.

'Or mine,' Mervyn added through a mouthful of quiche.

'I think Mummy is very generous to give up her room!' Beryl said.

'You would, wouldn't you? She's giving it up for your daughter!'

'And the baby,' Beryl pointed out. 'If it wasn't for the baby, I'm sure Fiona and David wouldn't mind where they slept.'

'It's all very well for you,' Maria said. 'Your beds are assured. You and Rodney *know* where you're sleeping.'

'I offered you and Mervyn bunks in the caravan,' Beryl reminded her.

'Don't worry,' Maria said. 'You didn't mean it, and I wouldn't. I've never slept in a caravan,' Maria said. 'I don't think I could.'

'It was surprisingly comfortable,' Mervyn said. He was quite enjoying Maria getting the worst of it. '*I* wouldn't mind.'

Oh dear, Poppy thought. That would simply make matters worse. If he did, and Maria wouldn't, he would take one bunk and the other would be spare – and who could she possibly put in the adjoining bunk to Mervyn? Only Maria was used to him and his snoring. In fact, the caravan wasn't a suitable place for Mervyn at all, the others wouldn't get a wink of sleep.

'I'm going to get a sheet of paper', she said, 'to write down all the permutations and see what comes out.'

There was no time for that, as it happened. None at all. The doorbell rang, and when she went to answer it there stood Fiona on the step with the baby in her arms.

Well, not exactly in her arms. Daisy, clad, in spite of the June day, in a top-to-toe white padded sort of spacesuit, as if she were about to be launched, reclined in a small plastic chair that swung by a sturdy handle from Fiona's hand like a basket of shopping.

'Hello, Grandma,' Fiona cried cheerfully. 'Or should I say Great-grandmama?'

If you must, Poppy thought. None of her grandchildren, Fiona included, had ever called her anything other than Poppy. It was particularly easy for children to pronounce.

'Whatever you like,' she said. 'We could even wait a bit and let Daisy choose for herself. Lovely to see you, darling. And dear little Daisy. What I can see of her!'

'She is gorgeous, isn't she?' Fiona said. 'David is unpacking.'

Poppy looked beyond Fiona and waved to David. He had opened the back of the estate car and was emptying the contents as if it were a removal van, and with a similar result, since what emerged covered several square metres of the drive. Cartons, cases, cushions, a cool box, two large quilted bags and a mysterious bundle from which poles protruded. Poles? Could they have brought a small tent? Poppy wondered. But why? Though it would certainly help with the sleeping problem.

'We'll leave him to it,' Fiona said, following Poppy into the house.

'I don't suppose you've eaten?' Poppy said.

'No,' Fiona confirmed. 'We're starving.'

Beryl, having heard her daughter's voice, was in the hall.

'Darling,' Beryl cried. As if, Poppy thought, they hadn't seen one another less than twenty-four hours ago and spoken on the telephone only this morning.

'Hello, Mummy.'

They kissed, the movement causing Daisy to be swung slightly in her chair, which was still suspended somewhere below Fiona's waist height. Daisy kept calm and went with the flow. Beryl bent down to release her granddaughter from her trappings.

'And here's my little Daisy flower! Come to Granny, then.'

'No, Mummy.' Fiona's tone was sharp. 'Leave her where she is for the moment. As soon as David's brought everything in I have to give her her dinner.'

'I could feed her while she's on my lap,' Beryl suggested.

'Mummy,' Fiona said patiently 'you know perfectly well she has her dinner while she's sitting in her chair. It's what she's used to.'

Beryl sighed. She wanted to give her gorgeous granddaughter a great big hug, and how could she do that when she was in a chair?

Poppy gave the baby a closer look. Dinner? Sitting in a chair? Surely at four months old she would be fed on what nature so conveniently and cheaply provides, ready to hand and at exactly the right temperature? Or, if not available, then something milky, in a bottle with a teat.

'What do you feed her?' she asked.

'She's well on to solids,' Fiona said. 'Cheese and butter beans today, I think. Or lentil and bacon. I've got a small jar of each, so we'll see which she prefers, though usually I blend my own. I do think it's important that everything's organic, don't you?'

'Oh, absolutely,' Poppy nodded vigorously.

'And banana custard to follow,' Fiona said.

'Wonderful. And what about milk? Don't you . . . ?' It would not surprise her to hear that the menu was rounded off with a nice cup of coffee.

'I weaned her,' Fiona said, 'but my milk didn't suit her. It was too rich and she threw up.'

'Ah, perhaps she prefers semi-skimmed?'

Poppy, observing Fiona's puzzled look, remembered that her granddaughter hadn't the slightest sense of humour. When she was small she would burst into tears because she didn't know what the others were laughing at.

'Not a good joke,' Poppy apologized.

'In the meantime, darling, come into the sitting room,' Beryl said. 'We're just about to move out of the dining room, and I know everyone's dying to see Daisy. If she has to stay in her chair, she can just as easily eat there.'

What bossy women her daughters were. They got it from their father. Edward had been in charge of everything – in his business, and his home. He made all decisions of any importance. She hadn't minded. It was one of his ways of spoiling her. He had spoiled her rotten, and she had loved it; she wished it could have lasted longer. If only he hadn't chosen to go to the lavatory at that particular moment!

David brought the contents of the car into the house, depositing things wherever there was space in the hall or on the stairs. How had this lot fitted into a small Renault? More importantly, how would it fit into her house, Poppy asked herself. The hall was already home to Maria and Mervyn's Louis Vuitton baggage, which sat uneasily, and disdainfully, beside a baby bath, buggy and a dozen other presumably absolute necessities of life for a four-month-old baby. And more was coming through the door.

Poppy left David to it and went into the sitting room. Fiona lowered Daisy, in her seat, to the floor in front of the sofa where Rodney was sitting, then returned to the hall to collect something from the heap. Rodney bent down, beamed at his grandchild and, when she grabbed at his hand, gave her his finger to suck, which she did avidly. He had large hands with long fingers, made for a baby to hang on to.

'And how's my little love?' he asked in a voice as sweet as treacle. 'Who's Grandpa's little flower, then?'

Daisy relinquished the finger and blew a bubble that burst and dribbled down her chin. Rodney took out a handkerchief and tenderly mopped her mouth.

Fiona chose that moment to return to the scene.

'Daddy!' she cried. 'Do *not* use your handkerchief on Daisy. It's *most* unhealthy.'

How fortunate, Poppy thought, that she had missed Daisy sucking her grandfather's finger.

'My handkerchief's quite clean,' Rodney protested. 'I'm not stupid.'

'David,' Fiona called out. 'Bring me the changing bag.'

David obliged. From one of its many pockets, Fiona took out a drum of baby wipes and expertly dealt with Daisy's face. Daisy responded by blowing another bubble, bigger and better, and bursting it down her chin.

My great-granddaughter is a rather clever child, Poppy decided.

'She's teething, poor love,' Fiona informed the assembled company.

Mervyn gave a nod of polite interest. He was not into teeth which had not yet made an appearance, and he had never been into babies, not even his own. Neither did Maria pretend any interest. Teething was just one of the things babies did, for God's sake, and a pain in the ass they were while they did it. Rodney and Beryl, on the other hand, received the wondrous news with delight, Rodney at once exploring Daisy's gums with his finger.

'Daddy,' Fiona screamed, 'you are the end. Don't you know better than to put your finger in a baby's mouth?'

'As a matter of fact,' Poppy said daringly, 'when my children were teething I used to massage their gums. It seemed to soothe them.'

Fiona gave Poppy a kind but pitying look. 'Of course you did, darling. That's what people did in your day. But you didn't know any better then. It's all different now.'

'I think you're a wee bit too fussy, Fiona dear,' Rodney said, not the least bit repentant.

'Oh no, I'm not,' Fiona answered. She did love her father and, quite rightly, he doted on Daisy, but her parents could be so ignorant. There was some excuse for Poppy. She was *really* old.

'Anyway, I'll change her,' she said. 'She'll be more comfortable to eat her dinner. David, will you get the changing mat?'

Like a well-trained retriever, he went into the hall and came back carrying it, though not in his teeth.

Fiona lifted Daisy from her chair and laid her on the mat. Daisy thrashed her arms and legs in her new-found freedom.

'Wouldn't you prefer to change her in the bathroom?' Poppy said in an encouraging voice.

'Oh, no. She's fine here,' Fiona replied. 'She

likes having people around her and, of course, we encourage that.'

'She'll certainly have that,' Poppy said.

There were seven people in the room, plus Daisy, and then eight, as Georgia entered, looking as if she were walking in her sleep. Would Daisy, when she was older, wish to know that eight people had witnessed her having her nappy changed and her bottom wiped?

'Ah,' Fiona said happily. 'Here's your Auntie Georgia.'

Georgia gave Daisy the briefest of looks and crossed to the other side of the room. From the bag, Fiona brought out baby cream, a pacifier in a sterile container, another space suit, a fluffy pink rabbit, a rattle and a clean nappy. Not that the nappy was instantly recognizable as such, at least not to Poppy.

'This is pretty,' she said, picking it up. 'What is it?' It was a bright yellow affair, with lace and bits of Velcro and pictures of characters from *Winnie-the-Pooh*.

Fiona gave her a strange look.

'It's a nappy. A designer nappy, actually.'

'A *designer* nappy?'

'Actually, Poppy, there're not much more expensive than the run-of-the-mill ones.' Fiona sounded a mite on the defensive.

'Oh. Are they . . . reusable, then?'

Fiona looked horrified.

'Good heavens, no. Whoever heard of reusable nappies?'

'I did,' Poppy said.

In no time at all Daisy was in her new nappy, as happy as a lark. Since she was lying on her back she was unable to see the Winnie-the-Pooh motifs, but they obviously pleased her mother.

'We've chosen the Shepherd illustrations for Winnie-the-Pooh rather than the Disney ones,' Fiona said. 'We want her to have an appreciation of art right from the beginning. In due course she'll have the books.' She turned to Poppy. 'I don't suppose there were many children's books around when you were a little girl?'

Poppy caught her breath.

'Oh, it wasn't too bad, dear. I read *Alice* before I went to school, and *Aesop's Fables*, and *The Railway Children*. I liked *The Railway Children* very much.'

'That was a film, Poppy!'

'I know, dear. I enjoyed the film, too – about thirty or forty years after I'd read the book. I didn't read *Winnie-the-Pooh* until I was nine. I got it from the library soon after it came out.'

'The library? You had libraries?' Fiona said.

'Of course. In fact, we were quite cultured, I suppose. Amazing, isn't it?'

'Absolutely,' Fiona agreed. She then said, 'I'll put Daisy in her playpen for a few minutes. She likes that. We've brought it with us. We've brought everything.'

Mervyn, who had rather enjoyed Poppy's

boasting, turned away and looked out of the window as Fiona resumed the topic of Daisy.

'There's a car stopping here,' he announced.

Poppy moved quickly to the window.

'It's Jeremy,' she said. 'And that must be Megan.'

6

I was due to leave school at the end of the summer term, five weeks after my sixteenth birthday. Esmé, though a year older, was staying on because, at eighteen, she would be going to teacher-training college. She was deeply disappointed that I was not to do the same.

'But you *must*,' she pleaded. 'Think of it; we'd both be away from home Monday to Friday every week. We'd have a marvellous time.'

The college was twenty miles away, and residential, though one was free to return home at weekends.

'You've got to persuade your mother,' she insisted.

'I've tried,' I told her. 'It's no use; she won't budge.'

One of the reasons for my mother's opposition was that she didn't like the idea of me being away from home, and especially not with Esmé.

'I'm not sure that girl is a good influence on

you,' she said. 'She's . . . . well, let's say she's *wayward*.'

Although, I had discovered, my mother had a fairly elastic moral code when applied to herself, where her dear and only daughter was concerned she was much more strict. She was not happy, for instance, that Esmé and I had discovered Saturday-night dances, and she only allowed me to attend because they were held in the church hall, were organized and supervised by responsible adults, including the curate, and finished at 11 p.m. prompt.

The curate did not dance with anyone, which was just as well, since had he shown the least inclination to do so at least half a dozen females, grown women as well as we teenagers, would have thrown themselves in his path. He looked like a dancer: he was tall and rangy, and walked about with vigorous grace, causing his cassock to swirl.

In fact, we knew he was not available to us because one Sunday morning he had told us so from the pulpit.

'I am married to the Church,' he declared, and several female hearts dropped to the floor. Not mine, though. Oh, I was as keen on him as anyone, but I was quite sure that I would be the one who would cause him to break his vow of celibacy and marry. We were made for each other, I reckoned. His hair was an even brighter red than mine. We would have a gaggle of red-haired, freckled children. None of it happened. He moved away.

Where was I? Oh yes. 'I dance with Esmé,' I told my mother. 'What's wrong with that?'

Nowadays, of course, there would have been a lot wrong with it, but not then. In any case, it was not quite true, or not the whole truth. Rather than sitting around waiting to be asked to dance – it wasn't *comme il faut* for us girls to do the asking – Esmé and I would set off together in a show of independence, in the hope that by the time we had made one circuit of the floor two youths – all hunting was done in pairs – would step in and break us up and we would each be wafted away by a member of the opposite sex, and preferably a good dancer.

We didn't take just anyone. We were acutely aware of the local talent – who had spots, who didn't wash often enough and who had sweaty palms. If we observed two predatory youths standing at the edge of the dance floor, ready to pounce, and we didn't like the look of them, then we had our own escape routine. 'Full steam ahead,' one of us would say to the other, and we would sail past them, eyes averted in a frenzy of fast dancing. On the other hand, if we liked the look of them – and we had our favourites, Laurence Butler was mine – then we would slow down in front of them and perhaps stop to adjust a shoe buckle, making it clear that we were available.

It was a ploy which did not often fail. Esmé and I seldom had any need to dance bust-to-bust for the rest of the evening. And we were both good dancers – foxtrot, waltz, quickstep, military two-step. Never the tango. The tango was not considered suitable for the church hall.

Then, as the church clock struck eleven, we would be rooted to the spot while the band played 'God Save the King', but as the last drawn-out note faded, Esmé and I would make a mad rush to collect our coats and leave. Alas, not with a male escort. They had been abandoned. The rush was because my mother would be waiting in the lobby to take us home, and we didn't wish our dancing partners to see we were being collected like small children from school.

It can't always have been easy for my mother to collect me. She had her own pursuits on Saturday evenings.

I was not deterred from bringing up the subject of teacher-training college again and again, and my mother had to find objections other than Esmé.

'And another thing,' she said, 'you are not cut out to be a teacher, Poppy dear.'

Though I never admitted it, I knew she was right, just as I recognized that Esmé *was* cut out for it. Esmé dispensed information to anyone who would listen, and she had a genuine empathy with children. I'm not sure I ever had.

'You wouldn't get far in life as a teacher,' my mother said. 'You wouldn't meet people. Not the kind of people I want you to meet. You'd probably end up marrying another teacher!'

'But surely—' I began.

'Oh, there's nothing wrong with teachers. Salt of the earth and all that. And there's no-one more respectable, which, of course, is something I would want you to be. But I have ambitions for you, Poppy. And with your looks and your capabilities you could go further than that. Much further.'

'You don't mean . . . ?'

For one glorious moment I thought she had come round to my own cherished ambition – frequently mentioned and always turned down flat – which was to be a dancer. On the stage, and preferably in the West End of London. By which I did not mean a ballet dancer with my hair scraped back severely in a bun. I did not have suitable hair for a ballet dancer; it was curly and refused to lie down. No, what I hankered after and dreamed of was the musical comedy stage – dressed in glamorous costumes and a blond wig, floating across the stage in the arms of a handsome man.

'No, I don't mean dancing,' my mother said. 'You've been going to the pictures too often. I have it all worked out for you. What I plan is this . . .' She paused.

I waited. This was going to be something new. I could tell by the look on her face – wary and eager at the same time – and the slight catch in her voice.

'I've given it a lot of thought,' she continued. 'What I plan is for you to go to Carson's Commercial College which, as everyone knows, is the best in the area, for a year's course, which I'm prepared to extend to two years if necessary.'

'But I don't—'

She took no notice of me.

'You would learn typing, shorthand, book-keeping, filing and secretarial skills like answering the telephone and making appointments. Possibly, you could do extra French. You've always been good at French. My plan', she said firmly, 'will give you a better life.'

I hardly knew how to answer. I was choked with rage.

'How will being a shorthand typist give me a better life?' She must have heard the fury in my voice, but she ignored it, answering me in a cheerful voice with a smiling face.

'You won't always be a shorthand typist, my dear. Oh, no. You might well start out as one, but it's my belief that you'll soon be a fully-fledged secretary. And then, who knows? A personal assistant. Probably to some important person. A bank manager, an MP or a surgeon.'

'It's a far cry from being a dancer,' I said crossly.

'Oh, Poppy love, it's no use thinking of being a dancer. It's an unstable life. Totally insecure. Not at all what I want for you. And what about when you get older and are too old to dance?'

That was no sort of argument to put to me. I saw myself for ever young, for ever comely, flitting across the stage, taking curtain calls to tumultuous applause, a queue of autograph-hunters at the stage door, my name in lights outside the theatre.

'No,' my mother said, breaking into my dream. 'A dancer is *quite* out of the question. Anyway, just think what happens to secretaries.'

'What does happen to them?'

'Why, they marry the boss. It's a well-known fact. Nurses marry doctors, teachers marry other teachers, secretaries marry the boss. You could end up the wife of a county court judge or a factory owner.'

I was lost for words, an unusual condition for me.

'I've got all the information from Carson's College,' she said. 'The brochures, the different courses and so on. We'll look at them together.'

Suddenly, I took comfort from the fact that, though my mother was quite good at getting what she wanted, this was pie in the sky for the simple reason that she could not possibly afford it. Carson's was the best and it wouldn't come cheaply.

'And how will you afford this wonderful plan?' I asked triumphantly.

The answer came pat.

'I would take in a lodger,' she said.

I stared at her, horrified. Then I let out a yell. 'No! Oh, no! Not another uncle.' I couldn't bear the thought.

She looked at me, clearly taken aback by my vehemence.

'But, Poppy love, it's the best possible way to earn the money. You know that.'

'We'll manage,' I said. 'I needn't go to Carson's. I don't want to go anyway.'

'We need the money apart from that,' she said. 'You've no idea how difficult it is to manage. I don't bother you with it, but it's a fact. And I can't get any more work.'

'Then I will,' I said. 'I'll be a shop assistant or a waitress. Or if I can't, then I'll go into service. I'll be a maid.'

'No daughter of mine will go into service,' my mother said firmly. 'You can put that right out of your mind. I didn't struggle bringing you up to have you be a skivvy.'

'I'd rather do that than have another so-called uncle live with us,' I said.

'You only called them uncle because you were much younger,' my mother said. 'You'd not need to do that now. He'd be a lodger or, as I'd rather put it, a "paying guest". Anyway, don't be so sniffy about it, my girl. If it hadn't been for Uncle Harry and Uncle Bob, you'd have been a sight worse off. How do you think I earned the money for your school uniform, hockey sticks, tennis rackets and school trips? All those extras. You never missed out on anything, did you? But without Harry and Bob I'd never even have had the money to send you to the high school.'

'I got a scholarship,' I reminded her.

'A scholarship doesn't pay for everything. I could have let you stay on at St Cuthbert's and leave at fourteen, take a job and earn money. But no, and why not? Because I wanted you to have a better life.'

She was crying now, with great tears running down her face. She took out a handkerchief and blew her nose. I felt terrible.

'I've always put you first.' She sobbed.

It was true. How could I be so mean?

'You've no idea how hard it is to make ends meet. And I still want to give you the best. Food on the table, decent clothes, new shoes . . .'

I took a deep breath.

'All right, Mother. You win. But no way will I call him "uncle".'

'Of course not,' she agreed.

She dried her eyes and smiled. It was like the sun coming out after a heavy rainstorm.

'And he needn't be here for ever,' I added. 'When I get this wonderful job, he can go. *I'll* be the wage-earner then.'

It didn't occur to me that, as well as money, my mother needed companionship, especially the companionship of a man. She was a woman who was only half alive without a man in her life, but I was too selfish then to understand that. Later, I did.

'We'll sort that out when the time comes,' she said. 'I think you'll like Mr Hargreaves; he's a nice man.'

'Mr Hargreaves? You mean you've got someone in mind? You've had him in mind all the time?'

'Not exactly,' she said. 'But I've been keeping my eyes open. I knew we'd need someone.' She meant *she* would need someone.

So, quick as a flash, Mr Hargreaves moved into the spare room. I never called him 'uncle'. Though friendly, he was not an avuncular man.

'No need to call me Mr Hargreaves,' he said. 'Raymond will do.'

My mother called him Ray and he called her Harriet, love. It occurred to me that she had known him longer than she admitted, but it didn't matter. He was quite nice, and he didn't interfere, not at first at any rate. And he made my mother happy, though she was never one bit less attentive to me, I'll give her that.

Before the summer term ended at my school I was enrolled to start at Carson's in September. Schoolfriends envied me a certain amount, but Esmé more so. She, after all, would be living away from home, totally emancipated.

'We'll still see each other every weekend,' she said on the day she left. 'We'll still do things together. We'll always be friends, you and me.'

And so we were. Though my mother heaved a sigh of relief as, from the front-room window on that September morning, she watched Esmé leave, carrying her new suitcase, she knew she couldn't keep us apart for ever.

I had already been at Carson's for a year, and would be starting my second year – the higher reaches of secretarial training – the very next day. Throughout that year Esmé and I had spent almost every weekend together.

'As thick as thieves, those two are, bless 'em,' Esmé's mother said to mine. My mother didn't reply. She couldn't deny it, but there was no way she was going to bless it.

Esmé and I had spent most of the summer Sunday evenings attending the brass-band concerts in Victoria Park. Well, not just attending the concerts, though strains of *Finlandia*, the 'Anvil Chorus' from *Il Trovatore, Poet and Peasant* and pieces of Gilbert and Sullivan made a pleasant background to the main reason for our presence in the park, which was, to put it bluntly, to attract members of the opposite sex.

The routine for this was as formal and set as that of mating birds, and not dissimilar, except that birds could be expected to complete the act, which we never did. At least Esmé and I never did. We would have run a mile first.

We would dress in our best – hats and gloves for the girls, the men in sporting attire: flannels and jackets, shirts and ties – in small groups. Esmé and I preferred our own group of just two; it worked better. We would parade up and down the boardwalk, passing and re-passing, catching the attention of our targeted males by laughing girlishly, or pretending to be affronted when the males called out some cheeky remark.

When we had passed and re-passed a few times – not for nothing was the boardwalk referred to as the promenade – we would pause and indulge in banter, which in turn would lead to male and female groups joining up. Never singly. We girls had been warned about that. If all went well, when the concert finished, which was usually with a hymn – 'The Day Thou Gavest, Lord, is Ended' or 'Abide With Me' – we would then be walked home, though only as far as the end of our street, never to the door. A chaste kiss might be exchanged but, unlike the birds, nothing was very serious. I never encountered anyone who had actually met their life's partner while parading at the band concert.

What we did when summer ended and the concerts ceased I can't now remember. It seems to me that life was mostly summer then.

A year later I had finished my course at Carson's. The less said about the college the better, not because it was awful, it wasn't; it did what it claimed to do. In the end, I could take down shorthand at 130 words a minute – and, what was more, translate my squiggles back into reasonable English – type at seventy words a minute, keep accounts neatly in a ledger, read a balance sheet and, my leaving certificate, ornately lettered in red and gold, said I was proficient in French. This last was without benefit of ever setting foot in France, and since my French teacher, Miss Schofield, was born and lived in Wakefield, I presume I spoke it with a Yorkshire accent. Which was no doubt why, when I finally went to France – Paris, 1938, honeymoon – no-one there understood a word I said.

Yes, Carson's teaching was all it was cracked up to be, and I, who had no feeling for any of it and spent a lot of time gazing out of the classroom window and dreaming of other things, actually won the college prize for all-round merit. It was presented to me on the final day by Alderman Binns, with my mother in seventh heaven in the audience, with tears of pride in her eyes.

The trouble with Carson's was that it was deadly dull. Everything about it – the building, the teachers, the uniform, even the porridge colour of the walls and the sludge green of the paint – was dull. Those two years, except for the weekends with Esmé, were the dullest of my life. Dullness, to me, was a cardinal sin. I daresay it still is.

On that prize-giving day, we went home to a celebration tea with a Fuller's walnut cake; and, as a further reward, I was allowed to invite Esmé, who was home for the holidays. Within minutes of reaching home my mother brought out a half-bottle of cream sherry and my health was drunk.

'I knew you could do it.' She beamed. 'I always knew you had it in you. Didn't I tell you, Poppy?'

'Well done, love,' Raymond said, raising his glass, swilling down the contents and pouring himself another.

'Chin-chin,' said Esmé, who still had a year to go.

'Now all you have to do', my mother said, 'is get yourself a job. With your qualifications' – she made it sound as though I had a double first from Oxford University – 'you should have no difficulty.'

My mother, usually so good at facing reality, was not doing so now. It was 1935. The country was only slowly emerging from a world depression and vast unemployment. There still weren't many jobs around, even for prize-winning shorthand-typists with added qualifications in bookkeeping.

'Well, now,' Raymond said, when only crumbs of the walnut cake remained and the half-bottle of sherry had been emptied – largely by Raymond and my mother; Esmé and I were restricted to the one glass each – 'I think another reward is in order. I'm going to treat you two girls to the pictures. Here's a two-shilling piece. That'll leave you enough over for ice-cream in the interval.'

'That's very kind of you, Ray,' my mother said. 'Very kind.' She was rosy pink, a flush not entirely due to my scholastic success.

We went to see Robert Donat in *The Thirty-Nine Steps*. So romantic. He was currently my hero, though that could change according to who was on next week.

'If you could choose,' Esmé said in the interval as we licked our choc-ices, 'what sort of a job would you *really* like to do? Only you can't choose dancing because that's right out. But what else?'

It didn't take me long to decide.

'I would like', I said, 'to be a mannequin.'

Esmé nodded approval.

'You'd do well at that. You suit clothes.'

'I know,' I said. I was tall and thin and intensely interested in fashion. What could be better than wearing loads of beautiful outfits and parading in front of people. And getting paid for it.

'Mannequin' was the word we used then. Models were women who took their clothes off and stood naked for artists to paint them. My mother would have had ten thousand fits at the thought of that, though long afterwards it occurred to me that she couldn't have been totally averse to taking her clothes off.

In spite of conditions, I was lucky enough to get a job quite soon after finishing at Carson's. Not as a mannequin, of course, and the word 'lucky' is a misnomer. I became a shorthand typist-cum-secretary to the two partners of a smallish firm, Tompkins, which sold – not manufactured, simply distributed – all kinds of screws, clamps, nails, brackets, nuts, bolts and hinges, which were referred to not by name but by mysterious combinations of letters and numbers.

'Wythenshaw's require ten gross HAG/52/17s by Thursday,' Mr Tompkins would say. 'Check the stock, Poppy.'

He didn't mean check the stock physically. I never handled or even saw screws, hinges, brackets and so on. They were letters and numbers in lists.

I didn't last long with Tompkins.

7

Poppy beat Beryl to the door. If there was one thing she liked to do it was open her own front door to visitors, or even casual callers.

'Hello, Grandma!' Jeremy said.

'Hello, darling. How nice to see you. And you must be Megan. Welcome.'

She tried to keep the surprise out of her voice. Why had neither Beryl or Rodney prepared her for Megan's appearance? From top to elegantly sandalled toe, she was stunningly beautiful. Blue-black hair which, from a cursory glance, owed everything to nature and nothing to the art of the hairdresser, fell thick, straight and shining to her shoulders, curving into her slender neck. Her skin was like cream, its even colour enhanced by a faint smudging of pink across her high cheekbones. Her smooth, full lips were a deeper shade of rose. Black lashes fringed eyes which had the colour and clarity of Maria's emerald ring. And, as if that was not enough, she was tall, rounded in the right places – bosom, hips – but curving into the most slender of waists.

Was my waist ever that small, Poppy asked herself? The answer was yes, but a long time ago.

'Thank you, Mrs Marsh,' Megan answered. Her voice was low and husky.

'Oh, Poppy please.'

She hardly thought of herself as Mrs Marsh these days. In any case, she had been usurped, if not legally, by the pseudo Mrs Marsh, who was probably now sunning herself on some golden Australian beach. Perhaps I should have gone back to being Mrs Baxter, she thought. There had been dignity in being Mrs Edward Baxter. Or Mrs Victor Worth.

'Do come in,' she urged. 'That is, if you can get in. I'm afraid we're rather overcrowded in the hall.'

'Easy to see my sister's arrived,' Jeremy said, but he spoke kindly.

Jeremy is a nice young man, Poppy thought, with a rush of affection for him. It was true that Joe had a very special place in her heart, perhaps because he was so far away that each moment spent with him was rare and doubly precious, but she was also fond of her other grandson.

Jeremy was an unassuming person. Nothing special to look at. Not quite as tall as his new-found girlfriend; brown-haired; grey-eyed; a slender, rather narrow figure; a pleasant but homely face, with humour in his eyes and mouth. He had done well not to be overwhelmed by a lifetime of Beryl's mother love and the attention of Fiona who, at almost five years older than he, had adopted him as *her* baby since she had first set eyes on him in his cot. Fiona had always been very much the big sister, guarding and protecting him. Since she now had her own baby to care for that might have died down a little. She also had more than a hint of her mother's bossiness.

Full marks to Jeremy, Poppy thought, that in spite of his seeming insignificance he had landed a girlfriend like Megan. She earnestly hoped that Megan would never let him down in favour of someone more glamorous.

They stepped over and around the impedimenta in the hall and went into the sitting room. At the sight of Megan, Mervyn sprang to his feet, followed by Rodney, who was a little slower because he had been on his knees amusing Daisy. Both men straightened themselves and smiled ingratiatingly at the vision that was Megan. Mervyn stepped forward and shook her warmly by the hand. There was no need of a handshake from Rodney, who had met her before, but his demeanour was no less welcoming than Mervyn's.

Maria gave a gracious nod and remained seated. Georgia, who had been lying back in her chair, possibly asleep, opened her eyes briefly, took in what she needed to of Megan in a single glance, then closed her eyes again. Perhaps it was the weight of the small silver sequins covering her eyelids which made it difficult for her to keep her eyes open, Poppy thought. She had behaved appallingly since she had set foot in the house, but she would give her the benefit of the doubt until she discovered the reason why. Georgia had not always been like this; in fact, she had been particularly pleasant as a child.

It was left to Daisy to divert the attention from Megan to herself. She had been uttering small whimpers ever since the newcomers had entered the room and now, her warning whimpers having achieved nothing, she broke into a full-throated yell, her body stiff, her face red, her hands and legs flailing. All heads, except Georgia's, turned to look at her.

'My goodness, that child sure has a temper,' Maria said.

'Not at all,' Beryl protested. 'She's the sweetest-tempered baby in the world. She hardly ever cries.'

'It's my opinion she's hungry,' Poppy said. 'All this talk about what she'll have to eat and nothing forthcoming. No wonder she's furious.'

'You're quite right, Mummy,' Beryl said.

'Don't sound so surprised, darling,' Poppy replied. 'I'm not so old that I can't recognize a baby's hunger cry when I hear it. Anyway, I had plenty of practice with you. You were the hungriest baby imaginable.'

'Was I really?' Beryl asked with interest. 'Well, I still have a good appetite. Perhaps Daisy takes after me?'

Fiona scooped Daisy up into her arms, which assuaged her grief a little – being picked up was usually the preliminary to something better to follow – so that her screams diminished into intermittent, though still accusing, sobs.

'David, darling, go and prepare her dinner, will you?' Fiona said. 'Be as quick as you can. Who's a hungry little girl then?' she enquired of Daisy.

'I'll give you a hand, David,' Poppy offered.

'Oh, he knows exactly what to do, Poppy,' Fiona said happily. 'Everything's in the food box – dishes, spoons – we're always well prepared.'

'Well, I'll see what I can do,' Poppy said, following David to the kitchen.

He put a pan of water on to heat, then carefully lowered the jars of prepared baby food into it. 'It's best to bring the food to blood heat,' he explained.

'You don't say,' Poppy looked at him with wide eyes.

'Why, yes.' He hesitated, not sure about her. 'Of course, I don't know what babies were like fifty years ago . . .'

'Oh, very much as they are now. I don't think there've been any fundamental changes. But fathers are better,' Poppy said with a smile.

He returned her smile. 'Do you really think so?'

'I'm sure of it. And you are a particularly good father.'

'Thank you.' He blushed with pleasure. 'We share everything, Fiona and I.'

Share you might, Poppy thought, but not share and share alike. I'm afraid my granddaughter takes advantage of you, she thought, and you are no match for her. On the other hand, they seemed happy enough.

He tested the contents of one of the jars on the back of his hand.

'Not quite warm enough,' he decided.

Did babies still have those rigid plastic bibs, Poppy wondered, with a sort of trough at the bottom to catch the bits of mashed-up food which didn't make it into the child's mouth – or did make it and were spat out again – and congregated at the bottom of the trough? She hoped not.

And why, she asked herself, when every nice woman I know loves all babies and their accoutrements and distasteful habits, do I like the babies but hardly any of the stuff that goes with them? Perhaps I'm just not a nice woman. Was I always like this?

She was sure she had loved both her daughters when they were babies, even though they had robbed her of sleep; Maria not going through the night before Beryl had arrived on the scene, and thereafter neither of them sleeping through for at least another year. And, of course, it had been she who'd had to get up and see to them. It was not man's work. Edward had to be refreshed for the next day's tasks. It seemed strange now that even though he had spoiled her in so many ways it had never occurred to him to let her sleep while he saw to the babies. Nor, in fact, would it have occurred to her, so closely were their jobs defined: man/woman, father/mother.

Richard, as a baby, had been quite different: placid, easygoing, sleeping when he should. There had been no need for Victor to raise a finger. She wondered what time Richard would arrive tomorrow; he would bring Graham, his partner. Would they expect to stay overnight? Since they lived in Croydon, she thought probably not.

'I reckon this is about right now,' David said.

He searched in the food box and found a dish and a spoon.

'Actually,' he said, 'we plan to have another baby in two years' time, a little boy, and then a girl two years after that.'

'Oh,' Poppy said. 'I didn't know one could do that. I mean, choose the sex.'

'You can't,' David admitted, 'but we live in hope. Fiona is very determined.'

'Well, I hope all your dreams come true,' Poppy said.

'Thank you. We were wondering, Fiona and I, that is . . .' He hesitated. 'But perhaps I should wait for Fiona to ask you.'

'No, you ask me,' Poppy said. What could it be? Perhaps they wanted to borrow money for something. They had a minuscule flat and needed to move into a house. David's salary wouldn't go far, especially with Fiona no longer working. She supposed she could help.

'So what is it?'

'We wondered . . . that is, we'd like it if you'd agree to be one of Daisy's godmothers? We'd very much like it, Poppy.'

She felt a rush of pleasure.

'How wonderful! I mean how wonderful even to be thought of! Of course, I couldn't do it: I'm much too old. I wouldn't live long enough to keep the promises, and I *do* think they're important. I wouldn't be around to carry them out. No, you must choose someone of your own generation, David. But thank you for asking me. I'm really chuffed.'

'It was only an idea,' David said.

'And I thank you for it. Do you think you should take the food in? Daisy is sounding quite impatient, poor love.'

'Of course,' David said.

He left. Poppy went to the dining room to rearrange the table for those who'd not yet eaten. Five of them. No, six, because Georgia hadn't been down earlier. Maria joined her.

'Thank God they're feeding that noisy baby,' she said. 'She is something else.'

'Nonsense.' Poppy surprised herself by the sharpness of her voice. 'I can remember you getting quite ratty when your meals weren't ready on time.' She found herself suddenly defensive about Daisy; it was something to do with being invited to be a godmother. She knew she could never do it, but she had a new feeling of protectiveness, as if she already was a godmother, not just a great-grandmother. I will guard her from the slings and arrows of outrageous fortune, she thought, including any barbs from Maria.

'And you didn't have the excuse of being a baby,' she added. 'I'm talking about when you were a schoolgirl. You expected your meal on the table the minute you came into the house.'

'And did I get it?' It was an accusation.

'Not always,' Poppy admitted.

'Half the time you were out.'

'Oh dear, you make me sound a bad mother.'

Why did her conversations with Maria so often verge on the unpleasant? It was a great pity because she seldom saw her, though perhaps that was just as well. Where did I go wrong? she asked herself. Wasn't that the question all parents asked at one time or another? Any day now Maria would ask herself the same thing about Georgia. Or she should do anyway.

'You weren't a *bad* mother,' Maria said. 'Not *bad*. In fact, you could be fun.'

It was an accolade of sorts, and about as far as Maria was likely to go. She was not one for compliments; criticism was more in her line, but there was something additional on this visit. Maria was not a happy woman, and it had nothing to do with the contretemps at the hotel, or with being cross at Mervyn about this and that. It went deeper. I might not see her often,

Poppy thought, and she might not be the most open person in the world, but I do know my daughter, and something is not right.

'You were a bit . . . inconsequential,' Maria said, whatever that meant. 'Anyway,' she continued, 'I need to call New York. I have a business deal going through . . . or not! I should be there. My cell phone doesn't seem to work.'

'Is it meant to, so far from New York?' Poppy asked. 'This is a bad area for mobiles. Use the phone in my bedroom; it's quiet there.'

Maria looked at her watch.

'Three o'clock,' she said. 'You're five hours ahead, so it'll be ten a.m. in New York. I'll give it until a quarter after ten before I call.'

'Are you worried?' Poppy enquired.

Perhaps it was business troubles that were making Maria so tetchy. And Mervyn was no better, though one wouldn't think a successful dentist would have those sorts of worries. From what she had seen and heard when she'd been in New York, he had patients queuing up for treatment. All the same, it couldn't be a soothing job, poking around in people's mouths day in and day out. It made her teeth ache to think of it. Perhaps they both worked too hard. People did these days, and no doubt more so in New York than East Sussex.

'I am,' Maria confessed. 'I'm bidding for another salon in midtown, on Forty-eighth and Madison. That's breaking new territory for me, but I want to move up.'

'So what *is* the worry?'

'The worry is,' Maria said, 'whether they'll accept my bid. I've gone as high as I can afford to, and Mervyn's too mean to stake me, though he could well afford to.'

'Perhaps he thinks you've got enough on your plate already,' Poppy suggested. Maria had three beauty salons in Manhattan, and they were all, as far as Poppy knew, successful.

'I'd be willing to sell Church Street,' Maria said. 'I do want to be in midtown. But there isn't time. There's another bidder. Anyway, I must make the call now. I don't want to be late; the timing's critical.'

She turned to go and, at that moment, the phone rang in the hall.

'Damn!' she said. 'Whoever that is, will you ask them to cut it short, Mummy?'

Jeremy, passing through the hall, picked up the phone on its second ring.

'Georgia,' he shouted, 'it's for you. Sounds like New York.'

Georgia suddenly came to life and arrived in the hall fractionally before her mother.

'Hi, Bill,' she said, her whole face coming alive. 'How are you? Are you OK? What's it like in New York? I wish I was there.'

'Hang up,' Maria hissed. 'Tell him to call you back. I've got to have that phone right now.'

Georgia ignored her completely. She was in another world, and if she had heard her mother's frantic commands she was certainly going to do nothing about it.

Maria gave a strangulated cry of rage, ran up the stairs to her mother's bedroom and picked up the phone by the bed.

'Bill dear,' she said sweetly, 'would you hang up and call back later? I have an important call to make.'

'Don't do that, Bill,' Georgia said fiercely. 'It's another of her ploys to separate us.'

'It's nothing of the kind,' Maria shouted. 'Please Bill.'

'Bill, don't you dare hang up,' Georgia yelled. 'If you do—'

The rest of her threat was drowned by simultaneous shrill cries from Maria. 'I need that phone. I need it NOW!'

The noise brought Mervyn from the living room and Poppy from the dining room into the hall.

'Georgia darling,' Poppy began.

'What the hell is going on?' Mervyn demanded.

'Ask my stupid mother upstairs,' Georgia snapped. 'Tell her to get off the line. This is *my* call.'

'If the two of you were standing closer I'd bang your heads together,' Mervyn retorted.

He started to climb the stairs, red in the face with rage and exertion. He really shouldn't be doing that, Poppy thought helplessly. He looked as though he would burst.

A plaintive cry came from Fiona in the living room.

'PLEASE! I'm trying to feed Daisy. It's very bad for her to have all this noise when she's eating. She needs peace and calm.'

At the same time as Mervyn entered the bedroom and his wife and daughter were both shouting down the telephone, somewhere in New York Bill quietly hung up.

There was a loud wail from Georgia. 'He's hung up on me,' she cried. 'It's her fault. It's all her fault. Why can't she leave me alone?'

In the bedroom, while Maria was still shouting at him, Mervyn grabbed the receiver from her and firmly replaced it in its cradle. 'That was Georgia's call,' he said. 'You had no business to interfere.'

'Don't be stupid,' Maria said. 'You don't approve of Bill any more than I do.'

'That's not the point,' Mervyn said. 'That's not the way to deal with it. Do you never think of anything other than what *you* want?'

'My business is more important than anything Georgia has to say,' Maria stormed.

In the hall Georgia was still holding on to the receiver. Poppy quietly took it from her and replaced it. 'Darling,' she said, 'that will give Bill a chance to ring back.'

'Then I shall stand here until he does,' Georgia said.

There were tears in her voice. Poppy's heart ached for her. Then, almost immediately, the phone rang again. Georgia snatched at it and her face transformed.

'Bill! I knew—' Her face fell.

'Yes, she's here.' She handed the phone to Poppy. 'It's Uncle Richard.'

'Mother.'

'Hello dear.'

'I've been trying to get you. You were engaged.' He sounded aggrieved.

'Ah, yes,' Poppy said. 'It's been a busy line. Well, now you're through, dear. What time will you be here tomorrow?'

'What time is the dinner?'

'Eight o'clock. But don't arrive at the last minute.'

'We'll be there at half seven. You know Graham's coming with me?'

'Of course, dear. I look forward to seeing you both. You're not staying over, are you?' Please let him say no, she prayed.

'No. We'll drive back to Croydon. One of us will keep off the wine.'

'Good. We'll see you tomorrow.'

'It sounds rather noisy there,' Richard said.

'High spirits, dear. Just high spirits,' Poppy said.

As she put down the receiver she could hear Maria and Mervyn going hammer and tongs at each other upstairs. Georgia was hovering in the hall in the hope that Bill would ring again. Then, suddenly, all went quiet in the bedroom and Mervyn stamped heavy-footed down the stairs, his face as dark as a thundercloud. He glared at Georgia.

'If you're waiting for that phone to ring again,' he said, 'you'll be unlucky. Your mother's already calling, and we all know how long *that* can take.' He turned to Poppy. 'I'm sorry we're hogging your phone like this. You must let me pay for the call. Knowing my wife, it's going to be expensive.'

'That's all right,' Poppy said. 'I'm sure she'll feel better for dealing with whatever it is.'

'Won't we all,' Mervyn said. 'And it's not necessary. The deal will go through – or not, depending on which way the wind blows – without Maria interfering.'

'She seemed worried,' Poppy kept her voice light. She didn't want to be involved.

'If my wife didn't have anything to worry about, she'd find something,' Mervyn grumbled.

'I know that,' Poppy answered. 'She's my daughter!' She doesn't take after me, she thought. By and large she was not a worrier, except about things like where everyone was going to sleep for the night, and at the moment that loomed large; even larger than these tiresome telephone calls.

'When will she finish?' Georgia demanded. 'I just *know* Bill will be trying to call me back, and how can he get through if she's always on the phone?'

'It's a business call, Georgia dear,' Poppy said. 'It's important to her.'

'Bill is important to me,' Georgia said, her voice trembling. 'They're always trying to stop me talking to him and seeing him.'

'Not true,' Mervyn said. 'Not true.' He marched off into the sitting room.

'It is so,' Georgia shouted after him.

'He'll ring again,' Poppy said. 'I'm sure he will.'

'If the line's busy every time he calls, he'll give up,' Georgia said.

'Wait until your mother's through, then you can go up to my room, call him and speak at your leisure,' Poppy suggested. 'No-one will interrupt you.'

What *was* she saying? At your leisure! No interruptions! Heaven knew what *that* would cost. Never mind, though. If it made Georgia happy. And was it true that Mervyn and Maria were trying to keep her apart from her boyfriend? If so, why? There must be a reason. She hated to see her granddaughter so unhappy, and whether it was her own fault or not, she could sympathize with her. She had never forgotten, and never would, what it was like to be cut off from one's beloved. It was like a death. Georgia, for all her air of sophistication, was a surprisingly immature eighteen-year-old. She needed someone to watch out for her, though through kinder eyes than her parents were viewing things at the moment.

She went back into the dining room. She absolutely must get on with the lunch. It was nearing teatime and those young people would be starving. As she started to re-lay the table she heard Maria coming down the stairs. Maria's footsteps were like her personality, short, swift and impatient, and on the uncarpeted oak treads the staccato sound was unmissable. No sooner had she reached the foot of the stairs than Georgia was running up them.

Beryl joined Poppy in the dining room.

'I'll give you a hand, Mummy,' she said.

'Thank you, dear,' Poppy said. 'You'll find more cutlery in the drawer. I always wondered why I needed so much cutlery and china, and now I know. All the same, I must get rid of things – and not just tableware. I'm beginning to run out of space.'

'I'm sure Fiona would be grateful for most things,' Beryl said quickly, 'especially if they manage to move into a house, which I hope they will, poor dears, only it's going to be such an expense.'

'I'll bear it in mind,' Poppy said. Would she be allowed to forget it? Beryl's hints were always so heavy.

'Maria doesn't change,' Beryl said. 'Still the same go-getter. I've never really warmed to Mervyn; I suspect he finds Rodney and me rather dull Stick-in-the-muds, but at the moment I feel a little bit sorry for him with both Maria and Georgia to contend with.'

So do I, Poppy thought, but I'm not going to say so.

'And Georgia, of course, is totally spoilt.

It would have paid Maria to spend more time with her daughter and less making money which she can't possibly need.' Beryl uttered her judgements in a perfectly pleasant voice, as if she were dispensing benign wisdom, rather than criticism – a view with which she would have agreed.

'Georgia is rather young, and in the throes of love,' Poppy said. 'It's a stage she's going through.'

'She's not all that much younger than Fiona,' Beryl pointed out. 'But Fiona never went through that awful stage; she's far too sensible. And then, her upbringing has been different. Perhaps it's the difference between England and America, or the difference between having parents of modest means and well-to-do parents who give you everything.'

'I don't think there's much wrong with Georgia that time won't heal,' Poppy said defensively. 'I think you exaggerate a little, dear.'

'Oh, do you, Mummy?' Beryl said equably.

Fiona came into the room carrying Daisy in her arms.

'There,' she said, 'she's had her dins; eaten it up like the good girl she is.'

'*You* must be hungry, dear,' Beryl said. 'In fact, you all must be, but it's just about ready. Will you tell the others?'

'If they're anything like me they won't need telling twice. I don't know where Georgia is, though.'

'She's in Mummy's bedroom, making a call to New York,' Beryl informed her.

'I'll tell her,' Poppy offered. She might, at the moment, be the only person to whom Georgia would be civil.

Georgia was sitting on the edge of the bed, the telephone held to her ear and a rapt expression on her face. All inertia had vanished; she was alive from head to toe. The sequins around her eyelids, which before had seemed only to weigh them down, now sparkled and lit her up. For a moment Poppy regretted that she had to interrupt her.

'I'm sorry, darling,' she said, 'your lunch is ready. I think you should come and eat.'

'I'll be right down,' Georgia said. 'Actually, I'm quite hungry now.'

In the sitting room, Fiona was settling Daisy into her chair and David was putting on a video. The others had gone in to lunch.

'We've brought the *Teletubbies*,' Fiona said. 'Daisy loves them. I'm sure she'd like you to watch with her, Poppy. And Uncle Mervyn and Auntie Maria.'

Do I want this? Poppy asked herself. Do I want to watch the *Teletubbies*, and in the presence of my daughter and her husband while they are at daggers drawn? At least they weren't shouting at each other, but nor were they on speaking terms. Oh, well. She concentrated on the screen. She had never seen the *Teletubbies* before, though it seemed everyone else in the world had.

There were four of them. It took her some time to sort them out because, although they addressed each other much of the time, they didn't speak in any recognizable language; it sounded to Poppy very like the noises babies make when they are first trying to talk. She could have done with an interpreter – Fiona or David, or perhaps even Daisy herself, who was watching the screen with rapt attention. Possibly she understood every move and every sound, who could say?

All four had round boneless faces, small noses, circular eyes that blinked, sticking-out ears, and things growing out of the tops of their heads which were, in the end, how she came to distinguish them. They danced to an insistent beat and repeated everything about twenty times. Occasionally they said words that Poppy could recognize. 'Toast', 'Oh!' and each other's names. She felt quite a sense of achievement when she recognized a word.

'This is a load of rubbish,' Maria cried.

'Daisy doesn't think so,' Poppy pointed out. 'Actually, I think I could get addicted to it. I might even learn the language.'

'Mummy, dear, don't be silly,' Maria said.

Mervyn jumped to his feet. 'I'm going to take a walk.'

Maria raised her eyebrows. 'So, you find this as stupid as I do, though I don't suppose you'll admit it. That would mean agreeing with me.' She turned to Poppy. 'Mervyn, let me tell you, does not take walks. He'd take a cab to the end of the block.'

Mervyn ignored her. 'Which way is the sea?' he enquired. 'I can't remember.'

'Turn right, and then left,' Poppy said. 'About ten minutes.'

'Wouldn't you like to have gone for a walk?' she asked Maria when Mervyn had marched out. 'It's a lovely day.'

'With my husband in the mood he's in! No thanks,' Maria said. 'Anyway, there still might be a phone call for me.'

'Did you get through earlier? Was everything all right?' It was a stupid question to ask. If it had been, why would Maria have been on tenter-hooks?

'Not really. Oh, I got through to Dan – he's my lawyer – but nothing's happening. He says not to rush it, let it take its course, but he doesn't understand my anxiety. He's exactly like Mervyn. I don't think men do. I don't think they worry about anything unless it's golf. Now that *is* important.'

'Your father never played golf,' Poppy mused. 'I could be wrong but I don't think there was all that much of it in the West Riding. Not then.'

'When is "then"?' Maria asked. Not that she particularly wanted to know.

'The late Thirties, I suppose. By the time you were born the war was on. There was no time for golf then; there were other things to worry about.'

Maria yawned. Poppy turned her attention back to the screen.

The Teletubbies were now waving interminable farewells before disappearing into holes in the ground.

'I don't think it's so much stupid,' Poppy said to Maria, 'as that we're too old to understand it. I liked the Flower Pot Men. Do you remember them?'

'They were stupid, too,' Maria said.

'Oh, do you think so? I could speak Flower Pot language quite fluently. I suppose Daisy could speak Teletubby language if she could speak at all.'

The credits rolled and the screen went blank. Daisy gave a small contented sigh, her head dropped forward and she was immediately fast asleep.

Fiona burst into the room, followed by everyone except Beryl and Rodney. Poppy put up a hand to silence them. 'Daisy has just fallen asleep.'

'Oh, bless her,' Fiona said. 'Did you all enjoy the Teletubbies?'

'Daisy did,' Poppy said.

There was a loud ring at the front door. Poppy went to open it and found Mervyn standing on the doorstep.

'I don't have a key.'

He followed her into the living room and, standing there in the middle, made his announcement, with a beaming smile on his face.

'I've done it,' he said. 'I've found us a place to stay. Or at least to sleep. A nice little bed and breakfast, or guest house or whatever you call them.'

Maria looked at him in horror.

'I'm not staying in any bed and breakfast place,' she said. 'Are you mad?'

8

I knew before the end of my first week at Tompkins that I would never settle there, and before the second week was over I was calling in at the public library on my way home from work to study the 'Situations Vacant' column in the *West Riding Gazette*, searching for something new – anything that wasn't to do with nuts, screws, bolts and clamps, and was not presided over by Mr Tompkins.

'You haven't given it a chance, Poppy,' my mother said when she discovered why I was late home from work every day. 'Give it another week or two and I'm sure you'll settle down.'

'That', I informed her, 'is the last thing I want to do *there*. It's a living death.'

'Oh, Poppy, you are so perverse,' she complained, 'and you do exaggerate. I'm sure Mr Tompkins is a good employer. What have you got against him?'

'He smells of tobacco and his teeth are yellow, but mainly it's his English,' I told her.

'His English? What do you mean?'

'He dictates things like "pursuant to my missive of the twentieth ult," and "We confirm the meeting on the twentieth proximo", and "Regarding your communication of the seventh inst. with reference to the non-delivery of 10 gross H72/BGS (female)" . . .'

'Female?'

'Yes, mother. There are bits of ironwork that are female and other bits that are male. Don't ask me why.'

'I expect', my mother said after a moment's thought, 'they fit into each other.' And then she went slightly pink.

'However,' she said, 'I see what you mean about the English.'

She did, too. Although my mother was not well educated, she was, courtesy of the public library, widely read. She spoke grammatically correctly in her Yorkshire accent and would allow no sloppy speech from me, so in this matter her sympathies were on my side.

'What's more,' I said, 'if I change even one word into proper English he makes me do the whole thing again.'

'All the same,' my mother said with a sigh, 'I don't know where you'll find something else. Jobs don't grow on trees these days.'

It was her first acknowledgement that the glittering path she had set out for me might possibly have obstacles in the way.

Nothing came of my assiduous attention to the

West Riding Gazette but, surprisingly, Raymond found the solution.

'I'll have a word with Albert Butterfield,' he said.

'Albert Butterfield?'

'You know Albert, Harriet love,' he said. 'He's an agent for Paragon Clothing Club. They're quite a set-up.'

'Oh, I know,' she said. 'Half the people around here exist on the Paragon Clothing Club, though I've managed not to do so myself.'

'Albert has to go into the offices regularly,' Raymond said. 'I'll ask him to make discreet enquiries.'

Almost unbelievably, it turned out that a young woman was shortly about to leave to get married, and her replacement had yet to be found. Even more unbelievably, she was part of the small team in that Holy of Holies, the managing director's office.

'I'll never land that job,' I said.

'Nonsense,' my mother protested. 'Why shouldn't you? You have all the qualifications.'

'Except experience,' I pointed out. 'Tompkins won't count for much.'

She brushed aside my objections. 'You must write at once,' she ordered. 'Write directly to the managing director; his name is Mr Edward Baxter.'

'How do you know his name?' I queried.

'Everyone does,' she said. 'He's a well-known important person, largely because his father was.

His father died suddenly not long ago and his son, his only son, took over. It was in the *Gazette* and the *Yorkshire Post*. He's quite young. We'll sit down right now and draft a letter.'

My mother should have been a writer, or perhaps a barrister, I thought, reading the finished letter. Without deviating from the literal truth, she could produce a glowing and enticing description of the subject in hand, in this case me.

'How can I live up to that?' I queried. 'If I get an interview at all, that is.'

'Of course you can,' she assured me. 'And of course you'll get an interview. Why not?'

Looking back, I reckon my mother's faith in me was one of the best things in my life. In this case it was justified: I was granted an interview. In the first instance I was interviewed by Miss Kingston, who was the personal and private secretary to Mr Baxter and ran his office, which consisted of Miss Simpkins – soon to be Mrs Stanley Ford – and Jessie Mackintosh, the office junior. In all the time I knew her, I never heard Miss Kingston addressed as anything other than Miss Kingston, though Jessie Mackintosh confided that her name was Lavinia, and in private the two of us referred to her as 'Lavvie', as in 'I'm going to the lavvie'. We thought that was quite funny.

Miss Kingston was thin, with straight brown hair cut into a fringe and a permanently worried look. Jessie said this was because she was twenty-nine and was not known to have a friend of the opposite sex, much less to be courting.

Interviewing me, she asked me all the usual questions, so there was no difficulty in giving answers, which she wrote down meticulously.

'You would be a junior secretary, responsible in the first place to me,' she said. 'I would supervise your work. You would be paid one pound a week and have one week's paid holiday in the summer. Mr Baxter is a generous employer. Is there anything you want to ask me?' she enquired in an effort to be fair. I knew I ought to ask questions, if only to show that I was intelligent, interested and paying attention, but I couldn't think of anything. 'Would I ever do work for Mr Baxter?' I said in the end.

'There would be no need,' she said. I later discovered that what she meant was 'over my dead body'. 'I do all Mr Baxter's work, unless I am off sick, which never happens.' That, I also discovered, seemed to be true – not so much that she was never sick, but that she would turn up at the office even if she had a temperature of 103 and a broken leg.

'Well, your qualifications are satisfactory,' she admitted, 'though I suppose Mr Baxter will want to see you.'

She gathered up her papers and went into his office, emerging two minutes later to beckon me in.

Mr Baxter, who wore a navy suit, a dazzlingly white shirt with a starched collar and a dark-blue tie with lighter blue stripes was sitting in an important-looking chair behind a large, rather tidy desk. Perhaps it was the size of the furniture, but he seemed smallish to me. He had a serious expression on a young face. Well, he *was* young; in his late twenties, my mother had calculated – 'calculated' being the *mot juste*. He was about the same age as Miss Kingston, who introduced me to him as one presenting a commoner to the King.

'Good morning, Miss Holdsworth,' he said, not rising to his feet.

'Good morning, Mr Baxter,' I replied. It was not to be Edward for some time yet, and even then never in the office.

He glanced at the sheet of paper in front of him.

'Let me see, you were at the high school before you went to Carson's, I believe?' I felt he was as short of questions as I'd been with Miss Kingston.

'That's right,' I agreed.

'Good,' he said. 'My father was a governor.'

It was a point in my favour.

'And I'm sure Miss Kingston has told you what Paragon is. What we do.'

'She has,' I confirmed.

In fact, my mother had told me much more about Paragon Clothing Club than Miss Kingston had. It had been started by Edward's father and was based on a simple idea which, very quickly, made him a well-to-do man. Through agents, Paragon would issue a cheque for one pound, which could be spent at any shop that took part in the scheme – mostly clothing and shoe shops. The loan would be paid back by the recipient at the rate of a shilling a week for twenty-one weeks, the extra shilling on each pound being Paragon's profit. The agent, sometimes called the tallyman, would call at houses each week to collect his dues, usually on Friday night because Friday was pay day. Paying the agent took priority over all other debts or needs, even the rent.

'You see, if you were a bad payer you wouldn't get another cheque when you needed one,' my mother explained. 'And because times were bad and so many people were out of work or on low wages, it was the only way some people could afford clothes, shoes and bed linen. But if you were a good payer, then you could usually get a new cheque when your current one was only part paid. Then you would owe two shillings a week, a fairly substantial sum.'

'My mother also told me about Paragon,' I informed Mr Baxter. 'Though she's never used the club herself.'

'It's a very fair system,' he said, a trifle sharply.

'Oh, I know,' I assured him. 'My mother says lots of people simply couldn't manage without it.'

He seemed somewhat mollified, and asked me a few more questions. 'And do you think you would settle here?' he enquired presently.

'Oh yes, I would,' I said with confidence. I

would settle anywhere which wasn't Tompkins and didn't deal in nails and screws.

'Well,' he said, 'when could you start, Miss Holdsworth? If you were to be offered the job, that is.'

'Tomorrow,' I wanted to say, even though Mr Tompkins would dock my wages if I left without notice. By this time I was desperate to land this job for which, Jessie Mackintosh had informed me, there were several other applicants. On the other hand, though I had no compunction about walking out on Mr Tompkins, there was another way. It was a gamble, but I decided to take it.

'I'm afraid it couldn't be until next Monday,' I said virtuously. 'I have to be fair to my present employer.' I held my breath.

To my great relief Mr Baxter nodded approval.

'Quite right, Miss Holdsworth,' he said. 'That does you credit. In fact, I am offering you the job. Shall we say next Monday, then?'

He stood up, and I realized that he was actually quite tall, almost six feet, most of which must have been in his legs.

'You are a very fortunate young woman,' Miss Kingston said to me when Mr Baxter had handed me back into her care. 'It is a privilege to work for Paragon.'

'And for Mr Baxter,' I said.

'Of course,' she agreed, 'you will not be doing a great deal of that, as such, though we all serve him in the end.'

'They also serve,' said Jessie, who had a surprisingly literary bent, 'who only stand and wait in the office, doing the filing.' Not that she was much good at filing. I discovered that, when in doubt, she filed letters under 'L' and memos under 'M'.

In a way, it was like any other office. On my heavy Remington typewriter I transcribed minutes of meetings from Miss Kingston's fortunately immaculate shorthand. She herself did all Mr Baxter's letters, so that I seldom set foot in his office, except for when Lavvie went to the lavvie, when I would hurry into the inner sanctum to put the file of letters on his desk for signature.

'How are you getting on, Miss Holdsworth?' he said to me on one such occasion.

'Quite well, I think,' I told him.

'And you enjoy the work?'

'Oh yes.'

I didn't particularly, though it was a thousand times better than Tompkins, and the monotony was sometimes broken by the visits of agents or shopkeepers who were on the Paragon list, or hoped to be.

'Good,' Mr Baxter said with a smile. He had a nice, though infrequent, smile. 'Don't hesitate to come to me if you have a problem. My door is always open.'

That was not true. It was firmly closed by Miss Kingston, and she would have liked to lock it and keep the key.

Only occasionally did Mr Baxter leave the privacy of his office and venture into the secretaries' domain; he had no need to as Miss Kingston was ever ready to run in at the first sound of his bell. Then one day when I suppose I'd been at Paragon for about a month, Jessie said, 'Mr Baxter pops in here much more than he used to. He's getting almost human.'

'I suspect he is doing it out of the kindness of his heart to save my legs,' Miss Kingston said. 'Though he knows he has no need to. He only has to ring for me. And I'll thank you, my girl, not to be so disrespectful.'

'All the same,' Jessie said when Miss Kingston was next out of the room, 'what I said is true. He didn't do it when Miss Simpkins was here, so it must be you.'

'Don't be silly,' I said. But I did wonder, just a bit.

Came the day when practically the whole of Akersfield was down with the flu and Miss Kingston, who had been valiantly fighting it off, succumbed. She was so ill, she had to be sent home in a taxi. She left amid a welter of instructions as to what I was, and wasn't, to do.

'But don't worry,' she said as I bundled her into the cab, 'I'll be back in a couple of days.'

'Poor Miss Kingston,' I said, firm in my own radiant health. 'I do feel sorry for her.'

'Poor Miss Kingston, but lucky you,' Jessie pointed out. 'You'll get to do all Mr Baxter's stuff.'

And so I did. And not for a day or two. Miss Kingston's influenza left behind a nasty bout of bronchitis and she was away for almost three weeks. We weren't much in touch because she wasn't on the telephone, but Jessie went to see her and took a bunch of flowers and a cream cake from both of us. It was not felt wise that I should visit, or at least not by my mother.

'It would be quite selfish,' she said. 'If you caught it from her, what would poor Mr Baxter do? He relies on you now. You owe it to him to keep well.'

It seemed that he did. He was always calling me into the office to dictate something or other. I was grateful now that mother had insisted that every evening I should listen to some dreary talk on the wireless and take it down in shorthand so as not to lose my speed. She was not to know that Miss Kingston would fall by the wayside, but she was a woman of foresight.

It seemed to me that he gave me more work than he had given Miss Kingston, so I often had to stay on into the evening. So did he, of course, and it seemed reasonable on a very wet night, when we both left the office after seven o'clock that he should offer me a lift home in his car.

'There is no need,' I said. 'I can get the bus.'

'Nonsense,' he said. 'I wouldn't dream of letting you stand at the bus stop in this weather.'

'You could have asked him in,' my mother said. 'Or perhaps not. Perhaps it's too soon. When is Miss Kingston due back?'

'According to her doctor, another week.'

'Poor girl,' my mother said insincerely.

But when Miss Kingston did return, she brought with her the biggest shock of all.

'I wish to announce', she said, her face lit by a radiant smile, 'that I am engaged to be married.'

We stared at her. Jessie was the first to speak. 'I'm ever so pleased, Miss Kingston. But how did it happen? We thought you'd been in bed, more or less, for three weeks.'

Miss Kingston nodded happily.

'And so I was.'

'Oh, I see,' Jessie said. 'You fell in love with the doctor and he with you. He looked into your eyes as he was taking your temperature. How romantic.'

'It *was* romantic,' Miss Kingston agreed. 'But not with the doctor. It was the milkman.' She went as red as a peony.

'The milkman?' It was Jessie who said it. I was struck dumb.

'Trevor,' Miss Kingston said. 'I've always quite liked him, and we often had a cheery word. And when I didn't come to the door for two days . . .'

It transpired that when she hadn't answered his ring at the door on the third day, he kept his finger on the bell until, in the end, she had to answer it.

'I must have looked a sight,' she said. 'I was in my . . .' she sought for the word '. . . in my *déshabillé*.'

'You mean your nightdress?' Jessie asked.

'*And* my dressing gown. I was certainly not at my best, but Trevor didn't seem to mind. He sent me straight back to bed, came in and made a pot of tea and some thin bread and butter.'

The next morning he had done likewise, and on the fifth day he had given her a lightly boiled egg. From there it had progressed to him having breakfast with her.

'Trevor is a born carer,' she said.

Having discovered how much they enjoyed having breakfast together, it was a short step to making it permanent.

'But he's not *just* a milkman,' Miss Kingston explained. 'It's his own business. He has a dairy. Eggs, cream, milk and so on. I shall keep the books and help him on the business side. He needs someone.'

'What will Mr Baxter say?' I asked her.

'Well, he'll be devastated, of course. But it can't be helped. Trevor wants us to be married quite soon. He's so impetuous.' She blushed again.

Mr Baxter took it with surprising calm, which he tried to hide from Miss Kingston, and lost no time in appointing me in her place. Miss Kingston didn't mind at all. She was as happy as Larry. All she could hear were wedding bells.

Events moved quickly after Miss Kingston's return. On her last day, she readily handed over the keys to the confidential files, which up to then she had guarded with her life. There was a whip-round at Paragon, and we bought her a set of three flying ducks for the wall, with which she seemed delighted. Her last words in the office were, 'I shall send you all a piece of wedding cake.'

A new secretary, Erin Donnelly, was appointed in my place and the office slipped back into its routine. Not quite its usual routine, though. I worked much more closely with Mr Baxter than Miss Kingston had, and I began to take an interest in the business. At the same time, Edward – I had stopped thinking of him as Mr Baxter – began to take even more interest in me.

It being spring, there was a surge of business at Paragon. There always was in the spring, Edward explained. In the brighter sunshine, household goods suddenly seemed shabby and dingy, and so did one's clothing. Also, Whitsuntide loomed, and it would be a disgrace not to put the children in new clothes for Whit Sunday and, if possible, a new hat, shoes and gloves, for oneself. So there was an almighty rush for club cheques. And since Edward was a hands-on managing director, he was as busy as anyone else, including me.

What I discovered was that working late with the boss several evenings a week was the way to get close to him. Not that I set out to do this. It just happened naturally, and it seemed equally natural that at the end of the evening he should offer me a lift home in his car.

'You've worked very hard, Miss Holdsworth,' he said. 'I couldn't think of letting you catch a bus. It's quite easy for me to go in your direction.'

It was a short step, once spring had merged into summer and the rush of work had died down, and there was no need to work late, for Edward to take me out for dinner.

'You deserve a little reward,' he said. 'We'll drive out to Ilkley or Harrogate.'

It was in Harrogate, in a restaurant overlooking the green acres of the Stray, where we ate fresh salmon, which I had never tasted before, that he began to call me Poppy.

'A lovely name. It suits you down to the ground,' he said.

'Thank you, Edward,' I said, greatly daring.

My mother was in seventh heaven. She made me two new blouses in white Swiss cotton with tiny flowers, and bought me a grey, accordion-pleated skirt. 'You must look your best at all times,' she said.

Esmé, who was in her last term at college and still came home at weekends, though not as often, was intrigued.

'I don't know how you do it,' she said, 'but good for you. Is he very passionate?'

'Don't be silly,' I said. 'I've only been out to dinner with him. You don't get passionate over grilled salmon.'

'Fish is an aphrodisiac,' Esmé informed me. She knew about things like that.

What I didn't tell her – indeed, I'd not yet told my mother – was that he wanted me to meet his family. He had already met my mother, on the night he brought me back from dinner in Harrogate, and she had totally approved of him.

'It shows he's serious, wanting you to meet his family,' my mother said. 'If you watch your Ps and Qs and mind your manners, you could be on to a good thing. I couldn't have hoped for anything better for you. We must sort out what you're going to wear.'

He lived with his mother, in the parental home, but when I arrived it was not just she: there were Aunts Gladys and Lily, with attendant husbands, Roland and Henry, plus an ancient great-aunt called Emily. They had all turned up to inspect me, though Edward said that wasn't so and that they came every Sunday to tea and supper and to play several games of cards. Only Great-Aunt Emily was allowed to opt out of playing cards, being too old to distinguish hearts from diamonds. Instead, she read the more scurrilous bits of the *News of the World* and ate chocolates.

And thus went by the Sundays of that beautiful summer. We were expected to stay in, with the curtains drawn against the evening sun, and we were never alone together for a minute. I think it was that which caused Edward to propose to me as he was taking me home after one particularly claustrophobic evening.

'Please say yes,' he begged. 'I love you, and I would look after you and be good to you. You'd want for nothing. And you do love me, Poppy, don't you?'

'Of course I do,' I told him. He was an easy man to love – kind, considerate, nice to be with, even though he was a little serious. Also, he was the first man I'd really known. So I said yes.

My mother was overjoyed.

'You see,' she said, 'I was right. Didn't I tell you that secretaries marry their bosses! And you'll have a good life with Edward, certainly no scrimping and scraping.'

'I'm not marrying him for his money,' I assured her.

'Of course not, Poppy,' she agreed. 'I know that. Never marry for money, but on the other hand, try to marry where money is.'

'I always knew you'd be the first of the two of us to marry,' Esmé said. 'Can I be your bridesmaid?'

'Of course,' I said. 'Isn't that what we always planned?'

I married Edward in the parish church in October. The *Akersfield Chronicle* did us proud with an eight-inch column headed LOCAL BUSINESS CHIEF WEDS.

> The bride, who was given away by Mr Raymond Wilson, family friend, wore an ankle-length cream satin gown with a cowl neck. Her embroidered veil was held in place by a chaplet of orange blossom, and she carried a bouquet of lilies, roses and

carnations. The bridesmaid, Miss Esmé Infield, was dressed in primrose-yellow taffeta and carried a sheaf of lily of the valley and roses . . .

And so on and so on. Mother of the bride, Mother of the groom, gift of the bridegroom to the bridesmaid – a silver bracelet, which Esmé adored. 'The happy couple left for a honeymoon in Paris.' Edward chose Paris because, he said, it might be our last chance to visit it for a long time. There was trouble brewing in Europe. Who knew what would happen?

I enjoyed my honeymoon. Thc act of sex came as a natural and great pleasure and, though I had no yardstick by which to measure him, it seemed to me that Edward was a competent lover.

Did I love him as much as he loved me? Looking back, I'm not sure. I *did* love him, but not with the passionate, consuming, earth-shattering love that I was one day to find with someone else. But, of course, that came too late.

9

'Don't be silly, Maria,' Mervyn said sharply, 'the place is fine. I checked it out. It's not the Waldorf, but it's OK.'

Maria dismissed him with a wave of her hand, as if she were brushing off an annoying fly. 'I don't care. I didn't travel three thousand miles to stay in some grotty little guest house. I expected to be in the Splendide.'

'It is not grotty. It's clean and looks comfortable.'

'I'm not going there,' Maria said.

Poppy intervened.

'Where is it, exactly? What's it called?'

'It's the Balmoral.' He heavily accented the last syllable. 'On Royal Avenue.'

'How very apt,' Poppy said. 'And how clever of you to find it. I didn't think it was on your route.'

She knew the road. It was quite pleasant, with largish, semi-detached, red-brick, late-Victorian houses and sycamore trees on both sides. She couldn't recall Balmoral; she didn't go that way often because it didn't lead to anywhere.

'I got lost,' Mervyn admitted. 'Somehow took a wrong turn and found myself outside the Balmoral by accident. There was a woman trimming the hedge and I asked her for directions. A lucky accident, I'd call it.'

'If you stay there,' Maria said, 'you stay on your own. And why would it have a vacancy when everywhere else is full? That says something about it.'

'What it says,' Mervyn replied, 'is that the owner does not like conference people. She reckons they're more suited to the centre of Eastbourne or Brighton, where they can stay out half the night and go clubbing. She seemed a very respectable woman.'

'She sounds a drag,' Maria said. 'Not that it matters to me because I shan't be meeting her.'

'What's her name?' Poppy asked. Not that that mattered either; it was just a way of filling the silence that followed Maria's declaration.

Mervyn took a card from his pocket and studied it. 'Mrs Bedlington-Smythe.'

What a perfect name, Poppy thought, for a lady who keeps a guest house named Balmoral, in Royal Avenue. And if Mervyn and Maria *would* stay there, though there was a great deal of ground to be covered before they reached agreement, it would go a little way to solving the question of beds, which loomed ever larger as the hours passed.

'Did you . . . ?' Poppy asked; she was curious about how Mervyn had engineered this. 'Did you know it was a guest house? Is there a sign outside?'

Mervyn shook his head.

'Just the name on the gate: Balmoral. I asked the way to the beach, which made it clear I was a stranger, and one thing led to another. I told Mrs Bedlington-Smythe just what I thought of the Splendide. And she agreed with me.'

'So then she told you she took guests?'

'Not exactly. She doesn't advertise. I guess she's quite fussy about whom she'll have. Usually, she told me, it's only on recommendation.'

'She must have taken to you,' Poppy said. And after all, why wouldn't she? Short and fat Mervyn might be, but he was well-dressed and he had a certain prosperous style to him, and if he had been booked in, or rather *not* booked in, at the Splendide, then he was not short of money. And, of course, he was American.

'I think maybe she did,' Mervyn admitted.

'And you clearly took a shine to her,' Maria said.

'She is a nice woman; very helpful in a totally professional way,' Mervyn said. 'The Splendide could learn a lot from Mrs Bedlington-Smythe. And she gave me a good rate, which included breakfast. I paid her cash in advance. I only had dollars, but she didn't mind.'

'Well, you've thrown your money away,' Maria

told him. 'That is, unless you mean to occupy the room on your own.'

Which wouldn't help me in the least, Poppy thought. What would I do with Maria?

'Two rooms,' Mervyn said. 'A double for us and a single for Georgia.'

Georgia ceased, for a moment, to flip over the pages of a magazine she was scanning and looked up. 'I', she announced in a clear voice, 'would sooner sleep on a bench in the park.'

'There is no call for drama,' Mervyn said furiously. 'I have booked a perfectly good room for you and you will occupy it.'

'Not unless you take me there by force and tie me to the bedpost.' She returned to her magazine.

Poor Mervyn, Poppy thought. He looked as though he'd like to do exactly that. His face was dark with anger, but against his implacable daughter he knew he was beaten. For a man at the top of his profession, he didn't get far with his womenfolk. And really, Georgia was being very naughty, though no doubt her attitude sprang from her unhappiness. She was stymied for the moment *vis-à-vis* Bill, and she would find every possible way of punishing her parents for that.

She was so like her mother – a chip off the old block. Almost from babyhood Maria had sought every cause to rebel, as if nothing was worth having for which she didn't have to put up a fight. Her food, her toys, her school from the very first day, and later her clothes and her choice of friends. Everything.

She studied Maria's thin bad-tempered face and the nervous movement of her beautifully manicured hands. I let her win far too often, she thought. I was lazy; I didn't know how to deal with her, and now she's paying for it more than I am.

Beryl had not been as difficult, but even as a child she had been a bossy little know-all. Well intentioned, though. As a nurse she could probably wield her authority without fear of contradiction. How awful, Poppy chided herself, that I should think of my children as *not* totally perfect.

Am I even a good grandmother, she wondered? She loved her grandchildren, she was sure of that, but it was a love that carried little responsibility, and it certainly didn't impede her lifestyle. She hoped her grandchildren loved her, but could she be sure? She had done nothing special to earn their love, except give a few lavish presents for birthdays and Christmas, or provide a computer, or fund riding lessons or a school holiday abroad. And did any of that count? Was that the way?

Ah well, there was still time. Fiona and her much-desired new house, Georgia, Jeremy – they would all have wants and needs. Distance, not money, was the drawback, and not just physical distance. She seldom saw them, and never for long enough to become close. On the other hand, did they seek her out? Did they telephone just to say, 'How are you, Poppy?' No, they did not!

Sighing, she turned her head and looked at Daisy, sleeping so peacefully in her chair. Now there was a new chance. Perhaps I could be the best great-grandmother ever.

Beryl broke in on her thoughts. 'In my opinion,' she said, 'Mervyn made a good move there. It would make things much easier.'

'Since you wouldn't be asked to take part in the arrangements my husband has made without consulting me, your opinion doesn't carry much weight,' Maria said. 'And you're all right, aren't you? You have your bed reserved in your little caravan.' She invested the last two words with patronizing disdain.

'And you and Mervyn could have had beds in our *little caravan*,' Beryl reminded her. 'The offer was made. It just wasn't good enough for you, was it?'

'Please,' Poppy begged, 'do we have to go on like this. Can't we just sit down and work things out.'

'Poppy is right,' Mervyn said. 'And it's wrong of you two to be spoiling her birthday with your silly arguing.'

'Don't accuse me, Mervyn dear,' Beryl said. 'I was on your side, remember? I think you did a most sensible thing.'

'Well, yes, thank you,' Mervyn acknowledged. 'But now, shall we move on?'

'I agree,' Poppy said. 'I'll get a sheet of paper and we'll write it all down and work out the permutations to see what we can come up with. I know it's not easy. There are twelve people – if Joe comes—'

'He will if he possibly can,' Maria interrupted.

'And ten bed spaces, which includes the caravan.'

'What about Richard and Graham?' Beryl asked.

'They'll go back to Croydon,' Poppy said. 'I haven't included them, though I *did* include Daisy, who will actually share her parents' room.'

'So the two rooms at the Balmoral will make it exactly right,' Mervyn said triumphantly.

'Except that I refuse to occupy one,' Maria said.

'Likewise,' said Georgia.

'Really, this is ridiculous,' Beryl said. 'Let's take each space in turn and decide who will occupy it. Start with the caravan. Rodney and I, Jeremy and Megan.'

Megan looked anxiously at Jeremy, who gave her a reassuring, almost imperceptible, shake of the head.

'I'll tell you what,' he offered, 'Megan and I will stay at the Balmoral, if no-one else wants to. How about that?'

'A good idea,' Maria said. 'So where do I sleep, Ma?'

'In that case,' Poppy offered, 'you and Mervyn can have the twin-bedded room here. That leaves a single bed upstairs and a camp bed in here, and I suppose the sofa for Georgia, Joe and me.'

'There would still be a perfectly good single room at the Balmoral, already paid for.'

Surely, Poppy thought, I am not expected to vacate my own house, as well as my room, and sleep in a strange place on the eve of my eightieth birthday? But Georgia would not stay there, and she hated the idea of Joe sleeping anywhere other than under her roof.

'The Balmoral would *not* be a good idea for Joe,' Maria said. 'Who knows what time he'll arrive—'

'If at all,' Beryl put in.

'For once, I agree with my wife,' Mervyn said. 'Mrs Bedlington-Smythe does not strike me as a lady who would want a young man arriving in the middle of the night.'

'Quite,' Maria said. 'And since she's so respectable, what's she going to say about an unmarried couple occupying a double room?'

Jeremy laughed. 'Don't worry, Auntie, Uncle Mervyn can introduce us as Mr and Mrs Dean.'

'Ooh,' Maria said. 'And what will your mummy say to *that*?'

Beryl, recognizing defeat, kept silent.

Georgia suddenly spoke up. 'It's quite simple. Poppy has the single room upstairs, which is her right. I'll have the sofa here, and if and when Joe arrives, he can have the camp bed in this room. I mean, he is my brother.' She hoped he would come. She counted on him to be on her side. He might even bring news of Bill.

I can't believe it, Poppy thought. She couldn't believe it was all settled. The feeling lingered that when bedtime came, one or other of them would be without a bed.

'And I', Mervyn said, 'will call Mrs Bedlington-Smythe and turn down the extra room she so kindly offered.' And he had paid for.

'Why don't you go and see her?' Maria said. 'I'm sure she'd just love that.'

'And so would I,' Mervyn said. 'That's exactly what I *will* do!'

He was sick of the whole thing. Moreover, his indigestion was playing up. He felt in his pocket, took out his tablets, and slipped one into his mouth.

'Megan and I will follow you a little later,' Jeremy said. 'We'll probably catch up with you.'

'A good idea,' Mervyn replied.

'Well,' Poppy said, 'we seem to have settled things. Let's hope it works.'

She turned to Maria. 'And now that you know where you and Mervyn are going to sleep, I'll help you take your cases upstairs to clear the hall.'

'You will do no such thing, Mummy,' Beryl said. 'Heaving other people's luggage about is *not* a thing you do the day before your eightieth birthday.'

'Don't pin it on me,' Maria snapped. 'It wasn't my idea. As far as I'm concerned it can all wait until Mervyn gets back from his dalliance with Mrs Bedlington-Smythe. *He* can take them upstairs. In fact,' she added, 'at least half the clutter in the hall is the baby's stuff. Perhaps someone should start moving that upstairs.'

'David will do that all in good time, Aunt Maria,' Fiona said. 'We're not going to start heaving things about while dear little Daisy is still asleep. Anyway, not all of it goes up to the bedroom.'

Then where *will* it go? Poppy asked herself.

'I can't see why one baby needs so much,' Maria said.

'You will, dear,' Beryl said smoothly, 'if ever you're a grandmother.'

Mervyn, glad to be out of the house, stepped out at a good pace. He looked forward to seeing Mrs Bedlington-Smythe, but he wasn't sure how she would take to the change of plan.

Jeremy and Megan followed at a more leisurely pace. Jeremy was in no hurry to catch up with Mervyn, he simply wanted to be alone with his beloved as, he was sure, she did with him. They hadn't had a minute together since they'd arrived at Poppy's.

They were in luck. Somewhere between Poppy's house and Royal Avenue they came across a small park. A board on the gate proclaimed that it was the Amos Thornton Memorial Park. 'No Dogs Allowed, No Bicycles, No Litter, Please Keep Off the Grass'.

'Didn't care much for mankind, Amos,' Jeremy said.

'Or animals,' Megan said.

Nevertheless, it worked out well for lovers. It was secluded, perhaps because there were no grassy areas where children could play, no swings or slides, just flowers, shrubs and a few seats. They quickly found a bench in a sheltered arbour and forgot the passage of time.

Mervyn, unusually nervous, rang the bell at Balmoral. How in the world would he explain that, for his wife, this place was not good enough and that she had totally refused even to enter it?

Mrs Bedlington-Smythe opened the door. 'Ah, Mr Leverson,' she said. 'Please come in. Oh dear, you do seem out of breath.'

'I guess I was in a rush,' Mervyn said.

'You naughty man,' said Mrs Bedlington-Smythe. 'You should never rush. You and I are at an age when we should take things more easily.'

It was not exactly what Mervyn wanted to hear, but coupling him with this charming Englishwoman made the words almost a compliment. A man did not have to be in the first flush of youth, or as thin as a stick, to be attractive. Or a woman either, come to that. Mrs Bedlington-Smythe was pleasantly rounded, her skin was pink and white English and, although she was a small woman, her confident bearing made her seem taller.

'Now, do sit down and get your breath back.'

And how kind.

'So you have come to claim your rooms,' she said. 'But where is your luggage? And your wife, whom I'm looking forward so much to meeting. Is she to follow?'

Mervyn shook his head. He would willingly have strangled Maria at that moment, not to mention Georgia.

'Alas, no,' he said, finding himself adopting Mrs Bedlington-Smythe's genteel intonation. 'My wife very much regrets that she cannot avail herself of your hospitality. The fact is . . .' he searched for inspiration '. . . her mother is not at all well.' For a moment he envisaged Poppy, who was probably fitter than most of them and would very much dislike being described as unwell. Thank goodness she would never know. 'After all, she is nearly eighty. And Maria sees her mother so seldom, though she'd like to see her more' – he was warming to his theme – 'so she feels she should spend every minute she can with her mother . . .' He ran out of steam.

'Oh, I do understand Mr Leverson.' Mrs Bedlington-Smythe laid a sympathetic hand on Mervyn's arm. 'I *am* sorry!'

'Thank you. Please call me Mervyn.'

'And you must call me Madeleine.'

'A beautiful name,' Mervyn said. 'Madeleine Bedlington-Smythe. It flows.'

'As long as you don't call me Mad,' she trilled. 'And what about your daughter? Where is she?'

'I'm afraid Georgia won't be here either,' Mervyn said. 'For the same reason. She's so devoted to her grandmother, you wouldn't believe.'

'How sweet. So I shall have you to myself?' she teased.

Oh, wouldn't that be great, Mervyn thought. What a haven of peace this would be.

He shook his head. 'I'm afraid not. It's not so easy. Oh, don't worry Madeleine. I know I've paid for the rooms, and there's no way I would expect a refund, even if we didn't use them . . .'

Nor would you get it, thought Mrs Bedlington-Smythe.

'. . . but we are very short of space at my mother-in-law's, which is why it was so good to find rooms here with you. As neither my wife or daughter can come, nor myself, I wonder if it would be OK if my nephew, Jeremy and his . . . and Megan . . . took the double room? You'd like them; they're a great couple.'

'Of course,' Mrs Bedlington-Smythe said. 'They'd be welcome, though I'm disappointed not to have you and your wife. And what about the single room? Perhaps you'd like to have that yourself, if your wife and daughter are going to be occupied with your mother-in-law, poor old lady?'

Wouldn't I just, Mervyn thought. But however much Maria irritated him, he had so far remained faithful to her, resisting temptation from more than one attractive patient who had hinted at repaying him in more than dollars for the loving care he had lavished on her teeth.

'I'm sorry,' he replied, 'I must be on hand, just in case I'm needed, though there is a chance that my son, Joe, might come in from New York. We don't know, but if he does and there's no room at the house, and if he arrives at a reasonable time, I'm sure he'd like to stay with you. He's a nice guy. You'll like him.'

'I'm sure I will,' Mrs Bedlington-Smythe agreed. 'If he comes, he'll be made welcome.'

But will his grandmother allow him to sleep under any roof other than hers? Mervyn asked himself.

'In fact,' he said, 'I expected Jeremy and Megan to be here before now. They planned to follow right after me.'

'Oh, I'm sure they'll find their way,' Mrs Bedlington-Smythe said. 'Perhaps you'll join me in a cup of tea while we wait?'

Mervyn, who actually disliked tea, was on his second cup and his third Bourbon cream biscuit when Jeremy and Megan arrived.

'Did you get lost?' he asked.

Jeremy smiled happily. 'You could say that. I'm afraid we've kept you waiting.'

Mervyn smiled equally happily, glancing at Mrs Bedlington-Smythe. 'It's been a pleasure,' he said gallantly.

Why didn't I say a word of protest about Jeremy and Megan? Beryl asked herself. But it was too late now, they had gone off to share a room at Mrs Whatever-her-name-was and, in any case, what could she have said that would have made the slightest difference? She was sadly aware that she was out of touch with the younger generation.

It had been so different for her, though she and Rodney had been an anachronism even in their own generation, which was busy flouting convention in the swinging Sixties. She had been a virgin when she'd married Rodney after a three-year courtship. She had been out of step, and old-fashioned then, so how could she be expected to reconcile herself to today's morals? By morals, she naturally meant sexual ones; the ones that counted.

In her heart, she blamed how she was on her mother. She'd had three husbands and, between and after them, no shortage of men friends. There had always been some man or other calling her up, taking her out or buying her presents. Sometimes they had given presents to herself and Maria, and though Maria had quite liked that, Beryl had hated it. Her mother was not like her friends' mothers. She felt she had to explain her to them, though, indeed, they were inclined to express envy of the fact that her mother was different, not to mention beautiful and glamorous.

Thank goodness it was not so now that her mother was getting old – well, *was* old. Her beauty had faded – though she is still more attractive than I will ever be, Beryl acknowledged to herself. There were, as far as Beryl knew, no longer any men in the offing. Surely not? In these later years she had grown quite fond of her mother. She was ready to look after her, keep an eye on her.

'Perhaps we should sort out what we're going to do tomorrow,' Poppy said. 'I mean, the dinner and so on. The seating.'

Fiona gave a sudden cry.

'Oh, look. Daisy is waking up. She always looks so sweet when she's waking out of her sleep. I shall change her, and then I'll take her out for a little trip in her buggy.'

Clever move, Maria thought. Trust her niece to wriggle out of anything that wasn't directly concerned with her baby.

'What about you, David?' Fiona said. 'Shall we both go for a walk with Daisy?'

'Since my husband and your brother seem to have deserted us,' Maria said in a sharp voice, 'I think we might need David's help here.'

Fiona lifted Daisy out of her pen, laid her on the changing mat and, kneeling beside her, removed her soiled garments and clothed her in fresh ones from tip to toe. Daisy lay on her back, kicking her legs, and allowed herself to be manhandled without protest.

'There,' Fiona said in a satisfied voice, 'who is Mummy's precious baby? Who is the best little girl in the whole world?'

Then, with great dexterity, amazing balance and fluidity of movement, she scooped up Daisy, brought them both to a standing position and immediately transferred the baby to Poppy's arms.

'Great-grandmama will look after you for just a teensy minute while I get your buggy ready for you,' she informed Daisy. Daisy regarded her great-grandmother with what Poppy felt sure was approval, indeed pleasure; her beautiful eyes opened wide and a faint smile played around her lips. She really is a poppet, Poppy thought. I wonder if she's at all like me, I mean, as I was as a baby? Was there an old photograph in the chest in the attic? Could she negotiate the loft ladder? It was ages since she'd been up there.

'Mummy,' Fiona said over her shoulder as she left the room 'would you be an angel and clear away the mat and the rest of the stuff?'

'Of course, darling,' Beryl said.

'And will you bring Daisy into the hall, Poppy?' Fiona called out. 'It won't take me two minutes to get the buggy ready.'

Nor would it have if it hadn't been buried under a pile of paraphernalia, but eventually it was unearthed. Fiona took the folded contraption by the handles and gave it a vigorous shake, whereupon it opened and magically transformed itself into a well-padded, miniature armchair on wheels.

'How comfortable it looks. And how sensible,' Poppy said, handing Daisy over to be trussed up and fastened in. 'When your mother was a baby she was pushed in a high, solid pram with springs. It was made of wood and polished a deep navy blue. "Coach built", they were called, and I reckon when it came to pushing it up hill it was as heavy as a coach. It was very smart, of course. There was fierce competition about who had the best perambulator.'

'It wasn't new,' Beryl said, passing through the hall with an armful of soiled clothes. 'Maria had it before me.' For years, almost everything she'd had as a child had been owned by Maria first: clothes, toys, shoes, pram, cot. She'd longed for something bought exclusively for her.

'That couldn't be helped,' Poppy said. 'It was wartime. We were lucky to have a halfway-decent pram.'

Old people, bless them, were always going on about the war, Fiona thought. 'Before the war . . .', 'during the war . . .', 'after the war . . .', as if the clock of their entire life was set by it. To her, the war was about as remote as the Battle of Hastings in 1066. It could get quite boring, but at this moment she didn't mind. She felt only benevolence towards the older generation. It was a lovely day, the sun was shining and she was about to take her darling baby for a walk. Nor did she mind too much that David wasn't accompanying her. He was the best of husbands, of course, but sometimes she wasn't sure he loved Daisy quite as much as she did. Anyway, there were times when she enjoyed being just with her baby, and now was one of them.

Her mother and grandmother stood in the

doorway, watching as she wheeled the buggy away down the drive and into the street.

'Take care,' her mother warned.

'Enjoy,' Poppy said.

Which way should she go? She had no plan; she would go where her feet took her. She turned left.

Mervyn had parted from Mrs Bedlington-Smythe reluctantly. Madeleine, he reminded himself. Madeleine. What a wonderful woman she was. Kind, uncomplicated, well-mannered. There was something about Englishwomen that he liked, which was why, he supposed, he had fallen for Maria in the first place. She had swept him off his feet all right. She was bright, clever, a real go-getter. He had been married to her almost before he knew it, and happy to be so. Once married, she'd been determined to further his career, which indeed she had done, cultivating all the right people so that he'd become not only a good dentist, but a fashionable one. He owed her that.

Over the years, though, she'd changed or, as she would have said, progressed. All the facets of her character, especially the annoying ones, had intensified, so that when she'd reached her goal of advancing *his* career, she'd started to make one for herself. The trouble with Maria was that she had too much energy, and some way or another it had to be channelled.

She had not kept her English ways for long.

She was now more American than the Americans, a successful New Yorker. Even so, he doubted if she was a happy woman, and when, as now, walking along this quiet English road in this temperate climate, he had time to think about himself, he doubted if he was a happy man.

Head down, deep in his thoughts, he saw nothing of Fiona, who was walking towards him; nor did Fiona, lost to the world, talking out loud to Daisy, see Mervyn approaching. She had almost run him down before they looked up and saw each other.

'Why, Uncle Mervyn,' Fiona cried. 'Fancy meeting you.'

10

The fact that I later found a love that surpassed all the others doesn't mean that I wasn't happy with Edward. I was; especially in the early days of our marriage. I had no idea then what was to come, let alone what love *could* be like. I was too inexperienced to have a yardstick. I suppose I looked forward to a contented life with Edward.

His choice of Paris for our honeymoon was a surprise. I'd already decided he wasn't a man of great imagination. A week at the Grand Hotel in Scarborough would appear to be more in his line, or, if he really wanted to venture far afield, then just possibly The Grand in Brighton. But no, he had set his mind on Paris, and nothing else would do.

'Why Paris?' I asked him as we sat at a pavement café on the Champs-Elysées drinking bitterly strong coffee. 'Had you been before? Or did you know someone who had?'

'Neither reason,' he admitted. 'I'd read about

it and seen it on the newsreels; it took my fancy and I was determined one day to see it for real.'

'Was it the place you planned to choose for your honeymoon?' I asked.

He smiled at me. He had a lovely warm, though infrequent, smile.

'I didn't give a thought to honeymoons until I met you,' he said. 'I was always too busy working. My father was a hard taskmaster; he made me toe the line, which was just as well, considering he died and left me to it.'

'Why did you engage Miss Kingston?' I said. I wanted to discover more about him. I didn't know much; I hadn't known him long enough.

'I didn't. She was my father's secretary and I inherited her. It was just as well I did because she knew about everything.' He called the waiter over and paid him, then he leaned across the table and took my hand in his.

'Let's go back to the hotel,' he suggested.

'Edward, it's the middle of the afternoon,' I said.

'I know, and we're on honeymoon.'

He stood up and pulled me to my feet, and we set off in the direction of the hotel, which was quite near, a little way down another of the wide avenues which led from the Arc de Triomphe.

Later, lying back against the pillows, momentarily satisfied, if not yet sated, with love and sex, I said, 'I'm glad you didn't fall in love with Miss Kingston and bring her to Paris for a honeymoon instead of me.'

He laughed at that. 'I hardly noticed her,' he confessed. 'She just got on with her job – very efficiently, of course.'

'Poor Miss Kingston,' I said. 'You know she was madly in love with you, at least until the milkman came along and swept her off her feet.'

'Why are we talking about Miss Kingston?' Edward protested. 'Come here.' He took me in his arms and we began to make love again.

In the time that could be spared from love-making during that week we did everything a tourist in Paris would do: a boat ride on the Seine, walks in the Tuileries gardens, the flea market, the *Folies Bergère*, restaurants, museums, shops, shops, shops. Edward was very generous to me.

Apart from my own heightened awareness of everything around, which the act of sex always seemed to give me, there was a feverishness about the city, as if it was waiting for something to happen, and meanwhile crowding everything into the time still left, a time of which no-one knew the length but feared was short. Later, when Paris was occupied by the Germans, I often thought back to our time there. Were the cafés in the Champs-Elysées crowded with German soldiers? Who was sleeping in our hotel bed-room?

Returning from our honeymoon, we stayed in London for a night, at a hotel near Marble Arch, before travelling back to Yorkshire. All the talk was of the war, which everyone agreed must come, and sooner rather than later. Here, also, there was a frenzied atmosphere, a mixture of doom and excitement and practical preparations. They were digging trenches in the park and some of the buildings were already sandbagged.

That day in London was the first time I felt a real prick of fear about what might happen. It seemed somehow closer in London than it had in Yorkshire. Until then most of the talk and conjecture had passed me by; I'd been too concerned with preparations for my wedding and the wedding itself to think much about preparations for war.

'It's been wonderful,' I said to Edward when we were in bed that night. 'I shan't ever forget it, but now I'm glad to be going home.'

'Me, too,' Edward agreed. 'There'll be a lot to think about; things to do.'

'Things to do in our new home,' I reminded him. 'I shall enjoy that.'

Shortly before we were to be married, Edward had bought a house called Two Elms. It was a few miles out from the town, but close enough for him to drive to work easily, and not too far from his mother, whose health, she insisted, was not too good. (Good health or bad, she wouldn't let him out of her sight for long.) His journey to and from work took him past her door, so there was no reason for him not to pop in most days to check on her.

I say Edward had bought a house because

that's exactly how it was. He came into the office one morning a bit late – I was already at work – and said, 'I've bought a house!'

I would have liked to help choose it. Not, when I went with him to see it that evening, that there was a single thing wrong with the house; I liked it. It was early Victorian, not too big and not too small; the rooms were spacious, with high ceilings and moulded cornices. I couldn't fault it; it was just that I would have liked to have had a hand in the choosing.

'We'll pop in on Mother,' Edward said as I got into the car to be driven back to my home. 'She likes to see you.'

'Well,' Mrs Baxter said, sitting in her chair, beaming. 'Did you like it?'

'The house? Why yes, it's wonderful,' I said.

She nodded agreement. 'I thought so. It will suit you both very well. I said so to Edward, didn't I, dear?' She looked up at him.

'You did, Mother,' he confirmed.

'Oh. You've seen it, then?' I tried not to sound annoyed.

'Of course, dear. Edward wanted my opinion. I told him I think it's a nice family house and it needs practically nothing doing to it. You'll hardly need to change a thing.'

That was the moment I decided I would probably change every single thing.

'You *do* like it, don't you?' Edward said, back in the car.

'Of course I do. It's just that . . . well . . . I'd like to have had a hand in the choosing.'

'Wouldn't you have chosen it?' he queried.

'Of course I would.' Why couldn't he understand?

'Well then, that's all right,' he said amicably. 'And you can pick the furniture. And all the decoration and furnishings and so on – curtains, cushions. That's a woman's job.' Buying bricks and mortar, in this case lovely, weathered local stone, was not.

I was to find out that there were women's jobs and men's jobs and, since I had lived with my mother all my life – I never thought of the uncles as permanent parts of the family – this was something that had never occurred to me. All decisions and most jobs had fallen to us.

Edward was true to his word. He gave me a free hand in furnishing the house and placed no restrictions on what I spent, apart from reminding me that almost anything that was needed could be had at wholesale prices from one or other of his business contacts. He tried hard to show an interest in colour schemes, fabrics and all the many small objects needed to turn an empty house into a home, but it was not his field. His talent was invested in Paragon.

'I don't have a good eye for colour,' he admitted, when I asked him to help me choose the precise shade of paint for the sitting room. 'It's really best left to you, love. Or you might like to ask Mother?'

It was the last thing I would do, so in the end my own taste prevailed throughout the house, and when it was all done, I must say I was pleased with it. It had a light, airy feel to it; fresh colours, nothing heavy or dark, except to give an accent here and there.

'You've done a good job,' Edward said.

'Very nice,' Mrs Baxter said. 'Light colours are pretty, though I'm afraid you'll find they show the dirt.'

As a married woman it was expected that I would give up my job and stay at home. I protested against this; I thought it was stupid, but I didn't win. 'I never went out to work for a single day after I married,' my mother-in-law said. 'My husband would never have allowed it.' And for once my own mother agreed with Mrs Baxter. 'One way or another I've had to earn money all my married life,' she said. 'It's not what I planned for you, Poppy love.'

Edward engaged a new secretary, Miss Carstairs.

'Is she all right?' I asked after a week or two.

He sighed. 'Not as good as you, love.'

'Serves you right,' I said. 'You should have kept me on.'

'Poppy,' he said, 'you know I couldn't do that. Men in Paragon don't have their wives working with them.'

'More fool them,' I retorted. 'But I shall have to find something to do, I'm bored.'

What everyone had expected, me included,

was that by this time I would be pregnant; but I wasn't, and who could say why? The ardour Edward had shown on our honeymoon was undiminished, but nothing came of it. I suppose it was assumed, even by me, that it was my fault.

It was the expectation of war that saved me. Suddenly there were all sorts of things for which women were wanted. Not paid work, of course; it was all voluntary. First Aid and Home Nursing courses; auxiliary nurses, who were actually allowed to set foot in hospital wards; Women's Voluntary Service, which did no end of things – or stood by, ready to do them in the event of war – and included a natty green uniform with a felt hat. It suddenly became quite the thing for stay-at-home ladies to join something.

'I shall do First Aid and Home Nursing,' I announced. 'And after that I shall be an auxiliary nurse. You have to do fifty hours on the wards for that, on top of your certificates.'

'*You*. Work in a hospital ward?' my mother cried. 'Why? You hate illness. If anyone was sick at school you had to go out and be sick with them. And you can't stand the sight of blood. What would you do with a wounded soldier?'

It was assumed that we would all be nursing the gravely wounded, or perhaps handing instruments to the surgeon in the operating theatre. 'Scalpel, nurse. Clamp, nurse.' Nothing as boring as elderly ladies with bronchitis.

'It's nothing more than the glamour of the uniform,' my mother declared.

'Oh no, it's not,' I said. 'And nursing is what I shall do.'

And I did. Every Wednesday I did First Aid and every Friday was Home Nursing. We worked in pairs, splinting or bandaging each other. My partner once bound me so tightly in a double-breast bandage that I started to go a funny colour from lack of air. In Home Nursing we applied mustard poultices, took temperatures and learned the day on which the rash first showed itself in various childhood illnesses – chickenpox the first day, measles the fourth.

Somehow, we all passed our exams and got the certificates to prove it. I don't remember anyone failing.

I completed my fifty hours in the local hospital, mostly getting under the feet of the real nurses. The one and only excitement was watching the doctor extract from the foot of a patient a fine sewing needle which had been lost on the floor. I didn't quite pass out unconscious.

'There you are, nurse!' the doctor said, holding the needle aloft. 'Always be careful where you drop these little fellows!' It was the first time a doctor had ever spoken to me, let alone called me 'Nurse'.

Now that I was a fully-fledged member of the nursing staff – though its lowest form of life – I worked two half-day shifts each week.

'I don't want you to be overtired,' Edward said. 'Remember, you have a house to run.'

I didn't really. At that time I had Elsie, a

competent housemaid, plus a daily for the rough, though Elsie left me later for the excitements of the ATS.

'I can hardly get tired,' I told Edward. 'There's practically nothing for me to do.'

'You wait until the balloon goes up,' Edward said. 'You'll not complain about nothing to do then.'

The official theory was that when the war started bombs would rain from the skies from the very first day. One hundred thousand would fall in the first two weeks, and then a thousand people a day would be killed in air raids. Naturally, all hospitals would be rammed to the gills with casualties.

'But at the moment,' I said, 'there are rows of beds reserved for the occasion, and none of them are occupied. There isn't enough work, even for the regular staff.'

It went on like that for months, long after the war had started. I cleaned lockers, washed and rolled bandages, tidied and retidied the linen room, with its piles of sheets, pillowcases and towels, waiting to be used. And I kept out of the way of Sister, who hated all auxiliaries because they'd been foisted upon her. Seldom did she allow one of us near a patient; even giving someone a bedpan was considered to be above our skills.

The hospital apart, there were suddenly many new rules and regulations, things we were commanded to do and other things we mustn't do.

Our lives were controlled. Edward, a strong supporter of Neville Chamberlain's government, obeyed them all implicitly, though he was niggled by the total ban on car lights.

'It won't work,' he said. 'We shall be bumping into each other all over the place.'

He was vindicated when it turned out that in the first month of the war the number of deaths arising from this ban doubled, while there were none from air raids. Later, the total ban was lifted and we were allowed one small slit of light from the cover of one headlamp.

'I knew they would see sense,' Edward said approvingly.

Several months afterwards we had our first bit of pleasurable excitement. So far the war in Akersfield had been mostly boring. Tedious, because rationing was now with us and we had the blackout with all its restrictions. As for the real war, we knew about that only from the news on the wireless. Akersfield might have been on another planet. The nearest we came to drama was on one occasion in the middle of the night, when the air-raid warning sounded and, at Edward's command, the four of us – me, Elsie, my mother, who was staying with us, and Edward himself – snatched at our dressing gowns and trooped into the Anderson shelter in the garden, along with the black beetles, spiders and earwigs.

'I think I'd rather face Hitler,' my mother said nervously as she and I watched a ferocious-looking spider climb up the inside of the shelter.

Our ordeal wasn't too long. Half an hour later the all-clear sounded and we went back to bed. It must have been the thought of danger that brought it on: Edward made love to me in the middle of the night. If this makes a baby, I thought, it will have an inborn fear of spiders.

The pleasurable excitement was the arrival of a regiment – or perhaps something not as large as a regiment – of the Royal Engineers. The soldiers were billeted in various places around the town, while the officers took over a large house halfway between the hospital and Two Elms. We would see them walking around, the officers usually in twos, looking well-groomed and immaculate in their ultra-clean uniforms, which showed no sign of having seen combat.

It appeared that they were waiting to be sent elsewhere, perhaps overseas. No-one knew where, but most people made guesses – all different. The officers, if they knew, said nothing. It all added a little welcome diversion.

It was Matron who announced *the* great excitement. In my humble role I had seldom set eyes on Matron, and then only from a distance; and as far as I knew she had never glanced in my direction. Nevertheless, when the invitation came, I was included in it.

She announced that the hospital would give a dance for the benefit of the officers and men. There was a large hut in the hospital grounds which could be made presentable, a local dance band was to be hired and there would be refreshments. Nothing elaborate because of rationing, though in my experience the hospital rations were far superior to those in my own home.

All grades of nurses who would be off duty were invited to attend, though none could bring partners because their function was to dance with the soldiers.

'I wonder,' I said to Edward, who had agreed to me going without him, seeing it as a patriotic duty on both my part and his, 'will the sisters dance with the officers, the staff nurses with the NCOs and the other nurses with other ranks?' And where would that leave we few auxiliaries?

'What I do want', Matron let it be known, 'is for my nurses to look their very best. Get out your dancing frocks. Dress up. Make this a special occasion for our brave soldiers, and a memory to take with them when they go into battle.'

I was agog with excitement, not because of the soldiers, but at the thought of dancing. I hadn't been to a dance since before I was married. Esmé was teaching at a school in Durham so, because of wartime travelling, I seldom saw her, but even if I had, I could no longer go to a public dance without my husband, and Edward was no dancing man.

There was no difficulty about what to wear, apart from choosing between three or four dresses which were languishing in my wardrobe. I chose a pale-green taffeta with a low square neckline, a fitted waist and an ankle-length full skirt. At the last minute I took a cream-coloured carnation from a vase, shortened the stem and pinned it on the bodice. It was a dress I was never to forget, though I've had many beautiful ones since. Year after year it hung at the back of my wardrobe. I never wore it again, but I couldn't bring myself to part with it.

'You look as pretty as a picture,' Edward said. 'You'll be the belle of the ball.'

There was a ring at the door.

'At last,' I said impatiently. 'Why is Caroline always late?'

Caroline was another auxiliary, who lived not far away. To save petrol, her father was to take us to the dance and Edward would fetch us home.

'I'll be there at eleven,' he promised as I rushed out to the car.

Matron had set eleven o'clock as the finishing time of the dance, strong in the belief that all her nurses should be in their beds, and hopefully asleep, by midnight. To this end, the doors of the nurses' home, where all except local nurses were housed, were locked and bolted at eleven fifteen sharp. Naturally, ways had been devised of getting in after that, ways known to all. A particular ground-floor bathroom window was so convenient that sometimes around midnight there would be a short, silent queue of nurses waiting to use it.

Caroline and I entered the hut to the sound of the four-piece band playing a quickstep. It was a large hut, with a small kitchen and two even smaller cloakrooms, and it had been transformed by the Parks and Gardens Department, who also looked after the hospital grounds. There were shrubs in tubs, the window sills were crammed with flowers against the blackout blinds, ivy grew magically up the walls and the band was almost hidden behind a screen of greenery. We hurried furtively to the cloakroom, shed our coats and, with no more than a quick glance in the mirror, reappeared to take our places on the chairs which were ranged in a straight line all around the room against the wall. Matron would not brook unpunctuality.

Should we, Caroline and I asked each other, dance together, or should we sit quietly on our chairs, like puppies in a pet-shop window waiting to be chosen by some kind person. Looking at the dance floor, we saw no nurses dancing together, all had khaki-clad partners.

'We'd better stay put,' Caroline said, 'and wait until someone asks us – if they ever do.'

I sat there with a smile on my face, trying to look interesting, the kind of girl any man would want to dance with. Inside I was all impatience. The band was playing, my feet were tapping, my whole body wanted to move with the rhythm. Dancing was the thing I liked best in the whole world. I suppose it still is, though at my age who would believe me.

I noticed Alun quite quickly, not that he was outstanding in any way. An officer, one pip, second lieutenant, his uniform quite new looking. He was a little taller than I was, with dark, straight hair, slightly built, his features regular but unremarkable. He was dancing with Staff Nurse Joan Dixon, and I saw at once that he wasn't among the world's best dancers. As the two of them passed close by, he turned his gaze away from his partner for a second and caught my eye. I knew, as sure as sure, that his next dance would be with me.

I was not wrong. I watched him take Staff Nurse Dixon back to her seat, then, the moment the band struck up the music again – a slow foxtrot – he was standing in front of me.

'Alun Griffiths,' he said. 'May I have this dance?' He had a soft, clear voice, with just the faintest trace of a Welsh accent.

I smiled and stood up. I can't remember what I said, if anything, and he led me away onto the floor.

He was not, as I'd already observed, the best of dancers. When it comes to ballroom dancing, the waltz and the quickstep are easy, but a slow foxtrot sorts out the good from the merely passable. Alun was passable. We circled the floor, but with none of those finely balanced turns, that daring to hover on the ball of the foot, that almost going against the beat but always knowing where it is.

A husky-voiced tenor began to sing 'Night and day'.

Except for the fact that the tune and words were something I would always remember, and would hear a thousand times over the years, I wasn't conscious of listening to the music, or considering how well or how badly we were dancing. It was a time and a place set apart. We might have been dancing in space, totally alone in the heavens. The floor was crowded, a mass of khaki uniforms and pretty dresses, but the other dancers seemed not to be there at all. Later, Alun told me that it had been exactly like that for him.

We didn't talk much, either, and then only about obvious things like [me to him] 'Where do you come from?' and [he to me] 'How long have you been a nurse?'

His home was in a village in Pembrokeshire. He had been a teacher for a short time before joining the Army. He didn't think he would go back to teaching. And so on.

At the end of the dance he took me back to my seat, then went to join his brother officers, but at the start of every dance he would stand in front of me again. We danced the next four dances together, and then the next one being an 'excuse me', one of the other officers broke in.

'We can't have Alun monopolizing you,' he said as he whisked me away. He was a much better dancer, but I resented him.

Alun was back again at the start of the next dance. 'I've been told I have to ask some of the wallflowers,' he said. 'So I shall for a while. But please save me the last waltz, and can I see you home?'

I hesitated for a second, then I came back to

earth. 'The last waltz, yes,' I said. 'But after that my husband is collecting me.'

He gave me a long look. 'I didn't know you were married,' he said in the end.

'I'm wearing a wedding ring,' I told him.

'I didn't notice. I'm sorry.'

'Please don't be sorry,' I said. 'I've enjoyed myself.' They seemed such empty, banal words. How did 'enjoy' begin to describe anything I'd felt.

'I'm sure we'll meet again,' I said. 'That is, if you're here for a while.'

'We don't know how long,' Alun said. 'I *must* see you again.'

It was when the last waltz ended that I came to and saw Edward, and realized that he was the last person on earth I wanted to see. I didn't have any shame about that, not at that moment. My feelings were beyond my control.

He had come into the dance to collect me, and he was standing by the door, talking to a senior officer. Alun walked with me towards them.

'Ah, there you are Poppy. Have you enjoyed yourself? I've just been saying to Major Betts here that we must have something or other at home. Entertain some of his men while they're still with us.'

11

'Why, Fiona, what a surprise,' Mervyn said. 'I didn't expect to see you.'

Nor was he sure he wanted to. He'd been walking along, wrapped in his thoughts, enjoying a rare moment of peace and quiet which he knew couldn't last, and now there was Fiona, plus the baby. He hardly knew her, and his memories of her, such as they were, were not entirely happy. She had been, what? He reckoned around thirteen years old when she'd visited New York with her parents. It had seemed a very long two weeks. Maria and Beryl had quarrelled frequently, Fiona and six-year-old Georgia, who'd had to share a room, had disliked each other on sight. Most of the time Fiona had refused to eat food that was strange to her, but had nevertheless thrown up in the car twice. Rodney had spent his time pouring oil on troubled waters, and cleaning up the car, while thankfully I, Mervyn remembered, had a very busy two weeks in the surgery.

'And I hadn't expected to see you,' Fiona said with a smile, 'but how nice. Were you out for a walk? It's quite different from New York, isn't it? Not that I remember much about New York, but one sees it all the time on TV. All those policemen.'

'It's not quite like that,' Mervyn said, 'but it sure is different. This is a pleasant change.'

'I wish Daisy was awake,' Fiona said. 'I'd like her to see you.'

'You would?' How about that. What a nice young woman his niece had grown into. Perhaps his memory of her was at fault; perhaps he had got her wrong.

'Oh yes, I would,' Fiona said. 'You are her only great-uncle. At least, you're her only *American* great-uncle,' she amended, suddenly remembering Richard, who had not taken the trouble to come to Daisy's christening, but had sent a single spoon, silver plated not silver, in the post. 'Oh yes, I would like her to know her family. I think it's good for children to know the family, don't you?'

'I suppose it is,' Mervyn said. 'I hadn't thought about it. I don't know much about babies. I suppose I was too busy when Joe and Georgia were that age to see much of them.'

'Oh, you poor man.' Fiona exuded genuine sympathy. 'How awful. We must see to it that you get to know Daisy while you are here.'

'Well, yes,' Mervyn said doubtfully. 'Of course, I shan't be here long.'

'I know,' Fiona said. 'Why don't we walk along together? Daisy is sure to waken soon, and when she does you could push the buggy. You can really look at each other.'

'Well, thank you,' Mervyn said. Not for one hour had he ever pushed his own children in their strollers.

'I won't suggest you do so while she's still asleep. If she were to wake and see a strange man looking at her, it might give her quite a fright. Oh dear, that does sound rather rude.'

'I quite understand,' Mervyn said, smiling. 'I never thought of myself as a guy who would frighten babies, but you never know.'

'I'm sure you won't frighten her once she gets used to you,' Fiona said kindly. 'Which way shall we go? Shall I turn round and make for home?'

'Good idea,' Mervyn agreed.

Fiona swung the buggy round and they set off.

'Most buggies,' Fiona informed Mervyn, 'have the baby facing forward, I suppose so that it can see where it's going, but I went to a lot of trouble to find one where Daisy and I could face each other. Apart from the fact that I can keep an eye on her, it helps the process of bonding, don't you think?'

'Undoubtedly,' Mervyn agreed.

'Oh, look,' Fiona cried, 'she's waking up, bless her.'

Daisy opened her eyes, stretched her mouth in a wide yawn and raised her fists in the air.

'She's waving to you,' Fiona said. 'That's right, sweetheart. Wave to Uncle Mervyn.'

Mervyn raised his own hand and tentatively wiggled his fingers in Daisy's direction.

'She's seen you,' Fiona said. 'Would you like to push her?' She was clearly conferring a favour.

Not without trepidation, Mervyn took over. Daisy stared hard at him, without flinching, grimacing or crying aloud. So, Mervyn thought with some pleasure, I know I'm no oil painting, but at least I don't frighten small babies.

'She's really taken to you,' Fiona said. 'I can tell she has. There you are, Daisy. Smile for Uncle Mervyn.'

Daisy, on command, bared her gums and gave a wide, toothless smile.

'She's a great-looking kid,' Mervyn stated.

'I knew the two of you would get on,' said Fiona.

And I like this particular kid's mother, Mervyn thought. She's a honey. She was so straightforward, so uncomplicated, so refreshing in her single-minded adoration of her baby. In fact, she was like no other young woman he had ever met, and totally unlike any other member of the family. She certainly did not take after her mother, whom he had never cared for, nor was she like her Aunt Maria. He wished Georgia was more like this sweet girl, trotting along by his side as he pushed the stroller.

Georgia had not always been difficult. As a small girl she'd been sweetly pretty and docile.

She was awkward as she moved into her teens, but what kid wasn't. Her mother had spoilt her, but it was Bill Cadell who had been her downfall. He was a singer, of sorts, with a fourth-rate unsuccessful group. He was ten years older than Georgia, married, and somewhere – though he seemed not to know where, and cared even less – he had two small children.

In the six months since Georgia had met him – was it only six months, Mervyn thought, it felt like six awful years – his daughter had completely changed. She was sullen, deceitful and totally rebellious. She could not see or hear beyond that guy's handsome face and silver tongue. If he had any faults, then she was confident she could reform him.

In Mervyn's view, Georgia's chief attraction for Bill Cadell was that she had a rich father, but Georgia couldn't believe that.

'He loves me,' she had said.

'Not a cent, not a single cent of my money will he ever see,' Mervyn had told her. 'Live with him and you'll live in squalor.'

'I'd rather live in poverty with Bill than in wealth with anyone else in the world,' Georgia had said.

Nevertheless, she *was* his daughter, and he loved her. But why couldn't she be more like Fiona? Why couldn't she choose a nice, decent guy? It didn't matter too much about money; he was prepared to be generous. He didn't even mind her marrying young if it was to the right man. He'd be glad to see her settled and with a baby of her own, like this cute little thing. 'It would be great', he said to Fiona, 'if you and Georgia could get to know each other and become friends. You're almost the same age.'

So they might be, he thought as soon as the words were out of his mouth, but otherwise they were worlds apart. Far more than the Atlantic separated them.

'Why, yes,' Fiona said amiably. 'Does Georgia like babies?'

Mervyn recognized it as a crucial question. 'She might,' he said cautiously. 'I don't think she's had a chance to get to know many. But I'm sure she'd love this little honey.' He looked approvingly at Daisy, who, already knowing approval when she saw it, treated him to one of her special smiles and a little splutter of bubbles.

'We're almost home,' Fiona said. 'How quickly the time has gone.'

'For me, too,' Mervyn said. 'That's because I've enjoyed your company.'

'And Daisy's. *She's* enjoyed it; I can tell.'

Maria, taking a temporary break from the kitchen, where Beryl, determined to be in charge, had driven her mad, was sipping a cup of coffee while glancing out of the sitting-room window. Suddenly she jumped to her feet.

'I don't believe it. I do not believe it. Georgia, do you see what I see?'

Since Georgia was lying back in the armchair

with closed eyes, she didn't see, and didn't bother to answer.

'You *must* take a look,' Maria said.

'Thanks, but no,' Georgia murmured. 'You tell me, if you must.'

'You will not believe it. Your father is walking along the road pushing a baby in a stroller.'

'So?'

'Never, not once, when you and Joe were babies, did your father do such a thing.'

'I believe you,' Georgia said.

'He dislikes children.'

'I know *that*,' Georgia interrupted.

'He even hates treating them. In fact he doesn't take them on unless they have extremely rich parents. But I assure you, he's pushing this one. And Fiona's allowing him to.'

'Another small miracle,' Georgia said, closing her eyes again. Where was Bill? What was he doing? And worse, who with? Why didn't he call? He'd told her he was going out and wasn't sure where he could be contacted. When, oh when, could she go back home? Could she get a flight first thing in the morning?

The doorbell rang. Beryl, who always liked to answer the door whether she was in her own house or not, rushed from the kitchen to answer it, but Maria beat her to it, which was surprising because it was one of the things she always left to others. Mervyn stood on the doorstep while Fiona took Daisy out of the buggy.

'Neither of us had a key,' Mervyn explained,

'though we didn't expect both of you to rush to the door. Quite a reception!'

'I suppose you guessed we were bringing Daisy back,' Fiona said. 'She's been such a good girl, and she's been bonding with her Uncle Mervyn.'

'Well done, Uncle Mervyn,' Maria said. 'Bonding *and* pushing the stroller. You must be quite worn out.'

'I'm no such thing,' Mervyn protested. 'I met Fiona quite unexpectedly, and we walked back together. It was very pleasant.'

'And what did you do with Mrs Bedlington-Smythe?' Maria enquired.

'I left her in her own home. She was particularly disappointed that you weren't with me. She'd looked forward to meeting you.'

'How sweet,' Maria said.

'I apologized on your behalf,' Mervyn said. 'Made up some tale to excuse you.'

'Oh, you needn't have. I don't feel the least need to apologize,' Maria said.

Mervyn felt his anger rise. He was not, and never had been, a violent man, but right now, and not for the first time, it was a recurring temptation. He would like to take her by the shoulders and shake her until she rattled. Then he felt annoyed with himself. Why did he let her get to him? Why couldn't he simply ignore her, and turn a deaf ear?

'More to the point,' Beryl demanded, 'where are Jeremy and Megan? I thought they were supposed to be with you?'

'I'm not in charge of them,' Mervyn snapped. 'They're not children. I fixed it with Madel—with Mrs Bedlington-Smythe for them to have the room. It's a very nice room, the one I should be occupying with Maria.' It still rankled with him that he was not. 'When they finally showed up I headed back.'

They all began to move out of the hall. 'At least', Beryl said in a clear voice while looking at no-one, 'I know where my son is. I wonder what's happened to Joe?'

Back in the kitchen, Poppy continued with the sandwiches she had been making. It had been decided, probably by Beryl, that since they'd all been eating at odd times they'd have a substantial high tea and skip supper. 'Then we can all have an early night,' Beryl had said.

Poppy stood at the worktop under the kitchen window which looked out over the garden. She was covering slices of wholemeal bread with some bright yellow spread to which she would not have given house room had she been on her own. She used butter for everything: sandwiches, cooking omelettes, piling on baked potatoes, generous dollops on all vegetables. Beryl and Maria, for once in agreement, had warned her that it was terribly unhealthy and had listed the ills to which it could lead, and it was Beryl, aware of her mother's propensity for butter, who had brought the large tub of the spread with her from Bath.

'Really, Mummy! Your diet! You need taking in hand,' she'd said.

Beryl, Poppy knew, was itching to do this. She would have liked to throw away the two packets of butter out of the fridge she was now rooting through. She had already been through the kitchen cupboards and consigned to the waste bin everything which had passed its use-by date, and now she was determined to clear the fridge. The fact that Beryl would do it from the kindness of her heart and real concern for her ageing parent only served to make Poppy more guilty, and even more resistant.

'Really, Mummy, you are so *careless*,' Beryl said.

'Since I've reached eighty without much mishap I can't have got too much wrong,' Poppy said. 'And I'm quite capable of reading the date on something and deciding what I'll do about it, thank you. Anyway, when you go back to Bath, you can take what's left of this spread. I assure you I'll never use it.'

'I do it for your sake, Mummy,' Beryl said patiently.

'I'm sure you do, dear,' Poppy said. 'And I'd rather you didn't.' She turned to carving succulent slices from a ham joint.

'Trim the fat off, Mummy,' Beryl said.

'Ham tastes all the better for a bit of fat,' Poppy said.

'You can put fat into *your* sandwich if you must,' Beryl said, 'but not in the rest. Also, we'll need some vegetarian sandwiches. Not everyone eats meat, you know.' She made a ham sandwich sound akin to cannibalism.

'Then you can do those, dear,' Poppy said.

She tore a piece from a slice of ham and popped it in her mouth. Yes, it was good. She had cooked it herself, gently boiling it first with cider and a generous glass or two of Calvados, then roasting it afterwards.

As she chewed, she looked out of the window, seeking the calm that the sight of the garden always gave her. It was looking particularly lovely, though the lawn was not as green as she would have liked because the weather had been too dry, and now there was the usual hosepipe ban. It was beyond her strength to carry enough cans of water to replenish the lawn. And next year, she told herself, I must have more peonies, both pale and deep pink ones. They had made such a lovely show.

Her thoughts turned to Joe. Where was he? What was he doing? It would be the middle of the day in New York. Why didn't he telephone? Not just his parents to tell them his plans, but his grandmother on the eve of her eightieth birthday. It was difficult to understand. She hoped he was all right, not ill or something. But that thought she would keep to herself. She had discovered that when old people voice concerns they are told not to worry, as if worry could be turned on and off like a tap.

Nevertheless, she knew one thing she *would* do, and without telling anyone. When they were all busy with tea, she would go up to her bedroom to call New York. She could at least try to find out what was happening.

'I'll do a few cheese and tomato sandwiches,' Beryl said. 'Will you pass the butter, Mummy?'

'Butter is not the word for it, but here you are, dear,' Poppy said.

'Thank you, Mummy.'

Her mother's gibe passed over Beryl's head, as indeed did most gibes, except Maria's. They were sharper, and aimed so accurately that they hit the spots no-one else could find. It was the result of lengthy practice; they had been at it for years.

While the others were at tea, Poppy slipped upstairs. In her bedroom she searched in her diary for Joe's number. She could probably remember it if she tried hard enough, but best to be on the safe side. It was a long number – thirteen digits in all.

She seated herself on the bed and tapped out the keys. Within a second of touching the last one she heard the long unbroken trill that told her the phone was ringing in Joe's New York studio. However often she called New York, she never ceased to be amazed at the speed with which she was connected over 3,000 miles of ocean. Listening to the telephone ringing, she could picture Joe's studio: large, untidy, canvases stacked against the wall and, on the easel, whatever he was engaged in at the moment. Something large, vibrantly colourful and abstract. She could smell the place, too: the oils, turps and varnish.

There was no reply. Perhaps she had mis-dialled and got through to a wrong number. It was easily done. She put down the receiver, then picked it up and started again. Still no reply, though she waited a long time.

Ah well, she thought, though reluctant to let go, I suppose he could have slipped out, gone shopping or something. But if he could do that, why couldn't he call England?

She went downstairs again. Beryl looked up, smiling, as she went into the room. 'Come and have your tea.' She made room beside her on the sofa.

Fiona, on her knees spooning something blancmange-like into the mouth of her chair-bound baby, looked up.

'Oh, Poppy, we were just looking at Daisy, trying to decide who she took after. We couldn't decide, but I wondered if she possibly had a look of her great-grandfather?'

'And only you can answer that,' Beryl broke in. 'Maria and I have no memories of how our father looked. How could we have? We were too young.'

'Of course you were,' Poppy agreed. 'But don't forget that, for my part, it's fifty-three years since your father died, and I only knew him when he was a man, not as a child.' Though in many ways she would never forget him, her memory of his physical appearance had dimmed.

'Aren't there any photographs of Grandpa?' Fiona asked.

'He wasn't one for having his photograph taken,' Poppy said, 'and we didn't take scores of snapshots then. There might be an odd one around.'

'Oh, I do hope so. I'd like to see it.' Fiona was enthusiastic. 'I would so like Daisy's great-grandfather to have known her. And she him, of course.'

'For that to happen he would have to be alive right now, and ninety-two,' Maria drawled. 'And what about Mummy's other husbands? Where would they have been?' She made it sound as if there had been a string of them. 'Not to mention Richard, who just wouldn't have existed.' And no great loss, she thought.

'I wasn't thinking of all that,' Fiona said defensively. 'I was just thinking about Daisy.'

'I'll go upstairs and try to find it,' Poppy offered.

The truth was, she wanted to make one more attempt to contact Joe. She went upstairs and dialled again. There was no reply, though she hung on a long time, hoping he might just walk in the door and catch it ringing. Leaving her bedroom, she stood on the landing trying to remember what else she had come upstairs for. Ah, yes! The photograph! She felt confident she could lay her hands on it quite easily. In those early days she had methodically pasted photographs into albums instead of, as now, pushing them into a drawer with the intention of doing something about them later.

She was about to move in the direction of the boxroom, where the albums were stored, when she saw Georgia climbing the stairs. How awful she looked. Pale and far too thin – which could be put down to fashion, of course, but that couldn't be said of her dark-ringed eyes or the drooping of her pretty mouth.

'Georgia,' Poppy said. 'Were you looking for me, dear?'

'Yes,' Georgia said. 'May I telephone New York again? There might be more chance of a reply this much later in the day. And could I do it from your bedroom?'

'Of course you can,' Poppy said. 'I hope you'll be more fortunate than I was just now. I tried to call Joe, but with no success. Anyway, come and sit down and talk to me for a minute or two. I haven't had more than half a dozen words with you since you arrived.'

Poppy went back into the bedroom, followed by Georgia. They sat side by side on the edge of the bed.

'I'm sorry,' Georgia said. 'I've not been very nice, have I?'

'Never mind. Tell me how everything's going.'

'Everything's awful,' Georgia said, 'just terrible. I'm sorry, but I don't want to be here. I didn't want to come. I know that sounds rude, but it's not against you; it's just that I want to be in New York. I *need* to be.'

'Because of Bill?'

'Yes. I wanted him to come here with me. I didn't think you'd mind. And at first he said he would, and then he found he couldn't. Something came up, he said, but I reckon he wouldn't come because of Mom and Dad. Mom hates him and Dad hates him even more.'

'Really? I wonder why?' Poppy said.

'They say he's too old for me. He's twenty-nine,' Georgia told her. 'And the fact that he's married.'

'I see.'

'But he doesn't love his wife,' Georgia said quickly. 'He doesn't love her any longer. He's going to leave her. He loves me.'

'I see,' Poppy said again. 'And when is he going to leave his wife? And does she know?'

'She doesn't yet, but he means to tell her quite soon,' Georgia said. 'Only it's not so easy; he has two little girls and he has to sort out what to do about them. I've told him that if he and I were together I could look after the children, but he doesn't seem to think I could.'

Poppy stopped herself from saying 'I see' yet again, though she most certainly did. Much as she loved Georgia, she could think of no-one less capable of looking after two young children. She wasn't yet mature enough to look after herself. She could now see Maria's and Mervyn's view of Bill, though whether they were dealing with things in the right way was another matter. But who am I to judge? she asked herself. She had never been the world's best mother.

'I think Bill might be right about that, Georgia dear,' she said gently. 'Looking after small children isn't easy. And do you suppose their mother would be willing to let them go?'

Georgia shrugged. All she knew was that she wanted Bill. If the children came as part of the package, then she would have them.

'It could all be worked out,' she said.

You mean to your advantage, Poppy thought. But Georgia was blinded by love, she couldn't see the world as it was. The point was, though, that she was also desperately unhappy, and a brisk talk of the pull-yourself-together-and-get-real kind would make matters worse. Right at this moment, it would be no help to Georgia to have her grandmother side with the enemy: her parents. Grandmothers were not supposed to do that.

'How old are the children? Do you know them? What are their names?' she enquired.

'They're three and five. They're called Amanda and Mary-Beth, but I don't know which is which. I haven't met them. But Poppy, I'm sure Bill and I between us could sort out the details.'

Details! Two small children, and a wife who might be awful or simply long-suffering. Poppy felt exceedingly angry, but tried hard not to show it, and succeeded – just. She couldn't trust herself to speak.

'So can I make the call?' Georgia asked.

'Go ahead,' Poppy said. What could she do to prevent it? And did she hope that Bill would be at the end of the line to smooth-talk Georgia even further into her childish dream, or that there would be no reply? She didn't know.

'I must find the photograph,' she said. 'And then go downstairs and lend a hand.'

Before she was quite out of the bedroom, Georgia had picked up the telephone and was tapping out the number.

Poppy went along to the boxroom. She hadn't had any reason go in there for some time now and it smelled dusty and foisty, a smell of old neglected things. She must do something about it sometime: throw things out and open the window.

She found the photograph without too much trouble. It was faded; it was, after all, more than sixty years since it had been taken. It was black and white, which in itself seemed strange. Only arty people took black and white photos these days.

My goodness, how young I look, she thought. But I suppose I was quite pretty then. At least by that day's standards. Neat, regular features, cupid's bow lips. Now one would have to have a bony face and a large mouth.

Edward looked exactly as she remembered him, but then he hadn't been allowed to grow old. She had never known him with wrinkles, or grey hair.

She had cheated on Edward. She was well aware of it, and had been at the time. She had done it with her eyes open, no excuses. Her only solace was that Edward had never known, or she truly believed and hoped that he had not.

Carrying the photograph album, she left the room. There was no sound from her bedroom as she passed the door. Did that mean Bill was speaking with Georgia? Seducing her with what must surely be false promises? Or simply that there was no reply?

12

From the night of the hospital dance, the doors of Two Elms were wide open to the officers, and nothing was too good for them. Food, drink, hot baths, music, the garden, books – whatever the heart of a soldier, bored with waiting around for the real thing to begin, desired was there for the taking.

This generosity on Edward's part, though he never said so, arose I think from a feeling of guilt that he wasn't taking a more positive part in defending his country. It was an unnecessary guilt because his eyesight was too bad for him ever to be accepted for active service. And later on, when civilians were called upon to do all manner of things, Edward was always in the thick of it: fire-watching, driving, fund raising – you name it, Edward did it. But for now he provided hospitality to the Army.

'Come and go as you please,' he said. 'I can't be there during the day, but my wife will look after you in my absence, except when she's busy nursing.' He always said that last bit with a teasing smile at me, as if nursing were a little game I liked to play, dressed up in a uniform.

Over the next few weeks, several officers accepted Edward's invitation to come and go, so the house became almost like a club. The men also enjoyed being helpful to me in various ways – gardening, mending fuses and fixing things. They said it made them feel at home. I did my best for them, providing endless tea, coffee, beers, snacks, quiet places to read or study, a radiogram and records, to which they added their own.

'Poppy is wonderful,' they said to Edward when they happened to see him.

'Of course she is,' he agreed.

He enjoyed my popularity with the men. I think he took it as a compliment to himself. After all, I belonged to him. Also, his faith in me was complete. It wouldn't have occurred to him to consider the attraction these young soldiers in their well-cut uniforms might have had for me. And if Alun had not regularly been one of them, Edward's faith would have been justified.

My head and heart were so filled with Alun that the rest seemed like shadows, moving in a dream in which only he and I were real. Even Dickie Philips, Alun's best friend and captain, though he tried to entice me in the way that best friends can do, failed to make any impression.

The fact was, though, that they *were* there; they were present. Most afternoons – none of them came in the mornings as they had soldierly things to do – there would be a group of them. Alun and I snatched brief conversations together, seldom uninterrupted. Even when we walked around the garden someone would inevitably join us.

'I can't stand this,' Alun said after the first week. 'I can't bear never to see you alone. What can we do?'

I knew the answer. I'd already worked it out in my mind, and it was this. The two afternoons the men knew they could not come to the house were Wednesdays and Fridays, because those were the days I did my hospital shifts. They were welcome in the evenings of those days, when Edward and I were at home, but never in the afternoon.

'On Wednesday,' I told Alun, 'I shall ring the hospital and say I can't be in, I have a migraine. Can you come on Wednesday?'

'Whenever you say,' Alun assured me. 'And whatever else happens. But are you sure?'

'I'm quite sure,' I told him. 'Sister won't care. I'm not needed. All those beds are still empty and waiting. Anyway, it'll reinforce her opinion of auxiliaries. She'll like that. And I'll give Elsie the half day off.'

He arrived at two o'clock. Though nothing had been put into words, we both knew why he was there. He came in and I closed the door behind him. Before we moved another step he took me in his arms. His kisses were hungry and urgent, and mine were no less so. I broke free, took him by the hand and led him through the hall, and me steady, he almost stumbling, we went upstairs. I was not so crass as to take him into the bedroom Edward and I shared. Instead, I led him to a bedroom at the back of the house which had never been used in the time I had lived there.

Garment by garment he undressed me, and then I did the same to him; neither of us hurrying; it was part of the lovemaking. Then we lay on the bed and gave everything we were, or had, or thought, or felt, to each other. Unstinting, no reserves, nothing held back.

There were to be times later, when Alun and the other soldiers had left and strict security regulations meant that I had no idea where they had been sent – except that they had been issued with tropical kit, but was that anything to go by? – when I would go into that room and lie on the bed. I would take the pillow in my arms and hold it close, as if I might be holding him, trying to summon his presence. I had to try hard not to cry. How would I explain red-rimmed eyes and a blotchy face to my loving husband?

We didn't know on that Wednesday afternoon that we had only exactly four weeks and two days left in which to snatch our opportunities to be together. We knew our time was limited, but nothing was precise. There were rumours and counter-rumours about when the men would move and where they were bound for.

'You would tell me, wouldn't you?' I begged

Alun. 'If you knew when you were going? Or where?'

'Poppy, love,' he said, 'you know I wouldn't. Even if I knew, which right now I don't.'

'But you won't keep it secret from me,' I said.

'Of course I will. I must. Surely you can see that.'

And, of course, I could. I wasn't all that naïve. It was just hoping against hope.

'And if you're wise,' Alun said, 'you'll take no notice of anything you hear.'

'What am I going to do without you?' I asked him.

'I don't know,' he admitted. 'Or I without you. What I do know is that if I get through I'll come back to you. And I also know that we must make the most of every day we have now.'

And so we did. I spoke to Sister and told her that, for domestic reasons, I could no longer do afternoon shifts; it would have to be mornings. It was surprisingly easy to arrange, and I told Edward, who wasn't particularly interested in days and times, that the rearrangement was the hospital's idea. I was therefore at home every afternoon, but Wednesdays and Fridays were for Alun alone. I had also managed to change Elsie's time off so that she was never in the house.

Alun and I made love, as we did every afternoon we were alone together. I had thought the first occasion was wonderful, incredible and that there was nothing in the world like it, but in fact, each time proved to be better than the last. The bedroom, door closed, chintz curtains drawn, the world shut out, became ours and ours alone.

'I shall never let anyone else use this room,' I said to Alun, as we lay together afterwards. 'No-one will ever sleep in this bed. Not ever.'

But it was not only lovemaking on those Wednesdays and Fridays. They were the times when we could talk to each other about anything and everything, and we did. Also, we started, after we had made love and gone back downstairs, to listen to music together. I had discovered earlier, on those occasions when there were several of us together at Two Elms, that Alun was a gifted pianist. Mostly he played jazz, rather in the style of 'Fats' Waller, but now, when we were alone, he searched among the small collection of records for classical pieces, and we listened to those.

On the Wednesday of the second week, when Alun arrived, he put a present into my hands.

'It's the Grieg piano concerto,' he said. 'Do you know it?'

'I've never heard it,' I admitted.

'I'm glad,' Alun said. 'I want to be the one to give it to you. It's one of my favourites. I wish I could play it for you, but I'll never be good enough for that.'

Sitting side by side on the sofa, we listened without speaking. In the crashing chords I heard thunderous waterfalls over huge rocks. I heard the lively sounds of lakeside villages in the fjords. In my mind's eye I saw quiet pools, dark caves, deep lakes and pine forests against high blue skies. In the arpeggios I heard fast-flowing streams in a cool north country.

'I would like to visit Norway,' I said.

'One day', Alun said, 'we will. Don't ask me how, or when. I don't know that. I just know we will.'

When we went up to the bedroom the sounds of the music were still in my head. It sounds trite, but how could I *not* say that I have never heard the Grieg since without thinking of Alun and almost feeling that he was there with me.

On the day before he left – by then we knew their departure was imminent – I gave him a copy of the same record, which he took with him and played on a not-very-good gramophone wherever he was. I know this because he wrote and told me so.

In our last week together he said, 'I can't bear it if I can't write to you or don't hear from you. What are we going to do?'

'I don't know,' I admitted. 'Perhaps I'll ask my mother if she'll help; if you can send letters to her address. I don't know whether she will or not.'

My mother, you see, was quite fond of Edward, and especially conscious of the security my marriage to him gave me.

'I don't like it,' she protested. 'It's not right, Poppy.'

'I know,' I acknowledged, 'but who knows where Alun will be or what sort of conditions he'll be fighting in. And what harm can letters do?'

'A great deal of harm,' she said.

Nevertheless, she gave in. I think she hoped it would all fizzle out quite quickly. She didn't know the extent of my relationship with Alun. Also, she didn't like to see me unhappy.

For several weeks no letter came. It seemed a lifetime. I said nothing to my mother because I trusted her, having said she would, to pass on anything that might arrive. I dare say she thought, and probably hoped, that Alun had changed his mind about writing, and that now it would all die down. As for me, though I waited anxiously, I never gave up hope.

'I miss the boys,' Edward said. 'The house seems quiet without them.' He always referred to them as 'the boys', though he was only a little older than most of them. 'You must miss them, too.'

'I do,' I agreed. 'But since we're so much busier in the hospital, I wouldn't have had as much time to entertain them.'

The empty beds had been filled, not by wounded soldiers or shot-down airmen, but by elderly, chronically-sick evacuees, most of whom had been long-term patients in the same hospital in the East End of London. They would, I quickly discovered, much rather have been left in London to take their chances than been banished to this outpost of civilization where the food was not what they were used to and absolutely no-one came to see them on visiting days.

The men, fewer in number, were put into one ward, and the women in the adjoining one. There was no mixing of the sexes. It might have cheered them up if there had been.

I worked in either ward, as needed, and there was no question now of not being needed. Even we auxiliaries had our value. Bedpans, sputum cups, soiled sheets and dirty bottoms became our special territory, along with bed-making, and bathing unwilling patients who felt that too much cleanliness wasn't healthy on our luckier days.

There was so much to be done that we were encouraged to work extra shifts, and this I did willingly. Work helped to pass the time and blot out, however briefly, the thought of Alun.

As often as seemed reasonable I caught the bus to see my mother. If she had been on the telephone I would have found an excuse to ring her every day. I was ashamed that my chief reason for visiting had nothing to do with her welfare; I was driven by the hope of finding a letter waiting for me.

And then one day I was rewarded. My mother handed me a thin air letter addressed to me in Alun's neat writing. She showed no pleasure in giving it to me, only disapproval.

'Quite apart from anything else,' she said, 'you're running a risk. Edward is a well-known man in the town, and the postman knows perfectly well that no Mrs Baxter lives here. He probably knows who you are, or he can put two and two together.'

'Baxter is a common enough name,' I said. I didn't much care.

In spite of her disapproval, she was kind enough to disappear into the kitchen so that I could be alone to read the letter. I looked in vain for the smallest clue as to where Alun was; there was nothing. Obviously no address, only an army post-office number. It was hot, he said. He was well, and hoped I was. He played the Grieg until everyone was sick of it, though he wasn't. He hoped I would write back, but they were always on the move, so he might not receive letters. And so on. He was not a good letter writer. The man I knew as warm and passionate did not come over as such on the page. Nevertheless, I read every word three times over before putting the letter into my handbag as my mother came back into the room.

'If you have any sense you will put that in the fire before you leave this house,' she said.

'I can't possibly do that,' I cried. 'I have to keep it. There's a war on. It might be the last I ever hear of him. I might never see him again. You don't understand.'

For a moment she looked at me as though I'd hit her. Then she said, 'I understand only too well. Why does one generation always think another generation doesn't understand? I know what it's like to wait for letters.' Her voice went very soft, as if she was half talking to herself. 'I also know what men are like when they've gone through a war. It does something to them that perhaps *you* can't understand. Sometimes I think it's better if they don't come back.'

I hardly knew how to speak. I was shaken by the quiet intensity of her voice. 'I'm sorry,' I said. 'I'm really sorry.'

'I'll make a cup of tea,' she said. 'I expect we could both do with one.' She went back into the kitchen.

I did not burn the letter, or the subsequent ones, at least not for a very long time. Life, at least its outward appearances, went on as normal. Every morning the sun rose, and every evening it set. Four days a week I worked in the hospital, where what was surreal passed for normal.

Mrs Baker, a seventy-eight-year-old weighing sixteen stones, regularly wet her bed. Miss Flower, a spinster of uncertain age, but old, continued to refuse to wear her knickers and hid them in her locker, together with scraps of cake and sandwiches she saved from tea. Mrs Poole mislaid her glass eye – the pride of her life – which she took out at night and placed in a cup of water on her locker, next to the cup containing her false teeth, and which was whisked away by a half asleep night nurse and rescued in the nick of time before it was swilled down the sink. Mr Chase in the men's ward died a nasty death. Mutton, boiled to a greyish colour, was served for four days a week to patients who were mostly toothless or had ill-fitting dentures.

This was normal life in the hospital, and at home I lived a normal life with Edward. It was part of my atonement to him that, even while keeping Alun's letters hidden away and thinking of him constantly, I would be a good wife to Edward. In my own way I loved him, and I was determined to act as if I loved him even more than I did.

I held nothing back, not in everyday life and not in bed. This was not as difficult as it sounds because, for me, the act of sex, once entered into, was enjoyable. My greatest and worst betrayal of Edward was that, when the climax of our lovemaking came, I was in Alun's arms, not Edward's. Time after time I betrayed Edward in this manner. It was something I could not help, and I thanked God that Edward never knew.

Then, several months later, and to my great surprise and Edward's, as we thought it would never happen, I found myself pregnant, and there could be no doubt that it was Edward's child.

Edward was ecstatic. 'It will be a boy,' he said. 'I shall have a son to inherit Paragon.'

'Don't be so sure,' I said. 'It could be a girl. After all, there's a fifty-fifty chance.'

'It will be a boy,' he said. 'I know it. What shall we call him?' He was full of joy and confidence. 'I know. We'll call him Thomas, after my father.'

'That's fine by me,' I assured him.

'And you will have to give up the hospital,' he said firmly. 'We can't take any risks, my love.'

I didn't want to do that. I didn't want to sit at home knitting tiny garments, but the doctor confirmed that I must.

'The nursing you're doing is heavy stuff,' he said. 'Not at all suitable for a pregnant woman. You don't want to risk losing this baby, do you?'

And of course I didn't, so I obeyed orders. I was sad about leaving the hospital. By now I had got to know the patients on both wards and, strangely, the most difficult ones were the ones I knew I would miss most. Flower – we had dropped the 'Miss' – announced that she, too, thought she might leave to have a baby. Mrs Baker said – they were all nasty to each other – that she was going the right way about it, leaving her knickers off, except that she was forty years too late. Mrs Baker said that she would miss me, and who was going to do for her when she had a little accident? She had decided from the first that I was the one she preferred to change her malodorous sheets and deal with her sopping nightdress. Sister suddenly became human and said, 'Look after yourself, Nurse.' All the nurses I knew went quite soggy at the thought of a baby.

My mother-in-law was delighted. I reckon from the moment we told her I was pregnant she decided to approve of me. I was doing what a wife should do. My mother was pleased, too. I think she thought it might settle me down, though I was still receiving letters from Alun.

'This will have to stop,' she warned me as she handed me a letter that had just been delivered.

I couldn't face that. I somehow convinced myself that the letters could continue. After all, who were they hurting? As for what might happen in the future, I refused to think about it. All the same, I knew I must tell Alun. I could deceive everyone else – though I had almost ceased to think of what I did as deceit – but not Alun.

By the time his reply came I was five months pregnant.

'For the last time, Poppy, this will *not* do,' my mother said. 'I will not be a party to it.'

As usual, she left the room while I opened the letter. I had not read even the first word when the most extraordinary thing happened; extraordinary because it was totally new to me. The baby inside me quickened for the very first time; a small but unmistakable movement, like nothing else I had ever experienced, as though it were saying, 'Hello. This is me. I'm here.'

I dropped the letter, and when the fluttering movement inside me had stopped, which it did almost at once, I bent down, picked it up and began to read it. '. . . You know what I wish about this child, don't you,' Alun wrote. 'But it can't be, and never could be . . .'

It was the last letter I ever had from him, though nowhere in it did he say that it would be. I wrote to him three times more, but nothing came back.

The rest of my pregnancy passed smoothly, at least physically, and to the eyes of any observer, except perhaps my mother, in whose look I would sometimes see compassion, though she said nothing. In my head, and in my heart, if that *is* the home of the emotions and not merely a super-efficient pump, it was different. There I lived another life. Never for long did I stop thinking about Alun. Every time the baby quickened, which it did with such vigour that I decided it would emerge a fully-fledged ballet dancer, was a sharp reminder of that first time.

If I was not to hear from him again, and as the months went by I reluctantly conceded that this could be so, how would I know where he was? How would I know if he had survived the war or if he had been killed in battle? How would I know if he had met someone else? These were the thoughts that filled my head, while to everyone else I was as I had always been – except twice the size!

My baby was born inconveniently at three in the morning, but otherwise the birth took place without fuss. I had never seen a new baby before. I was surprised at her shock of black hair, the redness of her face and her furious expression, as if she had been put to considerable disruption and would see that I paid for it.

When she and I had both been cleaned up, tidied and clothed in our new nightgowns, Edward was allowed into the room.

'I'm sorry,' I said. 'I know you wanted a son.'

'Did I?' he said gallantly. 'Well, now that she's here I'm more than happy with a daughter, especially if she turns out like her mother.'

'We can't call her Thomas,' I said.

'No. How about Maria? It was my grandmother's name. Mother would be pleased.'

'If you like,' I said. 'It's a nice name.'

'Are you sure you're all right, love?' he asked.

'I'm fine,' I assured him.

'Thank heaven,' he said. 'Oh, Poppy, what an experience it's been. I can't tell you what I've been through.'

I laughed. For the first time in months I laughed heartily at that.

13

Poppy walked into the kitchen, waving the photograph in her hand.

'Here it is,' she said. 'I found it at once.'

'Oh, did you?' Beryl said. 'I thought you must be having difficulty; you were rather a long time.'

'Was I? Well, you know how it is when you start looking at old photograph albums,' Poppy said. 'You don't notice the time.' She didn't intend to say she had been with Georgia who, because she took no part in anything, had possibly not been missed. 'Why? Did you want me for something, Beryl?' she added.

And if I meant that as a slight reprimand, she thought, which I did, because I don't wish to have my movements monitored, then it has fallen on deaf ears, because Beryl does not understand reprimands.

'Oh no, Mummy,' Beryl replied. 'I just wondered. Just let me finish this and I'll take a look.' She was up to her elbows in washing up.

'Why are you washing dishes, dear?' Poppy asked. 'Why don't you use the dishwasher?'

'I always like to wash up as I go along,' Beryl said. 'It keeps things tidy.'

Maria looked at her mother and shrugged.

'I'll bet my sister cleans the whole house before her help arrives,' she said.

'You're wrong there,' Beryl replied. 'I don't have help in the house. A teacher's and a nurse's salary, with Jeremy still at university, doesn't allow for luxuries.'

'OK. OK,' Maria said. 'Spare me the details.'

'Will you two please stop it,' Poppy said crossly. 'You hardly ever meet, and when you do you simply pick at each other all the time. Now if you want to look at this photograph, do so. If you don't, then say so and I'll take it in to Fiona.'

'Of course we do, Mummy.' Beryl dried her hands and the three of them stood round the table, gazing at the photograph.

'Oh, my.' Maria laughed. 'Doesn't Daddy look *funny*.'

'Funny? What's funny about him?' Poppy demanded. 'Your father was quite a handsome man.'

'I'm sorry, Mummy,' Beryl's voice was gentler, 'but I see what Maria means.'

'For once,' Poppy interrupted.

'He does look . . . well . . . funny. Stiff. As if he was standing to attention.'

'It was an important occasion,' Poppy pointed

out. 'We were at a wedding.' But the girls were right. Edward looked as stiff as a ramrod, as if he were on parade, which in a way he was. It *was* a formal occasion. It was also a photograph from a past age.

'*You* look OK, Ma,' Maria conceded.

'Yes, you do,' Beryl said. 'You look very pretty.'

'Thank you both,' Poppy said. 'Actually, I was then.'

'And you're not at all bad now,' Beryl said comfortingly.

If she says 'for your age' I shall scream, Poppy thought.

'. . . for your age,' Beryl continued.

Maria nodded in agreement. Poppy swallowed the scream. They meant well, and how wonderful to have them agree with each other for the second time in five minutes.

'Surely you've seen this photograph before?' she asked. 'You must have.'

'I think we have,' Maria said.

'I'd forgotten it,' Beryl conceded. 'In any case, as you know, I always thought of Pops as my father. I loved Pops.'

'And he loved you; both of you,' Poppy said. 'Yes, Pops was a very nice man. But don't forget that it was Edward's money that brought you up – and in quite comfortable circumstances, I must say. You went short of nothing. And Pops knew it was Edward's doing, though he never minded that.'

'I missed him so much after he died,' Beryl

said. 'I was only seven, but I remember it quite clearly.'

'You weren't the only one who missed him,' Maria said. 'I missed him, too.'

'Not as much as I did. I cried every night for ages.'

'Just because you cried more than I did doesn't mean you missed him more,' Maria said. 'Anyway, you cried about everything. You'd have cried if a snail died. In fact, you did. Remember Arthur? You cried buckets over him.'

'Arthur was not just a snail,' Beryl said hotly. 'Arthur was a *pet* snail. And there's nothing wrong with crying when someone dies, even if it *is* only a snail.'

'Please. Please,' Poppy begged.

'Well, is there?' Beryl demanded.

'No, of course not,' Poppy said.

The interesting thing was that now, and for a long time past, Beryl was never seen to cry, and Poppy doubted whether these days she ever did. She was so organized, so efficient, so much in command of every situation that there seemed no need for tears. Tears were for sorrow, frustration, even anger, which seemed to have no part in Beryl's life now.

'Poor Mummy,' Beryl said, suddenly sympathetic. 'You must have cried more than any of us. You must have missed him terribly.'

'Of course,' Poppy agreed. But had she cried as long as her little daughter? Beryl had been inconsolable.

'Though I had a great deal to do,' she said, trying to fight off an uncomfortable feeling. 'There always is when anything's so sudden.'

The fact that she had gone through it all after Edward's death didn't make things any easier. And when Victor died there'd been Richard to think of, though he had not seemed nearly as upset as Beryl had. He had been a stolid little boy, and he'd grown into a stolid man. The only emotion he allowed himself to show was for Graham, and even in that relationship they seemed like a long-married, middle-aged couple. Really, she thought, Richard had always been middle-aged. He had been a middle-aged small boy.

Rodney came into the kitchen. 'Where are the garden lights?' he asked.

'In two boxes in the garage,' Poppy said. 'On the left as you go in. But you can't do them on your own. It's not a single-handed job.'

'I know,' Rodney said. 'I'll get Jeremy to help when he's back.'

'What *can* they be doing?' Beryl asked.

As she spoke, Jeremy came in, hand in hand with Megan.

'There you are,' Rodney said. 'Good. I want you to give me a hand putting up the lights.'

'Dad, the party's not until tomorrow,' Jeremy protested.

'I know that,' Rodney said, 'but I'd rather get them done today, just in case there's anything wrong with them. They've not been used for ages.'

'Your father's right, Jeremy,' Beryl said. 'It would be awful if you found out at the last minute that they wouldn't work.'

'OK,' Jeremy said.

'If nobody minds,' Megan said, 'I'd like to do a spot of sunbathing. It's such a lovely afternoon and I'm dying to get a tan before Jerry and I go to Italy.'

Beryl's head shot up. 'Italy?'

What was this about? It was the first she'd heard of it. And she didn't like Jeremy's name being shortened to Jerry. They had always been most careful, she and Rodney, to call Jeremy by his proper name. However, she would go into both matters later, when there were fewer people about.

'Sunbathing is dangerous, Megan dear,' she said, kindly. 'You can get skin cancer from too much sunbathing.'

'Mother, you can get knocked down by a bus if you cross the road,' Jeremy said testily. 'It won't stop any one of us leaving the house.'

Beryl drew in her breath. There was a time, not long ago, when he would not have spoken to her like that.

'I shall need a ladder,' Rodney told Poppy.

'Also in the garage,' Poppy said. 'And the garden chairs are in the shed, but we won't put those out until tomorrow. There are two sun loungers, too.'

'Could I have one of those now?' Megan asked. 'Or would you like me to help in the house?'

It was a half-hearted suggestion which Poppy quickly but pleasantly refused.

'Not really,' she said. 'There simply isn't room. We're all falling over each other as it is. But thank you for the offer.'

'Yes,' Beryl said as Megan and the two men moved into the garden, 'it's nice when young people offer to help. But then, Rodney and I have always brought up Jeremy to do that. They follow their father's example.'

'If you are referring to the fact that Mervyn isn't dragging ladders around and fixing lights,' Maria drawled, 'then let me remind you that my husband is a dental surgeon. He cannot afford to damage his hands; he has delicate work to do. Moreover, if he were to make the smallest attempt to fix the lights he would probably electrocute himself, and whoever was standing near him!'

She said nothing about Georgia. She didn't know where Georgia was and she had no intention of finding out, though she would certainly have something to say to her when they were back in New York.

Georgia came into Poppy's mind. Where was she? Was she still upstairs? What was she doing?

'I'll be back in a minute,' she said as she left the kitchen. Walking through the hall she could hear Daisy crying lustily as she passed the sitting-room door. Her instinct was to investigate, but she stifled it and marched upstairs.

Georgia was indeed still in the bedroom, sitting on the bed, and at the moment Poppy entered, she replaced the telephone receiver in its cradle.

'Oh,' Poppy said, 'so you got through to Bill?'

It couldn't have been anything good; Georgia was the picture of despondency, her shoulders, face and every bit of her body, sagged.

'No, I didn't,' Georgia said. 'I've been trying every two minutes for . . . oh, I don't know how long. Ever since you left me.'

'Almost an hour,' Poppy said. 'And you've tried every two minutes?'

'At least! Where can he be?'

I must put a stop to this right now, Poppy thought. A whole hour with the phone virtually blocked off to any incoming calls. Supposing someone had been trying to get through? Supposing Joe had?

'Georgia dear, I'm sorry,' she said, 'but this won't do at all. I can't have you blocking the phone. In any case, it's doing you no good sitting here like this. Bill is clearly out.'

'Where?' Georgia wailed.

'How do I know? Why don't you give it a rest and go out into the garden? It's a lovely day. Megan is out there sunbathing. You could join her.' She realized as soon as she'd said it that it was a stupid idea. Megan and Georgia had nothing in common. And who would want to be with Georgia in her present mood?

'Or take yourself off for a walk. Such a shame to waste this lovely day,' she added.

'Poppy, how can I do that?' Georgia said reproachfully. 'Supposing Bill calls. Can't I just stay up here in your room?'

'I'm not sure,' Poppy said. She felt herself weakening. The girl looked so miserable. 'Don't you think you ought to be downstairs with the others? Won't your mother and father be worried about you?'

'They won't even notice I'm not there,' Georgia said.

'I'm sure they will,' Poppy said, though she was by *no* means sure. 'You could talk to Fiona.'

'That', said Georgia, with the first sign of animation she had shown, 'is the last thing in the world I would want to do. All Fiona talks about is her baby. She is unutterably boring.'

And no-one, Poppy thought in a flash of irritation, is as boring as you. I love you dearly, but you are both boring and incredibly selfish. Nevertheless, this was her granddaughter. She could remember occasions in her own life when she had shut herself in her room and refused to come out, in spite of her mother's entreaties, though oddly, although it had been so important then, she could no longer remember quite why. Had one occasion been something to do with wanting to have high-heeled court shoes, preferably in black patent leather, and being allowed only her usual school lace-ups?

'All right,' she conceded. 'You can stay here for a while. I shall tell the others that you have a headache, and that you're going to lie down until it's better. But don't be long, and please do *not* call New York again. I shall draw the curtains and perhaps you actually will have a little nap. I'm sure you'll feel better when you wake.'

'I shan't feel better until Bill calls me,' Georgia said.

Poppy went to the window and looked out on to the garden. Megan was lying full length, possibly asleep behind her dark glasses. How she envied her. It was exactly what she would like to do.

The garden looked nice and colourful. She had done very little gardening herself that year, but she had Arnold, who had come for one half day a week for years. He was possibly the world's worst gardener. She had to point out to him which were weeds and which were not, but at least he cut the grass reasonably well.

Rodney was up the ladder, draping the lights around the apple tree. It was strange, that apple tree; she never did a thing for it, didn't even prune it, but every year it produced a bumper crop of rather tasteless cooking apples of an unknown variety, most of which she gave to neighbours and friends.

Rodney was almost at the top of the ladder. What a nice man her son-in-law was. He would never set the world on fire, but he was no worse for that. She watched as he stretched out an arm, trying to hook the lights around a branch, and as he overstretched himself he lost his footing. The ladder went down, casting off Rodney, who described an arc through the air before landing on the lawn, where he lay quite still.

Poppy's scream mingled with loud cries from Megan and Jeremy as they ran to where Rodney lay. Poppy, shouting to Georgia, bolted out of the bedroom and down the stairs with a speed of which she would never have considered herself capable.

'Mervyn! Mervyn! Come quickly!' she cried as she ran through the hall. Why am I calling for Mervyn, she asked herself, without slackening her pace as she headed for the garden? What can a dentist do for a man who's fallen off a ladder? Did a dentist know first aid?

Beryl was already on her knees beside her husband, as were Jeremy and Megan.

'Rodney!' Beryl cried. 'Speak to me! Are you all right?'

'Of course I'm not all right,' he said. 'I've fallen off the bloody ladder. I reckon I've broken my ankle, or my leg.' He winced as a fresh stab of pain hit him.

Mervyn had joined them. 'We should call an ambulance,' he said. 'And, in the meantime, don't move him.'

'You're quite right,' Poppy agreed. 'I'll dial nine nine nine.'

'I'll do that,' Jeremy said.

'Thank you, darling,' Beryl said as Jeremy rushed away. 'And will someone please get a blanket? He's bound to be suffering from shock. And a cup of sweet tea.'

'Should he have anything by mouth?' Megan said hesitantly.

'I have broken a bone,' Rodney said faintly, 'I haven't swallowed poison. A cup of tea would be very welcome.' He closed his eyes again and grimaced with pain.

'Then I'll make it,' Megan said. 'I won't be a jiffy.'

'Lots of sugar, dear,' Beryl said.

'No bloody sugar. I hate sugar,' Rodney said.

'I know you do, darling,' Beryl said in a soothing voice, 'but on this occasion—'

She was interrupted by Jeremy. 'They're sending an ambulance from Brighton,' he said. 'It shouldn't be too long, Dad. In the meantime, don't try to move your leg.'

'I have no intention of moving my leg,' Rodney said wearily.

'Don't worry, dear,' Beryl said. 'I'm sure the ambulance won't be long, and I'll go with you.'

'So will I,' Jeremy said. 'Or I'll follow in my car, and then I'll be there to bring Mum back.'

'And me,' Rodney said. 'I don't intend to stay.' His leg hurt like hell. He wished the ambulance would come. He wished all these people hovering around him would go away – except Beryl, who was holding his hand.

David, who had come into the garden to see what the commotion was about, and had then gone back to inform Fiona, reappeared. 'Fiona says will you excuse her if she stays put until the ambulance has been and gone,' he said. 'She doesn't think it would be good for Daisy to see it all happening.'

'Fiona is very sensitive,' Beryl explained.

Megan hurried across the garden with a cup of tea, which Beryl, supporting Rodney with one arm, held to his lips.

'Thank you, darling,' he said. 'I do still have the use of my hands.' He grimaced as the sweetness of the tea hit his tongue. 'I really don't need it like this,' he complained.

'Yes you do,' Beryl insisted. 'You are suffering from shock.'

'I am *not* suffering from shock,' Rodney contradicted. 'I am suffering from a broken ankle, possibly even a broken leg. I am not fuzzy in the head and I do not need filthily sweet tea. Nor do I need a blanket when the sun is beating down on me.'

Poor Rodney, Poppy thought. He is possibly right. Perhaps it's the rest of us who are in shock? And why was Beryl, a trained nurse, behaving in this silly fashion? Did all one's training fly out of the window when dealing with a loved one?

Beryl looked around at the others. She shook her head and smiled patiently. 'My Rodney is never so short-tempered normally,' she apologized. 'You all know that. And he seldom swears. No matter what he says, it's the shock.'

'I am short-tempered', Rodney said in a tight voice, 'because my leg hurts like hell. And where is that sodding ambulance?'

'Any minute now, dear,' Beryl soothed. 'Any minute now.'

It's as well he's immobile, Poppy reckoned as she watched Rodney turn his head and bury his face in a cushion that someone had kindly provided, or I really do think he would rise up and clobber her. This was the nearest she had seen Rodney and Beryl to quarrelling.

'I'll go and watch for it,' she offered. 'I'll let you know the minute I see it coming up the road.'

There was a small window at the side of the front door, with a good view of the road, and there she took up her post. She could see as far as the corner, around which, hopefully any minute now, the ambulance would sweep. Would it come with lights flashing and sirens screaming? Probably not. A broken limb in a back garden was not on a level with a pile-up of cars in a street accident. And how silly of me, she thought, to imagine that watching out for something would make it arrive quicker.

She didn't have long to wait. The ambulance rounded the corner at a fast rate, though with no bells or sirens sounding, and turned into the drive as she was opening the door. A few minutes later Rodney, looking chalk-white, was borne out on a stretcher, the faithful Beryl at his side, and the rest of the attendant family, except Fiona, Daisy and Georgia, who had not appeared, gathered in the hall to wave him off.

'I'll follow right away,' Jeremy said.

'Would you like me to go with you?' Poppy offered.

'No thanks,' Jeremy said. 'You stay here. I expect you'll have things to do.'

The ambulance, followed by Jeremy in his car, drove away, waved off by the rest of them. Back in the house, Megan said, 'Shall I make us all a cup of tea?'

'You can, if you like,' Poppy replied. 'Count me out. I shall have a gin and tonic.'

'And me,' Mervyn said. 'And since we are now two men short on fixing the lights, I shall help – with David, that is.'

'I warn everyone', Maria said, 'not to let him do it. He's as likely to fuse everything in the house as not.'

And where is Georgia in all this? Poppy wondered as she mixed drinks. Surely she can't have missed hearing it? And she saw me run out of the room. Is she so incredibly self-centred that she can ignore it all?

She sipped her drink, then put it down on the table and went upstairs. Georgia lay on the bed, fast asleep, her arms curved around a pillow which she held close to her body, as if it were a living thing. There were black streaks around her eyes where tears had smudged the mascara.

A pillow to hold, Poppy thought, looking down on her granddaughter. How well I remember that. And dear Georgia, as I did then, is reaching for the unattainable.

She left her undisturbed, closing the bedroom door quietly behind her, and went downstairs, where she collected her drink and went into the sitting room. The only occupants were Fiona and Daisy; Daisy was fast asleep and Fiona was reading a book on childcare.

'It's nice and peaceful in here,' Poppy said.

'David and Uncle Mervyn are in the garden, seeing to the lights,' Fiona said. 'I think Aunt Maria is, too, or did she go to the hospital?'

'No, she didn't. I expect she *is* in the garden.' Which I shall avoid for the time being, Poppy decided.

'I do like a peaceful atmosphere around Daisy,' Fiona said earnestly. 'It's good for her spirit, don't you think?'

'Oh, I do indeed,' Poppy agreed. 'It would be good for my spirit.' But how often was it obtainable?

'Poor Poppy,' Fiona said. 'We all descend on you, meaning to cheer you up and make you happy for your birthday, and then things go wrong. You must wish we'd never come.'

'Oh, no, not at all. I'm pleased you're all here,' Poppy said, and realized she was telling the truth. 'Life can be too placid, especially when one is old.'

'Well, yours isn't that at the moment,' Fiona said.

'In any case,' Poppy said, 'my birthday isn't until tomorrow. Everything could be different by then.' It would be if Joe were to come. She hadn't quite given up hope, but there wasn't much time left.

It was almost three hours before they returned from the hospital. Rodney, white-faced, was helped from the car by Jeremy, with Beryl hovering close. His ankle was heavily bandaged and he limped towards the door, leaning heavily on a stick.

'Oh, you poor dear,' Poppy cried.

'It's OK, Poppy,' Rodney said bravely. He looked the most cheerful of the three. 'No bones broken, just a nasty sprain.'

'A *very* nasty sprain,' Beryl said,

'Oh dear. Is it painful?' Poppy asked.

'Very painful,' Beryl answered for him.

'It was, but not so much now. They've given me painkillers.'

'Which he won't like taking because he never has so much as an aspirin,' Beryl said. 'But I'll see that he does. And no more climbing up ladders.'

Rodney gave her the look of a man who had been at the receiving end of fatuous advice for several hours.

'No need,' Poppy said. 'Mervyn and David have seen to the lights. Everything seems to be in working order.'

'What about sleeping?' she asked. 'Will you be all right in the caravan?' She would go mad if she had to reorganize the sleeping arrangements once more.

'If not,' Beryl broke in, 'then I'm sure Mervyn and Maria will take the caravan, so we can have the bedroom.'

Stop it, Poppy thought. I can't bear it.

'Darling, will you just let it go,' Rodney implored. 'There are a dozen steps up to the bedroom and only two to the caravan. Of course I'll be all right in there.'

'I was only thinking of you,' Beryl said.

'Actually,' Rodney said, 'I'd be glad to go to bed pretty soon. One way or another, it's been a long day.'

'It certainly has,' Poppy agreed. 'Perhaps we'd all be glad of an early night.'

'A good idea, Grandma,' Jeremy said. 'I think Megan and I will make a move. I don't suppose Mrs Bedlington-Smythe will want us to be late.'

Beryl frowned, though she knew there was nothing she could do. How quickly one's children grew away from one.

A few minutes after Jeremy and Megan had left the telephone rang. Georgia, who had been driven out of Poppy's bedroom so that Daisy could be put to sleep there, sprang to her feet to answer it, but Poppy was there before her.

'Oh. Oh, my goodness,' she cried. 'Ten past six in the morning? Of course, dear. I expect your mother or father will meet you. I shall certainly come, too. No, it's not too early for me. Oh, all right. Goodbye for now, darling.'

'That was Joe,' she said, her face shining like the sun. 'He's at the airport. Newark, I think he said. He's due in at Gatwick at ten past six in the morning. He couldn't let us know any sooner, and he couldn't speak any longer because they were about to board. Isn't it wonderful.'

'I'll meet him,' Mervyn said.

Lying on the narrow bed in the small spare room which, because of the combination of fatigue and happiness which now suffused her, seemed much more comfortable than she remembered it from any previous occasion, Poppy lay thinking. When she woke in the morning she would be eighty years old. It was a solemn thought, but would she feel any different from this moment when she was only seventy-nine? It seemed so final because she couldn't imagine celebrating another decade, and couldn't see herself at ninety. She was not sure that she wanted to be ninety, though perhaps even then she would be the same inside as she was now, which was as she had always been.

I've forgotten many things and I remember a lot, she thought, but I've never forgotten what love was like, how passion felt, even after the fire had died down. The men she had known and loved, or who had loved her – and they were not necessarily the same – she remembered so clearly. Alun perhaps most of all, though she had known him for the shortest time. He could still be alive somewhere, but she had come to terms with the fact that she would never know.

Inside you, she thought, you don't age. Your body sags and your face wrinkles; you can't wear short skirts or sleeveless tops, or at least you shouldn't. But when you hear music you still want to dance; when you see a hill you want to climb it; when the water is in front of you, you want to jump in. How strange that the feelings never change, only the body they live in.

And tomorrow she would see Joe.

14

In celebration of Maria's birth, Edward, with characteristic generosity, gave me an eternity ring set with eighteen small, but fine-quality, rubies. It was stunningly beautiful.

I lay in my bed in the private room in Akersfield's most fashionable nursing home, with Maria in her cot near by and Edward sitting on a chair at my bedside, and I turned the ring round and round on my finger, watching the blood-red stones glow in the light, and I felt guilty because I didn't deserve it.

'It's wonderful,' I said. 'Oh, Edward, you are far too good to me!'

He took my hand – the one wearing the ring – and pressed it to his lips.

'I could never be too good to you,' he said. 'You're worth the whole world to me.'

'I'll try to be,' I said, and I meant it, though I didn't know how I'd carry it out.

'I can't stay, sweetheart,' he said. 'I have to go on duty. But I'll be in tomorrow.'

He went over to the cot and touched Maria's cheek gently with his finger. He was so proud to be a father.

'My two jewels,' he said. 'I can't wait to have you both home. A fortnight seems a long time.' Then he went off to his ARP post.

Edward worked so hard for the war effort: fund-raising, encouraging people to join war savings schemes and giving his own money to every possible cause. If we'd lived in an area that took in evacuee children I'm sure the house would have been full of them. Nevertheless, he felt that the things in which he was involved weren't enough. If he couldn't be in the army, then he wanted to do the nearest thing he could to defending his country, and it was for this reason that he worked regularly in the ARP post in the church hall. Being Edward, he had to do it the hard way, so every Tuesday he was on duty through the night.

He complained that there was seldom anything real to do. There were fewer than a dozen air raids on Akersfield during the whole of the war, and I reckon they were mostly unintended – pilots who had lost their way, or who'd jettisoned a spare bomb on their way home from somewhere else. So Edward, not normally much of a reader, ploughed his way with quiet desperation through several long novels, mostly Russian – *Anna Karenina*, *War and Peace*, and played hundreds of card games with his fellow wardens.

We all felt this urge to do something. While I

was pregnant I knitted scarves and balaclava helmets. I even brought my knitting into the nursing home and did several inches during my long labour. It was quite boring – the knitting, I mean. The only variety was in changing from air-force blue to khaki, and then to navy blue.

'Why don't you knit socks?' my mother asked me. 'They're always welcome.'

'You're joking,' I answered. 'Any soldier wearing socks I'd knitted would be crippled in a day. You never taught me to knit on four needles, did you?'

Later, when I had finished breast-feeding, I was able to leave Maria with my mother for two half days each week while I went back to work in the hospital. Sometimes I would take her to my mother's home, but more often my mother would come to Two Elms. She enjoyed that. She enjoyed the space and she liked pottering in the garden. Her house was poky and faced on to the street, with a small, square piece of lawn at the back and very few flowers.

Alun was never mentioned between us. It was as if he had never existed, and I think that was the way my mother wanted it. She took every opportunity to remind me, though never in so many words, how fortunate I was.

'I was talking to Mrs Infield yesterday,' she said one afternoon as we sat watching Maria crawling like lightning across the carpet. 'She's not at all happy about Esmé.'

'Why not?' I asked.

'Well,' she said, 'apart from the fact that Esmé doesn't like teaching – and we could have guessed that would happen, couldn't we – she's taken up with a most unsuitable man. He works at the Food Office.'

'How does that make him unsuitable?' I said. I knew I was being awkward. 'He might well slip her extra coupons.'

'You're so sharp, one of these days you'll cut yourself,' she said. 'He's unsuitable because he plays the field. He's not from round here. He was drafted in from somewhere or other. He's very good-looking, apparently, but not to be trusted.'

He sounded like the sort of man Esmé *would* fall for. He would also be a good dancer.

'Mrs Infield envies me,' my mother said. 'She said so straight out. "What wouldn't I give to have a daughter like your Poppy?" she said to me. "Nicely settled down with a good husband and a baby." '

I knew I was fortunate in Edward. I didn't need to have it rubbed in, I just wished there was someone to whom I could have spoken Alun's name. It would somehow have made him exist in the real world.

'I shall have to be going,' my mother said presently. 'Raymond will be wanting his tea. I was lucky this morning, I got a nice bit of haddock in the market. We haven't had fish for ages.'

Nor had we. I knew that in Edward's position, knowing so many people and not being short of money, we could have bought most things on the black market: meat, cheese, chicken, butter. Others did. They used their petrol ration – unless they had a source of black-market petrol – to drive up to the Dales, and they came back laden. But not Edward: he wouldn't get so much as a single extra egg to make a custard for Maria.

My mother picked up Maria and gave her a hug.

'Goodbye precious,' she said. 'Grandma'll come again next week.' She handed Maria over to me. 'She'll be walking before you know it, this one will.'

She was right. Maria walked on her first birthday. By that time I was already two months pregnant with Beryl.

'That's very quick, Poppy,' my mother said. 'Two babies in well under two years. What does Edward think?'

'He's delighted,' I told her. I supposed he was hoping for a son, and I hoped he would get one.

I don't remember that anyone else asked me what I thought about having another baby so soon, and if they did I'd hardly have known what to say. Since my life was not what I wanted it to be, I was still in that mood of thinking 'let it happen'. I would just do the best I could with whatever came.

Actually, though she didn't say so, I think my mother was pleased. I guessed she thought another child would keep me safely anchored to husband and home. From time to time, though,

I would catch her giving me anxious little glances. If she had anxieties about me, she never expressed them in words, not unless they were totally practical ones, such as was I eating enough and did I take enough rest.

'You'll have to give up the hospital,' she warned me. 'Looking after those old people is heavy work. You mustn't take any risks.'

I knew she was right, and when Edward said the same thing I agreed at once.

'We shall miss you,' Sister said. 'But your husband is quite right. And no more heaving Mrs Baker around, starting this minute.'

Mrs Baker was indignant at the news. She had recently been refusing to have her baths except when I was there to give them. I think she regarded me as her private nurse.

'What am I going to do?' she demanded. 'Couldn't you just come in to see to me?'

Then, as the weeks went by, I had something far more important to worry about, though I didn't understand in the beginning just how serious it was. I suppose I was absorbed by Maria, who was now into everything, and by the constant sickness of pregnancy, which I hadn't had my first time. I had a house to run single-handed, except for a Mrs Harper, who came twice a week to do the rough. Elsie had gone into the ATS, and after two or three letters I lost touch with her.

My mother visited me one Wednesday; she now came to me every week, insisting that it was easier for her to visit me than the other way around, which was true.

'By the way,' she said nonchalantly, as we were drinking tea and eating a fatless sponge cake she had brought with her – almost all cakes were fatless by then – 'I might have to go into hospital.'

I dropped my cake on the floor. 'Hospital?' I said, retrieving it. 'Whatever for?'

'Oh, nothing much,' she said. 'I've got this lump. The doctor thinks it's a cyst. They'll just take a look at it and they might take it out. I'm sure it's not serious.'

'Why didn't you tell me?' I demanded. 'How long has this been going on?'

'Only a few weeks,' she said. 'I didn't think it was worth bothering you with. You've got enough to think about right now, without worrying about me.'

'That's plain silly,' I said. 'You should have told me.' I know I sounded cross, but it was because I was anxious. My mother was never ill, she had never spent so much as a night in hospital. She was as tough as old boots, wasn't she?

'Don't worry,' she said. 'I just wanted to tell you I wouldn't be here next Wednesday. They're going to do it on Monday.'

'So soon?' I could hardly believe it. 'I thought they had a waiting list.'

'I think they had a space,' she said vaguely.

Edward took the news philosophically. 'I'm

sure your mother's right,' he said. 'A cyst doesn't sound too bad. They'll deal with it. And she must come here for a few days' convalescence.'

'She won't leave Raymond,' I told him. 'And in any case, he'll look after her.' Raymond was more and more devoted to my mother as time went by, and I'm sure she was to him, though neither of them was demonstrative.

She was in and out of hospital within the week and, as I expected, she refused to come and stay with me, but went straight home to Raymond, where I went to see her.

'That was quick,' I said. 'So how are you?'

'I'm fine,' she said. 'I told you it wouldn't take long.'

'And what did they say about it?' I queried.

'Oh, nothing much,' she said airily. 'They don't, do they? I expect because there's nothing to say. They have to wait for some tests, and they'll get in touch with Dr Harrison.'

A week later she went to see Dr Harrison. I wanted to go with her, but I was busy being sick, and also I had no-one with whom to leave Maria, so I telephoned her.

'I'll come down and see you as soon as Edward gets home,' I promised.

'Well,' I said, sitting down in front of her in her small front room, 'what did he say?'

'Everything's all right,' she answered in a bright voice. 'Nothing to worry about.'

'Are you sure?'

'Of course I'm sure,' she said crossly.

I didn't believe her. I was sure she was lying. Her eyes told a different story from her words. All the same, I decided that now was not the time to pursue the matter.

'Good,' I said. 'I can't stay. I have to get back to let Edward go on duty. You will let me know if there's anything you want? I'll give you a ring tomorrow.' I couldn't say any more. For once I didn't know what to say, and I sensed that she didn't want me there, not just then.

It turned out I was right. She *had* lied to me. It was ovarian cancer, but it was a long time before she admitted it. Even when she started a course of radiotherapy – there was no chemotherapy then – she tried to brush it aside.

'You know what hospitals are like,' she said. 'They always want to do things. They like experimenting on people, I reckon.'

Over the following weeks and months, while my body swelled with the child inside me, I watched my mother's body swell with the cancer. I watched her usual healthy, rose-tinted skin turn lemon yellow, as if there were no blood in her veins. I heard her vigorous, no-nonsense voice grow fainter, as if she didn't have the energy to talk. I watched her shrink until, at forty-six, she looked a tiny, wizened old woman. One long night, a month before my baby was born, I watched her die.

*　*　*

We named the baby Beryl. I did think about naming her Harriet, after my mother, but I couldn't bring myself to do it. My mother's death was so recent, and I was so raw, that I couldn't bear to think of anyone taking her name. It seemed almost as though I might be suggesting that my baby could take my mother's place, but no-one could ever do that. There was only one Harriet.

'Aunt Beryl would love to have the baby called after her,' Edward said.

Aunt Beryl was Edward's aunt; his father's sister. The man she had hoped to marry died in the Boer War, at Mafeking, so though she loved children she was never to have the joy of naming her own.

'That's a nice idea,' I said. I liked Aunt Beryl. She had accepted me much more quickly than the rest of Edward's family. 'And it's a pretty name.'

Beryl was a model baby, much easier than Maria had ever been. She did everything by the book: fed well, slept when she was supposed to and, when awake, she was lively and outgoing. With very little help from me she was an organized baby, almost as if she had been programmed. Edward adored her. Though I knew he had wanted a son, if he *was* disappointed he never let it show.

When the baby was six weeks old he gave me another ring; an eternity ring again, and this time set with sapphires.

'I had it specially made,' he said. 'That's why you've had to wait for it. It's exactly the same design as the ruby one, so if you wish you can wear them together.'

'Oh, Edward. It's beautiful,' I said. 'And I'm sorry I didn't give you a son.'

He waved my apologies away. 'Don't be sorry. I love both my little daughters. And there's plenty of time,' he said. 'When we have a son I'll give you emeralds.'

I was never to have my emeralds. On the day Beryl was six months old, sitting up unaided, her tiny first teeth showing in her gums, Edward was killed. There was no warning of the plane that jettisoned its bomb; I couldn't even remember having heard its engines. There was just this tremendous bang and thud as the bomb fell in the field that backed on to the large garden of Two Elms. It seemed uncertain what had killed him. It could have been the blast. No-one else was hurt in the least. The pilot continued on his way, leaving a solitary cow dead in the field, and Edward on the lavatory.

It was a cruel death for Edward. He was a rather proper, conventional man, well-mannered and reticent. Dignified even.

It was the first bomb to be dropped in our area for a long time, and the very last we were to experience. Though we didn't cease to be vigilant, I think we all felt the end of the war couldn't be far off. Sure enough, less than a year later, it came.

I was numbed and horrified by Edward's death, distraught and beside myself. Coming so soon after my mother's death and the birth of my baby, I couldn't face it; I could hardly believe it was true. Not Edward. Not Edward, of all people.

What I wanted, what I wanted most of all, was my mother. I had turned to my mother in every crisis in my life, large or small, from a bruised knee from falling in the school playground to Alun's departure. She had always been there, and now, when I needed her so desperately, she wasn't. I felt so angry with her that at one point I paced up and down the bedroom calling out to her. 'Why aren't you here?' I demanded. 'Why aren't you here?'

I felt no anger for Edward, only a very deep pity that he, who had always done his best for everyone, should have had his life cut short, and in such a manner. Underneath it all I felt guilty that I hadn't loved him as much as I should have done – in fact, that I'd betrayed him. If I'd been given time I would have made it up to him, but I was given no time at all.

And yet – and yet, what I still wanted was Alun. Grief and shock had not knocked that out of my system, possibly it had made it worse. I told myself that if he knew I was on my own he would surely come if he was able, or at least he would write. In desperation I wrote to him at the only address I had, his Army post office number. For weeks I watched and waited for the postman to bring me a reply. Nothing came. Was he dead? I decided he wasn't simply because I couldn't face another death. I told myself that it was just that he hadn't received my letter. One day he would; it would catch up with him. One read in the newspapers about letters being received months, even years, after they'd been posted. I stopped watching for every post, but I could never quite believe that one day I wouldn't find a thin, blue-grey air letter lying on the mat.

Somehow I had to get myself back into the land of the living. I had my two little girls to look after – Maria, missing her father, and at barely two years old unable to express it; Beryl, fractious because she was now teething in earnest.

It was at this point that Esmé Infield came back into my life; she literally turned up on the doorstep one Saturday afternoon.

I had not seen Esmé since my mother's funeral. She had not been to Edward's, I suppose because she and I drew apart a little after I married and she took a job some distance away. Also, Edward wasn't totally keen on her, and I think she perhaps realized that.

I answered the door with Beryl in my arms and Maria standing beside me. I could hardly believe what I saw – Esmé standing there, smartly dressed in spite of clothing coupons, her hair obviously straight from the ministrations of the hairdresser. She looked like something out of a magazine.

'Well,' she said, 'are you going to ask me in or aren't you?'

'I'm sorry,' I said. 'It's such a surprise to see you.'

'A pleasant one, I hope?' she said.

'Marvellous,' I assured her. 'Do come in. Do you mind if we go into the kitchen? I have to give the children their tea.'

She followed me through the hall. I put Beryl in her high chair, gave her a rusk and set about scrambling an egg for Maria.

'I'll make a cup of tea in a minute,' I said. 'Oh, Esmé it *is* good to see you.'

'If you'll tell me where things are, I'll make the tea,' she offered. 'You seem to have your hands full.'

'I don't have any help at weekends,' I told her, 'though Mrs Harper comes every weekday morning now to help with the housework.'

From Friday lunchtime to Monday morning was a desert to me. No-one came, and I couldn't always pull myself together enough to get the two children ready and take them out. Sometimes I took them to my mother-in-law's, but not often. Edward's mother professed herself pleased to see her grandchildren, but she was not a well woman and they quickly tired her, especially Maria, who was not always well-behaved.

When I'd seen to the children we all went into the sitting room. Beryl sat happily, playing with a rabbit my mother had knitted for her, but Maria constantly interrupted my conversation with Esmé, demanding to be noticed.

'You should try to get out more,' Esmé said. 'And I mean without the children.'

She had no idea how difficult, almost impossible, that was now. Until her illness, I'd always had my mother to turn to; and after she died Edward, especially at weekends, would look after the children so that I could be free for an hour or two.

I suppose it was true, and it left me with yet another feeling of guilt: that I missed my mother even more than I missed Edward – which is *not* to say that I didn't miss him. We had been so close, she and I. It had been just the two of us all the time I was growing up. There had been uncles, of course, but she'd never let them come between us; they never deflected her constant care for me. She shaped my life and saw to it that I was educated, trained for a job that would lead me to a better life than she'd ever had. She had values which she passed on to me. I always knew that, whatever I did, my mother would be there for me, even though she didn't always approve of what I did. I let her down over Alun, but she never loved me the less for it. And now she was not there. It was the first time in my life I had ever longed for a sister.

'I can't,' I said.

'You could,' Esmé said firmly. 'What's to stop you having a nanny? Don't tell me you're short of money.'

'I'm not,' I admitted. 'But most of the girls who might have been nannies seem to have gone into the Forces, or nursing. It seems as if they can't wait to get away from home.'

'I know the feeling,' Esmé said. 'Actually, the war will soon be over and they'll come flocking back. You'll be able to pick and choose then.'

'That doesn't help me now,' I pointed out, 'though as a matter of fact, I've heard of a girl who might do. She's only seventeen; too young to join up. Apparently she's the eldest of four, so she's experienced with children.'

'Then get hold of her at once,' Esmé said. 'You can't go on like this.'

And that, spurred on by Esmé, was how I came to acquire Jenny, and that led to other things.

Jenny was pleasant, likeable and completely untrained, unless you can call having three younger siblings training, but she got on well with Maria and Beryl, and she was kind – an important point to me. She played with the children in the house and garden, took them to the park, helped with their laundry and sometimes supervised them at mealtimes. What I did discover, quite quickly, was that what pleased her most about the job was that she had broken away from home, and what interested her most was her time off. About that she was demanding. What she wanted was time off in the evenings and at weekends so that she could meet her friends.

I gave in to her. If I hadn't I felt sure she

would have left. People were so eager for girls who would work in the house, or with children, that in spite of her inexperience she would have had the choice of half a dozen jobs. She knew this as well as I did.

In any case, I asked myself, where would I go if I *were* free in the evenings, or at weekends? My life had been bound by going to my mother's, or going out with Edward while my mother stayed with the children – and that wasn't often. Edward was a homebird when he had the chance.

So, for my time off I took to catching a bus into town and looking at the shops – anything for a change. While there I would often buy something for the children.

One Tuesday morning I said to Jenny, 'It's a nice day. I'll go into town and perhaps I'll have lunch; be back around three. You'll be all right, won't you?'

'Of course,' she said amiably. 'I might take the kiddies to the park. You go and enjoy yourself, Mrs Baxter.'

I wasn't sure that 'enjoy' was the right word, but at least I would be free for a little while and have time to myself, not bounded by the wants and needs of two small children, much as I loved them.

The bus passed my mother's house, where I'd lived for so much of my life. On the return journey – there was a stop right by her gate – the bus halted for a while to let off a woman with two small children and to take on two elderly ladies. I sat and stared at the house.

My mother hadn't owned the house; she'd rented it, which was what most people in our position did. Very soon after she'd died, Raymond had returned to his native Ireland. 'I can't stand to live here without Harriet,' he said. Now there were fancy lace curtains at the windows instead of my mother's plain net ones. Mrs Infield said the new tenant was a bit standoffish.

I had a terrible feeling of desolation. I wished the bus would move on, move away, which, of course, it did.

When I reached home Jenny said, 'There was a letter for you in the second post. I put it on the desk.'

Alun. It had to be from Alun, I thought. I rushed to pick it up. Of course it wasn't from Alun; it was from Esmé. I recognized her round, rather childish writing on the envelope.

'Arrange to be free next Saturday evening,' she ordered. 'I don't care how you do it, but arrange it. I am coming with two friends – male! – to pick you up, and we are going out for a meal. There will be dancing, so dress up. Don't let me down!'

And that was how I came to meet Victor.

15

When Poppy opened her eyes and saw the daylight filtering through the bedroom curtains, her first thought was to wonder whether she had overslept. Without raising her head from the pillow she turned to look at the clock. Ten minutes to five. Of course she wouldn't have overslept. She had set the alarm for five o'clock, and since it made about as much noise as a fire bell there was no way it wouldn't have woken her. She stretched out her arm and switched it off before it could erupt and wake the entire household, but especially Baby Daisy. This was no time for wide-awake babies.

Her second thought, following so quickly on the first that they seemed almost simultaneous, was that it was her birthday. It had come at last. She was, as of now, eighty years old. And since she had ten minutes to spare before she need get up, she could allow herself to wonder just how she felt about being a bona fide octogenarian. She lay quite still, savouring the moment.

I don't feel the least bit different from yesterday, when I was a mere seventy-nine, she decided. And what nonsense to think I should. And yet it was not quite nonsense. What made it different was the thought which suddenly came to her that she had now embarked on what might well be – it was odds on that it *would* be – the last decade of her life. There was nothing morbid in the thought. It was statistically unlikely that she would live into her nineties since she had already outlived, by several years, any known member of her family on either side. And did she want to be ninety? She thought not. But since almost ten years stretched ahead before that would be imminent, she didn't have to answer that question yet.

Since this probably *is* my last decade, she thought, I can use it to do whatever I want, not to mention refraining from doing the things I don't like, the boring things. She could be thoroughly selfish, and that would hopefully be excused on the grounds that she was old and all the time getting more eccentric.

It would have to be health and vigour permitting, of course, though lack of either would be a good reason for choosing *not* to do things. Her life was littered with things she had wanted to do and hadn't done, perhaps from lack of opportunity or from plain inertia, a lack of get up and go.

Skiing, for instance. It was too late now, but how often had she watched a film or a TV programme and imagined herself sliding down that dazzling white slope under a bright winter-blue sky? Never a spill, never a failure to stop dead, if she so wished, on an area the size of a table top. She had always thought it must be the nearest thing to flying. And in the realm of flying, why had she never done that parachute jump she'd said she quite fancied? Or even ventured up in a hot-air balloon? Perhaps that last ambition was even now not impossible?

What she *would* do was read more books and listen to more music. Perhaps she would go to more concerts, or the theatre, or movies. But with whom? Those were the things one wanted to do with a friend, and did she have many friends? And if not, why? Some she had lost because they'd died or moved away, but others, she was afraid, she had lost by neglect, because she hadn't made the effort to keep in touch. One had to work at friendship.

On the other hand, she thought, I'm not a person who dislikes being alone. I'm not one to feel lonely. It was simply that going to see a play, or a movie, especially to see something funny, called for a companion, though it had to be the right one. Laughter had to be shared or it hardly existed.

Where had they gone? Those friends she had made and presumably lost.

She thought about Esmé Infield. Esmé had died four years previously, aged seventy-seven, though they hadn't seen each other for some years before that. Their friendship had started to loosen soon after the move south with Victor. Esmé had visited twice, for summer holidays, the second time bringing her new husband. I didn't care for him, Poppy remembered. In the end, Esmé didn't care for him either. She'd divorced him after five years and there'd been no children.

She pulled herself back into the present. She must be up and ready to leave with Mervyn for Gatwick in half an hour. Then she would see Joe. That would be the best part of this birthday. Never mind the past.

She showered in a matter of minutes, and put on a pair of well-cut beige trousers, a silk blouse and a cream wool jacket, which she had remembered to rescue from her wardrobe yesterday before she gave up her bedroom to Fiona and David.

She was in the kitchen, the kettle coming to the boil, when Mervyn appeared. He was squeezed into a pair of blue jeans that were too tight for him, so that his ample girth was accentuated. His hair was tousled. He looked tired, not at all like a man who had just had a good night's sleep. Perhaps he hadn't?

'Good morning, Mervyn,' Poppy said. 'Did you sleep well?'

He shrugged. 'So so.'

'I never sleep as well away from home,' Poppy said. 'Would you like tea or coffee?'

'Tea,' he answered. 'I've developed a taste for tea.'

Poppy poured hot water into the teapot, swilled it around, then poured it away down the sink before putting in two English Breakfast teabags. 'I think of Americans as drinking coffee all day long,' Poppy said, giving the tea a stir.

'Some do,' Mervyn said. 'I don't go through all that routine when I make tea.'

'You should,' Poppy told him. 'It tastes better. Would you like toast or cereal? Or perhaps both?'

'Toast.' He sat down at the table.

'I almost forgot,' he said suddenly. 'Happy birthday, Poppy.'

'Thank you, Mervyn,' she said. 'I don't feel any older. One slice or two?'

'Two, please. You don't look any older. But at eighty you shouldn't be getting up at five in the morning to drive to the airport. I can do it.'

'It's no trouble,' Poppy assured him. 'And it's easier for me. I'm used to my car, and to driving on the left. Anyway, I usually wake early.' Also, of course, she wanted to be there to greet Joe.

'I'll get the car out,' she said.

'I'll be right there!' Mervyn spoke through a mouthful of toast and orange marmalade, scattering small crumbs.

Poppy drove her car out of the garage, then waited, drumming the steering wheel with her fingertips, for Mervyn to join her. They were short of time. The plane was due in at ten past six and she wanted to be there before it landed, never mind that everyone said it would be at least half an hour before anyone got through. She couldn't bear the thought that everything might be ahead of time and that there would be no-one there to greet Joe.

'Hey,' Mervyn said. 'Nice little car.'

She had never thought of her BMW as a nice little car, but no doubt it was compared to the great big thing Mervyn drove.

'I've had it quite some time,' she said. 'Probably too long. I used to change my car every two years, but now I don't bother. It's reliable and I'm rather fond of it. I think perhaps women do get fond of their cars.'

'How long to Gatwick?' Mervyn asked.

'About thirty minutes. At least the road will be clear at this time of day.'

Once on the M23 she drove fast. She had always been a fast driver. Noticing Mervyn's glance at the speedometer, she slowed down a little.

'Our speed limits are higher than yours,' she said, 'which surprises me. Victor always said I drove too fast.'

'Victor?'

'My second husband. You wouldn't have known him. You'd have been a teenager in New York in Victor's time. It was Victor who taught me to drive when we first came to Sussex.'

'He taught you well – even if everyone in Europe drives too fast,' Mervyn said.

They were silent for a while. There was

very little traffic, mostly trucks in the opposite direction, making for the channel ports.

'Pretty country,' Mervyn observed.

'Yes,' Poppy agreed, 'though when I first came south I thought it was too soft. I've grown used to it, and so I should after more than forty years. I've lived here longer than I lived in the North. Have you always lived in New York?'

'Always in Manhattan, as a matter of fact. We've bought this place upstate for weekends and so on. You haven't seen it yet, but I expect Maria's told you?'

'Briefly,' Poppy said. 'Are you enjoying it?'

'I hardly ever get there,' Mervyn admitted. 'Nor does Maria. It was supposed to be a place to relax, but we're both too busy to make it.'

'That's a pity,' Poppy said. 'I'm sure it would do you good to get away.'

'I know,' Mervyn admitted. 'You're right, but I never seem to have enough time. It's all go, go, go. Every day's filled with appointments. Everybody expects perfection all the time. And they pay for it.' His voice was tense, as if he were fighting something and not winning.

'I've got to slow down,' he said. 'My pressure's too high. I have medication – when I remember, that is. I know I've got to lose weight, but that's not easy, either.'

'I think you should do as you're told,' Poppy ventured. It was not something one said lightly to Mervyn. 'I dare say I shouldn't interfere, but you *are* my son-in-law, you *are* family.'

And on this visit, she thought, I think I like him more than I've ever done. In spite of his self-importance, underneath there is a vulnerable man.

She even began to find herself feeling sorry for him. He has a difficult wife – even if she *is* my daughter – a badly behaved daughter, plus the pressures of his job. I would actually, she realized, and was surprised at herself, like to give him a big hug, and say, 'There, there.'

'And what about Maria?' she asked. 'Is she likely to get this new salon she's so keen on?'

Mervyn sighed.

'I don't know. In one way I hope she does. She won't settle down until she has it.'

He means she won't be fit to live with, Poppy thought.

'On the other hand, if she gets it she'll be more overworked than ever. She's far too busy. We live in the same apartment and we hardly see each other.'

There seemed nothing useful Poppy could say. No wonder neither of them could deal with Georgia. And where did Joe fit in?

As if he could read her thoughts Mervyn said, 'And then there's Joe. I worry about him. Being an artist is no way to make a living, especially if you only paint what you want to. I mean, what pleases you instead of the customer.'

'I suppose that's what most painters prefer to do,' Poppy said.

'OK. But it doesn't bring in the dollars, does

it? If that's Joe's career – if you can call it a career – he'd be better off painting portraits. You paint them on demand and you get paid. And I think I could put work his way. I look after some of the most expensive teeth in New York. Their owners are rich, real rich, and when you're that successful you like having your portrait painted – and your wife's, your kid's, even the dog's. It could be a good business for Joe. He just laughs when I suggest it.'

'Has he ever painted your portrait?' Poppy asked.

'Mine?' He sounded surprised. 'God, no. Where would I find the time to be painted?'

'It might be quite relaxing,' Poppy suggested.

She didn't think it would be, really. And how, even if he decided to spare the time, would Mervyn sit still for so long?

'I'm not *against* art,' Mervyn explained. 'Quite the reverse. We try to go to all the big shows – the Met, the Guggenheim, MOMA. Most people do.'

She had a sudden memory of Mervyn and Maria's penthouse apartment on Park Avenue; its wonderful vista of New York and its furnishings: massive sofas; exquisite ceramics; small, beautiful bronzes; a mass of pink and white tulips on a low crystal table; and paintings – surely all original – on the stark, white walls. But, of course, it was all done, chosen, by the decorator.

'Not that I understand everything.'

'But you know what you like?'

Mervyn nodded agreement. 'Exactly.'

'Anyway,' he added, 'I'm glad Joe's coming over for your eightieth. Though I never thought he wouldn't. He thinks a lot of you.'

Poppy felt a warm glow of pleasure. 'And I of him,' she said, then added, 'As I do of all my grandchildren.'

She drove for a while in silence. Giant planes, which looked as though they might skim the treetops, crossed the sky in front of them.

'We must be close,' Mervyn said.

'We are,' Poppy agreed. 'It's the next exit.'

She parked the car and they hurried towards the South Terminal arrivals hall. 'It's only just six,' she said, 'but you never know. It could land early, flying west to east.' As indeed it had. 'Landed', the monitor said.

For twenty minutes they waited behind the barriers. No-one had yet appeared. Mervyn grew restless.

'He won't be the first out,' he said. 'Joe travels economy. They have to wait to the last for their baggage.' He spoke with the assurance of a man who never travelled except in first class.

'Why don't you take a little stroll,' Poppy suggested. 'I won't move from here.'

There was no way she'd be tempted to do that. She wanted to be right here to catch the first sight of Joe as he came through the doors. How silly I am, she chided herself. Eighty years old and acting like a young girl waiting for her lover.

Mervyn was wrong. Joe was amongst the first

to emerge. She saw him fractionally before he spotted her, standing at the front of the crowd. He was not, as she'd expected, pushing a baggage cart, and he carried only a single bag, slung from his shoulder.

Surely he had lost weight, which would explain why he looked taller than she remembered him. His dark hair, which had fallen over his collar when she'd last seen him, was cropped short. He looked pale and rather serious, but when she waved and he saw her, a wide smile lit up his face. He hurried towards her, and when he reached her he took her in his arms and held her in a tight hug. She felt his strength in spite of the fact that he was so thin.

'Poppy,' he said. 'Happy birthday.'

He held her at arm's length and inspected her, as she did him. He had dark rings around his eyes, no doubt from lack of sleep.

'You look great,' he said. 'You don't change a bit. As lovely as ever.'

'And you're still kissing the Blarney stone,' Poppy said, laughing. Oh, it was so good to see him. It had been so long.

'Your father's around somewhere,' she said. 'He didn't think you'd be through for a while.'

'I wouldn't have been,' Joe said, 'except that I only have a carry-on.'

Which means, Poppy thought, that he didn't plan a long stay. Well, she couldn't expect that, could she?

Mervyn joined them. She watched the two men

greet each other. They were amiable, friendly, but there was no overt show of affection between them. That wasn't Mervyn's style, though it might have been Joe's.

'Good flight?' Mervyn enquired. 'Did you sleep?'

'The flight was fine,' Joe said, 'but I never sleep on red-eyes.'

'If you want to, you can go to bed as soon as we get home,' Poppy promised him. She would give him her bed to begin with, see that he had a few quiet hours in a bedroom, though tonight he'd almost certainly be in the caravan. Or should I sleep in the caravan, she wondered? He probably wouldn't let her, and that would be a relief.

Joe sat beside her in the front of the car. Without protest, Mervyn took the back seat, and for the whole of the journey he hardly said a word. Once or twice, when she remembered that he was there, Poppy looked in her mirror to check on him. The first time he was looking out of the window, the second time his eyes were closed and his chin slumped on his chest. Poor Mervyn. He had been up very early; perhaps he was still suffering from jet lag. Why couldn't he have let her drive up to the airport on her own?

'I think your father's very tired,' she said quietly to Joe.

'He would be,' Joe agreed. 'He works like a maniac; never lets up. Ma is the same. But you can't stop them – at least I can't.'

'Are you enjoying living on your own?' Poppy asked.

'It's great having my own place,' Joe said. 'I couldn't have stayed at home. And the Lower East Side's a good place for a painter to live. Lots of other artists, always new shows. That's why I couldn't get to England as soon as the others. I had to finish a painting for a show which opens today. I came as soon as I could.'

'That's all right,' Poppy assured him. 'As long as you're here.'

'And by the way,' Joe said, 'I'm not living alone. I have a girlfriend. Anna. She's been with me two months. You'd like her.'

'I'm sure I would,' Poppy said.

They were reaching the end of the motorway. Poppy concentrated on the road while she changed lanes and made a left turn. That done, she said, 'Are you happy?'

'Absolutely,' Joe said. 'I can't tell you how happy.'

She could tell he was, simply by the warmth in his voice, but she took her eyes off the road for a moment and turned her head to look at him. His eyes met hers and, yes, he looked as happy as he sounded.

What a relief, she thought. What a wonder to have one member of her family totally happy and normal, not at odds with the world, not beset by problems.

'That's marvellous,' she said. 'Tell me what Anna's like. Have you got a photograph?'

'Sure,' Joe said. 'I'll show it to you later. She's tall, with dark curly hair, and green eyes.'

'Wow!' Poppy said. 'Is she American?'

'She was born in America. Her mother's French.'

'Could you have brought her with you?' she enquired.

'Not at the moment,' Joe said. 'She's working. She's an actress, and right now she's in an off-Broadway production. But when the run ends, then I will. Or why don't you come to New York?'

'Perhaps I will,' Poppy said.

Only yesterday she had doubted she'd ever go to New York again; she'd been in that sort of mood. This morning she felt differently. The prospect of spending time with Joe and meeting his girlfriend was a pleasant one.

'Yes, perhaps I will,' she repeated.

She glanced in the rear-view mirror. Mervyn was wide awake.

'Did you have a nice little sleep?' she asked.

'I did,' he answered.

'I was telling Poppy she should come to New York,' Joe said.

'Quite right,' Mervyn agreed.

'You're very kind, Mervyn,' Poppy told him.

He was always more welcoming than Maria. Maria didn't like spending time away from her businesses. Although, Poppy thought, I always get my hair done for free. And have a manicure and a facial. What with that and Mervyn giving her cut-price dentistry, and the fact that she could buy new clothes much cheaper than in England, she could easily persuade herself that it made economic sense for her to spend a few hundred pounds on a flight to New York.

'I'll give it serious thought,' she promised.

'You could come back with us,' Joe suggested.

'Oh, I don't think so.' She was startled at the suddenness of the idea. 'I would have to plan things.'

Yet what things? She had no animals, no-one was dependent on her and Edith Prince would keep an eye on the house. In fact, she was as free as air.

'One thing I have to confess,' Joe said. 'I haven't brought you a birthday present. But I *do* know what I'm going to give you, and I hope you'll like it.'

'I'm sure I shall,' Poppy said. 'Am I allowed to know what it is?'

'You'll have to. I can't do it without you. I want to paint your portrait. I want to do it today, on your birthday, or at least make a start on it.'

'My goodness,' Poppy said. 'I'm not sure that I'll have the time today. How long will it take?' How ungracious she sounded. 'But of course it would be a marvellous birthday present. It's just that—'

'You must find the time,' Joe insisted. 'Perhaps an hour today and the rest tomorrow. I'll do it in Conté, or crayon and perhaps give it a colour wash tomorrow.' The delicacy of her features and moulding of her high cheekbones would show best in a simple drawing rather than an oil painting, he thought. Her face was no longer young; there were well-defined lines from nose to chin and finer ones around her eyes. The flesh under her chin was no longer tight and her jawline sagged a little. Her eyes were deeper set than they had once been, the brows and lashes sparser, but the combination of all these things made an interesting face, and one which, for all its faults, had a beauty all its own.

'I didn't know you did portraits,' Poppy said.

'I don't really,' Joe agreed. 'That doesn't mean I never do.'

'I'd be thrilled,' Poppy said. 'If I'd known I'd have had my hair done.'

'Oh no,' Joe was adamant. 'That's what you mustn't do. And don't wear your best dress. I want you as you look every day, not dolled up.'

'If you say so,' Poppy agreed, though reluctantly. 'I suppose it's vanity to want to look my best. Unreasonable in the old.'

'Not unreasonable at all,' Joe said, 'but you look your best when everything about you is natural. At least to this painter's eyes you do.' He never wanted fashionable clothes or slick hair. They hid the person behind. But women, and in fact men, too, found that hard to believe.

'Well, somehow I'll find the time,' Poppy promised. 'But when are you going to get some sleep?'

'I'll sleep this morning, and start the drawing this afternoon,' Joe said.

They were home by half past seven. Stepping into the hall, they were met by silence.

'Everyone's still asleep,' Poppy said quietly. 'Let's go into the kitchen and I'll make some coffee.' It felt to her like the middle of the day.

'Good idea,' Mervyn said. In spite of liking tea there were some occasions when coffee is called for. 'Then I guess I'll follow Joe's example and grab a couple of hours' sleep.'

'Won't coffee keep you awake?' Poppy asked him. Poor Mervyn, he did look tired; far worse than Joe.

'Nothing will keep me awake,' Mervyn said.

Filling the kettle, Poppy looked out of the window. The garden was coming to life in the morning sun. It was going to be a good day. While she looked, Beryl, her hair in blue rollers, emerged from the caravan.

16

When the doorbell rang I said to Jenny, 'That must be my friends,' and went off to answer it. Answering the door was one of the things Jenny did *not* do. To her way of thinking, though she had neither qualifications nor training to back it up, she was a nanny. Nannies looked after children. Some of them also wore rather nice uniforms, which she would have liked, but I wasn't having that; it was too pretentious. Also, after five years of war, most of us were sick of the sight of uniforms.

Esmé stood on the top step, and behind her stood two men, one tall and plumpish, the other smaller and thin. A bit like Laurel and Hardy, only not so exaggerated.

'Are you ready?' Esmé asked.

'Almost,' I said. 'I just have to get my coat and take a last look at the children, though I think they're asleep. Please come in.'

They stepped into the hall.

'This is Charlie,' Esmé said, indicating the

smaller, thin one. 'And this is Victor.' She gave me a wink, not meant to be seen by them, which said, He's yours. 'And this is my friend, Poppy.'

'Pleased to meet you,' they said, more or less in unison.

'Come into the sitting room,' I said. 'I won't keep you long.'

'That's all right,' Victor replied, 'we're a bit early.'

'The early bird catches the worm,' Charlie said, smiling at his own wit. He had an unexpectedly hearty voice for his size, while Victor's gentler voice contrasted with his appearance.

'I'm sorry I can't offer you a drink,' I said. 'I don't have anything suitable.'

'Don't let that worry you,' Charlie said. 'There'll be plenty of that where we're going. Ha, ha!' He really did say 'Ha, ha', just like that.

'Oh,' I said. 'Thank you. I'll be back in a minute.'

'I'll come with you,' Esmé offered. 'I want to powder my nose. That is, if you two men can be trusted on your own.'

'You never know,' Charlie said. 'Just don't keep us dangling too long, that's all.'

'Cheeky,' Esmé said, following me out of the room.

'Well, what do you think?' she said as I took my coat out of the wardrobe.

'Charlie seems very . . . friendly,' I said.

She gave me a hard look. 'That wasn't the word you were looking for,' she said. 'I know you.

Actually, he's quite nice, and he's a bit of fun. I would have thought you could do with a bit of fun.'

'I'm sure I can,' I agreed. All the same, I was glad I'd drawn Victor and not Charlie.

'You'll need a headscarf,' Esmé said. 'They've got the hood down.'

'Whose car is it?' I asked.

'Victor's. Wait until you see it, that's all.'

It was a long, gleaming, dark-blue car with pale beige leather upholstery. I didn't know much about cars – Edward had always had a nice solid Morris – but I thought this was a Lagonda. At any rate, it was very impressive. Victor handed me into the front seat, then went round and took his place at the wheel. He pulled on a pair of fine leather gauntlet gloves.

'Off we go,' he said and the car leaped forward.

'Heigh ho for the open road,' Charlie called out from the back seat.

'Where are we going?' I ventured. I had to shout against the rushing wind and the noise of the car.

'Harrogate,' Victor said. 'There's a nice hotel there. Good food and dancing.' At least that was what I thought he said, though most of his words were carried away on the bitterly cold wind.

'Sounds nice!' I shouted.

We gave up the struggle to talk. It was the only conversation we had all the way to Harrogate, though Esmé and Charlie talked and screamed until the moment we drew up in front of the hotel and the concierge took the car away and parked it.

It was a large, posh hotel. We went straight to the bar.

'Little drinkies before we eat,' Charlie said. 'Of course, we should be having a bottle of bubbly. Nothing like a bottle of bubbly for a celebration, I always say. But the Frogs have got it all hidden away in their cellars. Anyway, the way the war is going it won't be long before the champers is flowing across the channel. What a celebration *that's* going to be. So what shall we have now?'

We settled on cocktails. I never knew what they were as Victor ordered them. I soon discovered that Charlie did the talking and Victor ordered and paid.

'We'd better go in,' Victor said after we'd had second drinks, 'while there's still something on the menu.'

The dining room, with tables arranged around a small dance floor, was crowded. Those men and women who were not in uniform – and a great many were, especially in Air Force uniforms – were smartly dressed. I was glad I'd done as Esmé had instructed and dressed up. Esmé always had an instinct for knowing exactly what to wear. It was to stay with her all her life. I didn't see her on her deathbed, but I'll wager she was wearing a sexy nightdress and had her make-up on.

It was the kind of hotel Edward could have

afforded to patronize every week of his life, but hardly ever did. He was never one for ostentation. Sometimes I'd wished he was.

Victor hadn't spoken too soon. The menu had started out well, but by the time we sat down to eat, the best dishes had gone. Still, it was wartime; it was what we were used to. And two cocktails apiece had raised our spirits and made food seem less important. Also, there was a bottle of wine to be had, though of indifferent quality.

We danced between courses; Esmé with Charlie, I with Victor. It was wonderful to be dancing again. Victor was good at it and I had lost none of my skill. Once a dancer, always a dancer. In fact, though, none of the dancing was quite as enjoyable as the Sunday School dances of my youth had been. For a start, there wasn't enough room on the postage stamp of a dance-floor; there was no twirling down something the length of the church hall. It was also more sedate; no abandoned stuff here. But then, I'm not sure that any dancing was as exciting as that of my teens. So romantic. All those slow foxtrots – 'I'm in the Mood for Love' and 'Smoke Gets in Your Eyes' danced cheek to cheek.

We stayed as long as we were allowed. We weren't exactly turned out, but the band had played the National Anthem, which seemed a broad enough hint. We were among the last to leave the dining room, and by now the bar was closed, except to those staying in the hotel.

I wasn't the least bit sorry. I'd enjoyed

the evening; it had been a pleasant change, especially the dancing, and I liked Victor, but I was tired and quite sleepy. What I most wanted was to put my head down on a soft pillow and nod off. I dare say that was partly the drink, which I wasn't used to. You don't drink much when you live alone, not if you have any sense. It was also partly, perhaps mainly, because I had young children. Nothing drains one's energy more than spending most of every day in the company of small children. Once they're off to school, that period of deadening fatigue goes. I bounced back as good as new, though I've since discovered that it returns, though not quite to the same extent, when one is old.

'Where shall we go now?' Charlie cried as we left the hotel, arm in arm with Esmé. 'The night is young. What do you say, Esmé?'

'*I* say the night is young!' She articulated clearly in a loud voice, looking as fresh as a daisy. 'We don't wanna go home, do we?' She turned to me. 'We could go to your place, Poppy. That's it everybody, we'll go to Poppy's.'

Victor must have seen the dismay on my face. 'I don't think so,' he said quickly. 'It's been a lovely evening, but it's quite late, and I for one have to make a very early start in the morning. I have to be in Liverpool by nine thirty. You will excuse me, Poppy, won't you?'

'Certainly,' I said. 'Perhaps some other time?'

'Spoil sport,' Esmé said. 'We'll go to Poppy's without you.'

Victor said nothing, the flaw in that suggestion was clear to the rest of us.

'We couldn't get home,' Charlie pointed out gloomily. 'Victor's the one with the car.'

Esmé pulled a face. 'Oh, shame,' she grumbled. 'Are you sure, Victor? Not for just a teensy-weensy bit longer?'

Victor shook his head.

Rather silently, we waited for the concierge to bring the car round to the front entrance.

'Would you like me to put the hood up, sir?' he asked when he arrived. 'It's turned rather cool.'

'Yes, please,' Victor said. 'That would be a good idea.'

Charlie and Esmé got into the back and I snuggled down in the front seat. There were a few giggles and whispers from the back, and then silence, but quite quickly, to my utter chagrin, I fell fast asleep, and didn't wake until I felt a hand on my shoulder.

'Here you are,' Victor said. 'Home. I'm dropping you first because you're the nearest.'

'Thank you for a lovely evening,' I said, trying to pull myself together. 'I did enjoy it.'

'So did I,' Victor said.

He got out of the car and walked with me to the front door, waiting until I'd turned the key in the lock.

'I'm sorry I fell asleep,' I said.

'Don't be. Can I telephone you when I get back from Liverpool?'

'I'd like that,' I told him.

Less than a week later, on a Thursday morning, Victor did telephone me. 'I'm back,' he said. 'When can I come and see you?'

Although he'd mentioned getting in touch with me again at the end of last Saturday's evening out, and I'd agreed to it, I wasn't sure now. I'd had a few days to think it over, and I'd done so quite a bit, but I had this uncertainty about what exactly he was after. I knew nothing about Victor, except that he was, presumably, a friend of Charlie's, which didn't seem a great recommendation. I was pretty certain what Charlie was after with Esmé, and it was not what I wanted.

I longed for companionship and I wanted comfort, but it was much too soon for anything else. Edward had been dead only a matter of months. Maria was not quite three, and I recognized that she was missing her father. Beryl was not yet a year old, and it was difficult to tell whether or not she missed Edward. I knew, however, quite clearly, that whatever *I* wanted, right now – and who could say for how long? – the girls had to be my priority.

It would have been different had I had women friends, but my closest woman friend had always been my mother. Esmé wasn't really in that class. Had we not lived next door to each other as children, attended the school and later shared a passion for dancing, I doubt we'd ever have been friends. I wouldn't have chosen her, nor would she have picked me. Because I had my mother, and she was a young mother – young in years and in her ways – I'd never felt the need for others. And now I regretted it.

Victor must have noticed my hesitation. He repeated his question. 'When may I come and see you? I would like to.'

'It's not easy,' I said. 'I'm nearly always with the children.'

'Does that matter?' he asked. 'Can't I come when the children are there? I like children. I promise not to frighten them.'

I laughed. He made it sound so easy.

'When would you like to come?' I asked him.

'As a matter of fact,' he said, 'I could come this afternoon.'

'Why not?' I said. 'About half past three?'

'I look forward to it,' he said.

So did I. From being cool and wary not many minutes before, I was suddenly like a heroine in a Victorian novel: all of a flutter. I went upstairs and surveyed the meagre wartime contents of my wardrobe, wondering what to wear. No way could I buy anything new; I had used all my clothing coupons. Now if it was *Charlie* who was interested in me, I told myself as I took down a navy skirt and pale-pink blouse from the rail, he would supply me with all the coupons I could ever want. I doubted that Esmé need ever go short of a new dress. But as far as I could judge, Victor was not like that.

I tried on the skirt and blouse. They were passable, except that I'd lost weight since I had last worn them, so I would have to move some buttons. What I didn't like the look of was my hair. It was too long and straggly. It hadn't seen a hairdresser in months.

I went downstairs and into the kitchen, where Jenny was giving the children their mid-morning milk and biscuits – in Beryl's case a Farley's rusk, which would end up a horrible soggy mess on her tray.

'I'm going into town for an hour or so to do a bit of shopping. Is there anything we want?'

'Lots of things,' Jenny said. 'Not that you'll get them.'

'Well, if I see a queue I'll join it,' I said. You never knew exactly what you were queuing for. Last time it had turned out to be kippers, which neither Jenny nor I liked, and the children couldn't eat because of the bones. But I was not on a food search today. My hair was the thing.

I was lucky that my hairdresser squeezed me in between two perms.

'And not before time, Mrs Baxter, if I may say so,' she said, holding up my tresses as if they were dead straw. 'So how do we want it?'

'Do whatever you can, Deirdre,' I told her. 'I'd just like to look glamorous.'

'Really?' she said.

Her eyes met mine in the mirror as she waited for an explanation, which I didn't give her. It was silly, anyway. Why did I want to look glamorous for a perfectly ordinary man I hardly knew who was simply coming to tea? No, the word had just slipped out, though I think it expressed a deep feeling that a great many women had in those last months of the war. We felt drab and tired; we were sick of short rations and make do and mend, and then to those feelings was added guilt because so many people were worse off than we were.

Deirdre worked wonders with my hair.

'I feel a new woman,' I said, tipping her lavishly.

I joined a queue at the baker's and emerged with six small jam tarts and two currant tea-cakes. Did I say currant teacakes? When you came across a currant you jumped up and shouted, 'Hallelujah!'

'Ooh,' Jenny said when I walked in. 'You've had your hair done. You didn't say you were going to the hairdresser.'

I handed her the paper bag. 'I was lucky at the baker's. Which is doubly lucky because a friend's popping in this afternoon. We can give him a cup of tea and a jam tart.'

'A friend?' Jenny queried.

'Mr Worth. You met him the other evening,' I reminded her.

'Oh, you mean the ones who took you out to dinner. Is Mr Worth the tall one or the short one?' she asked.

'The tall one.'

She nodded. 'That's all right then. I didn't think the short one was your style.'

'My style?' I said, nonchalantly. 'I don't know

that either one is my style. Mr Worth just happens to be in the neighbourhood this afternoon and said he'd drop in.'

'Would you like me to take the children out for a walk, then?' Jenny offered. If she'd been Esmé she'd have given me a wink.

'No thank you, Jenny.' I spoke quite firmly. 'I do not wish you to take the children out. In fact, Mr Worth quite wants to meet them. But if you want to be really helpful you can make tea when he comes.'

'Very well, Mrs Baxter,' she said pleasantly.

Usually, she would bridle at being asked to do something not strictly in her line of duty, but I realized she wanted to take a closer look at Victor, and perhaps even hear a snatch of conversation.

She called after me as I was leaving the kitchen. 'Shall I put out the best china?'

I pretended not to hear. The trouble with Jenny was, she read too many women's magazines.

Victor rang the bell at exactly three thirty.

'I'll go,' Jenny called from the hall.

I let her do so. It would not look good for two of us to rush to the door.

'Mr Worth, madam,' she said, showing him into the sitting room.

Madam? When had Jenny ever called me madam? She must be playing some kind of role.

Victor stepped forward and shook hands with me. That was strange, also, for a man with whom

I'd been dancing, held close, only a few days before, but I suppose he was picking up on the atmosphere. Jenny continued to stand there.

'Thank you, Jenny,' I said, playing her at her own game, 'that will be all.'

'Shall I take the children?' she asked.

'No thank you. They're fine.'

Beryl, crawling on the rug, ignored Victor. Maria, who was sitting at her own low table, gave him a cursory look, then went back to what she'd been doing, which was scribbling with coloured crayons.

'Perhaps you would make some tea, Jenny,' I said. She knew perfectly well what she was required to do. It had all been decided. She gave Victor a winning smile, then left.

'Do sit down, Victor,' I said.

I took a seat in the bay window and he sat in an armchair near by.

'Do you often go to Liverpool?' I asked. It was simply something to say.

'From time to time,' he answered.

I didn't really know what his job was. I had gathered from Esmé, the day after our evening in Harrogate, and she had heard it from Charlie, that he worked for the government, and that it was to do with armaments and was therefore hush-hush. She thought he might be some kind of an inspector, and if that was true it would explain why, though he seemed fit and healthy and was only in his thirties, he wasn't in the armed forces. He himself offered no explanation.

'It's a fine city,' he said, 'but it's taken a battering. What did your husband do?' he asked, changing the subject.

I told him about Paragon and explained how it worked.

'And has it kept going well during the war?' he enquired.

'Oh, very well,' I said. 'In a way, better than ever. People seem to need it. Of course, we've had staff shortages as the men were called up, but most of the jobs can be done by women, or older people, and the traders we deal with weren't exactly piled high with goods, but we managed quite well.'

'And do you take any part?' he asked.

'Not any longer. I used to, before I was married. As a matter of fact—'

I broke off as Jenny came into the room, pushing the tea trolley. I didn't particularly want her to hear what I'd been about to say. In fact, I wasn't quite sure why I was telling Victor, but somehow it seemed natural.

'Thank you, Jenny,' I said. 'I'll pour. Have you brought milk for the children?'

'Yes, madam,' she said.

'I'll ring when I want more hot water,' I told her.

It was all quite ridiculous. By now very few people had maidservants. No young woman would be expected to carry jugs of hot water from the kitchen to the drawing room for an able-bodied employer. We were all equal.

'You were about to say?' Victor began when Jenny had gone.

'Oh, yes. Do you take milk and sugar?'

'Milk,' he said. 'And you'll be pleased to hear I don't take sugar.'

I handed him his tea and then offered him the plate of jam tarts.

'Thank you,' he said. 'A real treat.'

'You were about to tell me what you did at Paragon,' he added.

'I wasn't, actually,' I corrected him. 'I was about to say that I was considering selling it. I've had a very good offer.'

'That *is* interesting,' he said, biting into a jam tart. I noticed that a little jam had attached itself to his moustache. Not a thin, spiv-like moustache, but a medium-sized, reddish-brown one, neatly cut. 'Do you think that would be a wise move?'

'I don't know,' I admitted. 'That's why I say I'm *considering* it. I'm not sure. But I don't really want to own something I don't take any part in.'

'Couldn't you play a part in it?' he asked. 'Women do all kinds of things now that they didn't do a few years ago.'

'I know,' I acknowledged. 'But women with small children are still tied to the home. I dare say they always will be. Will you have another jam tart?' He still had a small blob of raspberry jam on his moustache. If he didn't lick it off before it was time for him to leave, I would have to tell him.

He took another tart.

'I must give the children a drink of milk,' I said. 'Though nothing jammy until they're back in the kitchen.'

I poured a little milk into two small mugs, then picked up Beryl and sat her on my lap.

'Maria want drink,' my elder daughter demanded.

'Maria must wait,' I said. 'I have to see to Beryl first.'

'Let me see to Maria,' Victor said. He seemed quite eager.

'If you wish,' I said. 'If you put it on her table she can manage on her own, but she wants watching. Actually, what she wants is the attention. She doesn't like too much of it going to Beryl.'

'Then she can have my attention,' Victor said.

He put the mug of milk on Maria's table, then knelt down beside her. It seemed a long way down for a man so tall, but he was quite at ease. So was Maria. She was never shy with strangers. I think she saw them as yet more people who would do something for her, amuse her, whatever. And usually they did, though I hadn't expected it of Victor. But then, I didn't know anything about him, did I? For all I knew he could be married, have children of his own somewhere. Liverpool, perhaps? Was that why he went there?

No, I decided, it was not. He had no trace of

a Liverpool accent, or, in fact, of any north-country area. So where did he come from? That was something else I didn't know about him.

'You seem to have a way with children,' I said. Maria was making it plain that she wanted him to hold the mug to her lips, as I was doing for Beryl, and this he was quite pleasantly refusing to do. 'You're a big girl now,' he said. 'You can do it yourself.' And she did.

'You don't have children, do you?' I enquired.

'No,' he said. 'And I'm not married. But my sister has three. I don't see them, or her, now as often as I'd like to. They live too far away. In Brighton.'

'I've never been to Brighton,' I confessed. 'Indeed, I've not been to many places at all, though I did once go to Paris.'

My honeymoon in Paris had been only seven years before, yet it seemed as if it had been in another lifetime. I suppose anything that had happened before the war had that sort of feeling about it.

'You'd like Brighton,' Victor said.

'I expect I would,' I agreed. 'It always sounds interesting. Shall you go back there ever?'

'I don't know,' he said. 'My job ends when the war ends, but I don't know what I'll do, or where I'll do it.'

'It's going to be strange, isn't it?' I said. 'We shall all be living new lives, even if we're living them in the same place. Nothing will be the same.' But wherever my new life was, I thought, it would contain Alun. I would take him with me. And Alun was the reason why I would never want to leave Akersfield. It was the only place I had ever known him.

We chatted, Victor and I, for a little while longer – he was easy to talk to – and then the children grew restless. Beryl sat on the rug, threw her toys as far as she could, then started to grizzle, and Maria, with one sweep of her arms, sent her crayons flying across the floor.

'Maria hungry,' she announced.

'I'm sorry,' I said to Victor. 'I expect they both are, actually. They usually have a good meal at this time of day. It helps them to sleep better through the night. I'll hand them over to Jenny for a while.'

'No, don't do that, not unless you want to,' Victor said. 'In any case, I must be on my way. Thank you very much, Poppy. I've enjoyed myself, and I've enjoyed meeting the children.'

He stood up, as did I, and I accompanied him to the door.

'I wonder,' he said, standing on the doorstep, 'would you let me take you out to dinner somewhere?'

'Thank you. I'd like that,' I said.

'Not with Charlie and Esmé – unless that's what you'd prefer?'

'It isn't,' I said quickly. Charlie and Esmé had served their purpose, but I didn't want a repeat performance. Victor was a much nicer person without them.

'Then what about Thursday?' he asked. 'I have to be in Manchester the following week.'

'Thursday would be fine,' I told him. 'And can I say something else?'

'Certainly,' he said.

'You have a spot of jam on your moustache,' I told him.

'Thank you,' he said, and brought out an immaculate handkerchief.

'Let me,' I said. I took it from him, wiped away the offending jam, then handed it back.

As he walked down the drive I closed the door, went back into the sitting room and watched while he got into his elegant car and drove away.

17

Beryl came into the house, not expecting to see anyone. She liked to be up first and have the place to herself for a while, even when it was someone else's place. Seeing Joe, she came to a sudden stop and raised her hand to her rollers as if she had been caught indecently clad.

'Good heavens!' she said. 'You're here already. You quite startled me. I didn't hear the car. I thought you'd be ages yet.'

'Hi, Beryl!' Joe said, giving her a kiss. 'Great to see you. How are you?'

'Very well, thank you, Joe.' He always called her Beryl, never Aunt Beryl. She liked that. It made her feel acceptable. All the same . . .

'We expected you yesterday.' There was a slight note of reprimand in her voice.

'I know,' Joe said. 'I wanted to get here, but I had to finish some work.'

What kind of work did Joe have that could possibly keep him from anything he really wanted to do, Beryl asked herself. It sometimes seemed that all you had to do to be the favourite was to live 3,000 miles away, and then she chided herself for the thought.

'Well, you're here now,' she said. 'And it's nice to see you. I must say, I fully intended to be bathed and dressed and have your breakfast ready to be served by the time you arrived.'

'You look fine,' Joe assured her. 'Younger than ever.'

'I don't think I want breakfast,' Mervyn said. 'I'm going to bed for a couple of hours.'

She looked at him. Poor Mervyn; he did look rough. 'You'll sleep better and wake more refreshed if you have some food inside you,' she advised. 'If you don't want the whole works, then I could do you a lightly boiled egg and some toast.'

She will probably cut his toast into soldiers and let him dip them in the yolk, Poppy thought.

'Well, OK. Thank you. That's really very kind of you,' Mervyn said.

'What about you, Joe?' Beryl asked. 'You must be hungry. I dare say you didn't eat at all on the plane.'

'You've got that right, Beryl. I didn't. So what is the whole works?' Joe asked.

'Bacon, eggs, fried bread, mushrooms, tomatoes, or any combination from that.'

'Sounds great,' Joe said. 'I'll have the lot.'

Beryl beamed at him. She was never more

pleased than when she was putting good food into someone.

'What about you, Mummy?' she enquired. 'Can I tempt you? You know you never eat enough.'

'I can't eat the whole selection,' Poppy admitted, 'but I'll have one piece of bacon and an egg. I like my eggs—'

'Mummy, I *know* how you like your eggs. Flipped over and fried both sides.'

'That's right, dear. Oh, and perhaps a small piece of fried bread.'

'Good.' Beryl was now well on the way to happiness. 'You'll need to keep up your strength today,' she reminded Poppy. 'We all will. There's going to be a great deal to do.'

And you will no doubt organize us into doing it, Poppy thought.

'On the other hand,' Beryl said, 'it's not for you to do a lot. You're the birthday girl, remember? I'm sure you can leave it to the rest of us.'

'How kind,' Poppy said. 'And, in fact, I'll have to take some time out because Joe wants to paint my portrait. What do you think of that?'

'Your portrait? How wonderful.' Beryl turned to Joe. 'And I'm sure the minute you set eyes on her you'll just long to paint Daisy. You've not yet seen Daisy. She's an artist's dream, the most darling baby, isn't she?' She looked around for agreement, and received it. How could anyone deny her?

'There you are,' she said. 'We all think the

same. Or better still, Joe, you might like to do a mother-and-child portrait. Fiona and Daisy. That would be rather sweet.'

'I'll see how much time I have,' Joe said. 'Poppy is the first priority. It's a birthday portrait.'

Beryl busied herself at the stove. 'I shall cook your breakfast first,' she said to Joe. 'You must be hungry.'

'I am,' Joe admitted. 'Thanks.'

'In the meantime,' Poppy said, 'do you want to freshen up, or would you rather just take a look at the newspaper?' He suddenly looked too tired for any further small talk.

'I'll freshen up,' he said. 'Maybe then I'll take a look at one of your scandalous British papers. I didn't get to see one on the plane. They ran out.'

As he left the room, Beryl called after him, 'Don't be too long.'

Poppy joined Beryl at the stove. 'Can I do anything?' she offered.

'Not a thing. Not this morning.' Beryl was emphatic.

'I could pour some orange juice?'

'All right,' Beryl conceded. 'You can do that.'

'How is Rodney this morning?' Poppy asked Beryl. 'Is his ankle still painful?'

'I don't know,' Beryl said. 'I was careful not to wake him. Neither of us had a good night. He complained that I knocked into him and made his ankle twice as bad, poor lamb. In the end, I left him and went to sleep in one of the single bunks.'

'Poor Rodney,' Poppy said. 'He'll have to take it easy today.'

'Yes,' Beryl agreed. 'Though he could manage sitting-down jobs. Peeling potatoes and such like.'

'That doesn't sound very exciting,' Poppy pulled a face.

'It doesn't, does it? But then, as we all know, my Rodney will do anything for anyone. He's *too* willing, as I keep on telling him.'

Presently, Joe returned. Poppy handed him the paper. 'I'm afraid you'll have to make do with *The Times*.' Beryl broke an egg into the frying pan and flicked the hot fat over it.

'You'd better come and see if this egg's right for you, Joe,' she said.

He came over and looked at it.

'Sunny side up. Perfect,' he assured her.

She dished up his breakfast and set it in front of him before turning her attention to Mervyn's toast. His egg was boiling in the pan. Poppy would be served in due course. Whether Joe had been hungry or not, Beryl was a lady who always served the men first, no matter what. She would have served Prince Philip before the Queen.

'Are *you* going to eat, Beryl?' Poppy asked.

'All in good time,' Beryl said. She was also a lady who made a point of serving herself last, with whatever happened to be left. On this occasion it was one small piece of bacon, an egg, the yolk of which had broken on dropping it into the pan, and two mushrooms. The fried bread and tomatoes had run out.

'That doesn't look much, Beryl,' Joe said.

'I'm fine,' Beryl said. 'Really, I am.'

She was, too. These small sacrifices fed her happiness, especially if they happened to be noticed.

'That was very good!' Mervyn said presently, pushing his plate away. 'And now I really must go to bed. I'll set the alarm for eleven o'clock, and I'll be down to do whatever you require. I expect Maria will be down soon. If she's not awake yet, she will be when I get into bed.' He would like his wife to dally a little with him in bed, but there was little chance of that.

'I'll take myself off, as well,' Joe said.

'First give me ten minutes to get the room ready,' Poppy said. 'You're going to have my bed this morning, but you'll be somewhere else tonight.'

'That's OK by me,' Joe said. 'Whatever you say.'

By the time Poppy had returned and Joe had left the kitchen, Maria had drifted downstairs wearing a robe of black silk, embroidered with exotic flowers and birds of paradise, with matching slippers. Sounds of life, including small cries from Baby Daisy, could be heard from Fiona's bedroom.

'Good morning, Ma. Happy birthday,' Maria said. 'So where's my son?'

'Gone to bed,' Poppy said.

'Oh. Well, I did just think he might have waited to say hi to his mother,' Maria complained. 'But that's children for you, isn't it?'

'He was very tired,' Poppy said. To her way of thinking, Maria could have been on the scene to greet her son.

'Speaking of one's children,' Beryl said, 'since Fiona and David and the baby will be down any minute, and Georgia is presumably still asleep in the sitting room, she'll need to be woken, won't she?'

'Will she?' Maria said laconically. She seated herself at the table and poured a cup of coffee. 'But she's no longer a child, is she? I don't see it as part of my duty to wake her up in the morning.'

'In the circumstances,' Poppy said mildly, 'I think someone should, though no doubt Daisy will do that efficiently once she's down. I'll look in on her, shall I?' It would be kinder than having her woken by the full blast of Fiona and Daisy.

'That's kind of you, Ma,' Maria said, yawning. 'Have you all had breakfast?'

'We have,' Beryl said. 'It's all there, on the side.' She waved a hand in the direction of the eggs, the frying pan and the loaf of bread. 'And there's more bacon in the fridge.' Much as she enjoyed feeding the multitude, no way was she going to include Maria in that.

Maria shuddered and averted her gaze.

'I couldn't eat a morsel of *that*,' she said.

'I'll go and wake Georgia.' Poppy made her escape.

She tapped on the door of the sitting room, then, receiving no reply, went in.

Georgia lay on her side, her arm hanging down from the camp bed, the bedclothes pushed aside so that her shoulders and the upper part of her body were bare. She was fast asleep, her long dark eyelashes splayed against the flawless pale skin of her cheeks, her mouth ever so slightly open, her breathing quiet and even. She looked about twelve years old, untouched and vulnerable. She was quite beautiful.

This is the Georgia I know, Poppy thought.

She touched her granddaughter on her shoulder and spoke gently. 'Georgia, darling, It's time to wake up.'

'What? What's the matter?' Georgia said. Her eyes remained closed.

'Nothing's the matter, darling, except that any minute now Fiona will be down with the baby. You might want to be out of the way. The bathroom, perhaps?'

Georgia opened her eyes, troubled eyes, and looked at Poppy.

'Oh, shit!' she said. 'Shit, shit, shit!' The words sounded strange from her lovely morning-fresh face.

'What is it?' Poppy asked.

'I was dreaming I was in New York,' Georgia said. 'And I'm not.'

'Only a few more days,' Poppy said.

'Sorry. It's not you Poppy. It's just that . . .'

'I understand,' Poppy said. 'Now, if you'll get off to the bathroom, dear, I'll clear away your bed.'

'OK. Thanks. Hey, I just remembered. Happy birthday, Poppy.'

'When you've had your shower,' Poppy called after her, 'go to the kitchen and have a proper breakfast.'

She folded the sheets and blanket. She must stack them, and the bed, somewhere out of the way to make space for the playpen. The proper place for the camp bed was in the loft, which was accessible only from the room where Joe was now sleeping and she had no intention of disturbing him. She would dump it on the upstairs landing. Heigh-ho.

Camp bed in one hand, bedding and pillow under the other arm, she made for the stairs. Fiona was halfway down, carrying a whimpering Daisy in one arm and a bundle of dirty washing in the other.

'For goodness' sake!' Poppy said. 'You should *not* come down the stairs without a free hand for the banister, or at least not when you're carrying baby. Stay exactly where you are; I'll take Daisy.'

'You could take the washing,' Fiona suggested. 'Give it to Mummy. Happy birthday, Poppy darling.'

Poppy put down the camp bed and took the

bundle of washing. At the same moment Beryl, her ear finely attuned to any sound made by her granddaughter, rushed in from the kitchen.

'Daisy,' she cried, 'come to Grandma.'

Her cry fell on unreceptive ears. Daisy was caught up in exercising her lungs in the way best known to her.

In the very next second a shower of envelopes fell through the letterbox and landed on the mat, thus diverting Beryl.

'Oh, Mummy, the post,' she cried. 'Let me pick it up for you.'

'If you don't mind, dear,' Poppy said swiftly, 'I'd rather like to do that myself. It's kind of you, but I can still bend down to the floor. What you *can* do, if you like, is relieve me of the dirty laundry.'

Without waiting for Beryl's likes or dislikes, she thrust the bundle into her daughter's hands. What Beryl doesn't understand, Poppy thought – and why should she? – is that I have my own way of dealing with the post. She had her ritual, always mildly enjoyable, and today it would be more exciting because of it being her birthday.

Following her usual procedure she bent down and picked up each envelope separately, scrutinizing it, hazarding a guess as to what it contained and, if the sender's address was not printed on the outside, wondering who it was from. She preferred not to open any envelope until she had decided that. Then, following this preliminary inspection she would divide the envelopes into separate piles: appeals from charities – always the largest category, which would have to be subdivided into those she regularly supported, those she never supported and the few who merited further thought; gas, electric and telephone bills; mail-order catalogues – subdivided in much the same way as charities; leaflets – why were leaflets part of the post? – offering home or car insurance or the loan of large sums of money, and, lastly, personal mail. This category usually yielded the smallest harvest, but today was different. There were lots of large, stiff envelopes, some of them brightly coloured, and in every case her address was handwritten. Her method of dealing with the post had driven poor Edward mad, but she found it most satisfactory.

Joe lay in bed in his grandmother's spare room and waited for sleep. Though he could have fallen asleep at any point on the journey from the airport, or laid down his head on the breakfast table and nodded off, now that he was comfortable, the pillow soft, the curtains drawn, sleep eluded him.

He wondered where Anna was and what she was doing. He counted back the hours and decided that she would still be fast asleep in their bed. Or was she, too, awake and thinking of him? He did love her, though. They were so happy together. But then, he'd known the first time he'd set eyes on her that she was something special.

It had been in his mother's salon – the one on 17th Street. He'd been in the neighbourhood and had called in for a haircut. It was the one he usually went to because he liked the stylist and knew most of the staff, but Anna, seated at the reception desk, was new to him.

'Good morning, sir,' she'd said, with a wide smile that lit up her dark eyes and revealed teeth his father would have approved of. Her skin was the colour of *café au lait*, and glowed with health; her hair, close-cropped and curly, enhanced the shape of her head.

'I'd like a haircut,' he'd said.

'Do you have an appointment?' she'd asked.

He hadn't. He never had.

'My mother's always telling me I should be like other people, and make appointments,' he'd said.

Afterwards, she'd told him that she'd wondered why this otherwise normal-seeming young man was subject to his mother's advice. She'd have understood it better if he'd said, 'My wife'.

She pored over the appointments book before saying 'I'm sorry, sir, there doesn't seem to be a space anywhere.'

That had been the moment when Linda came back to the desk.

'Hi, Joe,' she'd said. 'I'm afraid Karl is on vacation. Do you mind if it's someone else?'

'Not at all,' he'd said. 'But I hear you're booked solid. Maybe I'll come back tomorrow?'

'No way, Joe,' Linda said. 'We'll fit you in somehow. Why don't you grab a seat.' She'd turned to Anna. 'Give Joe a coffee. Black, no sugar. I'll have a word with Raymond, see what he can do. Oh, by the way, Joe, you just missed your mother.'

He'd moved away and taken a seat. Anna had told him the next bit.

'Which one was his mother?' she'd asked Linda.

'He's Maria's son,' Linda said. 'A real nice guy. A pleasure to serve. Doesn't expect to be treated like the president.'

It had been Anna who'd come across to him a few minutes later, carrying coffee in an elegant white china mug.

'Raymond can do your hair in fifteen minutes, if that's OK?' she'd said.

'That's fine.'

'I'm sorry,' she'd said. 'I didn't know you. I'm new here.'

'No problem,' he'd assured her.

'It's my first day,' she'd confessed. 'I haven't done this sort of job before.'

He'd asked her what her usual job was.

'I'm a dancer,' she'd told him. 'Or an actress. Or preferably both – whenever I get the chance. In between I have to do whatever I can.'

He knew his mother frequently employed temporary staff, as receptionists, making coffee and running errands. They were quite often out-of-work actresses, and attractive, but not one had ever struck him like Anna. He'd watched her walk away. She was small and slender and moved elegantly, head held high; in fact, like a dancer. But she had something extra. He didn't know how to describe it, even to himself. Charisma perhaps.

Everything had moved quickly between them after that. Within a short time she had moved in with him. The thing was, they'd been so certain of each other. They still were.

She'd met his parents at their home. Mervyn had been courteous and welcoming, his mother courteous, but not quite so welcoming, not of Anna into her home, but of her into her son's life, and seemingly so permanently. Joe didn't know why and he wouldn't ask; he didn't want it to be an issue. He didn't think it was the fact that she was black. Was it because she worked for his mother? The only clue his mother had given was to ask him if moving in together wasn't a little too much, too soon. And, she had persisted, what did Anna's parents think? He had to be honest, he didn't know. Her parents lived in Washington and he hadn't met them or questioned Anna about their reaction, though they were aware of the relationship.

He and Anna had debated whether or not she should come to England with him for Poppy's birthday to meet the family en masse. Anna hadn't been sure that such a celebration would be the right time, but all that had been decided for them when she'd been offered a part in an off-Broadway musical. A smallish part – some dancing and a few lines – but there was no way she'd turn it down, nor would he want her to.

He'd have liked Poppy and Anna to meet. They'd have got on well. In some ways they were alike, both women of independent thought and action, and Poppy, he thought, had something of the actress in her, something which attracted attention. Style.

There was a feeling in the family – he had heard it touched on, but no more – that Poppy had had a racy past. Well, after all, three husbands! She could hardly have been a shrinking violet! And how many boyfriends had there been after her third husband had decamped? She'd been in her late fifties then. He couldn't imagine that in the last twenty years she'd had no relationships with the opposite sex.

But he would never know. He doubted any of them ever would. Way to go, Poppy!

His thoughts went back to Anna. He closed his eyes and slept.

And was Mervyn asleep? He was not. Mervyn was sexually frustrated, on this occasion because he had totally failed to persuade Maria to stay in bed long enough for them to make love. Worse than that, she had laughed at him; laughed outright!

'Don't be silly,' she said. 'In this house, with people swarming all over the place?'

'They're not swarming in here,' he'd said. 'We're quite private. And in any case, it's normal for married people to make love.'

There was very little sex in his life these days. He could hardly remember the last time. And on the very rare occasions when she made the first move, as rare as snow in summer, she always managed to pick the times when he was too tired to perform, and she didn't let him forget it.

He had hoped that, now they were away for a few days, relaxed, and not tied to business, it might just happen.

He watched her get out of bed and put on her robe. She was an attractive woman; she still had the power to excite him. But was she still attracted to him? Did *he* still have the power?

'Go back to sleep,' she said as she left the room. 'It will cool you down.'

Why was it like this? he asked himself. He had given her everything she could possibly want, and more. She had never gone short of anything. There had been no necessity for her to work, but he had supported her when she had made that choice. He had always been faithful to her, never looked anywhere else, though he could have, a man in his position. He had had his chances. Had she also had hers? He'd been tied to his job; perhaps he hadn't taken enough notice.

No, he was not a happy man. He took a couple of sleeping tablets, popped them in his mouth, and lay back against the pillows, waiting for sleep to come to him.

Poppy, Maria and Beryl sat at the kitchen table. Poppy had skimmed through her birthday cards – there were a surprising number – and would have put them away to be brought out and gloated over later, when she was alone, except that Beryl said, 'Oh no, Mummy, we must put them on show. In the sitting room I think, but a little later. For the moment we must sort out what's to be done and who's going to do it.'

'Very well,' Poppy said. She had no real objection to sitting back and being told what to do, knowing full well that if she didn't want to do something, she just wouldn't. But there was no point in saying that so early in the day.

'I'll make a nice cup of coffee for the three of us,' Beryl said. 'Practically everything is better when discussed over a cup of coffee. And then we'll look at the menu. You have written out a menu, Mummy dear?'

'Of course,' Poppy said. 'I'll get it.' It was on the dresser. 'And I've done the shopping for it.'

Beryl rose to her feet to make the coffee, Poppy moved to get the menu and Maria stayed where she was and continued to read the *Daily Mail*.

The back door opened and Edith Prince walked in, hung about with shopping bags.

'Sorry I'm a bit late, Mrs Marsh,' she said. 'Blame the buses.'

'I always do,' Poppy said.

'Happy birthday,' Edith said. 'And here's a little present. I hope you like it.'

Poppy would have preferred not to open it in Edith's presence. Being the recipient of birthday and Christmas gifts from her for several years, she was full of foreboding.

'Do open it,' Edith said, standing beside her. 'I want to see how you like it.'

Poppy did so. It was a lumpy parcel and she had no idea what it might be, but when the layers of flowered gift-wrap paper and several layers of tissue were removed, there it was in all its glory.

There was a short silence while four pairs of eyes took it in. Poppy was the first to break the silence. 'My goodness,' she said. 'Will you just look at that.'

It was a cart, the kind of cart a flower vendor might push, with deep sides and two large wheels. It was made of black plastic, designed to look like wrought iron, but failing to do so. It was filled to the top, and overflowing, with roses fashioned from puce pink and egg-yolk yellow pieces of sponge, one or two of which trailed artistically down the sides of the cart. Above it, going from stem to stern, was a banner which read, 'Happy Eightieth, Mrs Marsh'.

'My goodness,' Poppy repeated. 'This is something *else*.'

'I knew you'd like it,' Edith said. 'As soon as I laid eyes on it, I said to Ernie, "That's just the ticket for Mrs Marsh." I know how fond you are of flowers.'

'Thank you *very* much,' Poppy said. 'I shall treasure it.' And, of course, from one point of view she would. It had been chosen in all sincerity.

It reminded her vividly of an earlier birthday, when the girls had been young. They had saved their pennies and prevailed upon the Edith Prince of that era to take them to Woolworth's, where they had purchased a passe-partout framed portrait of outstanding hideosity; a crude and saccharine picture of a Continental saint – French or Spanish, perhaps – wrapped about with Madonna-blue draperies and wreathed in flowers. The girls had been ecstatic about it – for once they had agreed on something – and at their fervent request, she had hung it in a conspicuous spot in her carefully furnished sitting room.

For years she had found herself apologizing, in private, to friends for its presence. In the end, it was the girls themselves who administered the *coup de grâce*.

'Mummy,' Maria had said, 'how can you *bear* that awful picture on your wall?'

'I quite agree,' Beryl had said.

With a feigned show of reluctance, Poppy had removed it. She had no idea what had happened to it in the end.

'Thank you very much, Edith,' she said again. 'I shall find a suitable place to put it.'

'I wondered about the table in the hall,' Edith suggested. 'Just as you come in the door.'

As she struggled for a reply, the doors from the hall and the back door opened simultaneously on to the kitchen, Rodney hobbling in from the outside and Fiona, with Daisy in her arms, entering from the hall.

'Good morning, everyone,' Fiona said cheerfully. 'Wave a happy birthday to Great-grandma,' she instructed her daughter. 'And to Grandpa with a poorly ankle.' Perversely, Daisy turned her head away from the entire company.

'She wants her cereal,' Fiona explained.

'I'll get it, darling,' Beryl offered, jumping up from her seat.

'Really, Beryl, do you have to?' Maria demanded. 'Can't Fiona get her own child's breakfast? We're supposed to be sorting things out.'

'If I want to offer to give a hand with my own grandchild,' Beryl said, 'I'm quite entitled to do so.'

Before anyone could reply, David strode into the kitchen. 'Who's in the bathroom?' he said. 'I've been waiting for absolutely ages.'

No-one answered. Beryl did a head count and said, 'It has to be Georgia.'

'In that case, David,' Maria said, 'don't hold your breath waiting. Georgia can take for ever, just brushing her teeth.' She turned to Poppy. 'Ma, why did you never have that second bathroom put in?'

'I don't know, dear,' Poppy admitted. 'I just didn't get around to it, I suppose. And I never felt the need. I don't often have people staying. Certainly not a dozen!'

'It's just as well Jeremy and Megan slept elsewhere,' Maria said.

Beryl looked at her watch. 'They should be here by now. What *can* they be doing?'

In the silence which followed, Beryl realized that everyone was looking at her.

'Well,' Rodney said quickly, coming to her rescue, 'what about breakfast? I reckon I missed a meal last night.'

'I'll see to it,' Beryl said. 'Four of you, including Georgia. Does Georgia eat breakfast?' she asked Maria.

'Who knows?' Maria said. 'My daughter's a law unto herself. If I were to tell you she'd have breakfast, then she wouldn't. And vice versa.'

Edith Prince stood in the middle of the kitchen and spoke. 'May I make a suggestion, Mrs Marsh?' She looked directly at Poppy, ignoring everyone else. 'Why don't *I* make the breakfasts, and the rest of you clear out of the kitchen.' *My* kitchen is what she meant. 'And I'll see to the baby first.'

'Well, that sounds like a good idea, Mrs Prince,' Beryl said. 'If you're sure?'

Edith ignored her. 'Does that suit you, Mrs Marsh?' she asked.

'Ideally,' Poppy said.

'We could take Georgia's into the bathroom,' David muttered.

'So why don't you and I and Maria go into the dining room and discuss the menu and who's to do what?' Beryl said to her mother.

18

Thursday's dinner was the first of many I had with Victor. In between his trips around the country and beyond – he seemed to cover a wide area and was away from home for part of every week – he would call me and arrange to take me out. Sometimes it was at quite short notice, as on a Wednesday about six weeks after our first meeting. The telephone rang at half past ten in the morning.

'I'm in Sheffield,' Victor said. 'I shall finish earlier than I expected. I didn't plan to be home until tomorrow, but there's a late-afternoon train. I could be back in time to go to the pictures, or we could have a meal. If you've nothing better to do, I mean.'

How could I possibly have had anything better to do? Except when Victor was on the scene, each day was like every other, but he always made that polite sort of approach, as if my life were one long, mad social whirl and I would have to consult my diary to see if I could possibly fit him in. Naturally, I never told him that my diary was a succession of blank pages, with the occasional dental appointment. However, I hesitated a little, as a matter of form.

'Actually . . .' I began.

'Of course if it's not—'

'Oh, I didn't mean . . .' I broke in quickly. She who hesitates is lost, and I didn't intend to lose the chance of an evening out. 'I mean, I just have to be sure about Jenny.'

I knew perfectly well that it was Jenny's evening off, and that she would be away like the wind to meet her boyfriend, Ken. But I also knew how to counter that: if I gave her permission to entertain Ken at the house, she would probably leap at the chance – two or three hours, children permitting, of privacy, and in comfort. But until I was sure . . . . They might have tickets for something or other, or be going to a dance, though the latter was unlikely on a Wednesday.

'Assume that she is OK and come,' I said to Victor. 'If she's not, you'll have had a wasted journey.' Of course, I could have asked him to dinner, but that wasn't what I wanted.

'Not wasted,' Victor said. 'What would you like to do?'

'Whatever,' I told him.

'Then think about it and tell me when I arrive,' he said. 'What are you doing now?'

'Maria is out with Jenny, which is why I can't check what she's doing, and I've just put Beryl down for her mid-morning sleep.'

'So early in the day?' There spoke a man who'd never had children.

'It doesn't seem early to me,' I told him. 'They both wake before six, and there's no peace after that.'

'So what are you going to do now?' he wanted to know.

'This and that. There's always something.'

Actually, what I would do in view of the evening ahead was wash my hair, as there was no time to go into town, iron my best blouse and have a nice bath, throwing in a few precious drops of the Coty's L'Aimant he'd brought me back from one of his trips.

'I'll go home and collect the car and be with you around seven,' he said.

Victor never used his car for business trips. Whoever laid down the rules wouldn't permit petrol for that; he had to use the train, which he said he didn't mind. He always travelled first class anyway.

There was no difficulty with Jenny. She was delighted to be offered the house, especially when I said she could make Ken something to eat from whatever she could find in the larder. 'As long as you don't use all the rations,' I cautioned her. She seemed serious about Ken. She'd been going out with him for two months now, which was a long time for Jenny, who liked variety. She had also taken him to meet her mother – a serious step in Akersfield – who apparently didn't take to him.

Victor arrived at half past six. The children were bathed and in their pyjamas, ready to be put to bed, and Jenny had promised to read Maria a story. Beryl, thumb in mouth, always listened to the story, though she could have had no idea what it was about. I suppose the voice, either Jenny's or mine, sent her to sleep.

Victor and I looked at the *Akersfield Courier*, then decided that since there was nothing we wanted to see at the pictures we would have a meal somewhere.

Victor drove out of town and took the road north. We stopped at an inn in a small village on the edge of the moors.

'We should be all right here,' Victor said. 'There won't be anything fancy, just plain, good food; they're supplied by the neighbouring farm.'

We were shown to a table in the far corner of the bar. Victor was right about the food. We ate thick slices of home-cured ham, grilled to perfection, with eggs and tender young broad beans. It was a feast that left little room for the apple pie which followed, but we managed that, too. When it was finished, we sat back with satisfied smiles and waited for the coffee.

'Did things go well in Sheffield?' I asked.

'Very well,' Victor said. 'I'm almost at the stage of winding things down now. My part of the job is nearly over.'

'So what will you do next?' I said. 'Do you have plans?'

The coffee came; there was real cream. We busied ourselves, pouring, stirring, passing the sugar. Victor didn't answer my question immediately. In the end, when he'd taken his first sip of coffee, he said, 'I do. I want to start up on my own. I want to make my own decisions and follow my own rules, not someone else's. I feel I've spent too long being told where to go and what to do. Well, we all have, haven't we? That's wartime for you.'

'I suppose so.' I had never suspected this streak of rebellion in Victor. He seemed so in charge of himself. 'And how would you do that?' I enquired.

'I'm not totally sure,' he admitted. 'Whatever I do it has to be something I can take a real part in. I don't want to just sit back, watch the money and keep the books. The trouble is, I'm not certain exactly what I'm capable of, what I'd be best at, though I did wonder . . .' he hesitated.

'Yes?'

'I wondered about a guest house, or more probably a small hotel.'

He saw the expression on my face. I wasn't quick enough to hide it.

'Why do you look so surprised?' he asked.

'Do I? I don't know.' I floundered a bit. 'I suppose because it's something I'd never have thought of.'

'Well, I have,' he said. 'I know what's wanted.' He was a bit on the defensive. 'I've stayed in enough places up and down the country, and I usually find myself thinking how *I* would run it if it were mine. A lot of it's common sense and employing the right people.'

'Wouldn't it cost an awful lot to start up?' I asked. I knew Victor ran an expensive car and dressed well. He was also a most generous man – meals, drinks, presents for me and the children, always half-crown seats at the pictures, and once, when we went to the theatre, seats in the stalls – but I had no idea whether he was rich or not. I had never seen his house.

He shrugged. 'Quite likely. I might have to take on a guest house rather than a small hotel, but if I worked at that and made it pay, I could always move on to something better. I have a certain amount of capital. Enough to get me started, I think.'

'I see. Well, this is all a big surprise. Shall I pour you more coffee?' I was trying to be cool, though I wasn't happy inside. This was a Victor I didn't know.

He passed his cup and I refilled it.

'Where would you do this?' I asked.

He didn't answer at once. In fact, he looked embarrassed, or uncertain, as if he didn't know what to say.

'Would you like a liqueur?' he said quickly. 'A cherry brandy or something? I expect they'll have something hidden away.'

'No, thank you,' I said. He knew I never took liqueurs; I don't like them. 'But don't mind me if you want one.'

'I think I will,' he said. He called the landlord over and asked if a small brandy would be possible, which it was.

When he had the brandy and had taken the first sip, I repeated my question. 'Where would you do this? I mean, open a hotel.'

'Well,' he said. 'Well, I really don't think Akersfield would be the ideal place, not for what I have in mind. I envisage a place people will flock to for the holidays. Families and newly-weds. There'll be so many newly-weds once the men come home. And all the people who've had to stay put in this country haven't had a holiday in years. They'll be looking for a place with a bit of style.'

'And where do you think they'll find that?' I asked. I knew which way he was heading, but I had to hear it from him.

'I think . . . I'm pretty sure it has to be in the south. Oh, I admit I'm biased, because that's where I belong. It's not that I dislike Akersfield, especially recently as I've been so happy, but I don't see it as a holiday place. The weather, for a start, is against that. People on holiday want sun and warmth, as well as sea and sand and plenty to do.'

'You sound like a travel advertisement,' I told him. I didn't like what he was saying, though in my heart I recognized the truth of it. I just didn't like it. I surprised myself by how much I hated the thought of not being where he was; surprised because, though I liked him and enjoyed his company and being taken out and about by him – pampered, in fact – if I'd thought about it at all, I'd have said I could, in the end, take him or leave him. I had only to think of Alun for all other men to be as nothing.

'If I sound like a travel advertisement,' he said, 'it's because I think I'd have something to offer, something people want and would buy.'

'I would miss you,' I admitted.

He took a rather larger drink of his brandy, then looked me straight in the eye.

'You don't have to miss me,' he said. 'You could come with me.'

'But I don't . . .' I began.

He ignored me. 'Poppy, I'm asking you to marry me. I'm not doing it very well. For a start, I haven't told you I love you, but I do. I really do love you, Poppy.'

Again, I opened my mouth to say something, but he wouldn't let me.

'Please say you'll marry me, Poppy. I know I could make you happy.'

I was determined to speak. 'I've known you such a short time, Victor,' I said. 'I'm not sure that—'

'How long does it take to fall in love?' he asked. 'It took me ten minutes from the moment I set eyes on you.'

Well, I knew the truth of that, didn't I? I'd experienced love at first sight. I know, even now, that there's nothing like it. 'Whoever loved that loved not at first sight?' some poet wrote. I agree with him.

'Not that I expect you to be in love with me,' Victor said. 'Though it would be wonderful if you were. But you do like me, don't you? We get on well together. I'm sure we could be happy. And you know I love the children. I'd do my best to be a good father to them.'

I knew I sounded like someone in a Victorian novel, but all I could think of to say was: 'This is so sudden.' Which is precisely what I did say.

'It is to you,' he said, 'but not to me. If you can't say yes this minute, at least tell me you'll think about it. Don't turn me down right away.'

'All right,' I said. 'I *will* think about it. I'll give you an answer one way or another in a week's time. Could I have a sip of your brandy?' I wasn't as cool as I seemed; inside I was shaking.

'You can have one of your very own,' he said, 'even though you don't like it. Oh, Poppy, there's nothing you couldn't have.'

'Tell me more about your plans,' I said. 'Don't talk about me, just about what you want to do.'

'Very well,' he said, after a pause, 'if that's how you want it. In the first place, I'm fairly sure I'd go for Brighton. It's my belief that people will flock to Brighton again once the war's over, as they did before. It has everything I'm looking for, including the climate. And my roots are there, which I dare say makes a difference.'

What about *my* roots, I thought. No-one in my family – not that we were all that much of a family – had ever moved out of Yorkshire.

'And it would be wonderful for the children,' he continued.

'Please,' I said. 'You agreed you wouldn't talk about me, and that includes the children.'

He nodded. 'Sorry.' And then he began to elaborate on his plans. He had it so well thought out. It would be bed and breakfast, with guests taking their main meals in restaurants. 'When rationing ends,' he said, 'which can't be all that far away, there'll be good restaurants again. It's one of the things that will draw people.'

'In fact,' he said, 'opening a restaurant was one of the things I thought I might do, but I decided it needed more expertise than I possessed. Perhaps that might come later. Wouldn't it be a good thing to give the guests bed and breakfast, then send them to our own restaurant for the rest of their meals?'

He was full of enthusiasm. It was a side of Victor I hadn't seen before. My mind, though, was too full of ifs, buts, whys and wherefores for me to take part, and as he talked on, he clearly found it difficult to keep all mention of what I would do and where I would fit in out of the conversation.

I grew restless and looked away from Victor towards the bar. There were very few people left. 'I think we should leave,' I said. 'I don't like to keep Jenny up too late.'

Neither of us said much as we drove home. Victor concentrated on his driving. We were on country roads, there was no moon and the blackout was dense. For years now we had taken notice of the phases of the moon. With a full moon we could see where we were going, but so could enemy aircraft; with no moon we felt safer, though we couldn't see the way. As Victor turned into Two Elms we saw, in the dimmed lights of the car, Ken hurrying down the drive. He didn't stop and nor did we.

'Can I come in?' Victor asked as he drew up at the door.

'Honestly, Victor, I'd rather you didn't,' I told him. 'I'm quite tired, but thank you for a lovely evening.' It seemed a trite thing to say for a woman who had just received a proposal of marriage, plus the suggestion that she should up sticks, leave the only place she had ever known and go to live in a strange town at the other end of the country.

'All right,' Victor said. 'But you will think about it, Poppy? And don't keep me waiting too long. And you will remember I love you?'

'All those things,' I promised.

He held the car door open for me, and I ran up the steps and rang the bell, which Jenny answered quickly.

'Here she is,' Victor said to her. 'Safe and sound.'

I stood on the top step, watching him drive away, before I went into the house.

'Did you have a nice evening, Mrs Baxter?' Jenny asked.

'Very pleasant,' I said. 'Did you? Were the children good?'

'As good as gold,' she said. She looked flushed and bright-eyed. I reckoned she'd had a very enjoyable time.

'They're both sound asleep,' she said. 'Would you like me to make you some Ovaltine?'

'No thank you, Jenny,' I said. 'I shall lock up, take a peek at the children, then go straight to bed.' More than anything in the world I wanted to be on my own.

'Then I'll be off, too,' Jenny said.

I went to bed, but not to sleep. There was far too much to think about. Victor had made everything sound so simple, so easy. Pack up and go! But what was there behind that? Did Victor have his own reasons? I am, after all, a rich widow. I pushed the thought away. Not Victor. Definitely not Victor. So what about Paragon? The offer to buy was still open, and I would have to make a decision before too long, but I was still in two minds about it. It had meant so much to Edward, not to mention his elderly mother, whose husband had founded it. She wouldn't suffer financially, but how would she feel? If they promised to keep the name would that make her feel better? She'd never taken any part in the running of the business; the Baxter men hadn't wanted that, and I don't think she knew any of the present staff. All she did now was accept her regular cheque. As, of course, did I. I had no financial worries, but might I have in the future? Who knew what would happen after the war? And I had a long future ahead of me.

I tossed and turned in the bed I had shared with Edward, and where I still kept to my side of it. I switched on the light and tried to read, but the novel that had absorbed me on the previous night now made no sense.

Why couldn't I make up my mind? Why couldn't I just decide to go to Brighton and start a new life? It would almost certainly be a better place for the children: clean air, the sea, the beach. And whether I sold Paragon or not, there would be enough money from it to give me some independence, should I want that.

So what was keeping me? I knew it wasn't Paragon. Was it the memory of Edward? Or of my mother? Or the fact that I had never lived anywhere else and was too afraid, too cowardly, to take the plunge?

I closed my book, switched off the light and lay back, eyes still wide open. And in more ways than one my eyes were open because I knew perfectly well why I didn't want to move: I didn't want to leave Akersfield because of Alun. I didn't know whether he was dead or alive. If he was dead I would never know any more than I did then, no matter where I was. If he was alive, I asked myself, then why has he never got in touch with me? Why hasn't there been a single word from him?

And so it went on, back and forth, back and forth. I wish I could say that by the time daylight came I had made a decision, but it wouldn't be true. Exhausted, I simply fell asleep. It seemed no more than ten minutes later, though the clock said it was two hours, that I was woken by the children calling from their room, mercifully followed by the sound of Jenny going in to them. If I decided to go to Brighton, I thought as I turned over and pulled the bedclothes over my head, determined to snatch another thirty minutes' sleep, could I take Jenny with me? Would she want to go and leave Ken?

The post brought a letter from Mr Prendergast, spokesman for the group that wanted to buy Paragon. They didn't want to rush me unduly, he wrote, but was I any closer to making a decision? The thirtieth of the month had been the date agreed for my answer, but if I could give it before then it would be particularly convenient for them. 'We have other irons in the fire,' was the message that came over, though wrapped in the politest possible language.

I was still at breakfast when Victor phoned.

'Poppy, can I come and see you this morning?' he asked. 'I only have to go as far as York today, so I needn't leave until early afternoon. May I take you to lunch somewhere?'

'I'm not sure . . .' I began.

'*Please*, Poppy! I know I said I wouldn't rush you for an answer, and I won't, but surely we can talk about it? There's so much to say.'

Mr Prendergast's letter had been a sharp reminder of that. Also, I didn't fancy any more nights like the last one.

'I can't go out to lunch,' I said. 'Jenny has an appointment at the dentist's later this morning. I can't expect her to change it.'

'Then can I come to you? I'll bring something. You needn't cook.'

'No,' I said. 'I'll do the lunch. Come around twelve thirty if you have to leave to go to York. But don't expect answers from me; it's too soon.'

I gave the children their lunch at noon. They were just finishing when Victor arrived and, as always, they were delighted to see him, and he them. He had an easy way with children; I think almost more than I had, much as I loved them. Jenny arrived ten minutes later, having had two fillings.

'Are you all right?' I asked her.

'Perfectly,' she said.

'The children haven't had their morning nap,' I told her. 'Perhaps when they've digested their lunch you'll put them to bed while I give lunch to Mr Worth. He has to leave soon afterwards.'

Victor and I had our meal in peace, and while we were eating he didn't ask me too many questions, though I could tell he wanted to. He was holding back. I decided to show him Mr Prendergast's letter, which was very much on my mind.

'What shall I do?' I asked him.

'Poppy,' he said, 'you know perfectly well what

I would like you to do. I would like you to sell Paragon and move to Brighton with me. But I'm biased, so perhaps I shouldn't advise you.'

'I don't know who else would,' I said.

'There's one thing for sure,' Victor said, 'whatever money you might make from selling Paragon would have nothing whatsoever to do with me. I would neither need it nor want it. It would be my privilege to support you and the children.'

'Dear Victor,' I said. 'You make it sound so easy. But it isn't. Selling Paragon would perhaps be the easiest part – that's not so much to do with people – but leaving Akersfield, uprooting myself and the children is hard.'

'The children aren't old enough to have put down roots,' Victor said. 'And who is left of your roots? Perhaps there's some other reason?'

I shook my head. How could I tell him the truth? That I was still thinking about a man I was unlikely ever to see again.

'Perhaps', he said, 'it's that you don't like me enough, or don't love me, or can't trust me with your future. I admit that to do what I ask would be expecting you to trust me a great deal.'

I stretched my hand across the table and touched his.

'I can't think of anyone I'd trust more,' I told him. 'And, of course, I like you – very much indeed. And you would be an easy man to love.'

He took my hand in his and stroked my fingers. 'So?' he said.

'So,' I said, 'I will do this. I'll decide what to do about Paragon, and I will definitely decide by tomorrow.'

'And me?' he asked. 'Us?'

'I'll give you an answer in three days' time. Thursday at the very latest. I promise. I know it's quite wrong to keep you dangling. It's really not what I mean to do.'

'And between now and Thursday,' he said, 'am I allowed to do whatever I can to persuade you?'

'I won't try to prevent you, Victor,' I said. 'It wouldn't be fair.'

He looked at his watch. 'I shall have to leave, my love,' he said. 'Not that I want to. I'd like to stay every minute until Thursday trying to convince you.'

I saw him to the door and watched him as he drove off to York.

I had decided before I went to bed that night that I would sell Paragon. If I invested the money wisely it would bring in enough for me and the children to live on comfortably, and once they were old enough I could, if I wanted to, take a job.

So I sat down and wrote to Mr Prendergast with my decision, and posted the letter in the box at the end of the lane before I was tempted to change my mind. Not that I thought I *would* change it. When I got back home I phoned Victor and told him what I had done.

'Wonderful,' he said. 'How do you feel?'

'So much better for having made the decision,' I admitted.

'You see,' he said. 'And you will if you make the decision to marry me. Can I see you tomorrow evening? I have to be in Leeds all day.'

I hesitated only a little. I wanted to see him. The thought that I'd parted with Paragon made me feel bereft, which I knew was silly.

'You could come to supper,' I said. 'It's Jenny's half day off, so I can't go out in the evening. In the afternoon I shall take the children to see their grandmother and tell her what I've done.'

'Will she mind?' he asked.

I shook my head. 'I don't think so. She's very frail; she's not concerned about things these days, and, of course, she won't suffer financially.'

She might not be happy, I thought, should I decide to take her grandchildren to Brighton, though that was debatable. She had been pleased at the time to be made a grandmother, but she had never been close to either of the girls, though I had regularly taken them to see her. After fifteen minutes she was always ready for them to leave. Anyway, I told myself, I hadn't decided about Brighton, so I could put the thought out of my mind. I couldn't, of course; it was there all the time now; it never left me.

Victor arrived the next evening carrying red roses for me and sweets – on which he'd obviously spent the whole of his month's ration – for the children.

'Mummy, Mummy. I want a sweetie now,' Maria cried.

They were ready for bed; bathed, their teeth cleaned, rosy and sweet-smelling. I had kept them up so that they could see Victor and he them.

'Oh dear,' Victor said. 'I've timed this badly.'

'Please, Mummy,' Maria begged.

How could I resist her? 'Very well, then,' I agreed. 'Just one, and then you must clean your teeth again.'

When I had put them to bed, helped by Victor, I served the meal, a casserole which had been keeping hot in the oven. When we'd eaten we didn't bother to clear away, we left everything where it was on the table and moved into the sitting room, where we sat side by side on the sofa.

Though I had not meant to let it happen – I'd been determined to keep a cool head – in no time at all I was in Victor's arms and his mouth was on mine. And then we were lying on the hearthrug and making love. Now that it was happening, it seemed so natural, so real, so . . . inevitable. It was what, without acknowledging it to myself, I had been wanting, longing for, needing. I didn't want to do without this ever again.

'You are a woman made for love,' Victor said when it was over. '*Now* will you marry me?'

'Yes,' I said. 'I will.'

I knew I wasn't only promising to marry him, I

was saying that I would leave Akersfield, where I had been born and lived all my life, for an unknown future in a strange place. I also knew, even at that moment, that if I'd had the slightest sign that Alun was still alive and that he still cared for me, I wouldn't have done it. But there was nothing, and I faced the fact that I was not a woman to live alone for the rest of my life.

19

Beryl and Maria made a move towards the dining room; Poppy, following them, hesitated.

'If you should need me for anything, please do say,' she said to Edith Prince.

'Thank you, my dear,' Edith replied. 'I won't need you. I've worked in this house long enough to know where everything is, and no-one has ever said I didn't know how to cook a good breakfast.'

'Then I'll leave you to it, Edith,' Poppy said. 'Thank you.'

'I do think you let Edith take liberties, Mummy,' Beryl said when they were out of ear-shot. 'She's far too familiar.'

'Familiar?'

'Calling you "my dear". You shouldn't allow that.'

'Don't be silly, Beryl,' Poppy said impatiently. Perhaps it was the hierarchy of hospital life that made her daughter so rigid? 'Edith has worked for me for years, and there's never been a wrong word between us. We respect each other.'

'All the same—' Beryl began.

'I'm afraid you're a bit of a snob, darling,' Poppy said.

'She always was,' Maria interrupted. 'God knows why. Shall we get on with the menu?'

'A good idea,' Poppy said.

They seated themselves at the table and Poppy produced a notebook. 'I've written it all out,' she said, 'plus a list of various other things which mustn't be overlooked. Throw out dead flowers, check serving spoons, loo rolls, table mats—'

'The menu,' Maria said.

'Of course,' Poppy said. 'I did discuss it briefly with Beryl on the phone. I didn't think it was worthwhile calling you in New York, Maria.'

'Sure,' Maria agreed. 'So what is it?'

'It's quite simple,' Poppy said. 'I didn't want anything elaborate. But good food.' She read it out. 'Chilled watercress soup, Scotch salmon – nicely decorated—'

'Decorated?' Maria queried.

'Garnished. Cucumber and so on. Small new potatoes – Jersey Royals if they're still around, otherwise Charlottes – asparagus, *petits pois*—'

'We'll need another vegetable,' Beryl said.

'I was coming to it, dear,' Poppy said. 'Broad beans. I reckon I've got just enough ready in the garden. Still very young and tender.'

'Salad?' Maria queried.

'We could.' She had forgotten that Maria practically lived on salad. 'Of course we could. And for pudding I thought strawberries and cream, and I've made a batch of my brandied choc pots; they're in the freezer. And, of course, a cheeseboard.'

'Mervyn will certainly like the choc pots,' Maria said.

'I know,' Poppy said. She had made them when she'd last been in New York. Joe had liked them, too.

'You decided not to have meat?' Maria queried.

'Fiona and David are vegetarians,' Beryl said.

'But, of course,' Maria said. 'And so we will all fit in with *their* wishes. Let's hope Mrs Prince isn't persuading them to eat bacon right now.'

Poppy sighed. 'I thought salmon would suit everyone,' she said.

'Of course it will,' Maria conceded. 'It's a real nice English menu.'

'Thank you,' Poppy said. 'Then there'll be coffee and liqueurs, that sort of thing, if anyone wants them. And I've chosen a Sancerre with the salmon, plus a light Bardolino for those who prefer red to white whatever the food.'

'Oh, Mummy, Rodney would have chosen the wines for you if only you'd mentioned it,' Beryl said kindly.

'Thank you, darling.' Why would I need Rodney's help to choose wine, Poppy asked herself. She knew the answer, of course. Choosing wine was a *man's* job. 'And for the champagne,' she added – she wouldn't announce that Mervyn had funded it. No need to make Beryl uncomfortable – 'I opted for Lanson. It's a favourite of mine.'

Beryl laughed. 'Oh Mummy, you are funny. A favourite? How many brands of champagne do *you* know?' She said it without the slightest malice, almost affectionately.

'You'd be surprised, dear,' Poppy said. 'Not that I ever drank it out of a slipper! Anyway,' she continued, 'the salmon was delivered yesterday. It's in the freezer, and I must take it out soon, to let it thaw slowly. It takes very little time to cook.'

'And the soup?' Beryl queried.

'I've already made it. That's also in the freezer. We only have to sprinkle the herbs on it at the last minute. And I want it served really cold.'

'With a few croutons?' Beryl suggested.

'If you like, darling. You can see to that.'

'What about the rest?' Beryl asked. 'The vegetables? The strawberries? The cream?'

'They're being delivered this morning,' Poppy said. 'Except for the beans, which I'll pick myself.' She would also phone the greengrocer to add salad greens to her order.

'Why aren't you catering the whole thing?' Maria asked suddenly.

Beryl stared at her. 'Catering?'

'Yes. Why not? They'd come in and do everything. They'd even supply the china, and take it away and wash it up.'

'We know what they do,' Beryl said. 'We also know what it costs. It's not something *we* can afford or *you* could expect Mummy to pay.'

'Mervyn and I would have been pleased to pick up the tab,' Maria said. 'No trouble. It could have been part of our present.'

'In any case,' Beryl said dismissively, 'who would want a caterer for a family dinner?'

'Lots of people,' Maria said. 'You can cater for just two people if you've a mind to.'

Poppy had kept quiet, but now she intervened. 'It's a kind thought, Maria, but everything's arranged. This is a no-go discussion. We sit down to dinner in a few hours' time. I'm sure it will all go swimmingly.'

'OK, OK.' Maria waved her hands in dismissal. 'For a start, I'll volunteer to hull the strawberries.'

It was a not-unpleasant task which meant she could sit comfortably in the garden, though she must make certain she had the cordless phone in case there was a call from New York. Why hadn't they called? What might have gone wrong?

'Right,' Beryl said, pen in hand, notebook open in front of her, 'I shall list every job, and who's going to do it. That way nothing will be overlooked and there'll be no last-minute panic.'

'We shall decide who does what between us, by mutual consent,' Poppy said. 'And bear in mind that Joe is to do my portrait. I dare say that will take some time.' During which, she thought with satisfaction, I shall perforce be sitting quite still, doing absolutely nothing. They must choose a quiet place for her to sit, where the comings and goings of everyone else would not disturb them.

'And Fiona has to look after Daisy,' Beryl reminded them.

'One all,' Maria said.

Beryl drew in her breath audibly.

'Right,' she said. 'We must make a table plan. It's much better for everyone to know where they're to sit. Rodney can make place cards; he has particularly clear handwriting.'

'How nice,' Maria said.

Beryl wrote down the names, then counted them. When she reached the total she looked up in consternation.

'Oh dear. Oh dear,' she cried.

'What is it?' Poppy demanded. 'We can't possibly have missed anyone out, can we?'

'No, no,' Beryl announced. 'It's worse than that. We shall be thirteen at the table. That's *so* unlucky. We can't possibly allow it.'

'Good heavens,' Poppy said. 'I thought for a minute it was something serious.'

'But, Mummy darling, it *is* serious,' Beryl said. 'Nothing could be more unlucky. It means that something awful is bound to happen to one of us.'

'Don't be silly, dear.' Poppy's voice was sharp and impatient. 'That's nothing more than a stupid superstition. Now, if we had thirteen people and only twelve chairs—'

'We could play one round of musical chairs,' Maria suggested. 'Loser eats in the kitchen.'

'However, I *do* have thirteen,' Poppy said. 'Not matching, of course.'

'This is ludicrous,' Maria said.

Beryl shook her head. 'Oh no it's not. It's well known.' Then suddenly her face lit up as if a light had been switched on.

'I know,' she cried. 'I've got it. We can have Daisy as the fourteenth. She can be in her chair, close by. She won't actually be *at* the table, but she'll be in the room, part of the family. That should work.'

'Oh no.'

'I think not.'

Maria and Poppy spoke simultaneously.

'I don't think that would be at all suitable,' Poppy added firmly. 'In any case, it will be past her bedtime; she'll be asleep. We can't possibly let the poor child sacrifice her sleep for the sake of a silly superstition.'

'Too right,' Maria said. What could be worse than having a small baby at a celebration dinner, especially with a doting mother to hand. Babies are totally unpredictable in the most awful ways. Did they want Daisy doing a number two in the middle of the meal? No way.

'I think you're quite wrong.' Beryl sounded deeply affronted. 'All I can say is, be it on your own heads.'

'Right,' Poppy said in a no-nonsense voice. 'Let's get on with it, shall we? I shall lay the table and sort out the dishes we'll need. I know where everything is. And Rodney may write the place cards, but *I* shall decide where everyone is to sit.' Why, she asked herself, didn't I simply decide to take everyone to a restaurant and have Edith babysit for Daisy?

'Of course, Mummy,' Beryl said. 'I was only trying to be helpful.'

'Of course you were, dear,' Poppy said. 'Now, shall I take the list you've so kindly written?' She held out her hand and Beryl, with a slight show of reluctance, handed it over.

'I didn't want you to be working on your birthday,' Beryl explained.

If she says that once more I shall scream, Poppy thought, but she kept quiet and began to read.

'Potatoes to wash,' she said. 'Edith can do that. She leaves at noon, but there's enough time. Beryl, you can see to defrosting the salmon, which I will cook later. Maria, when you've finished the strawberries you can put the cream into jugs and make a French dressing for the salad. Jeremy and Megan can put out the garden chairs – we'll have champagne in the garden – and later on, Mervyn and David can find thirteen chairs for the dining room.'

She observed Beryl's rebellious expression at the mention of thirteen chairs and quelled her with a look. Then, without pausing, she reeled off the rest of the tasks on the list, and assigned each one of them.

'This way,' she told her family, 'you will all know what you are doing while I am having my portrait done. Other jobs will occur, of course; they always do. If you two, or any of the others, have any difficulty in dealing with them amicably, then I will step in. Otherwise, I shall leave you to get on with it.'

She knew she was treating her daughters like recalcitrant children, but then that was how they had behaved since the moment they'd set eyes on each other. She wasn't having it.

'Any questions?' Her voice challenged them to come up with even one.

'Seems clear enough to me,' Maria said.

'I only thought . . .' Beryl began.

'Good,' Poppy said. 'Then I'll phone the greengrocer about the salad. After that you can leave me to get on with the table. I shan't need any help.'

It was a plain dismissal. The three of them rose. 'By the way,' Poppy added, ' – and it wasn't on your list, Beryl – the white wine and champagne have to be chilled. The greengrocer will deliver two large bags of ice. Maria, will you tip it into two plastic garden bags and ask one of the men to lay the wine in them? Leave them in the garage.'

'Sure,' Maria said. There was something in her mother today which she had not seen for a long time; not, in fact, since they'd been children at home. As a young woman, she had been quick, decisive, knowing what had to be done and seeing that it was carried out, whether by herself or by her children. It was she who had seemed to be in command of family life rather than Pops; but, to be fair, what she remembered of Pops was his concentration on building up the small hotel he had run so successfully in Brighton.

Brighton was the seat of her earliest memories. She had no recollection of the north of England, or of her real father. Edward Baxter was no more than a name on her birth certificate; Pops had taken his place. She would like to have remembered her true father and had tried hard to do so, but without success. But, she reminded herself, she had been only three years old when they'd moved to Brighton. As far as she was concerned, Brighton was where her life had begun.

Her mother, she recalled, had not taken an active part in the running of the hotel. She had always been there because the top floor of the hotel had been their home. She had been nice to visitors, and when there were staff difficulties she would serve breakfasts, but she had her own small daughters to look after, and quite soon a baby son. Richard was Pops's own child but, to his credit, Pops had never treated Richard any differently from his stepdaughters. He had loved them all, and had been loved in return. But he had always been so busy.

Poor Pops, Maria thought, not for the first time; he wasn't around long enough to ease off work and enjoy his family.

She couldn't remember why or when her mother had changed from being a bright, bustling, beautiful woman into the serene, laid-back eighty-year-old she was now, nor could she remember whether the change had been sudden or gradual. She was still bright, of course – she had never lost that – still interested in what went on; still beautiful, but now with the particular beauty of old age. She was still sure of herself, too, but in a quieter, less abrasive way, as though she didn't have to prove anything. She seems, Maria thought, though I don't see much of her, to take life as it comes, to take what she wants from it and let the rest go. Perhaps that was the secret of a happy old age?

It had been all the more interesting, therefore, to see her a few minutes ago asserting herself and taking command, bringing them both to heel. Not that Beryl didn't deserve it. She grew bossier with every year.

Having no specific task assigned to her until the strawberries arrived, and not wishing on any account to be involved in whatever was going on in the kitchen, Maria went out by the French windows which led from the dining room into the garden, picking up the telephone from the sideboard as she passed. 'Please God,' she said to herself, 'or whoever you are, let it ring. And when it does, let it be from New York.' But how could it be? It was far too early there. There was no way she could possibly enjoy these celebrations unless she heard from New York first.

There was an iron table in the garden, with

four excessively uncomfortable iron chairs around it. She fetched the cushions from the conservatory, made herself comfortable and sat there doing nothing. She would have liked to have dipped into the newspaper, but that would mean joining the throng in the kitchen, so she would sit here and do nothing, even though everyone else in the house, except Joe and Mervyn, was presumably hard at it. And excepting Georgia, of course. In Georgia's present mood, which had lasted all too long, she wouldn't lift a finger to help anyone. What *were* they going to do about Georgia and her infatuation for that man? At least that was one subject on which Mervyn and she could agree.

Presently she heard the doorbell ring, and shortly after that Poppy came into the garden with a tray, on which were several punnets of strawberries and a large earthenware bowl.

'I thought you might like to do this in the garden,' Poppy said. 'There's more room. And it's such a lovely day. I often bring work into the garden.'

'We have a roof garden,' Maria reminded Poppy. 'Not that we ever have time to sit in it.'

'The ice has also arrived,' Poppy said. 'I had it put in the garage because that's the coolest place. Would you go and tip it into the big plastic bags? You'll find them in there.'

She was still in her brisk mood, Maria thought, though not unpleasantly so.

Going back into the house. Poppy encountered Edith Prince, who was alone in the kitchen. She had taken off her apron and was folding it up, prior to putting it in the ASDA carrier bag which accompanied her everywhere.

'I've done the potatoes,' she said, 'and I've left the kitchen nice and tidy – as far as I can with all the stuff around. I don't remember my children having all that paraphernalia, I must say.'

'Times change, Edith,' Poppy said.

'They certainly do,' Edith agreed. 'Mrs Dean has taken the salmon out of the freezer and it's thawing nicely in the larder. I reminded her the soup had to come out, but she said not yet; you're having it cold.'

'That's right,' Poppy confirmed.

'Cold soup. Whatever next? To my way of thinking, soup has to be drunk piping hot or not at all. However, not for me to pass comment. Don't you bother yourself clearing away tonight, Mrs Marsh. I'll be here in the morning to tackle the mess.'

She left with her usual banging of the kitchen door. One day, Poppy reckoned, it would come off its hinges.

Mervyn came into the kitchen. 'Here I am,' he said. 'What do you want me to do?'

'Nothing at this minute; we're well ahead,' Poppy told him. 'But I will need your help later. Did you have a nice sleep?'

Mervyn nodded. 'Yes, and I feel better for it. Where is everyone?'

'All around somewhere,' Poppy said. 'Except Fiona, who's taken Daisy for a walk. Joe is still in bed.'

'I think he's up and in the bathroom,' Mervyn said.

'Oh good!' She would make fresh coffee for him to come down to. 'Maria is in the garden,' she told Mervyn. 'Why don't you join her while you have the chance?'

'I'll do that,' Mervyn said.

He did so.

'Ah,' he said. 'Strawberries. That's something the English know how to grow.' He took one and bit into it. 'Delicious.' He reached for another.

'They're for dinner,' Maria reminded him. 'Not to eat now.'

'I'm sure Poppy wouldn't begrudge me one or two,' Mervyn said. 'I just asked her if there was anything I could do and she said not yet.'

'We all have our orders,' Maria said. 'When the time comes, yours will be to find thirteen chairs from somewhere in the house and assemble them round the table. But there's something you could do for me.' She explained about the bags of ice in the garage. 'And you could put the white wine and champagne on the ice at the same time, though strictly speaking that's assigned to Rodney. He won't mind, but best not to mention it to Beryl.'

'Why not?' Mervyn said, taking another strawberry.

'She doesn't like not being in command. My mother's relieved her of it. Also, she's having fits about thirteen of us sitting down at the table. Apparently something dreadful will happen.'

'Your sister is a silly woman,' Mervyn said.

The telephone rang. Maria, still not in tune with the time difference, grabbed it.

'Hi,' she said, then her expression of relief mixed with anxiety changed to one of disappointment. 'Oh, it's you,' she said. 'Mom's around somewhere; I'm not sure where. Richard, why don't you leave a message and I'll see that she gets it? You can't be here until eight o'clock? But we're eating at eight. Drinks at seven. She won't be pleased. I suggest you ask Graham to cut his meeting short. After all, it *is* your mother's birthday.' She paused and listened, but not for long. 'OK, OK. I'll tell her. But do your best.' She put down the receiver. 'Graham has a meeting, therefore Richard will be late for his mother's birthday. You'd think they could organize themselves to get here in time from Croydon. Anyway, you can give Poppy the message when you go in to do the ice.'

Lunch for everyone, except Daisy, was sandwiches, prepared by Beryl and served in the sitting room, Poppy having put the dining room totally out of bounds. Daisy had a sludgy green mixture of spinach and rice, and appeared to enjoy the small amount that had gone into her mouth and wasn't spread around her face or on her bib.

'OK, time for your portrait,' Joe said to Poppy. 'I'd like to do it in the garden. Is there a place where we won't be disturbed?'

'Certainly,' Poppy assured him. 'There's a seat at the top, by the fence. And I shall put it out of bounds to anyone else.'

She had looked forward to this since the moment Joe had mentioned it, not from vanity – she had no high hopes of how she would look – but because it would give her a little time alone with Joe, and that was easily the best birthday present she could ask for. Of course, she supposed, she would have to sit quite still and not talk, but never mind.

'This is a perfect place,' Joe said when she led him to it. 'And if you sit on this nice old seat and relax, it'll be great.'

He posed her as he wanted, her head slightly tilted in the way he thought was characteristic of her; her heavily ringed hands, shapely yet capable, loosely resting, not quite clasped, in her lap. She fell into the pose easily; no awkwardness, no stiffness, which meant she probably wouldn't wriggle.

'I'm going to use Conté,' he said. 'I'd have liked to do a watercolour, but there isn't time. Conté is nice and soft, though, and I can add a bit of colour. Your gold silk scarf, for instance.'

'That sounds fine,' Poppy said. 'I hope I don't fall asleep.' The sun was warm, but there was a slight breeze, which might help to keep her awake.

Joe set to work. For what seemed to Poppy a long time he simply looked at her, but then, when he did start, his brow knitted with concentration, he drew with firm, decisive strokes, as if he knew exactly where to place the crayon on the paper.

To Joe, it was not as easy as it seemed to Poppy, but he would enjoy the challenge. She had an interesting face, and the fact that she was old was no detriment. There was a lifetime of living in an elderly face. It was there to be seen, and beneath the etched lines, slacker muscles and a jawline which was no longer firm, he could see in his mind's eye something of how the young Poppy had looked. He found himself thinking, She must have been very attractive when she was younger. And then immediately he chided himself. Why didn't he think, You are very attractive *now*, though in a different way? Why did 'attractive' only apply to the young?

Her hands showed her age, though. Hands usually did. He paused. She was looking a little sleepy. 'Shall we break for a minute,' he suggested. 'Don't alter your pose, not unless you're uncomfortable. Tell me about your rings; they look interesting.' He wanted her to relax.

'They are,' Poppy agreed. 'I wear them all, all the time. The solitaire diamond and the eternity rings with sapphires and rubies were given to me by my first husband; the solitaire when we were engaged, the others when I had my daughters. It was Richard's father, Victor, who gave me this great big amethyst – one of my favourite stones.'

'And the opals? Who gave you those?'

'My third husband. Gregory Marsh,' Poppy said. 'He died before you were born. In Australia.'

'I didn't know you'd been to Australia,' Joe said. He had picked up his crayon and started to work again, and Poppy resumed her pose. Now, Joe noticed, there was a hint of bitterness in his grandmother's face, which he didn't want to include in the portrait.

'I haven't,' Poppy said.

'It's a pretty ring,' he said.

'Yes, it is.' Poppy twisted it on her finger. All her rings were getting a little loose. 'At the time, someone told me opals were for tears, but I was never one for superstitions.'

They both fell silent. There was no more talking; Joe was concentrating fiercely. Eventually, he sat back and took a long look at what he had done. 'That's it,' he said. 'Yes, that's it.'

'May I look at it?' Poppy asked.

'Sure. I hope you're going to like it.'

She did like it, very much indeed. It was a kind drawing, but without being flattering, as if he had caught something of the spirit beyond the physical. It was the face she had grown used to, the face that looked at her from her dressing-table mirror each morning.

'I'd really like to get it mounted and framed

right away,' Joe said. 'Complete it actually on your birthday. Is there somewhere locally I could do that?'

'There is in Brighton,' Poppy said.

'Then why don't I go there? Why don't you come with me and show me the way? Can you spare the time?'

'I can and I will,' Poppy said. 'I'll get the car out.'

'Right. While you're doing that, I'll spray the drawing very lightly with a fixative to keep it stable.' He looked at the portrait again. 'Yes. I'm pleased with it,' he said.

The birthday dinner is well under way. The champagne, sipped in a garden full of summer scents, is much appreciated – indeed, five bottles are drunk. Richard and Graham, immaculately attired but somewhat flustered by the rush, and clearly having had a tiff on the way, arrive in time to drink their fair share. Richard is bearing a large bunch of lilies, for which Poppy, irritatingly, has to break off her drink and find a vase. But he means well. Lilies are his style. Not for him anything understated.

Daisy, at Fiona's insistence, has sipped a few drops of champagne from a plastic spoon to celebrate her great-grandmother's birthday, and now she has been put to bed, Poppy very politely refusing to go in to the meal until that happens.

Rodney's place cards are most artistic, written with green ink in his best writing and embellished with tiny flower drawings. With their aid, Poppy secures herself a seat, with Rodney on her left and Joe on her right, and directly opposite Mervyn.

The watercress soup is exactly the right temperature: cold, but not icy cold. Edith Prince would have hated it. The salmon is delicious, which pleases Beryl because she got to cook it, Poppy's timetable having been thrown out of gear by her mad dash to Brighton with Joe.

The puddings are served and eaten with little murmurs of appreciation. Mervyn consumes a dish of strawberries and cream, plus two of Poppy's choc pots, and is now enjoying some rather good Stilton.

The sound level round the table is high, with everyone talking at the same time, but it is an entirely happy sound, with none of the acrimony that pervaded the earlier parts of the day. Only Poppy, because she is looking directly at him, notices that Mervyn is sweating profusely, the perspiration standing out in beads on his face. She hears his sharp, strangulated cry and sees him clutch at his chest. What reduces everyone else to silence is the thud with which he falls forward onto the table, knocking over his glass of port, which makes a large crimson stain on the white damask cloth.

The silence is broken, as Mervyn lies there, by Maria's scream.

20

Once I had said I would marry Victor and go to Brighton everything moved at top speed. That, I quickly discovered, was Victor's way. Give him something to do and he got on with it. Within days he was showing me details of small hotels and guest houses that he'd requested from estate agents in and around Brighton. There was a wide choice.

'I reckon owners who've been running this sort of business through the war years have had enough of restrictions and difficulties,' Victor said. 'They're tired and they want out, which is the best time for us to go in. Poppy, my love, I foresee a good future for us.' Victor was invariably optimistic, though usually with good reason.

'But you can't believe everything estate agents say. They get carried away. So I shall have to go and see for myself,' he added.

He had a few days' holiday to come – he had already given in his notice to leave his job – and he decided to spend a week in Brighton searching for the right business.

'I wish you could come with me,' he said. 'You're as much a part of this as I am.'

It wasn't possible. There was no-one with whom I could leave Maria and Beryl; they were far too young.

Matters moved with equal speed in other directions also. We planned to marry in Akersfield Registry Office in three weeks' time, and Esmé and Charlie were to be our witnesses. I reckoned Esmé was envious of my new future and of the way I was being whisked away by my Prince Charming.

'I never thought of Victor as being romantic,' she said. 'It just shows how wrong you can be.'

I didn't see it as romantic, though I never doubted that Victor was in love with me. I saw the plans for the future as a good business move on his part and acquiescence on mine, though I was stimulated by the speed of it all. On the day we were to be married, Victor was to move in with me. His own place was already on the market. Given the circumstances, even aside from the children, there would be no opportunity for a honeymoon. That would have to wait, and wait it did. After we moved to Brighton there was no time for such luxuries.

Victor set off for the south on a Monday morning. I gave him a kiss as he left, then watched him walk away down the drive.

'Don't forget, you're to telephone me,' I called after him. 'I want to know what's happening.'

'I've told you, I'll ring you every evening.'

He was as good as his word. At eight o'clock every evening, when he knew the children were in bed and we'd have time to talk, the phone would ring. For the first three days it was mostly a tale of woe. He saw some unspeakably awful places, but when he phoned on Thursday it was with a different story. 'I think I've found it,' he said.

It was, he told me, a small hotel in a road which ran off the seafront, just to the east of the Palace Pier. 'It's in an excellent position,' he said. 'Only a few yards up from the coast.' I couldn't picture it because I'd never set foot in Brighton, but his enthusiasm was catching.

'The Seagull Hotel,' he said. 'It's not large – eighteen bedrooms. Bed and breakfast. Evening meals by request, but we can discuss that. They're mostly commercial customers at the moment, reps and the like. Brighton wasn't considered a safe place for families to visit in wartime, because of being on the Channel coast, but it will be. I'm certain of that. They'll all be coming back: families, honeymoon couples, everyone.'

'So why is it for sale?' I asked.

The owners, he told me, were a couple who'd reached retirement age and now wanted to live closer to their daughter and grandchildren. The daughter and her husband had emigrated to

Canada before the war and were keen, now, to have the old people there.

'It's going to cost more than I bargained for,' Victor said, 'but they want a quick sale, so they might come down a bit.'

'Don't forget there's the money from Paragon,' I reminded him.

'I know, Poppy,' he said, 'and it's generous of you, but I don't want to use that. It's your nest egg. I don't want to touch it. Anyway, I've arranged to take a longer look at the place tomorrow to check out a lot of things, including the accounts. Oh, I do wish you were here.'

'So do I,' I said. 'But I trust your judgement.' I did, too, and now that I had got used to the idea of leaving Akersfield I was as anxious to be off as Victor was.

When he got back home on the Saturday, he filled me in on the details. The hotel had eighteen bedrooms, but not nearly enough bathrooms or showers. He planned to rectify that. 'Eventually,' he said, 'there will be a bathroom, or at least a shower, to every bedroom. That's the thing for the future.' There was an adequate breakfast room and a moderate-sized lounge. The basement kitchens were small and rather dark and needed new equipment. 'But I'll deal with that,' he said. There was no limit to his enthusiasm. Our living quarters would be a flat at the top of the hotel, which was where the present owners lived. It all sounded more than satisfactory.

VE Day came almost as an anticlimax, partly because we had been expecting it for some time and partly because we were so immersed in personal matters. The church bells rang and there were street parties in Akersfield but, not living in a street – Two Elms was rather isolated – we weren't involved in them. The children were too young to have much idea of what was going on. I did wonder about taking them to the parade in the town, but I've never liked parades, so I didn't. What we did have was a celebration dinner at a restaurant with Esmé and Charlie. Esmé and Charlie seemed to be growing quite close to each other, though there was no talk of marriage.

Four weeks after our wedding was the day set for leaving Akersfield. I spent those weeks packing, but I also managed to fit in a little visiting to say goodbye to friends and people I knew. It was chastening to discover how few of them there were. I paid a visit to Paragon, but everything was changing there and I felt like a fish out of water. I went to see Mrs Harris. I went to the hospital and bade my farewells to Matron. 'You would have made a good nurse,' she said. 'I always thought so. Who knows, you might have been a matron one day.' And, to her mind, nothing could be higher. When I enquired about the formidable Mrs Baker, I was told that she had died. 'The rest of the evacuees are to go back to London,' Matron said. 'Poor dears, they never really settled here. I'm not sure it was a good idea.'

After a lot of thought, and consultation with Victor, I asked Jenny if she would like to come with us. I would probably need someone to look after the children if I was to help Victor set up the business.

Her reply startled me. 'I'd like to very much, Mrs Worth,' she said. 'There's nothing I'd like better than to go and live in Brighton. But I can't. The fact is, I'm pregnant.'

'Oh. Oh dear. Is it . . . ?'

'Ken's? Yes it is.'

'So do you plan to get married?'

'I don't think Ken does,' she said. 'Anyway, I'm not sure it would work. We'd have to live at home; we can't afford anywhere, not with the men coming back from the war, and my Mum hates Ken.'

For one wild moment I wondered whether I'd say, You can come with us, but common sense prevailed. I was not the person to take on a single mother and a new baby, even if we hadn't been setting up a new business.

Victor sold his beautiful car, but not without regret; he was sorry to see it go, and so was I, but the hotel had very little parking space, and he didn't see much need for a car in the near future. 'In any case,' he pointed out, 'I couldn't get the petrol to drive to Brighton, nor would it be a suitable journey for the children.' So we travelled by train, the children clutching teddy bears. Maria was thrilled to be on the train; Beryl, at eighteen months, was indifferent. Mercifully, she slept a good deal of the way. The Petersons were there at the hotel to meet us. They had agreed to stay on for ten days to show us the ropes, but no longer, because even before they had sold the hotel they had booked their passage to Canada.

The fact that the business went well almost from the start was almost entirely due to Victor's hard work. He was determined to make a success of it, and he did so, though it was never easy. Food and other things were still rationed. Both materials and labour for making the changes we wanted to make – bathrooms, extra lavatories, dividing and refurnishing bedrooms and repairing war damage – were both scarce. Sometimes we would have the materials, but no workmen to use them, while at other times we would have a man available, but no materials. It was a slow and frustrating business. I wondered whether the day would ever come when the house would be free of workmen and their detritus.

It did, of course, and not only did we not lose the clients we had inherited, we gradually gained new ones. Victor had been quite right, people did start coming back to Brighton for holidays, and quite soon at that. This was in the years before they started flocking to Spain. They were good years, happy years. The children benefited from the clean air and enjoyed playing on the pebbly beach or going on the pier whenever I had time to take them. Soon, Maria started school and I found a place for Beryl in a day nursery. This gave me more time to help in the hotel, which I enjoyed.

Quite soon after this I found, to my great delight, and certainly to Victor's, that I was pregnant, and from that moment on Victor treated me as though I were made of cotton wool.

'You *must* have help,' he said. 'It's essential.'

In vain did I tell him I could manage, and then, as the weeks went by and school holidays loomed, I came round to his way of thinking.

'What about asking Jenny?' Victor suggested.

I had kept in a rather desultory touch with Jenny. She had never had the baby; at four months she had, to her relief, miscarried. The last I had heard she was working in the Co-op. Whether she was in the throes of another love affair from which she wouldn't be parted, I didn't know.

'It's worth asking,' Victor said. 'You always got on well with Jenny.'

As it turned out, she had just cast aside her boyfriend and was not only willing, but eager to try life in Brighton.

'I am sick to death of men,' she wrote. 'I've decided never to marry.' She was twenty-two!

Our son was born in September 1948. We named him Richard, for no particular reason that I can remember. He was a placid baby and a great delight to all of us. I was never sure what made him grow into a rather uninteresting young man. Perhaps he was *too* placid. Not that I didn't love him, and still do, of course.

If Victor loved him more than the others, because he was a boy and his own flesh and blood, he never showed it. He was equally loving to all three children.

These were happy days. I knew my good fortune. It was not that I ever forgot Alun, or ever would. Indeed, there was one week when we had a young Welsh guest staying in the hotel and just the sound of his voice was torture to me, but when he left I made a deliberate decision to put Alun out of my mind and concentrate on making Victor happy. And I succeeded in the latter.

This was the point at which I made a desperately painful decision. I had kept the few letters I'd had from Alun, via my mother, but I would now burn them. The time had come.

Even the small practicalities of that were difficult. I had to choose a time when the children and Victor were out of the hotel and I could rely on them not to return and interrupt me. This caused several days' wait, during which time I was frequently afraid I would lose my resolve, but in the end the opportunity came. Maria and Beryl were at school, Richard was out with Jenny and Victor had an appointment at the town hall with the planning officer about an alteration we wanted to make to the hotel.

I allowed myself to read the letters one last time; it didn't take long, as there were so few of them. As I read them, it was as if I could hear Alun's voice saying the tender, loving words. Then I took them to a bedroom which was not occupied, and burnt them in the fire grate; each one separately, watching the flames consume one before setting the match to the next. When the last small flame and curl of smoke had gone, I cleared away the ash and buried it in the dustbin.

You might suppose I felt better for all this; cleansed, forgiven, atoned. I didn't. All I knew was that I'd done what I could, what I had to do, and I could look Victor in the face again. I didn't waste time regretting it.

All went well for the next three years. Victor had managed to carry out many of the changes he wanted to make in the hotel, though there was always something more to be done. Maria and Beryl were now at a small private school in Kemptown, the fees of which I insisted upon paying out of the money Edward had left me, and Richard was a pleasant, easy-going three-year-old. We were a happy family.

The hotel was fully booked throughout the summer of 1950, with many of our guests returning after staying with us the previous year. Because we had families, we did more evening meals, and we still talked about opening a restaurant, but without any sense of hurry. There was plenty of time.

Little did we know, there was not much time. In the winter of 1951, Victor caught what at first seemed to be a nasty cold, but within hours proved to be influenza of a particularly virulent kind. It was not surprising that he caught it because there was a widespread epidemic. We had read in the paper that for six weeks there had been 10,000 deaths a week. The real surprise was that it was Victor who caught it. He was as strong as an ox and exceptionally healthy.

When the influenza turned to pneumonia the doctor, standing by Victor's bedside, looked grave. Afterwards, he told me that he had realized at that point that Victor was not likely to recover. There was a heliotrope coloration in his face and lips, which to a medical man bode ill.

He was right. Victor died within two days of that visit.

Even at this long distance I find it difficult to think about the period after Victor's death. How could anyone be widowed twice in less than seven years? Was it a punishment from heaven because I had wronged two good and honourable men? And in that case, why wasn't I the one to be struck down? I discovered, of course, that sometimes the worst punishment is to be left to go on living.

I thought I would go mad, but I didn't because there was no time for that. I had a hotel to run and three children to bring up, and for several years that's exactly what I did.

Looking back, I can be satisfied that I did it all reasonably well. The hotel prospered. Many of my visitors remained faithful to me for many years, perhaps because I was on my own. Even when people started holidaying abroad they would come to the Seagull for bank holiday weekends, or for the odd week in spring or autumn. The children, though they were shattered by their father's death – the girls more so than Richard – recovered, as children do. Jenny stayed on with me, and I don't know what I would have done without her.

'You've been good to me,' she said. 'I'll not leave you while you need me.'

As for me, though I coped with everything, I desperately missed Victor and then, as time went on, it was a man's company I missed. I had known when I'd married Victor that I was not a woman to live alone, yet while the children were growing up, that is what I did. Running a hotel, where reps and other businessmen frequently stayed on their own, I was not without opportunities. I dare say most people thought I took them, but I didn't.

I lived like that until 1968. By then Beryl had trained as a nurse and married Rodney, and Maria had married Mervyn and was living in New York. In 1966 Jenny, aged forty, who to my surprise had kept to her vow of never marrying, returned to Yorkshire. 'Mum's elderly now, and arthritic,' she said. 'I reckon she needs me.'

I reckoned it was the call of the north. After twenty years in Brighton, Jenny was still a northerner at heart. She had never quite settled in the south.

'Why don't you sell up, Mummy?' Beryl said to me. 'You've earned a rest. You could buy a nice little house in Bath. I could keep an eye on you, look after you.'

I was fifty-one; she made me feel eighty. I declined as politely as possible.

Maria, on the telephone from New York, made a similar suggestion about selling the hotel.

'You could come for a long holiday to New York,' she suggested. 'When did you last have a decent holiday?'

I wasn't sure that a few weeks in New York, with Maria and Mervyn both out at work every day, was what I needed. All the same, the idea of selling the Seagull was firmly planted in my head, and that was exactly what I did. In fact, I bought this house, in which I still live.

My plan was that I would sell the hotel, but hang on for the best price I could get; there was no desperate rush. I would then buy a house somewhere close to Brighton and, when I'd settled there, I would take myself off on a luxury cruise.

I had seen the advertisement for what I wanted. Gibraltar, Italy, Sardinia, Minorca, Spain. Eighteen days. The holiday of a lifetime. The only thing I wasn't sure about was whether I would buy the house or take the cruise first, and then I thought how nice it would be to have the house all ready and waiting for me when I returned.

The girls were happy about the house, but there were mixed feelings when I told them I'd booked a cruise.

'I don't like to think of you going on your own,' Beryl said. 'If you waited until the school holidays Rodney and I would gladly have come with you. You never know who you'll meet on a cruise.'

That was precisely my thought.

Who I met was Gregory Marsh. Gregory was tall, bronzed, had dark hair which fell in a rather boyish fashion over his forehead and was immaculately dressed in a nautical manner: blazer, cravat, white trousers, that sort of thing. He looked not unlike Gregory Peck and had the same gravelly kind of voice. He was six years younger than I was – a secret I kept from him for as long as I could – but he made me feel like a girl.

He singled me out on the second night aboard, and from then on he paid me the most delicate but insistent attention. I was swept off my feet; you could say literally, because when he invited himself into my first-class cabin I was delighted, and even more so by what followed. He was the most skilful of lovers. I can't tell you what that meant to me after years of starvation. Seduction was sweet.

So when, under a navy-blue sky and full moon, he asked me to marry him, I accepted without hesitation.

I didn't tell my children I intended to marry

until it was a *fait accompli*. They were furious. Appalled. Particularly Beryl.

'How *could* you, Mummy,' she demanded. 'It's dreadful! Disgusting!'

'It isn't actually,' I told her. 'It's rather nice.'

Maria, distanced by 3,000 miles of ocean, was censorious, but didn't go on at such length. Richard, who was now in his second year at Oxford, had come to terms with the fact that he was gay and had, moreover, fallen deeply in love with a young man there, so he was less concerned about his mother.

For a while my third marriage was happy, but Gregory soon became bored with the rather quiet life I led. It was not what he had envisaged. He took to looking for more fun in the hotel bars in Brighton. When he returned home, never quite sober, never actually drunk, hc would inevitably pick an argument, and it was in one of those regular quarrels that he took pleasure in informing me why he had gone on the cruise in the first place. He had, he told me, spent his last penny on the fare in the hope of meeting a rich woman who would keep him in the comfort he craved. And not only had he succeeded, he had the grace to tell me, but he had met one who was also beautiful and lively. 'Not to mention asking for it,' he added. 'You were a sitting target.'

You can understand, therefore, that when a few months later he hopped it to Australia in the company of a barmaid from the Queen's Hotel, I was not heartbroken. Good riddance, I thought – though not to my pearls, which he'd taken with him! Two years later the said barmaid, Maisie, wrote to inform me that he had been killed in a car accident.

I no longer have hard feelings about him. For a short time he made me happy. I wonder if Maisie still enjoys wearing my pearls?

I was fifty-four when Gregory decamped, and now I'm eighty. Twenty-six years on my own. Some of it I've hated; some of it I haven't minded. There are a few advantages to living alone, though I'd never say they outweigh the disadvantages. I know a lot of people, and some of them are friends. I know there's this opinion that I've had an adventurous past, even in the last twenty-six years. I think it's something to do with having had three husbands. I don't contradict it; in a way it's a compliment.

I enjoyed my children when they were young, as I now enjoy my grandchildren on the rare occasions I see them. I've no doubt I'll learn to like Daisy when she's more civilized and her mother is less besotted by her. Perhaps I should have told you more about my children, but right now I'm being self-indulgent, I'm thinking about *me*.

I look back with great affection on Edward and Victor, but to tell the truth, which I am doing, it is Alun who lives in my heart. His face has almost faded from my mind. I can hardly recall it, and I never had a photograph, but I remember his voice, with its slight Welsh accent. He had a beautiful speaking voice. Whenever I've heard Richard Burton over the years, I've heard Alun.

21

Both the silence which preceded it and Maria's scream seemed to last for ever, though it was not so. Almost before the scream had died in the air, Joe was leaning across the table to his father, and Fiona, who had been sitting next to Mervyn, was on her feet, her arm around him, stroking his head, all her maternal instincts to the fore. His eyes were closed, but he was still conscious, his face contorted with pain.

Rodney struggled to his feet and Richard and Graham leaped to theirs.

'I'll ring the doctor,' Richard said.

'Let me,' Graham echoed.

'No,' Poppy contradicted. 'Get the ambulance. There's no time to wait for the doctor.'

It came quickly. Maria, distraught, holding Mervyn's hand, went with the stretcher into the ambulance. I had not known my cool daughter was so capable of emotion. But then, they were all shattered, most of them standing around uncharacteristically silent, not knowing what to say or do. Georgia was shaking, white-faced and frightened. It was Fiona who moved to support her.

Poppy spoke to Joe. 'You and I and Georgia will follow in my car. Right away.' She turned to the others. 'We'll telephone you as soon as we can, as soon as there's any news.'

'Mummy, are you sure you don't want someone else to drive?' Beryl asked.

'No dear,' Poppy said. She was already walking out of the door. 'I'll be fine. Actually, I drank very little wine. Why don't you make everyone a cup of tea?'

She drove fast to the hospital, followed the signs to the Accident and Emergency wing. It seemed only a matter of hours, indeed it was, since Rodney had done the same journey. What else could go wrong on her birthday, and why, irrationally, did she feel that it was somehow her fault?

By the time she had parked the car and the three of them had gone into the waiting room, Mervyn had been whisked away and Maria, a forlorn woman, curiously out of place in her smart dress, sat alone on a chair close to the desk. She jumped to her feet as they entered. Joe embraced his mother and Georgia patted her arm.

'What's the news?' Joe asked.

'Nothing, so far. They're doing tests. They'll keep me in touch. They've been very kind.'

'I'll make myself known,' Joe said.

He went to the desk, had a brief conversation with the woman in charge there and rejoined his family. 'As you said, there appear to be various tests – blood tests and an electrocardiogram and so on – before they can make a diagnosis. She'll keep us in touch. In the meantime, as far as she knows, he's stable. How about I get us all a coffee from the machine? It might be a long wait.'

Maria shuddered. 'I couldn't drink a thing,' she said. 'Not yet.' What did 'stable' mean? she agonized. Even more, what did 'as far as she knows he's stable' mean? What *did* she know? How soon will we be informed?

It was, as Joe had said, a long wait. Poppy, sitting on the hard chair, her mind racing backwards and forwards, remembered how Edward had once told her that the longest waiting period of his life had been when she had been in labour with Maria. He had not been allowed anywhere near the labour room; it was forbidden territory to husbands then. But at least he had been waiting for new life, Poppy thought now. What are we waiting for? Naturally, she did not pass on her thoughts.

People came and went: nurses, stopping to have a chat with the staff behind the desk; a hospital porter pushing a man in a wheelchair. A child with his arm in a sling, accompanied by his mother, emerged from a door on the far side of the waiting room. They stopped to have a word at the desk and then left the hospital.

The woman in charge at the desk answered the phone several times. Each time it rang, Mervyn's family looked towards her expectantly, trying to hear what she was saying.

It was after midnight when she answered the phone yet again and, as she listened, looked towards them. Each one of them stiffened. Maria grabbed Joe's hand. When the woman put the phone down she called out, 'Mrs Leverson.'

Maria jumped to her feet and rushed to the desk, the three members of her family close behind.

'My husband . . . ?'

The woman smiled. 'The doctor will see you now, Mrs Leverson. Not all of you, but your son can go with you.'

'Is he . . . ?'

'Dr Mansfield will tell you everything. His office is the fourth door along the corridor.'

'Can't I go with them?' Georgia begged.

'I'm sorry. Only your mother and your brother at the moment.'

Poppy took Georgia's hand. 'I'll be glad of your company,' she said. 'I don't suppose we'll have to wait long.' But to hear what? she asked herself.

Dr Mansfield rose to his feet and held out his hand, first to Maria and then to Joe. 'Please sit down,' he said. There was no guessing whether the news was good or bad; he had the kind of face that would remain serious even while presenting a large win on the lottery.

'My husband . . . is he . . . ?' Maria began.

'Your husband has had a heart attack, Mrs Leverson,' Dr Mansfield said. He held up his hand to stop further questions.

'It was not the most serious attack I have ever seen; not by a long way. He is stable now, and we can expect him to improve, though he will need to stay in hospital for a day or two for further tests and treatment.'

'But he's going to be all right?' Maria insisted.

'I think so, Mrs Leverson.'

'Would it be better . . . please don't get me wrong, doctor, but would it be better to move him to a private hospital?' Maria asked. 'We have medical insurance.'

'I'm sure you have, Mrs Leverson,' the doctor said smoothly, 'but I would not be at all happy to see your husband moved in his present condition. Indeed, it would be your responsibility and not something I would endorse.'

'I think my mother thought—' Joe began.

'I understand, but your father is in an intensive care bed, where he is being looked after on a one-to-one basis by the most experienced nurses. You need have no worry at all about his treatment here. It could not be bettered.'

'Thank you. I'm sorry,' Maria said. 'Can we see him?'

'Both of you can see him for a few minutes,' Dr Mansfield said, 'and you will have unrestricted visiting tomorrow. If it were necessary, you could stay the night here, but I don't think it is. You would be well advised, when you've seen your husband, to go home and try to rest.'

How can I possibly rest, Maria thought. But wasn't it just the kind of thing doctors said? Like, 'Don't worry'.

In the intensive care ward a nurse sat at the side of Mervyn's bed. She gave up her chair for Maria and moved to the foot of the bed.

'He's just fallen asleep,' the nurse said. 'It would be best not to wake him.'

He was pale, but not as pale as that ghastly moment when he had been lying across the table. Maria would never forget that; never, ever.

She touched his hand gently and whispered his name.

'Are you sure he's all right?' she asked the nurse.

'He's doing well, though it's early days,' the nurse said. She had a calm, quiet voice.

'And you'll stay with him?'

'He won't be left, not while he's in intensive care,' the nurse assured her. She looked young for so much responsibility, Maria thought, hardly any older than Georgia, though presumably she must be.

'I think, perhaps, you should go now,' the nurse said.

'Very well,' Maria stood up, bent over the bed and touched a finger to Mervyn's cheek. 'Will you tell him I was here? And Joe.'

'Of course. And that you'll be back in the morning.'

‘First thing,’ Maria said.

Joe took her arm and they left. He gave her a tissue to wipe the tears which were coursing quietly down her cheeks.

It was half past one in the morning when they arrived home. Almost everyone was congregated in the sitting room, waiting anxiously for news.

‘Dad’s quite bad,’ Joe said. ‘It was a heart attack. He’s in intensive care right now, but we think he’s going to be OK.’

‘I’m sorry we didn’t phone,’ Poppy said. ‘Once we knew anything, there never seemed to be an opportunity.’

‘That’s all right,’ Beryl said. ‘And Fiona asked me to apologize that she’s gone to bed. She didn’t want to; she wanted to wait, but I insisted. Daisy doesn’t sleep through the night, and Fiona needs to get rest when she can.’

‘Quite right,’ Poppy said. ‘In fact, I think we should all go to bed. Unless there’s anything . . . ?’

‘There’s nothing to do. We’ve seen to everything,’ Beryl said.

‘I don’t think I can possibly sleep,’ Maria said.

‘You go up, ’Ria,’ Beryl said kindly. ‘I’ll bring you a warm drink and a couple of aspirin in a few minutes. And I’ve put a hot-water bottle in your bed. I know it’s not a cold night, but sometimes a hot-water bottle can be a great comfort.’

Especially when the other person isn’t there, Poppy thought. Don’t I know it! And really Beryl is so kind. I never give her enough credit for it.

And when did she last call her sister 'Ria? Not since they were children.

'Richard and Graham left,' Rodney said. 'They send their love, and they'll ring in the morning.'

Maria turned to Georgia, who had said nothing at all since they'd left the hospital.

'I think you should go to bed, honey.'

'OK,' Georgia agreed. Then she said, 'Mom, do you think I could sleep in your room, in Dad's bed?'

Maria tried not to show her surprise. 'Of course you can. In fact, I'd welcome it. Come on, let's go up, then.'

'Would you like a hot-water bottle, Georgia dear?' Beryl asked.

'I'm sure she would,' Maria said. 'How kind of you Beryl.'

'I'm just so pleased Mervyn's going to be all right,' Beryl said. 'We all are.'

Undressing for bed and cleaning her teeth, Maria found herself wondering that people cared so much about Mervyn. Had she herself fallen into the habit of not caring enough, or at least of not showing it, because, of course, she *did* love him.

When she went back into the bedroom Georgia was already in bed. 'Goodnight, Mom,' she said. 'He *is* going to be OK, isn't he?'

'Of course he is.' She spoke with more confidence than she felt. She was glad Georgia hadn't seen her father lying there, so still in the hospital bed, and all those tubes around.

'We should both try to get some sleep. I'm sure everything's going to seem better in the morning.'

She switched off the light and buried her face in the pillow. Oh, Mervyn, I do love you, she thought. Please get better.

Actually, she thought, she loved her whole family. Where would she be without them? Even Bossy Beryl.

Poppy lay in the narrow, uncomfortable bed in the spare room. Sleep seemed to have deserted her. Poor Mervyn. She'd grown quite fond of him on this visit. But the doctor had said he was stable, hadn't he? There was every reason why he should recover. But still the small doubt persisted in her mind. What if . . . ?

She couldn't bear to think of Maria experiencing what she herself had gone through twice.

'Please God,' she found herself praying; she who had given up such things years ago. 'Don't let Mervyn die.'

Everyone was up and about early the next morning. Maria and Poppy had both slept fitfully, more awake than asleep. In Georgia's case, youth had come to her aid and she'd slept soundly. Now, with the new day, anxiety returned.

At seven o'clock Maria rang the hospital, and waited with apprehension while the woman at the other end gathered information.

'I'm sorry to keep you waiting,' she said

presently. 'Your husband has had a reasonable night and his condition remains stable. He has more tests and more treatment to come quite soon. I'll be able to tell you more when those are done and the doctor's seen him.'

'I can visit him, can't I?' Maria asked.

'Certainly. It might be a good idea to wait for an hour or two. The doctor will have seen him and he'll be able to tell you more.'

'Very well. Thank you.' Maria put down the receiver and went into the kitchen. Poppy and Beryl were both there.

'You should try to eat a proper breakfast,' Beryl said. 'What would you like?'

'Anything. Whatever. But not too much.'

Yesterday she'd been irritated by Beryl's fuss about breakfast – she had *seen* it as fuss – but this morning she found it comforting.

'Scrambled egg?' Beryl suggested.

'Please.'

Georgia joined them. It was unheard of for Georgia to be around so early. Maria told her the result of the phone call.

'Can I come along with you?' Georgia asked. 'I haven't seen Dad. Joe has.'

'Why don't you both come?' Maria said. 'I expect you could see Dad in turn.'

'I'll drive you in,' Poppy said. 'Save you parking, which is almost impossible anywhere near the hospital.'

* * *

Before Maria and Georgia were taken to Mervyn's room, the Sister on duty said, 'Dr Mansfield would like a word with you. You know where his room is, don't you?'

Maria felt her head spin. She clutched at Georgia's arm. 'Is he worse? Is there something you're not telling me? When I called earlier . . .'

Sister smiled. 'Not at all, Mrs Leverson. The doctor simply wants to put you in the picture. It's the usual thing.'

Dr Mansfield's words, when they sat in front of him, were more encouraging than the habitually sombre expression on his face.

'Your husband is responding well,' he said. 'We're giving him anti-coagulant therapy, and monitoring that with regular blood tests—'

'Is he in pain?' Maria interrupted.

'We're dealing with that, too. We don't allow patients to suffer pain when we can prevent it.'

'I'm sorry,' Maria said.

'That's all right,' Dr Mansfield said. 'It's something everyone wants to know. As I said, your husband is responding well. Even so, I want him to stay in intensive care for at least thirty-six hours. After that, if all goes well . . .'

'He could be moved to a private hospital?' Maria said.

Dr Mansfield gave her a long look. 'After that, I was about to say, I would like to move him to a medical ward that specializes in cardiac care. They are very knowledgeable, very skilled; they have all the necessary equipment. It would be far better for him to be there than to be moved to another hospital. Just the move itself could be stressful, and stress is to be avoided.'

'Of course,' Maria said. 'I didn't mean . . . How long will he be here?'

'Up to a week, if all goes well. During that time he will be mobilized very gradually, so that by the time he's discharged he will be able to walk to and from the bathroom, shave himself and potter around a little more each day. Rest is also very important. We will see that he has all these things, as well as continuing his regular treatments.'

'You sound really hopeful,' Maria said.

'Oh, I am,' he assured her. 'If he keeps to the rules and follows a healthy lifestyle, with a low-fat diet and no more than a moderate intake of alcohol – and loses some weight – he could be back to normal within three months.'

'When will he be able to fly back to New York?' Maria asked.

He shook his head. 'It's too soon to decide that. Long flights can be stressful and, in my experience, busy airports are *always* stressful. So let's play that one by ear.' He stood up. 'And now I'm sure you both want to see him. Visiting is unrestricted, but it would be wise not to stay too long. Several short visits are better than one long one.'

'I understand. And thank you,' Maria said. 'Thank you for all you're doing.'

'I'll speak to you again,' the doctor said. 'Certainly before your husband leaves us.'

When they walked into Mervyn's room, he was awake and propped up against his pillows. To Maria's eyes he looked pale and ill, but he smiled at them, and she took comfort from what Dr Mansfield had said. She bent over and kissed him. Georgia did likewise.

'Oh, Dad, I do love you,' she said tearfully.

They stayed no more than fifteen minutes, at the end of which it was clear that Mervyn was tired.

'We'll leave you now,' Maria said. 'Joe would like to pop in for a couple of minutes.' She looked at the nurse for confirmation.

'As you say, Mrs Leverson. Two minutes.'

'And we'll be back again this afternoon, honey.'

When the three of them returned from their afternoon visit Rodney met them in the hall. 'How's Mervyn?' he asked.

'I think a little better. He seems very tired.'

'There was a phone call from New York,' Rodney said. 'They gave a number for you to call back.' He handed Maria a piece of paper. On it was Dan's number.

'Did you tell him why I wasn't here?' she asked Rodney.

'No. I just said I thought you'd be back shortly. He said would you call right away. Do you want me to do it for you?' He could see his sister-in-law was upset.

'That's kind, Rodney, but I'll do it myself.'

'Was there a call for me?' Georgia asked. She knew what the answer would be. If Bill had wanted to get in touch with her, he'd have done it before now.

'I'm sorry, no,' Rodney said.

'It's OK,' she said bleakly.

Maria tapped out the New York number. Within seconds it was answered.

'I'm returning a call from Dan. It's Maria Leverson,' she said.

He was on the line at once. 'Maria. Hi. Glad to hear from you. We've got a deal.'

'Congratulations,' she said. 'But—'

'How soon can you get a flight?' Dan said. 'You've got to sign things. Can you make it tomorrow?'

'I can't . . .'

'Oh, come on,' Dan interrupted. 'This is a real deal. The place is yours, Maria. Every which way we wanted it; pricewise, the lot.'

'I can't come,' Maria said.

'What do you mean, you can't come? You've got to. I've worked hard on this.'

'Will you listen. Mervyn's ill. He's had a heart attack.'

'You're not serious.'

'Of course I'm serious,' Maria said sharply. 'Would I say that for a joke? He's quite ill, but thank God he's going to be all right.'

'I'm sorry to hear that,' Dan said. 'I mean, I'm sorry to hear he's sick. Well, perhaps I could get them to hold for another twenty-four hours this end.' He sounded doubtful. 'Can you get a flight the day after tomorrow? Could you travel Concorde to save time?'

Maria sighed. 'Dan, I'm obviously not making myself clear. My husband is in intensive care. He'll be in hospital for at least another week. After that, I don't know, except that he won't be fit to fly home soon.'

There was silence from New York, then Dan said, 'But *you* could come. You're staying with your mother; won't she hold the fort? I mean, if he's being taken care of in hospital . . .'

'Will you *listen*?' Maria said. 'My husband is ill. There is no way I'll return to New York until he's well enough to do so. It's too early to say how long that will be. If it's several weeks, then that's how long I'll be staying here.'

'You can't miss this,' Dan said. 'I suppose, if it's the only way, I could get someone to fly to England . . . I don't know whether—'

'Don't even think about it,' Maria said.

'How about you giving me power of attorney. I'd have to send you the papers. You'd have to go through them, sign things, get them witnessed.'

'Dan, right now I have no intention of signing anything. My mind isn't on new salons; it's on Mervyn.'

'But you were dead set on this,' Dan said furiously. 'It was what you wanted most in the world. How can you have changed your mind? I've gone to a lot of trouble.'

'I'm truly sorry about that,' Maria said. 'Of course, bill me for all your time. Let's just say I've changed my priorities. I'm staying with Mervyn for as long as he needs me.' No-one would ever know how she'd felt when she'd seen Mervyn slumped across the table. There'd been a moment when she'd thought he was dead.

'So that's it, Dan,' she said. 'I've got to go now. Goodbye.'

She hung up before he could reply, and only then did she realize that Georgia was standing beside her, and perhaps had been for most of the time.

'Thank you, Mom,' Georgia said. 'And I'll stay with you. As long as you have to stay here with Dad, I'll stay.'

'It's not a case of having to,' Maria said. 'It's that there's no way I'd think of doing otherwise. I'll go back home when Dad goes, and not before.'

It was amazing how much better she felt having put that decision into words.

With a somewhat lighter, or at least more settled, heart, Maria visited the hospital again that evening, this time accompanied by Joe. Mervyn, to all appearances, seemed much the same.

'In fact,' Sister said, 'his tests show he's slightly improved. Steady progress is the best and, if he keeps it up, we should be able to move him on to the cardiac ward tomorrow. He's likely to improve quickly there; there's a different atmosphere, with people beginning to do things, people recovering.'

'What about home?' Mervyn asked before Maria and Joe left. 'When . . . ?' He looked anxious.

'All in good time,' Maria said cheerfully. 'Joe's going back. He's already spoken to your surgery and they're taking care of things at their end. Don't bother about anything, just get well.'

'And you?' he asked Maria.

'Me?' she said. 'Well, honey, I'm here while you are, and we go home together. Whenever.'

Mervyn smiled. 'Thank you,' he said. He stretched out his hand and took hers.

'You didn't suppose I'd go back without you, did you?' Maria asked. And how close was I, she wondered, to having to do just that? The thought was horrendous, and she put it away from her, confident now that it wasn't going to happen.

'I'll see you during the day tomorrow,' Joe said to Mervyn. 'I have to get the late flight back. I've got paintings in a show. I've got to put in an appearance; I promised my agent before I left – and now that you're getting better . . .'

'Let me know how it goes,' Mervyn said.

'I will,' Joe promised. 'And you'll be in good hands here. And when you leave the hospital, you've got Mom and Poppy and Georgia to spoil you.'

'Georgia?' Mervyn queried.

'She's determined not to go back until you do,' Maria said.

On the way back to Poppy's, Joe said, 'Shall I go round to the salons and check everything's OK? See if there's anything I can do?'

'I'd like that,' Maria said. 'I plan to call them and explain the situation; tell them I'll keep in touch. I know I've always thought they couldn't function without me popping in all the time, but I guess that's not true.'

'I'm glad Georgia's staying with you,' Joe said. 'She could stay with me and Anna, of course, but I don't like the thought of her hanging about in New York, able to see Bill whenever he beckons.'

'I think that relationship's dying the death,' Maria said. 'He hasn't called, and I think she's got the message. Poor Georgia. I feel sorry for her. It does hurt, you know. You think nothing will ever hurt as much.'

When they reached Poppy's, it was to find everyone discussing when they would leave.

'It's not that we *want* to go, 'Ria,' Beryl explained, 'but Rodney has to get back to school, sprained ankle or not, and I want him to look after himself in the circumstances.'

'Of course,' Maria said. She had an inkling, which she would not have had before, of how Beryl felt.

'And I should go back tomorrow, Aunt Maria,' Fiona said. 'It's Daisy's baby clinic the day after. I wouldn't want her to miss it. I think it's very important to keep a check on her progress, don't you?'

'Oh, absolutely,' Maria agreed.

'And you have enjoyed meeting her, haven't you? You and Uncle Mervyn. And do give him lots of love from me and Daisy, and David, of course, every time you see him.'

'I will,' Maria promised.

Fiona and her family left soon after breakfast the following morning, thus reducing the clutter in the house by at least 50 per cent. Jeremy and Megan, together with Beryl and Rodney, left in the caravan soon afterwards. It was curiously peaceful in the house, and a little bit empty, Poppy thought. But, looking on the bright side, she would have her own lovely bed back. Her greatest regret was that Joe must return in the evening.

'You must come and visit us *soon*,' he said, as he ate a light meal before she drove him to Gatwick. 'We don't see you nearly often enough. And anyway, I want you to meet Anna.'

The day after Joe had left, Poppy went with Maria and Georgia to visit Mervyn. He had been moved into the cardiac ward, which was not, as Poppy had envisaged, a huge ward with twenty or more beds, but a small room with only three other occupants.

'Mr Leverson is doing very well indeed,' the nurse said. 'It's possible he'll be home within the week. And Dr Mansfield would like to see you when you come tomorrow.'

'I know what he's going to say,' Maria said to Poppy as they left the hospital. 'He's going to tell me there's no way he can fly home just yet. Actually, I think he's right.'

'You know you are welcome to stay with me for as long as it takes,' Poppy said. 'Most welcome.'

'I do know, and I'm grateful,' Maria said.

It was Poppy who had the bright idea that same evening, as they were watching a rather boring programme on television.

'I've just had a brilliant thought,' she said suddenly. 'Why don't you scrub the idea of flying home when Mervyn's well enough. Why don't you go by ship?'

'Ship?' Maria queried.

'Yes. The *QE2* sails from Southampton to New York. I think it's the start of a cruise to the Caribbean or somewhere. I don't know when, of course, and it mightn't be a convenient date, but I could phone Cunard.'

'*That*,' Maria said, 'is quite an idea.'

'Shall I phone Cunard in the morning?' Poppy asked.

'Why not? Of course, I'll have to see what Dr Mansfield thinks.'

'Naturally,' Poppy agreed. 'Though I can't imagine he wouldn't think it was an improvement on flying – I mean, for a man in Mervyn's condition. Four whole days of rest, a little exercise, the right food and no stress. And, of course, they have doctors and all sorts of equipment I don't doubt. He'd be able to have all his treatments.'

'Georgia might enjoy it, too,' Maria said.

What Poppy discovered was that the *QE2* would sail from Southampton in four weeks' time, and that there was a first-class suite, suitable for three, suddenly available because of a cancellation. 'Though it's a horrendous price,' she told Maria.

Maria shrugged. 'What does *that* matter,' she said. 'This is something special. I can hardly wait to see what the doctor says, but I shall take his advice. I'm not going to run any risks.'

When she walked into the cardiac ward with Georgia – Poppy would visit later in the day – it was to see Mervyn in his robe, walking towards them, a nurse by his side. Maria's immediate impulse was to run towards him, but Georgia put out a restraining hand.

'No, Mom,' she said. 'Let him come to you. He knows what he's doing.'

So Maria stood there and waited for him, her arms outstretched, trying without success to blink back the tears which filled her eyes.

'Hi there,' Mervyn said as he reached her.

'Hi.' It was all Maria could say.

'Well done,' the nurse said. 'And now back to bed. Perhaps you'd like to take your wife's arm?' She turned to Maria. 'Your husband's doing very well, this is his second walk; he had the first last night.'

Mervyn, his wife and daughter on either side of him, walked slowly but steadily back to his bed.

'I'd like to see Dr Mansfield this morning, if that's possible,' Maria told the nurse.

'I expect it will be,' the nurse said. 'Actually, he's due here in a few minutes.'

'Why do you want to see the doctor?' Mervyn asked Maria when the nurse had left them.

She told him.

'Hey,' he said. 'That sounds great. The *QE2*. I've always fancied sailing on her – the two of us, that is – but somehow there's never been time.'

'It would be the three of us,' Maria said. 'Georgia's staying until you're fit to travel. We'll all travel back together.'

'Better still.'

Dr Mansfield had no objections. 'Quite the best thing,' he said. 'Especially since she doesn't sail for another four weeks. If you do as you're told between now and then, you should feel well enough to enjoy the voyage. Of course, you must keep up your regime, and as soon as you get back to New York you must see your own physician.'

'I'll make sure he does that,' Maria promised. 'And when do you think he'll leave here?'

'By the end of the week, providing there are no set-backs, and I don't expect any,' Dr Mansfield said.

On a morning four weeks later, Poppy watches the Louis Vuitton baggage being loaded into the limousine that is to take her family to

Southampton. Maria, Mervyn and Georgia are standing in the hall. Farewells have been said at least three times over, tearful ones on the part of Maria and Georgia, and even Mervyn is finding it difficult to keep his countenance.

'I think that's it, sir,' the chauffeur says. 'If you're ready . . . don't let me rush you.'

At this stage they are all relieved to be rushed; partings don't improve by being prolonged. They follow the chauffeur out of the house, with Poppy bringing up the rear.

'Now don't forget, Mummy,' Maria says, 'you're to come to us for Thanksgiving. You know you promised.'

'And I'll keep my promise,' Poppy says.

'I'll be cross if you don't,' Mervyn says.

'Disappointed, but not *cross*. You have promised not to get cross; it's bad for you,' Maria reminds him.

Georgia flings her arms around her grandmother for one last time. 'Oh, Poppy, thank you for everything,' she cries.

'Have a wonderful time on the ship,' Poppy says to Georgia. She is sure she will.

At last they are all in the car and the engine is purring, eager to move.

'Take care. *Bon voyage*. Telephone me. See you at Thanksgiving. Take care. Take care,' everyone shouts as the car moves down the drive and turns into the road.

Poppy walks to the bottom of the drive and watches them go out of sight, then she goes back into the house. Well, it was a strange birthday, she thinks. Certainly the most eventful she has ever had. Taking it as a whole, though, everything has worked out well.

THE END

MIDSUMMER MEETING
by Elvi Rhodes

It was an unexpected legacy which brought Petra to the close village community of Mindon. An imposing stone house in the middle of the village, left to her by an old friend of her mother's, promised a very different way of life from Petra's lonely and unsettled life in Yorkshire, and she was immediately made welcome by the local residents – in particular, by the members of the local Amateur Dramatic Society. Presided over by the formidable Ursula, who liked to run things her way, the ambitious decision had been made (mainly by Ursula herself) to put on *A Midsummer Night's Dream* as the next production. Petra, to her surprise and pleasure, was put in charge of the scenery.

Rivalries, squabbles, love affairs and seething resentments threatened to scupper the production, and all Ursula's management skills were needed to prevent disaster. But Petra had more pressing things on her mind than the set designs. A mystery from the past had begun to haunt her – and the answer to that mystery might solve the puzzle of why she had been left such a beautiful house by a total stranger.

0 552 14715 X

SPRING MUSIC
by Elvi Rhodes

Naomi had been contentedly and, she thought, happily married for nearly all of her adult life when her husband Edward explained kindly to her one day that he had fallen in love with a twenty-six-year-old and wanted a divorce. She had to leave the comfortable home she had shared with Edward and their three children, now all grown-up, and move into a small flat in the middle of Bath. The dramatic change in her lifestyle threatened to overwhelm her.

But gradually Naomi began to appreciate the changes, and even to enjoy them. For the first time in her life she could do what she liked, and make her own friends. If these included men friends – well, why not? Unfortunately her children could think of many reasons why not, and Naomi began a battle to establish her own independence, and to persuade her family that she had moved into the springtime of a whole new life.

0 552 14655 2

PORTRAIT OF CHLOE
by Elvi Rhodes

She was born plain Dora, in a bleak northern town where her future seemed all too predictable. But from her earliest childhood she always went after what she wanted, and at the age of eighteen she wanted freedom and a new life – and a new name, Chloe. She moved to Brighton, to work as a mother's help to a Member of Parliament and his wife, and she glimpsed for the first time a life of luxury and wealth – a life which, she believed, could be hers. But her new circumstances brought with them difficulties which she could not have foretold, including the passionate interest of her boss and the unexpected bond which she discovered with the small children in whose charge she had been put.

Torn between the interest of an attractive older man and her feelings of affection and loyalty towards his wife and children, Chloe embarked upon a dangerous course. Then a near tragedy changed everything for her, although it also brought a new love into her life and helped her to grow up and to appreciate what she had.

0 552 14577 7